A ghost story, lessons in kindness and love, and truly comic first-person narrations: they are all here in a delightful mixture of short stories published long ago by L. M. Montgomery but not since republished. We find her writing in different voices and for different audiences—and the collection has the bonus for scholars and fans of having the stories in chronological order by publication. Imagine Emily's Disappointed House showing up in a new and charming setting, and subplots from *Magic for Marigold* tickling audiences as early as 1918. For Montgomery fans, for those sampling her writing, and for those studying her narrative strategies, [this book is] not to be missed!

> —Elizabeth Rollins Epperly, Lucy Maud Montgomery
> Institute (LMMI) Founder, Professor Emerita, UPEI

L. M. Montgomery's short stories show the same insight, wit, and charm as her novels. This collection of newly discovered examples of her skill, presented by Montgomery experts Carolyn Collins and Christy Woster, includes a fine preface and notes relating each story to Montgomery's development as a writer between 1900 and 1939. Here are stories to delight "Anne fans" and to bring new readers into the worldwide circle of Montgomery's admirers.

> —Elizabeth Waterston, Professor Emerita,
> University of Guelph

It's always a joy to find new writings by L. M. Montgomery, and these stories do not disappoint. They are set in earlier eras, but her understanding of human nature keeps them fresh. Spanning the years from 1900 to 1939, they show Canadian life moving from agrarian pre-war Prince Edward Island to postwar Ontario, reflecting the changing cultural attitudes and lifestyles. Because Montgomery builds so many of her stories out of her own emotions—her deepest fears, most painful longings, and greatest joys—they provide another level of interest for those who try to decode her creative process.

—Mary Henley Rubio, author of *Lucy Maud Montgomery: The Gift of Wings* and co-editor, with Elizabeth Waterston, of Montgomery's "selected" journals

✣   ✣

When a reader has finished all of L. M. Montgomery's books, there is a hunger for more. Montgomery's short stories are literary hors d'oeuvres for that desire. Stories bring a different experience to the reader, often a simple moment in time, yet they also invite us to recognize the seeds of personalities, places, and lessons that grow into fullness in the author's novels. There is always something new to discover about Montgomery's work, and this publication shows, happily, that there is more to be revealed.

—Mary Beth Cavert, independent L. M. Montgomery scholar, publisher of *The Shining Scroll*

After Many Years

Twenty-one "Long-Lost" Stories

L. M. Montgomery

Selected & edited by
Carolyn Strom Collins
& Christy Woster

NIMBUS
PUBLISHING LTD
nimbus.ca

Nimbus Publishing Limited
3731 Mackintosh St, Halifax, NS B3K 5A5
(902) 455-4286 nimbus.ca

NB1309
Printed and bound in Canada
Design: Heather Bryan

Library and Archives Canada Cataloguing in Publication

Montgomery, L. M. (Lucy Maud), 1874-1942
[Short stories. Selections]
After many years : twenty-one "long-lost" stories by L.M. Montgomery /
edited by Carolyn Strom Collins and Christy Woster.
ISBN 978-1-77108-499-4 (softcover)

I. Collins, Carolyn, editor II. Woster, Christy, editor III. Title.

PS8526.O55A6 2017   C813'.52   C2016-908061-7

Nimbus Publishing acknowledges the financial support for its publishing
activities from the Government of Canada, the Canada Council for the
Arts, and from the Province of Nova Scotia. We are pleased to work in
partnership with the Province of Nova Scotia to develop and promote our
creative industries for the benefit of all Nova Scotians.

The L. M. Montgomery Institute (lmmontgomery.ca) promotes research
into, and informed celebration of, the life, works, culture, and influence
of the Prince Edward Island-born acclaimed Canadian writer, L. M.
Montgomery.

L. M. Montgomery is a trademark of Heirs of L. M. Montgomery Inc.

MIX
Paper from
responsible sources
FSC
www.fsc.org   FSC® C103113

Dedicated to the memory of
Christy Schreck Woster
who died April 29, 2016

PREFACE

In addition to writing *Anne of Green Gables* and other novels, L. M. Montgomery also wrote over five hundred stories and five hundred poems which were published in her lifetime (1874–1942). She pasted many of those stories and poems into twelve scrapbooks. In the 1970s, Rea Wilmshurst noticed those scrapbooks while visiting Montgomery's birthplace in New London, Prince Edward Island, and quickly began to search for bibliographic information on the stories and poems she found in them. Soon she discovered that Montgomery had made a handwritten record of most of her publications in her "ledger list," now part of the University of Guelph Archives. Using these resources, Wilmshurst found many references for Montgomery's stories and poems, eventually publishing them as a part of *Lucy Maud Montgomery: A Preliminary Bibliography*, published in 1986 by the University of Waterloo. (Ruth Weber Russell and D. W. Russell compiled the portion of the bibliography on Montgomery's novels and Wilmshurst produced the portion of the bibliography on Montgomery's stories, poems, and miscellaneous pieces.)

Some years ago, using the 1986 *Preliminary Bibliography* as a guide, several independent researchers interested in the works of L. M. Montgomery began to find additional references for the stories and poems in Wilmshurst's list as well as references to titles she had not been able to locate before her list was published. (These titles are listed in the "Unverified Ledger Titles" in her bibliography.) In the process, several stories were found that were not listed at all in the Wilmshurst bibliography. Twenty-one of those stories are presented here for the first time since their original publications.

Seven of the stories found by a "team" of Montgomery bibliographic researchers (even though they often did not know each other's discoveries or sources) were published before Montgomery's first and best-known novel, *Anne of Green Gables*, was published in 1908. Like many of Montgomery's earliest stories, most of these were published in the *Western Christian Advocate*, which she termed "a Sunday School paper," and featured school-aged children as the main characters.

"The Chivers Light" (1924) was first published in 1900 as "The Glenn's Light." Jack Haslit, aged fourteen, is left in charge of the lighthouse while his father, the lighthouse keeper, has to go away overnight. A sudden storm comes up and Jack, having left the island for a few hours, is unable to get back in time to light the lamp, endangering the lives of sailors depending on it to guide them into the harbour.

"Elvie's Necklace" (1906) concerns a young girl who has lost a treasured gold necklace and blames the hired boy for its disappearance, ruining his reputation in the community. "What Happened at Brixley's" (1906) is the story of a group of boys being threatened by another rougher group of boys and how they managed to end the bullying by their wits and tricks. In "Janie's Bouquet" (1907), a young girl wants to find a way to show her friend who is in the hospital how much she misses her. The very poor Jean Watson in "Jean's Birthday Party" (1907) is ashamed that her family cannot host her birthday party for her school friends as promised. A lost and neglected kitten shows up at little Maggie Taylor's house but since Maggie's mother does not like cats, Maggie has to find another home for it in "Maggie's Kitten" (1907).

"The Old Homestead" (1907), one of the stories that was not in the 1986 bibliography, was found by two researchers who shared their discoveries for this present collection. The story was first published in *The Kentuckian* (and other newspapers) and is the story of a couple who feel it is time to sell their family farm and make their home in the city.

About the time *Anne of Green Gables* was published, "The Pineapple Apron" (1908) and "How Bobby Got to the Picnic" (1909) appeared in the *Western Christian Advocate*. "The Pineapple Apron" shows us how girls in school vied with each other to create new patterns for knitted and crocheted lace and how friendships were affected by the rivalry that sometimes ensued. (Readers of *Anne of Green Gables* may remember that "Sophia Sloane offered to teach her a perfectly elegant pattern for knit lace" in Chapter XVII.) The story of "How Bobby Got to the Picnic" (1909) is similar to the story of the Sunday School picnic in *Anne of Green Gables* but features a poor schoolboy as the main character. "Peter of the Lane" (1909) recounts the blossoming friendship between an elderly and very dignified Judge Raymond and a precocious seven-year-old Peter who has just moved to the neighbourhood.

"For the Good of Anthony" (1910) was published in the *Sunday Magazine* supplement of many newspapers. By that time, Montgomery had published two more novels—*Anne of Avonlea* and *Kilmeny of the Orchard*—and clearly was beginning to write for adult audiences, publishing in more sophisticated periodicals. This story was a romance that was being threatened by a misunderstanding but was saved by a very determined young lady who meant to see her sister and Anthony Allen reunited.

"Our Neighbours at the Tansy Patch" (1918) is the rather comical story of very different sorts of neighbours: one set is decidedly traditional and the other set is completely non-traditional with a vicious-tongued Granny as the head of the eccentric family.

A year later, "The Matchmaker" (1919) was published, featuring a busybody woman who decided to use "reverse psychology" to bring a couple together by commenting at every opportunity on why they should *not* get together. Montgomery used this story twenty years later in *Anne of Ingleside* with Anne as the so-called "matchmaker."

"The Bloom of May" (1921) is an unusual story with a beautifully blossoming apple tree as its main "character." The apple tree offers shelter and respite for several members of the surrounding community as they pass by it over the course of one day at the height of its bloom.

More than a short story, the novelette "Hill o' the Winds" (1923) is the story of a romance between two young people who seem determined not to fall in love with each other.

Idealistic schoolmaster Jim Kennedy enlists the aid of a shy, plain young woman to help him decorate and furnish a cottage for his intended bride in "Jim's House" (1926). In a somewhat darker plot than is usually associated with Montgomery, "The Mirror" (1931) reveals the story of a young woman who died suddenly before her wedding and then prevents what could have been the disastrous marriage of her sister.

In "Tomorrow Comes" (1934) we see overtones of Montgomery's novel *Jane of Lantern Hill* (1937) when a young girl discovers that the father she had been told was dead is actually alive and still in love with her mother.

Amanda Page, paralyzed for ten years and resigned to her fate, has once again turned down the proposal of Captain Jonas because she no longer has "The Use of Her Legs" (1936). The sudden appearance of a madman who is determined to "sacrifice" Amanda to save his own soul changes Amanda's—and Captain Jonas's—life forever.

Orphaned as a baby, Janet Stannard had been taken in by

her aunt and cousins but was treated more as a servant and was always given hand-me-down dresses to wear, to her great humiliation. On an impulse, she rebels by wearing a gingham school dress to a society wedding rather than the made-over formal gown in "Janet's Rebellion" (1938).

Finally, "More Blessed to Give" (1939)—not listed in the 1986 bibliography and discovered a few years ago—tells the story of Helen Lewis, the best student in her college class, who cannot return for her senior year due to her family's financial situation. A friend offers to pay for her final year in order to maintain the high ranking of the class but Helen cannot accept the offer out of personal pride. An overheard discussion on the "gracious acceptance of a favour" helps her reconsider her position.

After each of the stories in this collection, a note on its publication history and those who located it (and shared their discovery with us) is included, along with a bit about Montgomery's own story taking place at the time the story was published. We also note when a story appears in the online Ryrie-Campbell periodical collection, *KindredSpaces*.

This volume of long-lost stories joins other volumes of L. M. Montgomery's collected stories, beginning with her own selections in *Chronicles of Avonlea* (1912). A few years later, her publisher L. C. Page produced another collection he entitled *Further Chronicles of Avonlea* (1920). This resulted in Montgomery successfully suing Page for his audacity and greed in publishing this collection without her permission. Two more volumes of stories were published a number of years after Montgomery died: *The Road to Yesterday* (1974) [re-published in its entirety and restored to its original form as *The Blythes are Quoted*, edited by Dr. Benjamin Lefebvre in 2009] and *The Doctor's Sweetheart* (1979). In the 1980s, Rea Wilmshurst began publishing more Montgomery stories in eight themed collections: *Akin to Anne:*

Tales of Other Orphans(1988); *Along the Shore: Adventures by the Sea* (1989); *Among the Shadows: Tales from the Darker Side* (1990); *After Many Days: Tales of Time Passed* (1991); *Against the Odds: Tales of Achievement* (1993); *At the Altar: Matrimonial Tales* (1994); *Across the Miles: Tales of Correspondence* (1995); and *Christmas with Anne (and other Holiday Stories)* (1995). These collections contained from fourteen to twenty stories each.

Of the approximately five hundred stories that Montgomery wrote and published in her career, less than half have appeared in print since their original publications; thus, these collections represent only a part of her work. We hope that more of her stories can be made available, in the near future, to today's readers.

—Carolyn Strom Collins and Christy Woster, March 2016

FOREWORD

As one of L. M. Montgomery's granddaughters, I am proud and delighted that these short stories are now available for a wider audience. Even though my grandmother died before I was born, she was a large presence in my life. I grew up with great pride in her achievements and continue to honour her legacy to this day.

After Many Years is a delicious collection of my grandmother's "long-lost" stories. I love reading short fiction; perhaps it's because of time restraints of a busy life, or perhaps it's the satisfaction of completing a story in a relatively short period of time. It's also fun to begin and end a story before falling asleep! For me, the editorial notes at the end of each story in this collection make this a most fulfilling read. These notes often answered questions that were in the back of my mind, and illuminated my reading experience.

My father, Stuart, sitting at the dining room table of our family home in Toronto, would recount story after story about growing up in Leaskdale and Norval, Ontario, with his family and his famous mother. Stuart was also a talented storyteller and I only wish he had pursued his desire to be a writer as well; I think he would have been a good one!

Thank you to Carolyn Strom Collins, Christy Woster, and all the independent researchers involved in this project for seeing it through and adding these stories to the other published collections of my grandmother's work. Thank you as well to the L. M. Montgomery Institute and its founder, Dr. Elizabeth Epperly, for supporting the project—I am grateful to you all for your efforts.

I would also like to add my profound sadness to the late Christy Woster's family and friends that she is not here to enjoy the publication of this book; her warmth and dedication to the world of L. M. Montgomery and her zest for life are missed by all who knew her.

—Kate Macdonald Butler, February 2017

TABLE OF CONTENTS

THE CHIVERS LIGHT
(1900/1924)

"Jack," said William Haslit one morning, as they sat down to breakfast in the lighthouse, "your mother and I have had bad news. Word has just come that your Aunt Grace is very ill, and we must go at once. Most likely we shall not be back until tomorrow, if then, and we must leave you in charge. You must not leave the Chivers to-day, and be very careful about the light."

"But, father, the cycle races over at Southport!" exclaimed Jack. "I want to see them. There will be plenty of time to get back after they are over."

Haslit shook his head gravely. "I'm very sorry, my boy, but I can't let you go. The wind sometimes blows up so quickly in the afternoon that you might not be able to get back, and that would be a terrible thing. Vessels might be wrecked and lives lost; and at the best I should lose my job."

"But Father," pleaded Jack, "I'd be careful, and if I saw the least sign of a gale I'd start home at once."

"No, Jack, you mustn't go; I can't take the risk. I know what you are like too well. If you went over to Southport and got watching the races, a hurricane might come up without your noticing it. I don't like to disappoint you, as you well know, but it can't be helped, so don't let us hear anything more about it."

When his father spoke in that tone Jack knew it was no use to plead, but he felt that he was a very ill-used boy and ate his breakfast in sulky silence.

After breakfast Mr. and Mrs. Haslit started. They had to sail across to the mainland and take the train at St. Eleanor's. Chivers

Island, on which the lighthouse was built, was a tiny bit of rock at the mouth of the harbour. The Haslits were the only people living on it, so it could not be called very lively. But it was within an hour's sail of Southport and St. Eleanor's and other villages, and Jack liked the life very well.

Haslit did not feel any anxiety at leaving Jack in sole charge. He had often done so before. Jack was a tall, strong lad of fourteen and understood the lighting-up thoroughly. He did not mind being left alone, and was proud of the responsibility.

But to-day he was in a very different mood. He had set his heart on going to the cycle races over at Southport, and he thought his father very unreasonable.

"It's going to be a splendid day," he muttered, kicking a pebble angrily into the water as he watched his father's boat skimming over the bay. "Just a fine breeze for sailing! The races would be over by four, and I'd be back by five–three hours before dark. It's too bad."

The longer Jack thought about it the worse he was convinced it was. His chum, Oscar Norton, would be expecting him at Southport, and they had planned to have such a splendid time. The races would be the last of the season, and it was unjust and unkind of his father to forbid him to go.

The morning wore away slowly. Jack hadn't enough to do to keep him out of mischief. He got his dinner and then went down to the little point where his own pretty boat, *The Pearl*, with her glistening white sides and new sail, was anchored.

It was a glorious day: a splendid breeze was blowing up the bay from just the right quarter, the sky was blue and clear, there was no sign of a storm. Jack came to a sudden conclusion. He would go to the races. His father need never know, and he would be back long before dark. In a few minutes *The Pearl's* white sails were filling merrily away before the breeze, and

Chivers Island, with its huge white tower, was growing dim and misty behind her.

Jack reached Southport in an hour. Oscar Norton and several other boys whom Jack knew were at the wharf and greeted him hilariously. In a few minutes they were hurrying through the streets to the park, and Jack had forgotten all about Chivers Island and the lighthouse.

They were soon absorbed in the races. The bay could not be seen from the park, and so excited were they all that they did not notice how strongly the wind was blowing up. Jack, as his father had foretold, forgot everything he ought to have remembered, and thought of nothing but the track and the whirling figures on it.

At four o'clock the races were over and Oscar proposed a trip to a restaurant by way of a wind-up to the day. Jack had awakened to the fact that a stiff wind was blowing and that it might be wiser for him to hurry home. But the track was sheltered and he did not realise how much the gale had increased. The other boys assured him that there was plenty of time, and in the end he went with them, so that it was fully five o'clock before he and Oscar found themselves again at the wharf.

"Great Scott! Jack, you can't get home to-night," exclaimed Oscar, as they came in sight of the bay. "Why, I had no idea it was such a gale. It's a regular young hurricane. Whew! Look at those waves!"

Jack looked about him in dismay. Far and wide the bay was an expanse of rough waves, and far out Chivers Island lighthouse loomed dimly through a haze of spray. Too late he wished that he had obeyed his father.

"I *must* get home!" he exclaimed desperately. "Why, Oscar, Father and Mother are away and there's nobody to light up."
Oscar looked grave.

"I don't see how you can get there, Jack. You can't do it in your own boat, that is sure. She would swamp in a jiffy. What is to be done?"

"I'll have to get some of the men here to take me over in a big boat," said Jack. "There is no time to lose, either. Well, this scrape serves me right. If I get out of it I'll mind what Father says next time, you can be sure of that."

But "getting out of it" was no easy matter. Not a man could Jack find willing to risk an attempt to reach Chivers in that storm. One and all shook their heads; and though they looked grave enough when Jack explained the state of affairs, they persisted in assuring him that the thing was impossible.

"There ain't a boat in Southport that would take you to Chivers to-night," said old Sam Buxton, who knew the bay if any one did; "nor a man rash enough to try it. You'll have to make up your mind to stay here."

"But the light!" gasped Jack. "There is no one there to light up. Father'll lose his place—and maybe there'll be vessels wrecked!"

"You should have thought of that before you came away," said old Sam, grimly. "It's a bad piece of business, but you can't better it by drowning yourself. You can't get home to-night, no matter what happens, and that is the long and short of it."

Poor Jack was in a terrible state of mind. Oscar wanted him to go home with him, but Jack refused to leave the wharf, although he knew quite well that there was no likelihood of the storm abating that night. He was very miserable. If he had only obeyed his father! What if a vessel should be coming in, amid all that tempest and darkness, with no beacon to guide her! If lives were lost, he, Jack Haslit, would be a murderer!

The boys were cold and drenched with spray, but Jack was determined to stay at the shore; Oscar stayed too, for he felt himself a little responsible for the state of affairs, since he had helped to delay Jack.

The night came down early. They knew when the sun set by the faint glow of light among the wind-rent clouds far out to sea.

Suddenly Oscar gave a start of surprise and exclaimed: "Jack, Jack, look! There's Chivers' light. It is all right, old fellow!"

Jack, who had been sitting with his face buried in his hands, sprang up; then he gave a gasp of joy and almost reeled against his friend, so great was his relief. For there, clear and bright across the harbour, through the stormy night, shone the beacon of Chivers Island lighthouse.

"Thank God!" Jack muttered huskily. "Father must have got home after all."

The appearance of the light was a great relief to many others along the shore, for the men had been very anxious. Jack consented to go home with Oscar, but he did not sleep much that night, and when he did it was to live over in dreams the horror of the last few hours. He was sure that never, as long as he lived, could he forget it.

It was the afternoon of the next day before the wind calmed enough to permit Jack to go home. Even then he had an exciting passage. As he drew near to Chivers a boy came running down from the lighthouse, and when Jack sprang ashore he saw that it was his cousin Alec, who lived at St. Eleanor's.

"Where's Father? Isn't he here?" he asked, as they shook hands.

"No. Where on earth have you been? Uncle John and Aunt May called at our place yesterday morning and said they were going to be away all night and you'd be here all alone, and wouldn't I come over? So I sailed merrily over yesterday afternoon, and this is the first I see of you."

"I went over to the races at Southport," said Jack, shamefacedly. "I oughtn't to have gone—Father told me not to—but I was sure I'd get back in time. Then the storm came up and I couldn't. I nearly went crazy. You don't know how thankful I felt when I saw the light flash out! Did you light it?"

"Yes, I hung around waiting for you until it got too late to go home—and, anyway, I knew somebody ought to be here. When it got dark I managed to light up. I had seen Uncle John do it lots of times. Then I stayed up all night for fear something would go wrong. A nice, cheerful time I had, you may be sure, with the waves crashing out there and not a creature to speak to but the cat! Besides, I was afraid that you had tried to come home and had got drowned."

"I've got off better than I deserved," said Jack humbly. "I'll never do the like again, and I'm grateful to you beyond words, Alec."

Jack's father came home the next day. Jack did not try to hide the story from him, but confessed all frankly. Haslit did not scold him very much, for he knew the lad's punishment had already been severe enough. All he said was: "You see, my son, what your disobedience might have cost you and us. Let this be a lesson to you."

"It will indeed, Father, I'm sure," said Jack earnestly.

And it was.

❦   ❧

Editors' note: "The Chivers Light" was published in *Children's Companion Annual* (London) in 1924. It was not listed by this title in the 1986 bibliography. This was a repeat, with the change of the name of the light, of L. M. Montgomery's story "The Glenn's Light," published in *Good Cheer* in October 1900. "The Chivers Light" was found by Joanne Lebold and is available to view online in the Ryrie-Campbell Collection.

It is possible that Montgomery had Summerside in mind for "Southport" in this story and the Indian Head lighthouse at the entrance to Summerside Harbour may have been her model for the Chivers Island light. It had been built in 1881 on a "circular pier" and originally had a two-storey dwelling beneath the light tower. It still stands guard at the mouth of the harbour.

Montgomery had spent part of 1898 teaching in the one-room school in Lower Bedeque, across the harbour from Summerside and a short distance by road from Indian Head Lighthouse. It is likely that she saw the lighthouse from that vantage point as well as passing by it when taking the ferry from Summerside to and from the mainland.

Lighthouses (and range lights) dot Prince Edward Island's north and south coasts from "up west" at North Cape to East Point. They were vital to the safety of sailors in fishing boats, merchant crafts, and those who sailed for pleasure in the Gulf of St. Lawrence and the Northumberland Strait. In the middle of the twentieth century, electric lamps began to replace the oil-powered lamps that demanded the presence of a lighthouse keeper. In recent years, lighthouses have become almost obsolete due to electronic navigation systems.

Readers of *Anne's House of Dreams* will recall the colourful "Captain Jim" who kept the lighthouse near Anne and Gilbert's cottage at "Four Winds Harbour." "Captain Jim's" lighthouse is widely believed to have been the one located at Cape Tryon on the north shore of Prince Edward Island until the 1960s when it was moved; an electric light replaced it [see the article on "A Visit to Captain Jim's Lighthouse" in *The Shining Scroll* (2010, Part 3)].

ELVIE'S NECKLACE
(1906)

Elvie Floyd was dressing to go to Nellie Howard's birthday party, and Mrs. Floyd had permitted her, as it was a special occasion, to wear her gold chain necklace.

Elvie was not often allowed to wear it because she was only a little girl and the necklace was very beautiful. It was a finely chased gold chain of exquisite workmanship. Elvie's globe-trotting Uncle Raymond had brought it home for his little niece from his last trip to Europe.

Elvie stood before the glass, looking very dainty and pretty in her white dress, with her long brown curls tied back from her face in the very latest fashion for twelve-year-old misses. The chain was lying in its silk-lined box on her dressing table, and Elvie picked it up and ran it admiringly through her fingers. It was a lovely afternoon for a party. So thought Elvie, as she moved over to the window and looked out into the garden where Dannie Haven was just finishing weeding the onion bed.

Dannie was a boy of twelve. His mother was a widow, and she and Dannie lived in a little house down the village street. There were always little jobs to be done that people were glad to have Dannie do and just now it looked as if Mr. Floyd had a good deal of work for him in his garden. Dannie straightened up and bowed as Elvie came to the window.

Just then Aunt Anna called "Elvie" from upstairs. Elvie knew Aunt Anna did not like to be kept waiting. She hastily laid her chain on the broad window-sill and ran upstairs to her aunt's room. Aunt Anna was an invalid and needed a good deal of waiting on. This time she wanted Elvie to hold a skein of yarn for her while she wound it. When that was done it was time to go to the party, and Elvie suddenly remembered the chain which she had left lying on the window-sill. She ran down to her own room. The chain was gone!

Elvie stared at the bare sill in dismay. It had not fallen on the floor; it could not have fallen out of the window, for the sill was fenced in by her mignonette box. Yet gone it was, and all Elvie's searching failed to discover it.

Elvie burst into tears, forgetting all about the party. Her lovely chain was gone; somebody must have taken it, but who could it be? Mrs. Floyd was out; there was nobody in the house but Aunt Anna and Elvie.

Suddenly Elvie remembered Dannie Haven. He had been there when she was at the window—he must have seen her lay her chain down—and when she came back he was gone. Elvie's eyes sparkled and her cheeks flushed with indignation.

It was one of Elvie's faults that she was too quick at jumping to a conclusion and acting upon it. She did not pause to consider that Dannie had always been looked upon as an honest and reliable boy, and that she ought to be very careful about casting suspicion on him. She felt too worried and troubled to go to the party, and when Mrs. Floyd came home she was met by a very woe-begone little maid and a sobbing tale of the lost necklace.

"And I'm sure Dannie Haven must have taken it, Mamma," said Elvie. "It couldn't have fallen off the sill. There was nobody else near, and he saw me put it there."

Mrs. Floyd was troubled, but warned Elvie that they must not be too ready to accuse Dannie. In her heart she thought it very strange, and so did her husband when he heard the story. He was a quick, impulsive man, and, like Elvie, he at once believed in Dannie Haven's guilt.

"I'll go right down and see Dan and his mother about this," he declared. "I never thought it of the boy—he always seemed so honest and obliging."

Mr. Floyd's visit to the Havens' did not result very satisfactorily. Dannie listened to the accusation like a boy turned to stone. Then he grew crimson and straightened up his shoulders indignantly.

"Mr. Floyd, I never touched Elvie's chain," he cried. "I never even saw it. I'm poor, sir, but I'm honest, and always have been."

Mrs. Haven cried bitterly, and assured Mr. Floyd that Dannie would never do such a thing. Mr. Floyd was distressed but not convinced. He believed that Dannie was guilty, but he would not be too hard on him.

"Look here, Dan," he said kindly. "As you say, you have always been an honest boy, and I am sure this was a great temptation. Elvie had no business to leave such a valuable trinket lying carelessly about. I believe you simply yielded to a sudden wrong impulse, and if you will confess and give back the chain I'll say no more about it."

"I can't give back what I haven't got, Mr. Floyd," said Dannie firmly—stubbornly, Mr. Floyd thought—"I never saw Elvie's chain, and would not have touched it if I had."

And in this statement he persisted. Mr. Floyd grew angry and left the cottage with threatening words. When he had gone, Dannie threw himself into a chair and cried. The accusation had stung him to the heart; and he also foresaw the harm it would do him.

It all came about as Dannie feared. Mr. Floyd was firmly convinced of his guilt, and the story soon spread through the village. Dannie found himself coldly received everywhere. Nobody had any work for him, and on all sides he was treated as a "suspect." His Sunday School teacher looked at him with grieved eyes; his few friends refused to have anything further to do with him.

Elvie, after crying her pretty eyes half out, had resigned herself to the loss of her chain. The cherry blossoms that had bloomed when the necklace disappeared had now changed to tempting fruit. The big tree outside of Elvie's window was loaded and haunted by piratical robins, who feasted royally on cherries all day, and grew so saucy and bold that they hopped into Elvie's room and twittered about the window-sill as if they were old friends of hers.

One day her cousin Will came to see her, and they went out to the garden to eat cherries.

"What a splendid old tree!" exclaimed Will, when he caught sight of the one at the window. "And I say, Elvie, look at all those beauties up on the top boughs. Aren't they big and red though! I'm going to climb up and get them."

Will was soon high up among the topmost boughs.

"I tell you, Elvie, it's a great place up here," he shouted. "I can see clear over the whole village."

Will in the tree, and Elvie on the grass below, ate cherries until they both declared they couldn't eat another one.

"Guess I'll come down," said Will, with a sigh over his limited capacity. "What a time those robins must have! There's a nest of them up here, away over on the other side of the tree. I'm going to scramble over and have a look at it, though I guess there is nothing in it."

Will swung himself over to a big bough which hung out over the roof. The robin's nest proved empty, and he was about to descend when something caught his eye. He peered closer, then, with a long whistle of astonishment, he tore the nest from its place and quickly scrambled down.

"Elvie, look here," he said excitedly.

Elvie stood up with a cry of wonder. There, wound in and out among the twigs and grasses on the outside of the nest was her long-lost gold chain necklace!

"O, Will," she cried, "the robins must have taken it from the window-sill that day. And O, Will, we blamed Dannie Haven for it. O, we have been dreadfully unjust to him."

Mr. and Mrs. Floyd realized this, too, when Will and Elvie ran breathlessly into the house with the necklace and the story.

"We must go at once and apologize to Dannie," said the former. "It is too bad, the way we have treated that boy. Elvie, you must come with me, and we will go straight to Mrs. Haven's now."

Dannie's feelings can be better imagined than described when Mr. Floyd told him the story, and Elvie, with tears in her pretty blue eyes, begged him to forgive her for suspecting him.

"We will do our best to atone to you, my boy," said Mr. Floyd. Mr. Dille was asking me only yesterday if I knew of a boy about your age whom I could recommend for a vacant place in his factory. If you will take it, I will see that you get it."

If he would take it! Dannie was overjoyed at his double good fortune. But things cleared themselves up some way, and when the Floyds went home they left two happy hearts behind them in the little Haven cottage.

The gold chain was quite unharmed, save for a little tarnish that the jeweler soon removed. And Elvie, when she once more clasped it around her neck, fingered it thoughtfully.

"I think I've learned a lesson, Mamma," she said, frankly. "I feel as if I could never forgive myself for all poor Dannie Haven must have suffered this summer."

৩   ৶

Editors' note: "Elvie's Necklace" was published in the *Western Christian Advocate* on May 9, 1906. It was listed in the "Unverified Ledger Titles" in the 1986 bibliography and was found by Alan John Radmore and Christy Woster.

Montgomery published over forty stories in 1906 in addition to about thirty poems.

Earlier in 1906, L. M. Montgomery, living in Cavendish, PEI, with her Grandmother Macneill, became interested in "table rapping" and other "psychic phenomena," encouraged by the ministers in the area. She was also forming deep and meaningful friendships with Frederica Campbell, who became her best friend, and Ewan Macdonald, to whom she became engaged in October 1906. They married in July 1911.

WHAT HAPPENED
AT BRIXLEY'S
(1906)

"It's a downright shame the way Alf Logan and all those Cornertown Road boys persecute Lige Vondy," said Frank Sheraton, dropping down on the porch steps.

"What do they do?" asked his cousin Fred, looking up from his book.

"Everything. I was down at the blacksmith's forge this evening, and Alf was there with a crowd of his satellites, bullying and bragging as usual. Lige came along and they guyed him in every way they could. He feels so badly over it, too. He almost cried to-day. Alf jeered at him, and the other boys laughed and applauded. I told Alf it was a shame, but I was only one against them all. Lige was on his way to the brook for a pail of water, and when he was coming back Tom Clark pretended to run into him and tripped him up. The water was all spilled, and it's no easy job for Lige with his weak back to carry a bucket up that hill. I went and carried the second one for him, and those Cornertown bullies didn't meddle with us. They play every kind of mean trick on Lige, but he doesn't mind that as much as the fun they make of him. It makes him wild to be laughed at, and they know it. The rest of the boys wouldn't be so bad if it wasn't for Alf Logan. He has a kind of chieftainship over them some way—what with his bluster and his boasting they think him a regular hero—and they follow his example in everything."

"I believe Alf Logan is a coward at heart," said Fred.

"Of course he is. Do you suppose a boy who wasn't a coward could take pleasure in persecuting a poor, simple chap like Lige? Alf likes to bully boys who can't defend themselves, but he's mighty careful to keep clear of those who can. I'd like to give him a settling down, but I don't want to get into a scrap with Cornertown rowdies, even for Lige's sake."

"Of course not," agreed Fred, "but perhaps we'll get a chance to take Alf Logan down a little yet. If we could only make him ridiculous in the eyes of his admirers it might destroy his influence, and maybe they'd leave Lige in peace."

About a week later Frank came home with another story.

"I tell you, Fred, there was some fun on foot at the forge to-day. Alf Logan was there, and was giving the details of some wonderful adventures of his down at the harbour and the crowd was drinking it all in when Lige came ambling along and began to tell his story. You know that old tumbledown shanty in the hollow of the Jersey road that the Brixleys used to live in? Folks say it's haunted. Goodness knows why it should be, for I'm sure the poor Brixleys were nearly as silly and quite as harmless as Lige himself. But that's the report, and skeery people give that house a wide berth after night. Well, it appears that Lige was coming past there about nine o'clock last night, and just as he got opposite the door—you know it's right close to the road—a great, tall, white figure popped out and flew at him! Lige is a truthful fellow, so he must have seen something—a white cow or horse, or perhaps a wind-blown paper. He took to his heels and ran for dear life with the ghost chasing him as far as Stanley's hill, when it suddenly disappeared. Well, Lige reeled all this rigmarole off in his own peculiar fashion, and dilated on the scare he had got quite proudly. The boys pretended they didn't believe a word of his yarn, and badgered him until he got mad as hops. Alf Logan had the most to say, of course. He didn't believe in ghosts, not he! And if he was to meet one he wouldn't be scared of it—not much! He'd ask no better fun. He'd march right up to it and ask it what it wanted. You wouldn't catch him running away like a scared baby!

"Lige may be simple-witted, but he has his cute moments, too. He spoke right up, and told Alf that he wouldn't go past the old Brixley house himself after dark. Alf said he'd just as leave go past it and through it on the darkest night that ever was as not, and then Lige up and dared him to do it.

"I couldn't help chuckling—Alf looked so flat. But he couldn't back out after all his bragging.

"'Of course, I'll go,' he said loftily. 'Don't some of you fellows want to come along too, for the fun of it?'

"I thought that was a pretty barefaced dodge to get company for the escapade, but it seemed to pass. Tom Clark and Chad Morrow, Ned and Jim Bowley said they'd go. Chad is a bit jealous of Alf, so he'll see there's no shirking. They're to go tomorrow night, and look here, Fred! Alf Logan is going to see a ghost then if he never saw one before, and never will again. And I want you to help me a bit."

The next night was just such a one as a ghost, if at all particular in his choice of scenic effects, would have chosen to walk abroad in. It was cloudy, but a full moon behind the clouds gave a dim, weird light, and a chill east wind moaned and shivered among the trees. Alf Logan and his cronies, walking by no means briskly up the Jersey road, shivered, too. Just at that moment Alf would have given a good deal to be well out of the adventure.

"There ain't no such things as ghosts, anyhow," said Tom Clark, breaking a disagreeable silence.

"'Course, there ain't," said Alf loftily. "Nobody believes in 'em nowadays, except fools."

"Then what was it that Lige saw?" whispered Ned Bowley nervously.

"Shut up," growled Alf. "Lige'd be skeered of his own shadow. I don't believe he saw anything; he was just yarning."

"Supposin' we do see something," suggested Chad Morrison. "What will you do, Alf?"

"You heard me say what I'd do, didn't you?" retorted Alf, angrily. "Shut up your talk about ghosts! You'll skeer yourselves and be running off and leaving me first thing."

The other boys resented this slur on their courage, and relapsed into sulky silence. As they neared the dreaded hollow, dark and mysterious in the shadow of the fire that surrounded it, they drew closer together and glanced nervously from side to side. The old Brixley house was indeed a tumbledown place. It had almost fallen into ruins. Doors and windows were gone, and the framework was decayed and rotten. With hesitating steps Alf and his comrades shuffled through the weeds of the old yard and stood at the entrance of the kitchen.

"Well, ain't you goin' in?" asked Chad, rather tauntingly, as Alf peered doubtfully into the darkness.

"Yes, I am," said Alf desperately. "Come on, you fellows! What's here to be skeered of?"

In another moment they had crossed the threshold and were in a small, square room that had once served the Brixleys as a kitchen and parlor and dining-room. All was quiet and dark. Something scurried overhead—a rat or a squirrel, but the sound made Alf break out into a cold perspiration. He laughed nervously.

"Well, there ain't no ghost yet, boys."

"You've got to go through every room in the house, you know," said Chad. "There's a bedroom at 'tother side of this, and two more up in the loft. That was the bargain."

Alf, with a forlorn attempt at a whistle, started across the creaking floor. They had almost reached the door of the inner room when a dreadful thing happened.

In the doorway appeared a tall, white figure, whose head reached quite to the ceiling. Huge, shadowy wings flapped and

waved about it, and apparently in the middle of this horrible appa-
rition was a flaming face with hollow, cavernous eyes. At the same
time a wail of the most discordant agony that ever fell on human
ears resounded through the house.

With a yell of terror Alf Logan wheeled about and made a
blind dash for the door, followed by his terror-stricken comrades.
Across the yard, over the hollow, and up the hill they flew with
frantic speed, never daring to glance behind, although the dismal
wails still followed them on the wind.

When the last echo of their flying feet had died away the ghost
burst into a shout of very human laughter, and proceeded to take
off the pillow slip stuffed with shavings that was on his head.

"Come here, Fred, and unpin a fellow," he called. "I'll never get
these sheets off alone."

Fred Sheraton popped out of the inner room, laying an old
fiddle on the window-ledge.

"Did you ever see anything so funny?" he laughed. "How those
fellows did run!"

"They're running yet, I'll bet," said Frank. "That fearful noise
you made on the fiddle scared them worse than I did, I believe.
Alf'll never hear the last of this."

If Alf Logan cherished any hope that his ghostly adventure
might remain a secret, that hope vanished when he went to the
forge the next day. He was greeted with derision by all the men
and boys assembled there. Lige Vondy had at last turned the
tables on his old tormentor. Chad Morrow, who had not made
any pretensions to valor in the matter of ghosts, and so did not
mind owning to a scare, had told the whole story of Alf's panic
and flight. To make matters worse the truth of the story soon
leaked out, and Alf had not even the consolation of thinking it
was a real ghost he had run from. "Alf Logan's homemade ghost"
passed into a byword along the Cornertown Road, and Alf's

chieftainship among the boys was gone forever. He had shown himself both a braggart and a coward. Thereafter Lige Vondy was left in peace.

As Frank said to Fred: "Our grand ghost act was a decided success, old fellow."

❦   ❧

Editors' note: "What Happened at Brixley's" was published in *Western Christian Advocate* on May 16, 1906. It was listed in the "Unverified Ledger Titles" section of the 1986 Bibliography as "The Ghost at Barclay's." It was found by Christy Woster and Alan John Radmore. This story had also been published in *Young Americans* in November 1904 under the title of "The Ghost at Brixley's" and was found by Donna Campbell. It is available to view online in the Ryrie-Campbell Collection.

In October 1904, a month before this story appeared in *Young Americans*, Montgomery was able to have a rare vacation from her life with her grandmother Macneill in Cavendish and spent some time with her friend Nora Lefurgey in St. Eleanor's, near Summerside. She went from there out to O'Leary to visit her college friend Mary Campbell Beaton, and finally to "town" (Charlottetown) for a week. Travel across the Island was reasonably convenient, thanks to the railroad.

Montgomery published over forty stories and thirty poems in 1904.

In 1906, L. M. Montgomery was still living in the Macneill homestead in Cavendish, caring for her grandmother. By May of that year she had already published about two hundred stories (since 1895), and at least that many poems. About a year earlier, she had begun writing *Anne of Green Gables*. Two other Montgomery stories published in May 1906 were "The Prodigal Brother" and "Aunt Meg's Reporter."

JANIE'S BOUQUET
(1907)

Janie was down in the garden behind the sweet-pea trellis... crying! It was not often Janie cried, but when she did—and if it were summertime—she always hid behind the sweet-pea trellis and had it out. Nobody could see her there until it was all over, and the sweet peas were usually splendid comforters. They were always so bright and lighthearted that they simply cheered small girls up in spite of themselves.

But even the sweet peas could not comfort Janie this time; she didn't even want to see them, they looked so provokingly happy. They had never been disappointed in the dearest wish of their hearts; why, sweet peas simply did not know what trouble was!

Dear knows how long Janie would have sat there and cried if Aunt Margaret had not found her out. Perhaps Aunt Margaret, from an upstairs window of her house next door, had seen a small disconsolate figure behind the sweet peas, but that is neither here nor there; Janie thought that Aunt Margaret had just happened along.

"Why, what is the matter, Janie-girl?" asked Aunt Margaret.

"O, Aunt Maggie, I'm so—so—d-d-disappointed," sobbed Janie. "O, I am sure I shall never get over it."

"Tell me all about it, dearie," said Aunt Margaret sympathetically.

"Papa was going to Raleigh to-morrow...with Aunt Ethel, and they were going to take me. I've never been to town, Aunt Maggie, but that isn't what I'm crying about. It is because I wanted to see Miss Edna so much. You don't know Miss Edna, Aunty, 'cause you didn't live in Hexham last summer, but she is a teacher in the city and she boarded in Hexham last summer in her vacation…right across there at old Mrs. Fraser's. She was just lovely, Aunt Maggie; we were the most intimate friends. She was going to come again this summer, but she can't because she's sick in the hospital. And that is why I wanted to go to Raleigh, 'cause Papa said he would take me to see her. And now Papa can't go and of course I can't either, 'cause Aunt Ethel isn't coming back. O, I'm so disappointed that I just can't feel cheered up."

Aunt Margaret smiled as she patted the curly head of her little nine-year-old niece.

"It's too bad, sweetness. But never mind. I'll tell you something to do. Pick a nice sweet bouquet of your very nicest, sweetest flowers and send it to Miss Edna. Aunt Ethel will take it…she has to spend four hours in Raleigh. Perhaps you might write a little note to go with it, too."

Janie jumped up smiling through tear-stains.

"O, Aunt Maggie, you're a splendid hand to think of things. I hope I'll be as clever as you when I grow up. That is just what I'll do. I'll send Miss Edna the loveliest bouquet I can pick and I'll write the note, too. I can't write very well and my spelling isn't very good, but I know Miss Edna won't mind that. She's as good at understanding as you are, Aunt Maggie."

On the afternoon of the next day two of the hospital doctors were anxiously discussing the case of a patient in Ward Three.

"I'm not satisfied," one of them was saying. "She isn't making the progress she should. The operation was successful and there is no reason why she shouldn't recover rapidly; but there seems to be a lack of vitality. I should say the girl doesn't want to live… doesn't seem to have any interest in living, in fact. If she can't be roused soon there is no hope for her. Such a case is the hardest we have to deal with. When nature refuses to aid us we can do very little. The girl is dying simply because she isn't trying to live."

Meanwhile, Edna Bruce was lying on her cot with closed eyes and a listless white face. She felt O so tired; she didn't care whether she got better or not. There was nothing to get better for…there was nobody who cared whether she lived or died. She was quite alone in the big city where she had not lived long enough to have made any friends. No, she didn't care; she was too tired and lonely to want to live; it wasn't worthwhile.

Presently one of the nurses came to her. "Miss Bruce, here is a bouquet for you. It was left by a lady a few moments ago."

Miss Bruce opened her eyes to see a lovely bouquet of pink and white sweet peas; a bouquet that suddenly recalled to her mind a big, old-fashioned garden in which she had spent many happy hours in the summer of a year ago, and a little blue-eyed, curly-haired maiden with whom she had had many an interesting chat. A new light replaced the languid wistfulness of her eyes as she opened and read the little note that came with it.

"My dearest Miss Edna," it ran in Janie's rather uncertain hand-writing, "I wanted so much to go in and see you, but I couldn't because Papa has so much bus'ness. You know bus'ness is a very important thing and has to be attended to. I went out and cried behind the sweet peas when I couldn't go. But Aunt Maggie said to send you some flowers, and I thought it would be nice too. I picked them all off my own sweet peas. Mother has lots more and hers are bigger, but I wanted to give you some of my very own because I love you so much, Miss Edna. I'm so sorry you're sick and I want you to get better right away. I pray for you every night and lots of times through the day when I think of it. You promised to come and see me this summer and you must get well and keep your promis', and Aunt Maggie says so, too. Good-bye with ever so much love. Yours respectfully, Miss Janie Miller."

Miss Edna wiped the tears from her eyes with her thin white fingers. But she was smiling. Something glad and happy stirred in her heart. Somebody did care...somebody loved her...somebody thought of her. She must get well; she wanted to get well and go back to work and visit that dear old garden again. After all, life was worth living, worth striving for. The hopeless, indifferent look was quite gone from her face.

A few days afterwards the same doctor was talking of the same patient. "She's coming on all right. Will be as well as ever shortly. She seemed to rouse herself all at once and take an interest in life again and that was all that was necessary. It was one of those cases where everything depends on the patients themselves."

Before the summer ended Miss Edna had redeemed her "promis,'" for she spent a fortnight in Hexham before going back to work. She and Janie had delightful times together and Janie learned, to her delight and astonishment, the part her flowers had played in Miss Edna's recovery.

"O," she said happily. "I'm so glad that I have an Aunt Maggie. She suggested it, you know. It's a splendid thing to have an Aunt Maggie in a family."

"Yes; and it's a splendid thing to have a little girl with a warm, loving heart in a family, too," said Miss Edna with a kiss.

∽ ∾

Editors' note: "Janie's Bouquet" was published in *Western Christian Advocate* on June 5, 1907. It is listed in the "Unverified Ledger Titles" in the 1986 bibliography and was found by Alan John Radmore.

In April 1907, L. M. Montgomery received a letter from L. C. Page and Company that they would publish her novel *Anne of Green Gables*. In October, she began working on the sequel, *Anne of Avonlea*.

Over forty of Montgomery's stories were published in 1907 along with over twenty poems.

JEAN'S BIRTHDAY PARTY
(1907)

I t was the afternoon recess at Burnley School and all the third class girls were sitting in a circle under the clump of spruce trees in the corner of Mr. Strong's field just behind the schoolhouse. This clump of trees was the third class's own private and particular resort; the fourth and fifth classes respected their claim and the primary grades would never have dared to go there.

Generally the third class played games and were jolly. Just now they all sat still and looked at each other in perplexity. All? No, not all. Jean Watson wasn't there. Jean had been there at first and Jean had looked very sober. But nobody had noticed this and Carrie Deane had asked gaily, "Your birthday party is next week, isn't it, Jean?"

To the surprise of everybody Jean's eyes suddenly brimmed up with tears.

"No-o-o," she said miserably, "it isn't. I'm not going to have a birthday party at all."

"Why, Jean Watson," said all the class together. They couldn't believe their ears. Everybody in the class had had a birthday party that summer and they knew that Jean's mother had promised her one. To be sure the Watsons were poor and Jean never had very nice clothes and always brought very plain lunches. But then— her mother had promised.

"No, I can't have it," said Jean. "Mother told me so last night. We—we can't afford it. Bob has been sick so long and there's such a big doctor's bill. Mother is awful sorry, but I can't have the party."

At this point Jean broke down altogether and ran away to the schoolhouse; and the rest of the girls sat down to talk the matter over.

"It's just too mean," said Georgia Smith. "Jean is awfully disappointed. She never had a birthday party and she'll feel so bad to be the only girl in the class who didn't have one."

"Ma says she doesn't understand how the Watsons manage to get on at all," said Emily Sharpe. "Jean's father drinks—everybody knows that—and he doesn't get much work to do, and they have so much sickness and there is such a lot of them. Ma says she doesn't know how Mrs. Watson could ever have dreamed of giving Jean a birthday party, anyhow."

Nothing more was said about the birthday party by either Jean or the other girls; but the next Monday morning Jennie White came to school with news.

"Girls, what do you think? Jean has sprained her ankle and she has to lie on the sofa for a whole week. I was in to see her on the way to school this morning and she is feeling dreadfully lonesome. We must all go and see her often and keep her cheered up."

"And Thursday is her birthday," said Georgia. "It is too bad to have to spend one's birthday lying on a sofa. It's worse even than not having a birthday party."

"Jean is feeling bad about that party yet," said Jennie. "I know she is, although she never speaks of it. She was dreadfully disappointed."

"Girls," said Carrie Deane, "I have a plan—O, it's a real nice plan—it just came to me this minute."

When Jean's birthday arrived it was a lovely day, all breeze and sunshine and blue. But to Jean, lying on her sofa, there really didn't seem much beauty about it. There wasn't a great deal of fun in a birthday when you had a sprained ankle and didn't have the party to which you had been looking forward so long. Jean felt that she could never get over the disgrace of not having a birthday party when all the other girls in their class had had one. Jean did not mind having poorer lunches and shabbier dresses than her classmates. But at nine years old Jean thought that her whole life was darkened because she couldn't have a birthday party.

Somehow the morning dragged by. Jean thought she had never spent such a long morning.

"I wish the day were over," she thought. "A birthday like this seems as if it would never end. Maybe when it is yesterday I won't mind not having a party any more."

But Jean's birthday surprise was already on its way to her. Early in the afternoon a knock came at the door, and when Mrs. Watson opened it, Jean, looking past her, gave a little cry of astonishment. There on the platform stood all the girls of the third class. Every girl was dressed in her very finest dress and every girl carried a big bunch of flowers in one hand and a covered basket in the other.

"Many happy returns of the day, Jean," cried Carrie. "We've brought your birthday party to you."

"O girls," said Jean, wondering whether she meant to laugh or cry and doing a little of both finally. "O, this is just lovely of you."

They had a splendid time that afternoon and every girl there thought it was the very nicest birthday party she had ever been at. They played games galore—such games as Jean could join in, lying on the sofa; and then they had lunch out under the apple trees in the little orchard. Mrs. Watson and Jean's big brother carried Jean and her sofa right out to it. It was a lovely lunch for every girl had coaxed her mother to make the nicest things possible, and the result was that there hadn't been a spread at any of the parties equal to the one at Jean's.

When evening came and the little girls went home, Jean said to her mother happily, "O Mother, wasn't it all splendid? And so sweet of the girls? I'm perfectly happy for I've had a birthday party after all."

That night Carrie Deane said to her mother, "What do you suppose made Jean's party so much nicer than all the others, Mother? We had a lovely time and nobody got cross or offended or sulky as somebody mostly did at all the other parties."

"I think," said Mrs. Deane with a kiss, "that it was because you were all thinking of Jean and trying to give her a good time and not of yourselves. Unselfishness is the secret of it all, little daughter."

❦   ❦

Editors' note: "Jean's Birthday Party" was published in the *Western Christian Advocate*, June 12, 1907. It was listed in the "Unverified Ledger Titles" section of the 1986 bibliography and was found by Alan John Radmore.

The winter of 1906–07 had been a difficult one for L. M. Montgomery. The weather had kept her in much of the time, her grandmother was growing more senile, and her fiancé, Ewan Macdonald, studying in Scotland, wrote depressing and glum letters. But the news from the L. C. Page Company offering to publish *Anne of Green Gables* heartened her considerably. It would be published in 1908 and proved so popular it has never been out of print since. Montgomery continued to publish stories and poems in a number of magazines and newspapers as well as twenty more novels after *Anne of Green Gables*.

MAGGIE'S KITTEN
(1907)

It was noon recess at the Plympton School, and Maggie Taylor had slipped away to the brook to eat her lunch alone. She never had anything but bread and butter—not always the butter. Her schoolmates laughed at her for this, and they sometimes made fun of her patched dresses and shabby hats. So she preferred to go away alone.

She would not have minded this if she could only have had a pet of some kind. She envied those of her schoolmates who had a dog or cat. Maggie was very fond of cats. She thought it would be lovely to have a dear little kitten like Lucy Miller's.

There was a small, marshy fen a little distance down the brook from where Maggie sat, and presently she heard a faint cry coming from it. It sounded like a kitten's cry. Maggie sprang to her feet and picked her way down to the reeds.

"Pussy, pussy!" she called, peering into the tangled thicket with excited blue eyes. The pitiful cry came again in answer. Maggie stopped and parted a clump of reeds. Underneath them, crouched in a little islet of turf, was a small yellow kitten with shining, famished eyes.

Maggie caught the poor little creature indignantly from the damp earth. She knew the habit which certain people in Plympton had of leaving kittens they did not want to keep in the woods to die of hunger. This poor little morsel of yellow fur had evidently been cruelly cast away for this purpose. Its bones were almost sticking through its skin.

Maggie ran with it back to a spot where she had eaten her lunch. She had not been hungry, and there was a slice of bread and butter left. She broke off little bits and fed them to the starving kitten. She felt a sense of delight and satisfaction. This was *her* pet—her own.

She knew very well that she would never be allowed to keep the kitten at home. Her mother, overworked and impatient, did not like cats. Often as Maggie had pleaded for a kitten, she had been refused.

Down the brook, visible from where she sat, was an old mouldering shanty. It was a mere box of a place, which had been used years ago by a party of sportsmen who were accustomed to spend a week or two there in the duck season. Of late years it had remained unused, and was fast going to decay. She decided to keep her kitten there. She could bring it food every day when she came to school.

When the school bell rang she gave her new-found and now purring pet a regretful hug, then ran with it to the old shooting-box, put it inside with a crust of bread, pulled to the sagging door, and left it.

She slipped down to see her pet when the school came out. Fluff, as she had decided to call him, seemed quite contented in his new home. It was a good distance from the school and road. Maggie had little fear that anyone would discover her pet. She went home as if she trod on air.

She had not far to go. The little house in which she lived was only a quarter of a mile from the school. Maggie sat down on the doorstep to eat her supper of bread and milk. In the stuffy little kitchen behind her the pale, tired mother was ironing. In the yard her father was cutting wood. He was a tall, thin, bent man, with slow motions and a brooding, discontented face.

Maggie ate half her bread and milk. The remainder she poured into a rusty tin pint and hid it under the step. She meant to run up to the old shooting-box with it at dusk.

L. M. MONTGOMERY

From where she sat she could see Aunt Jessie Brewster's house. She wondered what it must be like to live in a big, roomy house like that, with great orchards and barns.

Maggie knew very little about her Aunt Jessie beyond the fact that she had never spoken to or noticed her small niece and that nothing made her father so angry as any mention of Aunt Jessie's name. Maggie did not know why, but everybody else in Plympton knew.

Years before, when old Mr. Brewster had died, he left all his property to his daughter, completely ignoring his disliked stepson, James Taylor. But Plympton people said that Jessie Brewster had done well by her half-brother at first. He remained with her as overseer, and got on well until he married. Miss Brewster did not approve of his selection of a wife. She told him so plainly, and a bitter quarrel was the result.

He built a tiny house down by the pond and tried to make a living by all-round jobs. He worked hard and incessantly, but he seemed to be one of those people who are always unlucky. He never got on. Jessie Brewster did not relent. Apparently it mattered nothing to her if her half-brother and his family were to starve on the roadside. He struggled feebly on in his slow, ineffectual way. The little family would more than once have suffered actual want if it had not been for his hard-working wife. By her needle and washtub she earned the greater part of their subsistence.

Of all this—the old quarrels and heart-burnings, the pinching, and the toiling—Maggie was as yet happily ignorant. Her only real trouble had been the lack of playmates and pets. This lack was now supplied, at least in part. She had Fluff.

On this yellow waif Maggie poured out all the affection of her warm, little heart. Often she denied herself food that Fluff might sup unstintingly. All her spare time she spent at the old box, playing with and chattering to her pet.

It was in August when she found him. When the chill
November days came Maggie began to wonder uneasily how Fluff
was to be kept through the winter. He could not live in the old
shanty, that was certain; he would freeze to death. Neither could
she take him home. She knew quite well that no pleadings would
win this privilege.

One morning a plan darted into her head. It was a gloomy,
bitter morning, and there had been hard frost in the night. Fluff
mewed with the cold, and crept into her lap for warmth, shaking
his chilled paws comically. Maggie patted him softly, and brooded
over her plan.

She knew her Aunt Jessie was very fond of cats. Once she had
heard her father say bitterly that Jessie Brewster thought more of
her cats than she did of her own flesh and blood.

"If I go up to Aunt Jessie," said Maggie tremulously to Fluff,
"and tell her what a dear, good kitten you are, "I'm 'most sure she
would keep you for the winter. I'd never see you—and O, Fluffy,
I don't know what I'll do without you. But it's the only way I can
think of. I'll take you up to-night."

That evening at dusk Maggie set off. Her heart beat painfully
at the thought of facing Aunt Jessie's keen eyes and grim face. But
Fluff's precious life was a stake.

Fluff ran out to meet her; he was cold and hungry. Maggie put
down the milk she had brought for him, and cried softly as he
lapped it up.

"I'll be so lonesome without you, Fluffy. And p'raps in the
spring you won't know me and won't come back to me. And, O
Fluffy, dear, I'm so afraid of Aunt Jessie! P'raps she won't take you
in at all, and then I don't know what we'll do, you poor, dear, little
thing!"

Fluff purred hopefully. Maggie tucked him away under her
shawl, and set her little blue lips firmly. She must lose no time.

There was a shortcut up through the woods to the brown house. It seemed very short to Maggie. And it was a very trembling, small figure that crept up to the front door with Fluff cuddled invisibly under her shawl. The warmth from his little body and his deep-toned purr alone gave her courage. But when she heard steps in the hall, after she had knocked, she would have run if her feet would have carried her. The door opened, and Miss Brewster stood on the threshold, looking down with questioning surprise at the small, shrinking figure on her doorstep.

Miss Brewster was a tall, handsome woman, with keen, dark eyes. She looked like an obstinate woman, but not quite an unkind one.

"What little girl are you?" she said, quite gently for her had Maggie but known it. But to the frightened child her voice sounded cold and forbidding.

"Maggie Taylor, ma'am," she whispered tremulously.

A change came over Miss Brewster's face at once.

"What do you want?" she demanded coldly.

Maggie felt the change. She was in dire distress, lest all hope for Fluff were gone. Every word of the little pleading she had thought out so carefully vanished from her mind. Yet she must say something before Aunt Jessie would step back and shut the door in her face. In desperation she held forth Fluff, warm and frightened and squirming, to Miss Brewster.

"Please, ma'am," stammered poor Maggie, "I thought maybe you'd take Fluffy; I'm afraid he'll freeze and he's an awful good cat. O, I'm 'most sure he won't be any trouble. Please, *please*, take him—he's such a good cat, and he can't live in the old shanty all winter, and they won't let me take him home."

The tears came then, and rolled down her cheeks. Fluff had ceased to squirm, evidently realizing that his fate hung in the balance. His head and tail hung down forlornly.

Miss Brewster had listened in blank amazement. Something like amusement now dawned on her face; but she still spoke suspiciously.

"Who told you to come here?"

"Nobody, ma'am," sobbed Maggie. "I heard you were good to cats, and I couldn't bear to see Fluffy freeze to death; so I just thought I'd come and ask you to take him. I didn't mean any harm. And I know he will be good. He doesn't eat much—truly, he doesn't eat much."

"Come in," said Miss Brewster briefly.

Maggie followed her timidly into the sitting-room. Miss Brewster placed a chair before the fire and motioned Maggie to sit down.

"Now, Maggie, if that's your name, tell me all about this. Don't be afraid, child. I'm not going to eat either you or your cat."

Maggie drew a long breath and told her aunt it all unhesitatingly: how she had found Fluff starving in the woods and had kept him in the old shanty; how he had grown fat and cunning and so good; how fond she was of him; how she was so afraid he would freeze or get lost when winter came; and how the only way she could think of to save him was to bring him to her Aunt Jessie, who was fond of cats, and might be good to him just for the winter.

"I suppose," said Miss Brewster severely when the little plaintive voice eased, "that you would be wanting to run up here every day to see him."

"O, no," said Maggie quickly, "I know I could not do that; but I thought perhaps I might come to the edge of the woods just once or twice in the whole winter, and you might let Fluffy come down to see me."

"Well, I'll keep him for you," said Miss Brewster, looking meditatively into the glow of the fire.

Maggie stood up, feeling both glad and sorry. She kissed Fluff's head and whispered a tearful good-bye into his yellow ear before she let him slip to the rug.

"Wait a minute, child," said Miss Brewster abruptly.

She went out of the room, and soon returned with a tray in one hand and a hat and coat in the other. On the tray was a plate of cake and a glass of some warm drink.

"Eat that, Maggie," she said kindly, "and warm yourself well. You aren't half-clothed. I should think you'd be in more danger of freezing to death this winter than that fat kitten. I'll be good to him, never fear. When you have finished your lunch I'll go a little way down the road with you. It's too dark for you to be travelling around alone."

When Maggie had eaten her cake, Miss Brewster put on her hat and coat, and they walked down the road in silence. When Maggie discovered that her aunt evidently intended to go all the way home with her she began for the first time to wonder what her father and mother would think of it all.

At first, when Miss Brewster and the frightened Maggie walked into the tiny kitchen, Mr. and Mrs. Taylor were too much taken by surprise to think or say anything. Before either of them found tongue, Miss Brewster spoke.

"I never thought to cross your threshold, James, but I don't mind acknowledging that I've been a fool. And I want you to forgive me. I've wanted it for years, but I'd never have come to tell you so if it hadn't been for that mite of a child of yours. She has got genuine spunk in her. I'm pleased with her and I want to cultivate her acquaintance."

Maggie had listened to this speech with bewildered eyes, seeing which, her mother told her to go to bed. Maggie obeyed at once, so she did not hear any more of the conversation, which must have been a long one, for it was quite late when Miss Brewster took her leave.

But Maggie did know that very soon after she and her father and mother all went to live in the big house with Aunt Jessie, where she had nice and good food and all the love her heart craved.

Besides, she had Fluff, who lived to a green old age, and waxed fat and valiant; and though Maggie spoiled him atrociously, she was nothing to Aunt Jessie, who was guilty of such unheard-of indulgences as would have ruined any ordinary cat.

But then, both Maggie and Aunt Jessie knew that Fluff was not an ordinary cat.

∽ ∾

Editors' note: "Maggie's Kitten" was published in the *Western Christian Advocate* on November 13, 1907. It was listed in the "Unverified Ledger Titles" section of the 1986 bibliography (as "Maggie's Kilter") and was found by Alan John Radmore.

L. M. Montgomery loved cats and felt they had very human qualities. In her personal scrapbooks of mementoes, she pasted bits of fur from many of the cats that were her pets in Cavendish. She dedicated her novel *Jane of Lantern Hill* (1937) to her favourite cat, "Good Luck."

THE OLD HOMESTEAD
(1907)

Stephen Winslow backed his horses down to the brook to drink before turning in at his gate, as had been his lifelong custom. To-day he felt tired, and even after the animals had lifted their heads from the water he still sat there, leaning back contentedly against the sacks of flour piled up behind him.

"I shouldn't wonder if I missed that brook," said Stephen reflectively. "When you've heard a thing for sixty-odd years, it's apt to ring in your dreams, maybe."

Stephen was a small, lean old man, half lost in loose clothes that seemed far too large for himself. His white beard combed into straggling locks by his nervous fingers, flowed in a patriarchal fashion over his breast. Presently he chirruped to his horses and they lumbered along through the water and up the steep little rise to the turn. As he drove through the open gate a woman came out of the house.

"Well, everything is about wound up at last, Pris," he said contentedly. "I went into Dan McCulloch's on my way to the mill and we made the dicker. He's rented the farm for a year. Laws, Pris, it makes me young again to think of it! Seems 'sif we were starting out in life all over again, don't it now?"

Priscilla smiled.

"Maybe you'll be wanting to get back before you've lived long in Redmond," she said.

Stephen chuckled, as if at a joke.

"That was all the talk at the store to-day. Peter Shackleford says, says he: 'Winslow, you'll never be contented in city life. You'll be wild to get back here afore next spring,' says he, Shackleford-like, as if he knew it all."

"I don't know that I care a great deal myself," said Priscilla placidly. "But I'm tired of this lonesome life too, now that the children have all gone. I'm sure of myself, but I'm not so sure of you, Father. You are as full of enthusiasm as a boy over moving to the city, but perhaps you won't find it all you expect, and you may feel discontented."

"No, I won't, Pris," protested Stephen. "I've thought it all out, I tell you. There'll be no hankering for Roseneath on my part. You'll more likely be homesick yourself."

∽✄　☞∾

Stephen and Priscilla Winslow had decided to sell or rent their farm and move to Redmond for the remainder of their days. Their three children were settled there and they wished to be near them. Gordon, the oldest, was president of the university. Besides the natural tie, there was a bond of intellectual comradeship between him and his mother, from whom he had inherited his most marked characteristics. Theodore, commonly called Ted, was a prominent Redmond lawyer, and Edith, who was the youngest, had recently been graduated from college and was the teacher of mathematics in the Redmond seminary.

By Christmas they were settled down.

"I'm glad it's finished," said Priscilla. "I've had enough of shopping and 'harmonizing.' I must say I like the result, though. Don't you, Father?"

"Yes," piped Stephen with alacrity. In his heart he was wondering if he would ever feel like anything but a visitor in this fine new house of his. But he would not say so to Priscilla. He was ashamed and alarmed to find that he was longing for Roseneath—"after all my bragging," he reflected sheepishly. He grew more ashamed as the winter went by. He could not feel like anything but a stranger in the city. He missed his old cronies at the store. He had been wont to laugh at them to Priscilla but he had, in reality, enjoyed his simple preeminence among them. He had been looked up to as a clever, well-read man. Now, he did not like being a nobody. Above all, Priscilla must never suspect it—Priscilla, who so evidently enjoyed the new life as fully as she had predicted.

When April came his homesickness grew worse. The spring air wakened in him a keen desire to get back to the farm and its old, homely ways. One day it overpowered him.

"Things'll be wakening up in Roseneath by now," he thought. "These evenings the store'll be full. Wish't I could drop in. S'pose Dan'll be getting ready to work the farm. Wonder what he'll put in the south hill field? 'Tought to be wheat, but like as not he'll sow it with oats."

Presently Priscilla came in, flushed and bright-eyed. "Father," she said abruptly, "do you think you can get along without me for a couple of days next week? The—the Mothers' Council meets in St. Andrew's then, and I've been appointed one of the delegates."

"Think of that, now!" said Stephen admiringly. "Of course you must go. I'll be all right. I'll be as jolly as a sand-boy."

"If I go I will leave here Tuesday morning and not be back until Wednesday evening. Why, Father, what's the matter?"

Stephen sat bolt upright with an exclamation.

"Nothing, nothing," he said hastily, as he subsided. "I just thought of something I'd—I'd forgotten. But it's of no importance. Yes, you were saying you'd go on Tuesday, Pris. Well, all right, all right."

Left alone, the weazened little figure in the wicker chair sat up and slapped its right leg smartly thrice.

"I'll do it," said Stephen excitedly. "I'll do it! She'll never know. I'll come back Tuesday night."

He was silent for a minute, then added explosively: "I am dodgasted sick of the town!"

Early Tuesday morning he went to the station with her and saw her off on the St. Andrew's flyer. His own train did not leave until later. It landed him at Roseneath station in the mid-forenoon.

Roseneath proper was three miles from the station, and Stephen started to walk it, over the long, moist road that wound and twisted up to the wooded hills, through the young green saplings.

He stood with his arms on the yard gate, feasting his eyes on the gray buildings and gardens. There was a lonely, deserted look about the place that hurt him, but it was home. He would spend the whole afternoon here. He would go over the farm in its length and breadth and visit every field and nook.

He was down on his knees by the day-lily plot when he heard the eastern gate swing back with its old peculiar creak. Stephen hastily got upon his feet. A woman was coming through it. "I'll be dod-gasted if it 'taint Priscilla," he said, helplessly.

Priscilla it was. She did not see Stephen until she came round the last cherry tree on the path.

"Father!" she exclaimed.

They stood and looked at each other in silence for a few moments. Stephen's brain worked in a succession of jerks. He had begun to understand things before Priscilla had recovered herself.

"Priscilla, Priscilla," he said solemnly, but with a twinkle in his mild. "Where are the mothers?"

Priscilla had to laugh.

"They're at St. Andrew's, no doubt, Father. You know I didn't tell you I was going there. I just said the council met there and I was appointed one of the delegates. I never meant to go. I meant to come here, but I couldn't bear to admit to you that I was so crazy for Roseneath that I had to start off in mud and mire for it. And after all our talk last fall, too! How did you find out I came here?"

"I didn't know you did come," he answered. "I thought you was safe in St. Andrew's. I came on my own account, because I was so homesick I couldn't stand it a day longer, and because I was lit'rally dying to get out of sight and sound of that town, if only for a day."

"Why, Father," said Priscilla, in astonishment, "you don't mean to say that you are not contented in town! Why, you seemed so interested in everything—I thought you were just as happy as you expected to be!"

"All put on, Pris, all put on," said Stephen. "I've hated it—name o' goodness, what a relief it is to say it at last! But I wouldn't let on for the world for fear you'd laugh at me and say you told me so, for all my brag. I didn't think you were hankering for Roseneath. You seemed so taken up with everything in town and as busy and happy as if you were just in the place that fitted you,"

"O, I just pretended, to hide the truth from you," cried Priscilla. "I—I—couldn't bear to admit how disappointed I was after being so sure of myself. I wanted to be back here. Why, Father, I missed the loneliness of it! I just wanted to feel lonely again, with all my heart. And the worst of it was, it came between us. I was determined you should not suspect what I felt like. I don't care now, when you're feeling the same way. So I came out to-day. I brought a lunch with me, and I meant to stay all night at the Hendersons'. I've been all over the farm already. I wish we'd never left it. We were old fools to run after new things at our time of life. Good as they are, it's too late."

"We can come back, Pris," said Stephen eagerly.

"O, if we only could!" cried Priscilla. "But the children—"

THE OLD HOMESTEAD 43

"Never mind the children! See here, Pris. It's not going to do them any good for us to be miserable. They'll be willing enough to let us come when they find out how we feel. And we'll come, whether or so, We're our own bosses yet, I guess, Pris. We'll move out as soon as come good roads. Won't them Shacklefords cackle with delight over my back-down! But I don't care a mite since you're in it, too. I can just snap my fingers at the whole world."

He laughed squeakily with joy. Priscilla smiled and drew a long breath.

᷎ ᷎

Editors' note: This story was not listed in the 1986 bibliography. It was found in *The Kentuckian* (November 14, 1907) by Christy Woster and Alan John Radmore. It is an abbreviated version of Montgomery's story "The Jewel of Consistency," published in *Ladies' World* (April 1905), which is available online in the Ryrie-Campbell collection.

Other Montgomery stories published in November 1907 included "Aunt Susanna's Thanksgiving Dinner" (in *Housewife*); "The Old Fowler Clock" (in *Boys' World*); and "The Genesis of the Doughnut Club" (in *Epworth Herald*).

THE PINEAPPLE APRON
(1908)

All the girls in our class that winter were crazy over lace patterns. The fifth class girls were making patchwork quilts and the third class were collecting postage stamps; but we went in for crocheting lace, and our greatest ambition was to get a pattern nobody else had. We felt so triumphant when we succeeded, and so vexed and mortified when some other girl came out with it, too. Only we never showed that we were vexed; we just said we were tired of that pattern, it was getting so common, and we never did any more of it.

We took our lace to school and worked at recesses. Josie Pate was actually caught crocheting under her desk in school hours once but she never did it again, for the teacher made her copy out the pattern and give it to every other girl in the class.

Peggy Reid was my chum, and we always lent our patterns to each other at first. One day Peggy came to school with an elegant new spotted muslin apron on, trimmed with the sweetest edging in a brand-new design. She said her aunt out west had sent it to her, and all the girls were in raptures over it. I thought it real mean in Peggy never to have shown it to me, and she must have had it quite a while to have crocheted such a long piece of lace; for the apron was frilled and the lace sewn on the frill, and Peggy hasn't much spare time, for there are six children in her family younger than she is, and she is only twelve.

I didn't say anything, however, for I thought that perhaps Peggy would offer to show me the pattern when we walked home from school that night. But she never so much as mentioned it, and so, of course, I didn't either. Peggy told Julia Simmonds the next day that I was real jealous of her new apron, because I'd never said a word about it. Julia told me, of course—Julia is the worst tell-tale in school—and I felt that Peggy had acted mean right through. I was pretty cool and dignified to her after that, I can tell you; but I didn't stop speaking to her, of course, for I wouldn't have shown for anything that I cared whether she gave me the pattern or not. Meanwhile, all the other girls seemed to be constantly discovering new patterns, but I hadn't a bit of luck that way.

Then a really brilliant idea struck me—all at once, one day in geography class, when I was trying to bound Brazil. It was: "why not invent a pattern of your very own?" I was so excited I could hardly wait until school was out, and then I raced home and shut myself up in the garret.

I can't tell you what a time I had inventing that pattern. It took me three weeks. I got right down to the foot of my class and lost marks in everything because I was thinking of it all the time. Mother said it wasn't safe to send me on an errand, because I was sure to make a muddle of it; some nights I actually couldn't sleep. But in the end I succeeded. It was a pineapple design, but not a bit like any of the other pineapple patterns the girls had, and it was really sweetly pretty. None of the other girls had ever thought of such a thing.

I decided I wouldn't tell them at first that I had invented it; it would be fun to see them trying to get it, and hunting old maga-zines through, and writing away to all their friends for it—and I knowing all the time that there was no other copy of it in the world.

I crocheted enough of it to trim an apron, and then one day I wore the apron to school. The girls were wild over the lace, and said it was the prettiest pineapple pattern they had ever seen but Peggy never so much as referred to it.

Of course, nobody could get the pattern, and soon it got around that there was some mystery about it. Peggy told Julia that someone would soon get hold of it, and when Julia told me, I said it wouldn't be Peggy Reid, anyhow. Julia told Peggy that, and Peggy said she could find out that pattern in a fortnight, if it was worth finding out, but it wasn't. I walked home from school with Maggie Brown that night.

The next day was washing day, and mother washed my pineapple apron and hung it out on the line. It was a lovely moonlight night when we went to bed—clear as day—but before morning it was quite a snowstorm. When I went out to bring the clothes in after breakfast, my pineapple apron was gone. Mother said it must have blown away; I looked everywhere but couldn't find it.

Peggy wasn't in school all the next week. She was sick with a cold, but I didn't know that, or, of course, I would have gone over to see her. I thought she just had to stay home to help her mother. She often had to.

But one morning when I went to school, there was Peggy in the midst of a group of girls, all laughing and talking. As soon as I went in, Josie Pate called out: "You said nobody would ever get your pineapple pattern, Alice, but Peggy has."

Then they all stood back, and there was Peggy looking so triumphant, wearing an apron trimmed with my pineapple-pattern lace.

O, I can tell you I just flared up. It was really too much.

"Peggy Reid, you took my apron off the line, and that is how you got the pattern," I cried. "You couldn't have got it any other way, because I invented that pattern myself!"

Of course, I didn't mean that Peggy stole the apron. I meant she'd just borrowed it without asking to get the pattern, and a pretty mean thing I thought it. Peggy turned red, and then she turned white.

"I guess I'm not a thief, Alice Morley," she snapped out. "I don't know where your old apron is, and I don't care. You're just mad because I've got the pattern when you said I couldn't, and I don't believe you made it out of your own head."

Miss Westcott came in then, and we couldn't say anything more. But from that cut I was done with Peggy. It was dreadfully lonesome, and none of the other girls was really half so nice as Peggy; but I thought she had behaved dreadfully, and I vowed I'd never forgive her. I always walked home with Maggie Brown, and I never spoke to or looked at Peggy.

Things went on like this until the middle of the winter. The pineapple lace fuss all seemed far away by that time, and I began to wish I hadn't got so mad over it. After all, perhaps Peggy only meant it as a joke on me for boasting that nobody could ever get that pattern; and although she certainly had been horrid, I had been—a little—horrid, too. But the mischief was done, and how it could be undone I couldn't see, for I was bound I wouldn't be the first to try to make up, and Peggy just went by me with her head in the air. The very sight of a crochet hook made me sick.

One day Mother got a letter from Miss Newell, and everybody in our house went straightway into a red-hot state of excitement. Miss Newell is an old school friend of Mother's, and she is a famous writer. Her books are splendid, and Peggy and I just revelled in them. Peggy always thought it wonderful that I should have a mother who was Miss Newell's friend, and I had always promised that if Miss Newell ever came to visit Mother I'd have Peggy over to meet her.

And now Miss Newell was really coming. She wrote that she would be passing through Bingham on Tuesday, and would drive out to Westford between trains to have tea with mother, for the sake of Auld Lang Syne. This was Monday already, so Miss Newell would be here the next day. I was too excited to eat or study or do a single thing except plead with Mother to let me put my front hair up in curlers that night. Mother doesn't approve of it as a frequent occurrence, but I felt that I simply could not face Miss Newell with straight hair, for all her heroines have curly hair.

Then I thought of Peggy and my old promise to her. I was in a regular fix. Of course, Peggy had acted meanly, but a promise is a promise, and Mother had brought us up to keep one whenever we made it. Besides, you couldn't read one of Miss Newell's books without discovering what opinion she would have of a girl who would break a promise. I didn't know what to do, but I felt I must decide that night. It would never do to leave it till the next morning, for that wouldn't give Peggy a chance to curl her hair. Finally, just at dusk, I marched over to Peggy's through the fir grove. Peggy saw me coming and she met me at the door, but she didn't speak.

"Miss Newell is coming to our place to-morrow afternoon," I said just as stiffly and politely as anything you ever heard, "and I have come to ask you over because I promised long ago that I would."

Peggy caught me by the arm and pulled me right into the hall.

"O, Alice, do forgive me," she said. "It's lovely of you to ask me over to meet Miss Newell. And honestly, Alice, I didn't take your apron, but—"

"I never supposed you stole it," I broke in. "I thought you'd just borrowed it to tease me. But since you say you didn't, of course it is all right, and—"

"But it isn't all right," interrupted Peggy, looking miserable. "I—I have something to confess. I was bound to show you I could get that pattern, and that night your apron was out I slipped over into your yard and examined the lace until I was sure I could do it. But I never took the apron off the line, and it was there when I left. It—it wasn't ladylike," said Peggy, beginning to cry, "and please don't tell Miss Newell I did it. But you provoked me so, telling Julia I couldn't get it, and I thought you were real mean not to lend me the pattern."

"But you didn't lend me the pattern of that lace your aunt sent you," I said reproachfully.

Peggy opened her eyes wide.

"But she didn't send me the pattern," she said. "She sent me lace and apron and all, and I couldn't make out how the pattern went, either. I thought you knew that; all the other girls did. I thought you were jealous of my present, because you never said a word about it."

Peggy and I just sat down with our arms around each other and explained everything out. O, it was so jolly to be friends with Peggy once more. She came over and stayed all night with me, and we both put our hair in curlers.

Miss Newell came next day, and we had a real nice time. But I think both Peggy and I were just the least little bit disappointed, although we would never admit it even to each other. Miss Newell was very nice, but she didn't talk a bit cleverly, and she was short and stout and quite gray. Of course, that wasn't to be wondered at, really, when you come to think that she was as old as Mother. But I had never thought of Miss Newell being gray, and it was a great shock to me.

About the pineapple apron? O, yes: a big thaw came in March, and I found it under the lilac bush. It wasn't hurt a bit, but I couldn't bear the sight of it, so I put it in the missionary box. I think Peggy put hers in, too, for I never saw her wear it again, and the missionary's wife wrote to mother saying that she gave the two pineapple aprons as prizes in the Native school. So I suppose they did some good in the world after all.

Editors' note: "The Pineapple Apron" was published in the *Western Christian Advocate* (August 26, 1908), shortly after Montgomery received her first copy of *Anne of Green Gables* in June 1908. It is listed in the "Unverified Ledger Titles" section of the 1986 bibliography and was found by Carolyn Strom Collins. Nineteen Montgomery stories were published in 1908, including "The Proving of Russell" (in *Sabbath-School Visitor*) and "A Will, A Way, and A Woman" (in *American Agriculturist*), both published in August.

Like most women of her era, L. M. Montgomery was an expert in many kinds of needlework, including crochet, knitting, embroidery, and patchwork. Many references to needlework can be found in Montgomery's books, stories, and poems. She herself invented a "netted doily" pattern for a centerpiece that was published in *Modern Priscilla* magazine in April 1903.

HOW BOBBY GOT TO
THE PICNIC
(1909)

Bobby was lying prone among the lush grasses behind the dairy, crying as if his heart would break. The maple trees over him were whispering softly, and sunbeams flickered down through their boughs to dance over Bobby's tow-coloured hair and play bo-peep with each other; a robin perched on a bough and twittered an invitation to Bobby to cheer up; and a big, golden bee hummed in the air above him. But Bobby refused to be comforted.

Now, who was Bobby, and why was he crying behind the dairy on such a lovely, sunshiny summer morning, when everything in the world—boys, birds, and bees—ought to have been as happy as the sunshine?

Bobby had been Bobby, and nothing else, as long as he could remember. But a year ago he had come from the Orphan's Home to live with Mr. and Mrs. Johnson, and since then he had been called Bobby Johnson. He was about twelve years old, and he had been happy enough since he had come to the farm. Mr. and Mrs. Johnson meant to "do well" by the boy they had adopted, and certainly as far as material comfort went, Bobby had nothing to complain of. But the Johnsons had never had any children of their own, and it was so long since they had been children themselves that they had forgotten what it was like. So Bobby would have been a rather lonely little fellow if there had not always been so many chores and errands to keep his hands and thoughts occupied.

Bobby should have been down in the orchard picking currants

instead of crying behind the dairy. And after the currants there would be something else. Bobby was willing to work, but who could pick currants with big tears rolling down his face? He must cry out his dreadful disappointment first.

Another boy came whistling around the dairy presently and stopped in astonishment at the unusual sight of Bobby crying. The newcomer was about Bobby's age, but he was dressed in a very natty suit of clothes and wore a white collar and tie; his hair was carefully cut, and altogether he did not look like a Butternut Ridge boy.

"I say, Bob, what on earth is the matter?"

Bob twisted himself around until his disconsolate, freckled face, stained with tears, came into sight. He was past caring whether Frank Rexford or anybody else caught him crying. They might call him baby if they would; nothing mattered after his crushing disappointment.

"It's the Picnic," wailed Bob, contriving even in the depths of his despair, to pronounce the word with a capital. "My clothes got b-b-urned up, and I can't go-o-o."

His head went down again and he gave such a big sob that it almost choked him.

Frank whistled again, and sat down on a convenient stump.

"Look here, Bob, crying isn't going to help matters any. Sit up straight and tell me the whole business."

Thus adjured, disconsolate Bobby sat up and dashed his fists across his eyes.

"You don't know," he sobbed. "You've been to dozens of picnics, and I've never been to a single one. And I did want to go to this one awful bad. All the boys of my class are going. And they're going away up the river in the boat, and going to have swings and ice-cream and fireworks at night—and a splendid time—and now I can't go."

Frank knew all about this picnic. He had come down to

Butternut Ridge on the train the night before for the very purpose of attending it, because his Aunt Agnes, who lived next door to the Johnsons, and who was a power in the Sunday School, had invited him. Frank had been spending a month with her in the earlier part of the summer, and this was how he came to know Bobby well. They had been "great chums."

"What do you mean by saying your clothes were burned up?" he asked.

"My good clothes," said Bobby, sorrowfully. "They were hanging up in the kitchen chamber closet, you know, along with Uncle Hezekiah's good trousers and Aunt Mary's Sunday dress and the kitchen pipe goes right up through. This morning Aunt Mary smelled something queer and run up and opened the closet and it was all full of smoke. The things had caught fire from the pipe. They had an awful time to get it put out—and when they did my clothes were all burnt into holes. They ain't any more good at all—and I haven't got anything fit to wear to the picnic."

Bobby filled up again.

"It's too bad, old chap," said Frank sympathetically, "but you ought to be thankful the house didn't burn down."

"And I am," said Bobby indignantly, "awful thankful. And I never let on to Aunt Mary how bad I felt. I just was bound I wouldn't. But when she said at dinner time that I'd have to stay home from the picnic 'cause I hadn't any clothes to wear I couldn't stand it. 'Course I knew it before, but when I heard her *say* it—O, dear!"

"Well, I'm awful sorry, Bob," said Frank slowly. "If I'd any more clothes down with me, I'd lend them in a minute. But I haven't because I'm going right back the next day."

"O, it's just my luck," said Bobby drearily. "I've never been at a picnic in my life, and I've been thinking about this all summer and planning such a good time. And I was to carry the flag at the head of the procession, too. Miss Helen picked me 'cause, she said, I was so straight. And I never tasted ice-cream or saw skyrockets."

Frank dug his heels uncomfortably into the ground.

"I'm sorry," was all he seemed able to say. "I wish you could go, Bob, but I don't see how it could be managed."

"O, it can't. I know that well enough. If it could, do you s'pose I'd be here crying? No, sir, I'd be busy managing it. Well, I've got to go and pick the currants now."

Frank walked home in a brown study. He was trying to fight down a sudden idea that had come to him. Picnics, as Bobby had said, were common things in his experience—he had been to four that summer already. But the Butternut Ridge picnic was always a tip-top affair—more fun than a dozen ordinary picnics put together. This one promised to be particularly good, and he had been thinking about it for a week, ever since Aunt Agnes sent him word that it was to take place. It was no use talking, he simply *had* to go. Of course, he was sorry for Bobby. But there would be another picnic next summer, and Bobby would get to that and forget all about this disappointment.

Frank thought he had settled the question, but some way it wouldn't stay settled. He was very silent and preoccupied all the rest of the day. Over and over something kept saying to him: "You have been going to picnics all your life and Bobby has never been to one; he never has any fun. You are a selfish boy, I'm afraid, Frank Rexford."

Aunt Agnes wondered what had come over her lively nephew. She had no boys of her own, and Frank was a particular pet of hers. At twilight she said to him: "Frank, you will turn brown for good if you keep on meditating much longer. Of what are you thinking so deeply?"

Frank stuck his hands in his pockets and looked out of the

window.

"I've been trying to make up my mind to do something I don't want to do, Aunt Agnes," he said slowly, "but I think I ought to do it. I wouldn't mind staying in bed all day so much, but I'd hate to miss the picnic."

"Stay in bed! Frank, what on earth do you mean?" exclaimed his aunt in bewilderment.

Thereupon Frank explained matters, and they had a long talk. It ended with Aunt Agnes saying gently: "Well, do just as you like about it, Frank. I shan't object."

The picnickers were all to meet at the wharf the next morning at ten o'clock, and at nine a very disconsolate Bobby was feeding the pigs, pouring great milky streams into the troughs under the apple trees and trying with all his might and main to forget what a glorious day it was for a picnic. Suddenly Frank dashed around the corner, caught Bobby by the shoulder, and whirled him about.

"Bobby Johnson, do you know what you are going to do to-day? You are going to the picnic. I'm going to lend you my clothes. They'll fit you all right. You are to come right over to Aunt Agnes's now and get them on. Hurry up, too; you won't have any too much time to get dressed and get down to the wharf by ten o'clock."

"But what will you do, Frank? Have you another suit?"

"O, I'm not going after all—changed my mind since last night. Bobby Johnson, why don't you hurry?"

"O, I won't go," cried Bobby, as the nature of Frank's sacrifice dawned on him. "You are going to give me your clothes and stay home yourself. O, I'm not so mean as that, Frank."

"Look here, Bob, be sensible. Why, I've been to four picnics this summer already. If you won't go to this one I won't, either—that's flat. You have just *got* to go."

After a little more argument and persuasion Bobby yielded,

tipped the last foaming bucket over the fence, got Mrs. Johnson's permission, and hurried off with Frank in a high state of excitement. Frank's trim suit fitted Bobby admirably, and Frank did not have to go to bed after all, for Aunt Agnes had found in the garret an old discarded suit of his, left there after a vacation two years ago. It was badly torn and faded and very tight, but it served the purpose, and Frank stood at the door and watched Bobby and Aunt Agnes drive away with a much lighter heart than he had expected. After all, he didn't mind missing the picnic *very* much; Bobby was so happy.

Frank found the day a pretty long and lonely one. But he read a sea story Aunt Agnes had given him, and ate the lovely lunch she had left, and in the afternoon he took a long nap. And so the day wore away, and at last Aunt Agnes came home.

"Well, Frank, here we are back. Have you been lonely?"

"No, Aunty, really not much at all, only since it got dark. Where's Bob?"

"He is coming up with the other boys. Frank, if you could have seen that child to-day, you would have felt more than repaid for staying home. I really never saw any one look so happy. I am sure he enjoyed every minute of the time, and he was so careful of your clothes. But he will tell you all about it himself."

Presently Bobby came running breathlessly in, and as he got out of Frank's clothes and into his own patched ones, he gave an animated account of the picnic.

"O, Frank, it was just splendid. At first I felt bad about your staying home, and thought I oughtn't to have let you. But after a while I just couldn't think of anything but what was going on. We had a splendid sail, and when we got up to the island we landed and had lovely games, and the procession and all, and I carried the flag. And when it got dark we had the fireworks— O, my! And then we came home. Frank, I'm just awful much obliged to you."

"That's all right," said Frank cheerily. "I'm glad you had such a good time, Bobby."

When tired, happy Bobby had gone home across the dewy fields, Frank turned to his aunt and said: "I'm so glad I did it, Aunt Agnes. If I hadn't, I'd have been the meanest-feeling boy in Butternut Ridge to-night; and as it is, I'm the happiest."

Aunt Agnes smiled and patted Frank's shoulder tenderly.

"Picnics by proxy are not bad things sometimes, are they, Frank? I dare say you *are* the happiest boy in Butternut Ridge to-night, because you have been kind and unselfish; but I am sure Bobby thinks *he* is. He has had the desire of his heart. I wish you could have seen his eyes shining at the picnic, Frank."

⤙ ⤚

Editors' note: "How Bobby Got to the Picnic" was published in the *Western Christian Advocate* on September 29, 1909. It is listed in the "Unverified Ledger Titles" section of the 1986 bibliography as "Bobby's Picnic." It was found by Carolyn Strom Collins.

There are similarities in this story to the scene in *Anne of Green Gables* when Anne was forbidden to go to the Avonlea picnic until she "confessed" to stealing Marilla's amethyst brooch. Because she had never been to a picnic before and had never tasted ice cream (like Bobby), she finally confessed to something she didn't do in order to go to the picnic. The rest of the story is in Chapters XIII and XIV ("The Delights of Anticipation" and "Anne's Confession") of *Anne of Green Gables*. "How Bobby Got to the Picnic" was published a year after *Anne of Green Gables* and about the time *Anne of Avonlea* was published.

PETER OF THE LANE
(1909)

Judge Raymond was taking his morning constitutional in the lane. It was a fine old lane, running just back of Elmcroft, under big chestnuts, and debouching into a sunny by-street below, whereon lived people whom to know was to be unknown. None of them ever ventured into the lane, for it was part of the Elmcroft estate, and everybody in Marsden knew that the judge did not like trespassers. He had never met anyone there in his morning walks, and he had come to look upon the lane as the one place where he was perfectly safe from all interruption; consequently he carried there his griefs and anxieties and walked them off or wrestled them down, going back to the world the same suave, courtly man of iron it thought it knew so well.

This particular morning the judge especially desired to be alone, for it was the tenth of June and he had a bitter reason for hating the date. Therefore he was surprised and displeased on coming out from the chestnut shade into the sunny space at the end of the lane to find somebody sitting on the big gray boulder by the fence.

This somebody was a small boy, most immaculately arrayed in white trousers and stiffly starched white blouse. He had his hands in his pockets, and although his face was very sober and care visible on his brow, he evidently did not realize in the least what an offense he was committing in sitting thus unconcernedly on Judge Raymond's boulder. His hat was pushed back on his head and the face beneath it, rimmed about with yellow curls, was very pink and white and wholesome—a woman would have called it "kissable," but, of course, such a thought never entered into Judge Raymond's head. The latter stopped, folded both hands over the top of his cane and looked frowningly into the lad's blue eyes.

"Who are you?" he said stiffly.

The scowling, bushy eyebrows, before which every other small boy in Marsden would have fled aghast, disturbed the serenity of this self-possessed interloper not at all. He got up briskly with a sigh of relief, and said clearly: "I am Peter, and I am very glad to see you because I want to ask a favor of you. Will you please come and help me get my kitten out of the well? She fell in two hours ago, and Aunt Mary Ellen is away waiting on a sick lady."

"Bless my soul, child," grumbled the judge, "if your cat fell into the water two hours ago it must be drowned by this time."

"O, no, she's not in the water," explained Peter cheerfully. "She fell into the water, I expect, but she climbed out of it into a little hole between the stones; I can see her eyes and hear her crying. Will you please tell me if you will help me to get her out? Because if you can't I must look for someone else. Aunt Mary Ellen told me I mustn't associate with anybody 'round here, but I thought it wouldn't be any harm to ask you—you look so respectable."

Judge Raymond, even when much younger and nimbler than he was then, had not been in the habit of rescuing cats from wells, but now he asked briefly where the well was. "Come," said Peter with equal brevity, extending a plump little paw. The judge took it and was led to a small gap in the fence palings. Peter measured the gap and the judge ruthlessly with his eye.

"You can't go through it. You'll have to climb over."

The judge meekly climbed over. He found himself in the trim little yard of a small brown house all grown over with vines. In the middle of the yard was the well with an old-fashioned open hood, windlass, and chain. To it Peter dragged the judge and peered over.

"She's all right yet," he announced. "There is a ladder on the kitchen roof. Will you get it, please? And I'll hold it steady while you go down the well and bring her up."

With an effort the judge shook off the mesmeric influence which had already made him take three steps toward the ladder.

"My dear Peter," he said firmly, "I can't with my years and—ahem—weight go down a well on a ladder after a kitten. Instead, I'll go home and send my man Jenkins over. He will do it."

Peter thrust his hands into his pockets, threw back his head and looked scrutinizingly at the judge.

"Is your man Jenkins respectable?" he demanded.

"Very much so," assured the judge.

"Well, I'll take your word for it," said Peter confidingly. "It's not that I'm so particular myself, but Aunt Mary Ellen is. You may send Jenkins."

Accordingly Jenkins was sent, so dizzy with amazement over such an unheard-of order from the judge that he was barely capable of obeying Peter's concise and pointed directions. Eventually the kitten was rescued, as the judge, who was posed unseen behind the chestnut trees, saw. Upon Jenkins' return he condescended to question him.

"Do you know who those people are, Jenkins? I thought old Mr. Morrison lived there alone."

"He used to, sir, but he died very suddenly a month ago, and I understand, sir, that his property went to a cousin of his. She only came last week, sir. The little chap is her nephew, and a fine, manly little fellow he is."

"Was the—ahem—the kitten uninjured, Jenkins?"

"It hadn't lost more than one of its nine lives, sir. Very wet and muddy, sir. Peter made me carry it into the kitchen and lay it on the rug, because he said his aunt had told him on no account to dirty his clean clothes, and he always obeyed her when he could because there were often times when he couldn't."

The next morning Peter was sitting on the boulder again. The judge halted before him and smiled.

"I hope the kitten hasn't fallen into the well again, Peter."

"O, no; such a thing isn't likely to happen *every* morning," said Peter, "and Aunt Mary Ellen is going to have a pump put in. She says I'll be falling into the well myself the next thing if she don't. Aunt Mary Ellen is bringing me up, you know, because my parents are dead, and she takes a great deal of trouble with me. But I came out this morning for two reasons. One was that I wanted to thank you for helping me yesterday. I'm very much obliged to you, and if you ever want *me* to do anything for *you* you've only to mention it."

"Thank you; I will," said the judge. "What was your other reason?"

Peter sighed.

"I was lonesome," he said frankly. "I've nobody to talk to, and I thought maybe you'd let me talk with you for a spell."

"Certainly, certainly. Only I've grown so unaccustomed to conversing with boys that I'm afraid you'll have to do most of the talking."

"O, I'm well able to do that," said Peter confidently, getting up and falling into step with the judge. "Aunt Mary Ellen says I talk a great deal too much, and sometimes when I'm very bad she punishes me by forbidding me to say a word for one hour by the clock. You've no idea how long an hour like that can be. But the time seems very long anyhow in Marsden."

"Where did you live before you came here?" asked the judge.

"In Westville."

The judge frowned. He had his own reasons for disliking the name of Westville but Peter, striding blithely along with his hands

L. M. MONTGOMERY

in his pockets, did not see the frown, and perhaps would not have cared in the least if he had.

"Westville's a dandy place. I had so many friends there—one very dear friend in particular. It's a terrible thing to part with your friends, isn't it? It hurts your feelings so much, doesn't it?"

"Yes, it hurts them so much that they sometimes never get over it," said the judge gruffly. Perhaps he was gruff because he was so unaccustomed to talking about his feelings. Marsden people would have said he hadn't any to talk about.

"Will you please tell me what your name is?" said Peter. "It's not that I care myself what it is, because I'd like you if you hadn't any name *at all*. But Aunt Mary Ellen does. She is very particular who I associate with, as I told you. I couldn't tell her your name yesterday, and she didn't much like the sound of Jenkins."

"People call me Judge Raymond."

Peter looked up with a radiant smile.

"O, I'm so glad. Raymond is a fav'rite name of mine. You see" —confidentially—"it's the name of my promised wife."

The judge gasped.

"Your—your—well! I understand that the rising generation is very precocious, but aren't you *rather* young to be engaged?"

"Far too young," agreed Peter promptly. "I'm only seven. But you see I couldn't leave her in Westville without making sure of her, 'specially when Roger Mitchell was to go on living there after I left. So I asked her to marry me, and she said she would and she promised she'd never play with Roger any more. She'll keep her word, too, for she is that sort of a girl. So I'm quite easy in my mind. Of course, we don't intend to be married till we're grown up."

"Come, come; that's a relief, anyhow. What is your fair lady's name?"

"Averil Raymond."

The judge gave an inarticulate exclamation and stopped short. His face grew purple and his eyebrows drew down in such a black scowl that his deep-set black eyes could hardly be seen. Peter looked up in astonishment.

"What is the matter?"

"Nothing, nothing," said the judge with an effort and walked on.

"I wouldn't look like that over nothing," said Peter indignantly. "You gave me a fright. I thought you were sick. I expect I look like that when I take stomach cramps. Well, I was telling you about Averil. I'm so glad I've found somebody I can talk to about her—somebody who is sym'thetic. Aunt Mary Ellen isn't very sym'thetic. She liked Averil, though—everybody likes Averil. But Aunt Mary Ellen laughs at a fellow when he talks about his girl. You won't laugh, will you?"

"No, I won't laugh," promised the judge; and to do him justice he didn't look in the least like laughing.

"They lived right next door to us in Westville, Averil and her mother. Her father was dead, but they had his picture hanging in the sitting room, and Averil said her prayers to it every night. She said her mother thought she was saying them to God, but it was her father all the time, because she felt so much better acquainted with him. He died when Averil was four, so she remembers him. She is six now. They were dreadfully poor—poorer even than Aunt Mary Ellen and me, and goodness knows we were poor enough then. But Aunt Mary Ellen said they came of good stock, so she let me associate with them. Aunt Mary Ellen was pretty thick with Averil's mother herself. Averil's mother gave music lessons and she always looked sad and tired. But Averil didn't look sad—no, sir. She was laughing all the time. I like a girl who laughs, don't you?"

"I suppose it is pleasanter," conceded the judge.

"Averil is the prettiest girl in Westville. She has long brown curls and big brown eyes and a muscle like a Sullivan. She knocked Roger Mitchell clean over once because he tried to kiss her. But she's a very ladylike girl for all that. I tell you I felt awful bad when I came away, and so did she. But, of course, we'll write. I can't write very well yet, and Averil can only print. I wrote her yesterday and I know I spelled half the words wrong. I didn't like to ask Aunt Mary Ellen how to spell them for fear she'd laugh, because some of them were very affectionate. Look here, will you help me with my spelling when I'm writing to Averil?"

"I will if you will come and walk with me now and then in the lane," said the judge.

"O, I was expecting to do that, anyway," said Peter comfortably. "I'll come as often as you like. I think you are a very int'resting person. Any time I'm not here and you want me just come to the gap and whistle and I'll come if I hear you. You can whistle, I suppose?"

"I used to be able to," said the judge, who hadn't whistled since he was ten.

The judge and Peter continued to walk in the lane for over an hour, deep in conversation. Marsden people wouldn't have believed their eyes if they had seen it. Jenkins did see it and had to seek out the housekeeper to relieve his feelings.

"Yes, Mrs. Moody, as true as I stand here, the judge is walking out there with that little fellow from across the lane. Him that's never looked at a child for years. What do you think of that?"

Mrs. Moody looked sourly at Jenkins, to whom she accorded very scant approval.

"I think the judge is capable of attending to his own business; and if it pleases him to take up with strangers after the way he used his own flesh and blood I don't think it is any concern of yours or mine, Mr. Jenkins."

"It's just two years yesterday since Master Cecil died," said the unabashed Jenkins. "D'ye suppose the judge will ever make up with the widow and the little girl?"

"No, he never will," said Mrs. Moody shortly. "He's as bitter as ever against her. An angel from heaven couldn't induce him to forgive her."

Every day through that summer the judge and Peter grew better friends. The judge never missed his morning walk now. Peter was generally on the boulder or playing in the yard of the brown house. Jenkins declared that the judge was infatuated.

They had long, absorbing conversations. Peter sought the judge's aid frequently in his epistolary struggles and the judge learned more loving words than he had ever known were in the dictionary.

"Do you think 'sweetheart' or 'darling' is the tenderer word?" Peter once wanted to know.

"*I* should use them turn about," advised the judge gravely.

"Averil has sent you a kiss," said Peter on another day. "I wrote her about you and what good friends we were and how you helped with the spelling, and that's why she sent it. If you will stoop down I'll give it to you."

For a moment the judge looked as if he meant to refuse; then he stooped down and Peter gave him a hearty smack.

"Shall I tell Averil you sent her a kiss back?" he questioned blithely.

"No," said the judge. He said it with such a black frown that Peter looked at him curiously.

"Do you know," he said reflectively, "there are times when it almost seems to me that you don't like Averil. I suppose it's a ridic'lous idea, but it *does* seem so at times."

"How can I either like or dislike her when I've never seen her?" said the judge coldly.

"Well, *that's* what I say to myself when the idea comes to me," agreed Peter. "Of course, it's nonsense. Nobody could help liking Averil."

"Do you like her better than anyone else in the world?" asked the judge. An older listener might have detected a wistful note in his voice.

"'Course I do. Then Aunt Mary Ellen, and then you."

"So I must be content with the third place," said the judge bitterly. The judge did not like third place nor second place. He wanted to be first—he had always wanted it with anybody he loved. Peter divined that the old man was hurt by his answer. He slipped his hand into the judge's.

"You know, I think an awful lot of you," he said, looking up with his own winsome smile. "I believe I'd like you better than Aunt Mary Ellen if it wasn't my duty to like her best. But you can see it is my duty because she's bringing me up and she isn't very well off, though not so poor as she was before cousin Mr. Morrison died. It's very good of her to take so much trouble with me, and I'm bound to like her second best. But I do wish she'd stick to the one way of punishing me when I'm bad. She thinks out so many different ways I never know what to expect."

"Are you bad very often?" queried the judge with a twinkle.

"Quite often," said Peter candidly. "Aunt Mary Ellen says I'm awful stubborn. Aunt Mary Ellen is stubborn, too—but *she* calls it determined—so, of course, there's bound to be trouble when we don't have the same opinion. But I tell you Aunt Mary Ellen is a fine woman, a very fine woman."

One morning it rained so hard that the judge could not walk in the lane. When it cleared up in the afternoon he sallied forth, but no Peter was to be seen. The judge walked up and down the lane for some time; the blinds were down in the brown house and there was no sign of life about it except Peter's kitten basking contentedly on the platform of the new pump. Finally the judge whistled. He whistled several times without result, and was just turning away in disappointment when something crept reluctantly through the gap in the fence. The judge nearly whistled again in amazement. *What* was it? *Who* was it? It had Peter's head and face certainly, but below head and face was a blue-checked gingham dress and girl's pinafore.

"Peter, is this you?" demanded the astonished judge.

Peter, red as a beet, nodded miserably, tried to thrust his hands into his pockets and failed, because there were no pockets.

"What has happened?"

"Aunt Mary Ellen and I had a diff'rence of opinion this morning," explained Peter in anguish. "It was about that porridge. I hate porridge, but Aunt Mary Ellen says I've got to eat it or I'll never amount to anything. She won't give me anything else till I've finished a whole plate of porridge, and there's always so much of it that then I'm not hungry for anything more. This morning I said firmly that I wouldn't eat it because there were sausages, and I didn't want to be filled so full with porridge that there wouldn't be any room for sausages. Aunt Mary Ellen was very angry, and she punished me by dressing me in some girl's clothes that belonged to a niece of hers that visited her last summer. It's a brand new punishment and it's the worst yet. Just think, if Averil knew it! Aunt Mary Ellen went away this afternoon, and when she was gone I hunted for my own clothes, but she'd locked them up. I was so ashamed that I thought I couldn't come to you when you whistled; but then I thought it was my *duty* to come, because I told you I'd always come when I heard you whistle. So I'm here," concluded Peter, hanging his head dejectedly like one disgraced forever.

The judge looked indignant. "Come right over to Elmcroft with me, he said peremptorily.

Peter look scandalized.

"Not like this," he protested.

"Nobody will see you like that except my housekeeper, and she won't see you like that long. It's a shame. Come, I say. There are—there ought to be—some boy's clothes in my house somewhere. We'll see what can be done."

Peter would have gone anywhere with anyone in the hope of getting rid of the shameful feminine garments. Mrs. Moody was presently amazed at the tableau which met her eye.

"Mrs. Moody," said the judge sternly, "take this boy and see if you can find suitable clothes for him."

When Mrs. Moody brought Peter back the latter held his head erect once more, but the judge looked suddenly away from him with a peculiar expression on his grim face. An old memory, once sweet, now bitter, came to him of a boy who had worn that self-same velvet suit and lace collar long ago. That boy had not looked like the yellow-haired Peter; he had been dark and black-eyed, like the judge himself.

"I feel lots better," announced Peter, "but I'd like to know how you came to have a suit of clothes that fit me. Did you ever have a little boy?"

"Yes—once."

"What became of him, then?" asked Peter, picking out a very comfortable chair and depositing himself in it. In his velvet and lace, with his fair curls and rosy face, he made a bright spot in the dim, stately room. He was as much at home there and fitted as harmoniously into his surroundings as if he had been on the old boulder in the lane. The judge noticed this and felt a certain satisfaction in it.

"He grew up and broke my heart," said the latter grimly.

"How did he break your heart?"

"Listen, I will tell you," said the judge, as if he were talking to a person of his own age. "I had one son. I idolized him and lavished everything on him. I never denied him a wish. I had great hopes, great ambitions, for him. He repaid me with ingratitude and disobedience. He fell in love with a girl far beneath him—a wretched little music-teacher. He married her in defiance of my wishes—my commands. I told him never to darken my doors again. He did not. I never saw him again. He was killed in a railroad accident two years ago. But he died to me on the day he disobeyed me."

"You are worse than Aunt Mary Ellen, I do believe," said Peter tranquilly. "She makes me eat porridge when I don't like it, but I'm sure she wouldn't try to prevent me from marrying anybody I wanted if I was old enough. I think that you did very wrong. Did your son have any little boys?"

"No. He left a daughter, I believe. I don't know anything about her—at least, I mean I've never seen her or her mother—and I never want to. I hate them both." The judge thumped his cane savagely on the floor.

"I'm sorry for that little girl if you hate her, because she has missed a splendid grandfather," said Peter. "You *would* make a splendid grandfather, you know, if you had a little practice."

"How would you like to have me for your grandfather?" asked the judge.

"I think I'd like it very much, but it can't be. Grandfathers have to be born."

"They might be adopted, mightn't they?" queried the judge. "I wish you would adopt me as a grandfather. Wouldn't you like to come here and live?"

"I would get you a pony and a St. Bernard and everything you wanted."

"I think I'd like it," Peter said cautiously, "but I don't know what Aunt Mary Ellen would say. Maybe she'd think with such a good aunt as her I didn't need a grandfather. But she says I'm a terrible responsibility, so perhaps she'll be glad to get clear of me."

"I'll have a talk with your aunt about it some of these days," said the judge, looking at Peter with affectionate pride.

But the judge's plans were upset—not by Aunt Mary Ellen, but by Peter himself. The next day Peter sat on the boulder and looked disapprovingly at the judge.

"What is the matter?" inquired the latter anxiously. Peter's good opinion had come to be very precious to him.

"Matter enough." Peter's eyes and voice were reproachful. "I think you might have told me that Averil was your granddaughter."

"Who told you?" asked the judge angrily.

"Aunt Mary Ellen. She only found out lately. I don't think you've been fair at all. You let me talk about Averil and I let you help me with my letters. Do you suppose I'd have done that if I'd known you were hating her all the time?"

"I'm sorry," said the judge humbly. "Can't you forgive me?"

"Yes, I can forgive you because I think so much of you. But I can never talk about Averil to you again and you needn't expect me to. And another thing: you needn't speak to Aunt Mary Ellen about that matter we were 'scussing. I can't adopt you for a grandfather because it wouldn't be fair to Averil. You ought to be *her* grandfather and it's my duty to think of her rights. Of course, if you feel like being grandfather to us *both*—"

"Never!" interrupted the judge, scowling blackly. "I'll never have anything to do with that woman or her child. Peter, you don't understand—you *can't* understand."

"Well, it isn't a nice subject," conceded Peter, "but I'll keep on feeling that way."

"We'll see what difference a year or two will make," the judge said to himself. But he did not have to wait so long.

One September afternoon when the judge came in from a drive, Jenkins met him with a very sober face.

"There's trouble at the little house, sir. The boy has been badly hurt; he was run over by young Blair's automobile and he's been asking for you."

Without a word the judge went down the lane to the little brown house. He met the doctor at the door.

"How is he?" whispered the judge. The doctor looked at him curiously. He had never seen Judge Raymond so moved before.

"There's no hope," he said. "It's only a question of a very short time. I always knew that drunken Blair would wind up by killing somebody. But the boy is quite conscious and wants to see you."

He ushered the judge into the spotless little bedroom. A tall, plain-faced woman with deep, kindly eyes was bending over the bed where the little fellow lay. The pink was all gone from Peter's face, but the big, bright eyes looked out undauntedly.

"My boy," said the judge, his voice breaking in a sob. Peter smiled gallantly.

"I'm glad you've come," he said faintly. There's something very important I want to say to you, and I guess there isn't much time. I wanted to see you about Averil. Aunt Mary Ellen says it's such a hard world for women. You see, Averil's my promised wife and when I'm dead she'll be my promised widow, and I feel that it's my duty to provide for her. Won't you be her grandfather, sir—just as much her grandfather as you'd have been mine?"

The thing he had never dreamed of saying came willingly, even eagerly, from the old man's lips: "Yes, yes, I'll look after Averil, and her mother, too. They shall come and live with me."

"And you'll love her, won't you?" persisted Peter. "Because it wouldn't—be much—use—to do things—for her—if you didn't—love her."

"I'll give her the love I would have given you, Peter."

"It's a promise—isn't it?"

"Yes, it is a promise," said the judge. And whatever might have been said of Judge Raymond, his worst enemy could not have said that he ever broke a promise.

"I'm so glad. It's a great—weight—off my mind. Don't cry—dear Aunt Mary Ellen. You've been—very good to me—and I'm sorry—I was ever naughty—about the porridge. Please be good—to my kitten—and tell Averil—tell Averil…."

But the little knight's message to his lady went with him into the shadow.

⋞⋟ ⋞⋟

Editors' note: "Peter of the Lane" was published in *Pictorial Review* in August 1909. It was listed in the 1986 bibliography under "Unverified Ledger Titles" and was found by Donna Campbell. It is available to view online in the Ryrie-Campbell Collection.

Adoption is frequently a topic in L. M. Montgomery's novels and stories but it usually involves adults adopting children rather than is the case in this story in which an adult wishes to be adopted—as a grandfather—by a child.

Prince Edward Island has an unusual history regarding the automobile. There were a few cars on the Island in early days, the first one—a "horseless carriage"—having been brought in by Father G. A. Belcourt of Rustico in 1866. By 1905, a few years before "Peter of the Lane" was published, there were at least five cars on the Island. They were hated so much by most Islanders that a law was passed in 1908 banning their use on the public roads. However, by 1913, the idea of the automobile had become more accepted and cars were permitted to be driven on the roads three days a week. It was not until 1918 that automobiles were legal to drive on all days of the week in Prince Edward Island. (For more information on the history of the automobile in Prince Edward Island, see Deborah Stewart's article, "The Island Meets the Auto," in the 1978 Fall/Winter issue of *The Island Magazine*, available to view online in the Island Archives.)

Peter's comment that Averil had "a muscle like a Sullivan" was a reference to the famous American heavy-weight champion boxer John L. Sullivan, still active at the time of this story's publication.

Early in the summer of 1909, L. M. Montgomery began work on her book, *The Story Girl*. She also observed many visitors coming to Cavendish to look for Lover's Lane, made famous the year before in *Anne of Green Gables*.

Several of Montgomery's stories published in earlier years were republished in August 1909. Two new stories were published that year as well: "The Life-Book of Uncle Jesse" (which she later adapted for chapters in *Anne's House of Dreams*), and "The Little Black Doll."

FOR THE GOOD
OF ANTHONY
(1910)

My very dear Coz: What shall I say? I am tired—so
tired!—having reached Halifax at three yesterday and
Beechlands half an hour later. Yet tired as I am, I am
in the seventh heaven of delight. Halifax is a dear, quaint, grimy,
romantic place, and so charmingly old! There is none of our blatant Western newness about it. Then, too, what a flavor life must
have in a garrison town! I feel already as if I were living in one of
Kipling's stories. But my impressions of "the warden of the honour of the north" are yet too raw to be of any value, and well do
I know that if they were finished to the nicest degree they would
only bore you. You want to hear about Beechlands, Aunt Clara,
Uncle Maurice, and Elizabeth. Well, you shall have the very best
picture my weary pen can sketch.

Beechlands is delightful, a stanch old house of mellow red brick,
looking as if it had been steeped in the sunshine of a century's
summers, with ivy and the glamour of royalty hanging about it.
For you must know, dear Mils, as Uncle Maurice did not fail to tell
me before I was well under his roof, that the Duke of Kent lived at
Beechlands for as long as six weeks during his ancient sojourn in
Halifax. And it is said that he planted the aforesaid ivy with his own
royal hands—which you may believe or not, as you like—but on no
account let Uncle Maurice suspect your heresy if you do not. The
grounds were also laid out under the same princely supervision,
and do credit to his taste, being magnificent. Such trees, dear Mils,
you never saw! And the view of the harbour is the finest in Halifax.

Uncle and Aunt are kind, old-fashioned folk, much surprised to find that I am not still the little girl of ten from whom they parted nine years ago. And Elizabeth! Ah, now you are interested, much more interested than in all my chatter of Beechlands and its ducal memories! You want to hear all about this cousin of yours and sister of mine whom you have never seen and I have not seen for ten years, ever since our mother died and your parents took me into your Western home, while Elizabeth came to Beechlands.

Well, Elizabeth is very beautiful. And I am so like her that when we look in the glass together I am half puzzled to know which is my own face. Are you shocked at my vanity? My dear, it is the simple truth. Elizabeth and I are marvelously alike. In spite of ten years' seniority we might, as Uncle assures us, be taken for twins. The only noticeable difference is that I have colour, while Elizabeth is pale.

But with our looks all resemblance between us ends. I am, as you know, a most friendly creature; Elizabeth is cold and reserved in manner. I laugh always; Elizabeth never, though her smile is sweet enough to atone for the absence of laughter. I prattle my secrets to all and sundry; alas! Elizabeth shows no sign of being confidential. I have no dignity; Elizabeth is dignity incarnate. I am capable of holding resentment long enough for it to be serviceable; but I am much mistaken if my stately, sweetly smiling sister has not a most high spirit to resent an injury, and a strength of will—stubbornness, if you think it the more honest word—to sustain it for longer than is wise. With it all, she is charming and I love her dearly already.

I shall write more of Elizabeth in a few days, when my Western breeziness and her Eastern conventionality shall have been mutually adjusted.

Until then, dear Coz,

I am your most affectionate and most weary, Eve.

Dear Coz: A week has gone by, and I have not wasted it. I have found out the secret of Elizabeth's romance. For Elizabeth has a romance and has shared it with me—very unwillingly, be it confessed—and only because she could not help herself. I fear that Elizabeth has a most unsisterly disapproval of me, in spite of the fact that I think she loves me also.

At first I did not suspect Elizabeth of human weakness, although it struck even my frivolous perception that in repose or solitude her face was much sadder than the face of a beautiful girl of nineteen ought to be. But I did not speak of this to her. Nor would you, dear Mils. There is a fire in Elizabeth's dark eyes which would daunt any unwarranted curiosity. I think those eyes of hers can flash fiercely upon occasion. She has even favoured me with some glances, far from loving. And yet if you only knew how charming she is with it all! Even her very pride and coldness seem virtues in her.

One day at luncheon Uncle Maurice remarked casually that Anthony Allen would return from New York next week. Now, I had never heard of Anthony Allen and Uncle's item of news, and it would have gone in at one of my small ears and out of the other if I had not at that very moment happened to glance at Elizabeth. Wonder of wonders! My sister's eyes were studiously cast down at her plate; but the point of dissemblance between us was gone, for Elizabeth was no longer pale. Pale, dear Mils? You never saw a rose so crimson! From the tip of her deliciously pointed chin to the "moonshine parting" in her hair was all one painful blush. So amazed was I that I stared at her, quite forgetful of all good form, until she looked haughtily up and, finding my curious eyes upon her, favoured me with an indignant flash of those before -mentioned proud, dark orbs. I looked promptly away, and was just in time to intercept an amused family look on its way from Uncle Maurice to Aunt Clara. Not being duller than most people, I could divine a meaning in all this; but what meaning? Who was Anthony Allen, and why should Elizabeth Stuart blush so painfully at the mere mention of his name? I determined to find out—and you, dear Mils, who know me tolerably well, do not need to be told that I succeeded in my determination—at the cost, I fear, of some of Elizabeth's affection; for she loves me none the better for compelling her confidence.

After luncheon that day I followed Elizabeth to her room, and found her standing at the window looking out on the Pine Walk. She was pale again and her eyes were sad, but O, how proud her face was!

"Elizabeth," said I, sitting down in a chair whence I could see her profile, "who is Anthony Allen?"

Again that magnificent colour! But her voice was steady and even-toned as she answered, without turning her head, "He is the son of our neighbour, Mr. Allen. They live over there at Rockywold; you can see the house over the pines of the walk."

"Is he your lover, Elizabeth?" I asked daringly.

Elizabeth flashed round upon me in right royal anger. "How dare you, Evelyn?" She cried. "No, no, no!"

"'Methinks the lady doth protest too much,'" I quoted provokingly. "One 'no' would have been more convincing."

"Anthony Allen is nothing to me," said Elizabeth coldly, mastering that blaze of temper instantly.

"I should not put myself to blush over the name of a man who was nothing to me," I said with a smile.

How angry she was, and how well she hid it! She did not deign to answer me; but turned haughtily away to her contemplation of the Pine Walk. I went over and slipped my arm about her.

"Sister mine, tell me all about it," I coaxed.

"There is nothing to tell," said Elizabeth freezingly.

"Then Aunt Clara can tell it as well as another," said I.

"You would not ask her!" cried Elizabeth. "O, Evelyn, you are cruel! I—I—since you will have the truth of the matter, take it! Anthony Allen and I were to have been married this fall; but his conduct was so—he behaved disgracefully to me, and I broke the engagement. I do not repent it. I do not care for him in the least—now."

That was a fib, dear Mils, and I knew it. This little bit of femininity endeared Elizabeth to me wonderfully. "Does he care?" I asked sympathetically.

"He has tried to make our quarrel up," she answered reluctantly, "but he need not, for I will never forgive him."

And if you had seen the light in her eyes and the haughty curve of her lips as she spoke you would have thought poor Anthony's chances about as fair as I do. Then, after having told me so much, she took leave to be angry with me and told me never to speak of the matter to her again. But I shall please myself about that. And I know quite well that Elizabeth is breaking her heart in secret over this same Anthony.

Aunt Clara has since told me something of him. He is, she says, a gay, handsome fellow, frank and friendly, and very fond— or so it would appear—of jesting and talking with our sex, among whom he is a decided favorite. Not at all a flirt, you understand; but simply as Nature made him. And this, it seems, Elizabeth does not like. O, in spite of her queenliness, she is not above a little honest human jealousy. Hence her quarrel with Anthony, and the present deplorable state of affairs. Yet Aunt says that Anthony cares for no woman in the world except Elizabeth, and never has cared for any other. But such is my sister's pride that she will not listen for a moment to any pleas of his for forgiveness and has sent back all his letters unopened.

Now, I love my sister who is unhappy: and, although I have never seen him, I also like this Anthony, who is very certainly unhappy, too. Would that I could unravel this tangle in their loves! Perhaps Fate has brought me to Halifax for no other purpose; and, though I must confess that I do not at present see any way of helping this unlucky pair of lovers out of their dilemma, still, my vision may be clearer later on. It is on the knees of the gods. Be assured that if I can do anything, I shall, even if, as I suspect, this strange Elizabeth would resent successful interference as keenly as failure.

But her anger shall not daunt me from doing her a sisterly kindness!

I am, dear Coz,

Your most affectionate, Eve.

◌◌

Dear Coz: Did I not tell you that Fate was mixed up in this matter? When you hear my story you will doubtless say that Evelyn Stuart seems to have taken a much more prominent part in it than Fate; but that will be your shortness of sight, my dear, even as Elizabeth persists in being angry with me. For two whole days she has not vouchsafed me a word or a look; but I have the approval of my conscience. And, besides, I think Elizabeth will come to her senses and forgive me in time.

But to my story. O, my dear, such a story! And remember it is a secret which none but you and I and my lovely and provoking sister must ever know; least of all Anthony, who must go to his grave in ignorance of it.

Four days ago I was curled up comfortably in the library at dusk, indulging in brilliant day dreams, when one of the maids entered with a letter which she said had just been left at the door for me. I took it, opened it without looking at the address, and walked to the window to read it by the fast fading light. Well, the letter was not for me. It began, "My Dear Elizabeth," and was signed, "Yours repentantly, Anthony Allen."

I picked up the envelope, which was addressed plainly enough to Miss Elizabeth Stuart. In the dim light the maid had mistaken me for her, which happens frequently. Did I read the letter? You ask. Verily, yes; or, rather, when I glanced at it the meaning of the few lines written on the page was borne in upon me without any effort on my part. As nearly as I can remember—for I had no after opportunity of refreshing my memory—the letter being in ashes five minutes later, they ran thus:

For the last time I implore your forgiveness. On Friday morning I sail for England. I am going there on business; but I shall remain there indefinitely if you will not pardon me. Will you meet me at the old spot at the end of the Pine Walk to-morrow evening at sunset? If you do not come, I shall know that you have wholly ceased to care for me, and I shall never trouble you again.

I went to Elizabeth with the letter. "The maid brought me this," I said, laying it on the table before her. "I opened it and caught the sense of it before I knew it was not mine."

Elizabeth snatched up the letter, glanced at it, and flung it into the smoldering fire in the grate beside her. With all her beauty and dignity, I must say that for the moment she looked the shrew and vixen and nothing else.

"O, Elizabeth!" I cried in dismay. "Won't you forgive him? Won't you go to the Pine Walk?" Which was a foolish speech; for I had had time enough to learn right well that my sister goes by contraries.

"No!" said Elizabeth, all her pride and anger flaming in her face and behind it the heartbreak looking out of her eyes.

"But he is going away," I pleaded, still unwisely, "and he will not come back unless you forgive him! You are setting the feet of your pride on the neck of your happiness, Dearest."

"Do not speak of this again, Evelyn, if you value my affection," said Elizabeth in her haughtiest manner. "Once and for all, I will not go to meet Anthony Allen!"

I said no more then but ventured to hope that she hardly meant it. Anxiously all the next day I watched for a hint of relenting. No such hint came. Dearly would I have loved to shake the girl! At sunset I went to her again as she was reading in the library. I say 'reading,' dear Mils, but considering the fact that she was holding the book upside down, I take the liberty to think that the pain of deciphering it must have overweighed the pleasure of the story.

"Elizabeth," I said pleadingly, "he is waiting there for you now. Think of it! Won't you go?"

"Evelyn Stuart," said she icily, "must I tell you in plain English that I permit no interference with my affairs, before you will cease to intrude yourself into that which does not concern you?"

Indeed, at that I had almost left her to her fate. And I should have had she alone been concerned—but there was Anthony. It was for his good I did what I did.

I ran upstairs to her room, whipped her crimson dress out of her wardrobe, and hastened to my own. The dress fitted me perfectly, and, when I had wrapped Elizabeth's red scarf around my head to shade my face and peered into the mirror, I was well satisfied. True, it was a very rosy Elizabeth I saw; but surely even she, at such a time, would be flushed, and by now the light would be very dim in the Pine Walk.

I slipped out of the side door and hurried down past the pines. A curve in the walk shut me from the house just before

I came to the hedge between the demesnes of Beechwood and Rockywold. There at the gate was a manly figure. Indeed, my heart could not have beaten more uncomfortably if I had been Elizabeth herself.

At sight of me he sprang over the gate and hastened toward me. O, dear Mils, he was very handsome, this same Anthony! No wonder that Elizabeth loves him in spite of herself! A dash of fair hair over a sunburned brow, a pair of frank, blue eyes, a laughing mouth—so much I had time to see before I found myself engulfed in his arms.

"Elizabeth!" he cried. "My darling, my darling!"

And then—and then—but I really could not help it, dear Mils, and I took good care that it should not happen again; for I drew myself quite haughtily away and averted my face.

"You have forgiven me?" he said, holding my hand.

"Yes," I whispered, "but I cannot stay any longer now. I must hurry back, Anthony. You have forgotten that this is the night of Mrs. Dacre's dance and I have yet to dress."

"O, yes," he cried gaily. "I wasn't going but now I will. And I shall meet you there, my sweet?"

"Yes," I promised, although I had my painful doubts.

"Wait just another moment," he entreated. He put his hand into his vest pocket, and the next moment I felt something slipped over my finger.

"That is never to be taken from its rightful place again!" he said triumphantly, and then he bent his head but I broke away and fairly ran back through the Pine Walk.

Arriving at the house, I went straight to the library again. Dear Mils, surely my errand was a righteous one, and I needed that assurance to sustain me.

"Elizabeth," I said, "it is time you were dressing for Dacre's dance. Remember, it is six miles out to the place."

"I am not going," said Elizabeth without looking up from her book. And, indeed it had been arranged that Aunt Clara and I should go without her.

"O, yes, you are," I said. "I have just been down to the Pine Walk to meet Anthony. He took me for you, not unnaturally, and I forgave him most wholeheartedly and promised him that you would meet him at the dance."

"Evelyn!" Elizabeth stood up. If you could have seen her, dear Mils! For once in my life I was frightened, but I would not show it.

"Don't eat me, dear sister," I said. "I knew you wanted to forgive Anthony and that your pride would not let you. You ought to be very grateful to me for having spared you the trouble and humiliation. I shall not go to the dance—and you will. If you keep your own counsel, Anthony will never know it was not you he met in the Pine Walk. And here is your ring."

I laid it on the table beside her and got myself out of the room for, dear Mils, she looked as if she might throw it at me. And I was not at all easy in my mind either, for I had not the least idea whether she would go to the dance or not.

But go she did, with mystified Aunt Clara, and I stayed home. The next day Aunt Clara told me that Anthony and Elizabeth were reconciled.

"She was very gracious to him at Dacre's last night," said our good, unsuspecting aunt. "I was a little surprised, for the child is so proud and so resentful when her anger is really aroused that I feared she would never forgive him. But I suppose that when she found out he was going away her love got the better of her pride."

It was hardly that way, dear Mils, but I did not say so to Aunt Clara—and all is well that ends well. Elizabeth will be long in forgiving me; but I think that in time she will. As for Anthony, he is safely off to England, and before he returns I shall be gone. So he will never suspect that the girl of the Pine Walk was not his stately Elizabeth, after all. Dear Mils, is it not all a delightful little comedy? I laugh merrily to myself about it. Laugh with me when you read this.

Your affectionate Coz, Eve.

⋙ ⋘

Editors' note: This story was published in the *Sunday Magazine of the New York Tribune* and other metropolitan papers (October 23, 1910), illustrated by John Newton Howitt (1885–1958). It was found by Christy Woster (in the *New York Tribune*), Benjamin Lefebvre (in the *Boston Sunday Post*), and Donna Campbell (in the *Philadelphia Press*). This story is available to view online in the Ryrie-Campbell collection.

L. M. Montgomery had lived in Halifax, Nova Scotia, while attending Dalhousie College in 1895–96 and again when she went to work for the Halifax *Echo* newspaper in 1901–02. Later, she set her third "Anne" book, *Anne of the Island*, in Halifax, which she called "Kingsport." By 1910 when "For the Good of Anthony" was published, she had published *Anne of Green Gables, Anne of Avonlea, Kilmeny of the Orchard*, and many other stories and poems while living in Cavendish, PEI, caring for her elderly grandmother Macneill. She was also finishing up her work on her fourth novel, *The Story Girl*, at this time.

Nine other Montgomery stories were published in 1910, along with twelve poems.

OUR NEIGHBOURS AT THE TANSY PATCH
(1918)

Part I

When, during our second summer at the Tansy Patch, the whiskers of one of our cats were cut off mysteriously, we always blamed a small boy pertaining to a family living near us, behind a thick spruce grove. Whether we were right or wrong in this conclusion I cannot say. None of us, not even our redoubtable Salome, cared to accuse any member of this family openly. We had too well-founded dread of "Granny's" tongue. So nothing was ever said about "Doc's" whiskers, and our amiable relations with our neighbours remained undisturbed.

They were certainly a curious assortment. Salome always referred to them as "them lunatics behind the bush," and asserted vehemently that "every one of them is crazier than the others ma'am." She thought it quite dreadful that Dick and I should allow the children to consort with them so freely; but the children liked them, and we ourselves found an endless source of amusement in their peculiarities. They were even better fun than our cats, we thought.

The head of the house was a handsome, middle-aged man whom we seldom saw and with whom, save on one memorable occasion, we never had any conversation. His legal name appeared to be William Conway. His offspring called him "Paw." Aunt Lily always referred to him pathetically as "my poor brother," and Granny called him "my worthless skinamulinx of a son-in-law." What his wife had called him I wot not. She had died, it appears, eight years previously, when Millicent Mary Selina Munn Cook Conway had been born. If she resembled her mother it is not probable that her bereaved spouse sorrowed as one without hope.

When Timothy Benjamin, the oldest son—better known, it may be said as T. B.—paid us a long, friendly, first call, Salome had asked him bluntly, "What does your father do for a living?"

"Nawthing, mostly," was T. B.'s frank and laconic response.

"Then how do you get along?" demanded Salome.

"My old beast of a granny has a little money. We live on that," said T. B. easily. "Folks round here call paw lazy, but he says no, he's just contented."

"Does he never work?"

"Nope. He fiddles and fishes. And he hunts for buried treasure."

"Buried treasure?"

"Yip—down on them sand-hills 'cross from the hotel. He says Captain Kidd buried millions there. He keeps a-digging for it, paw does. Says when he finds it we'll all be rich."

"Your father'd better be digging in his garden," said Salome, severely. "I never saw such a scandal of weeds."

"That's what Granny says," retorted T. B.

Salome was squelched for the time being. The thought that she and Granny could be of the same opinion about anything enraged her into silence.

Of Mr. Conway's prowess as fisherman and treasure-seeker I know nothing, but I can testify to his ability as a violinist. When he fiddled, on his tumble-down "back stoop," on the summer evenings, the music that drifted over to the Tansy Patch, through the arches of the spruce wood, was enchanting. Even Salome, who prided herself on her ear for music, admitted that.

"It's angelic, ma'am, that's what it is," she said with solemn reluctance. "And to think that lazy good-for-nothing could make it! What could Providence have been thinking of, ma'am? My good, hard-working brother John tried all his life to learn to play well on the fiddle and he never could. And this Bill Conway can do it without trying. Why, he can almost make me dance, ma'am."

That would have been a miracle, indeed! But Dick and I often did dance, on our own stoop, in time to the witching lilts of the invisible musician beyond the spruces.

In appearance Mr. Conway looked like a poet run to seed. He had a shock of wavy, dark auburn hair, a drooping moustache and a goatee, and brilliant brown eyes. He was either shy or unsociable; we did not know which. At all events, he never came near us. "Jest too lazy to talk, that's all." T. B. assured us. "Paw hasn't nothin' again' yous."

The first member of the family to call on us—and the only one who ever paid us a formal call—was Aunt Lily (Miss Lilian Alethea Conway, according to the limp, broken-cornered card she left behind). The formality of her call consisted in her leaving this card. For the rest, she stayed the afternoon, took supper with us, and then remained for the evening.

"I am not, my dear Mrs. Bruce, a soulless society woman," was her somewhat unnecessary introductory remark. She swam up the steps—she really had a very graceful walk—and subsided limply into a rocker. She wore a rumpled dress of pale blue muslin with a complicated adornment of black velvet ribbon, and her long, thin arms were encased in cream lace gloves—remarkably nice gloves, of their kind, at that. Some of Granny's money must have gone into those gloves. She had a pale, freckled face and reddish hair. Yet she was not absolutely lacking in beauty. Later on I saw her once in the moonlight and was surprised by her good looks. Her features were quite classical and if she had known how to do anything with her hair she would have been a pretty woman.

I asked her to come into the house, but she assured me she preferred to remain outside.

"I love to sit and watch the golden bees plundering the sweets of the clover," she said dreamily, clasping her lace-covered hands. Neither bees nor clover were noticeable about the Tansy Patch, but that did not worry Aunt Lily. She rolled her large, blue eyes upon me and added.

"I adore the country, Mrs. Bruce. The city is so artificial. Don't you truly think the city is so artificial? There can be no real interchange of soul in the city. Here, in the beautiful country under God's blue sky, human beings can be their real and highest selves. I am sure you agree with me, Mrs. Bruce."

I did, or pretended to. Salome and I knitted the afternoon away while Aunt Lily swayed idly and unceasingly in her rocker, and talked quite as idly and unceasingly. She told us all there was to be told about her family and herself. She kept a diary, it appeared.

"I must have some place to pour out my soul in, Mrs. Bruce," she said pathetically. "Some day, if you wish, I will show you my journal. It is a self-revelation. And yet I cannot write out what burns in my bosom. I envy my niece Dorinda her powers of expression. Dorinda is a poetess, Mrs. Bruce. She experiences the divine afflatus. My poor brother can express the deepest emotions of his soul in music, but I can only wield my halting pen. Yet my journal is not devoid of interest, Mrs. Bruce, and I should not object to sharing it with a sympathetic friend."

"I should like to see it," I assured her—sincerely enough—for I suspected that journal would be rather good fun.

"I will bring it to you some day then," said Aunt Lily, "and when you read it, remember—O, pray remember—that it was written by a being with a tired heart. I suffer greatly, Mrs. Bruce, from a tired heart."

I did not know whether this was a physical or an emotional ailment. Salome understood it to be the former and asked quite sympathetically,

"Did you every try a mustard plaster at the pit of your stomach, Miss?"

"I fear that would not benefit a weary heart, Miss Silversides," sighed Aunt Lily. "Possibly you have never suffered, as I have, from a weary, wounded heart."

"No, thank the Lord, my heart's all right," said Salome, briskly. "My only trouble is rheumatism in the knee j'int. Ever have rheumatism in your knee j'int, Miss?"

No, Aunt Lily's knee joints were all right. In fact, Aunt Lily proved to be a remarkably healthy woman. Her wearied heart evidently found no difficulty in pumping sufficient blood through her body and her appetite, as suppertime showed, as anything but feeble.

"When I can forget what might have been, I am happy," she sighed, "I have had my romance, Mrs. Bruce. Alas, that it should be in the past tense! I once thought I had found my true soul mate, Mrs. Bruce, and I dreamed of happy, real marriage."

"What happened that you didn't get married?" queried Salome, pricking up her ears. Salome is always rather interested in blighted romances, despite her grim exterior.

"A misunderstanding, Miss Silversides. A misunderstanding that severed two fond hearts. He wedded another. Never since that sad day have I met a man who could stir the dead ashes of my heart to tingling life again. But let us not talk of my sorrows, dear friends. Will you tell me how to can peas?"

When Aunt Lily went away I asked her to come again and she assured me that she would.

"I think you will understand me—I have always been misunderstood," she said. Then she trailed her blue draperies down the hill to the wood, looking, when kindly distance had lent enchantment, quite a graceful, romantic and attractive figure.

"Did you ever hear such a lunatic, ma'am?" demanded Salome. "Her and her soulmates and her tired hearts! Her hair looks as if she'd swept it up with a broom and her nails weren't cleaned and her stockings were scandalous dirty. And yet, for all, there's something about the creature I like, ma'am."

That was the eventual verdict of our household upon Aunt Lily. In spite of everything there was a queer charm about her to which we succumbed. The same thing could be said of that absurd diary of hers, which she brought over to us during our second summer. It was as ridiculous and sentimental, and lackadaisical as Aunt Lily herself. And yet there was an odd fragrance about it that lingered in our memories. We could not, somehow, laugh quite as much over it as we wanted to.

T. B. was also an early and frequent caller. He was thirteen years old, in our first summer at the Patch. He had thick, fair, thatch-like hair and deep blue eyes—the only intelligent eyes in the family. He was, it developed, much addicted to creeping and crawling things; he always had bugs, toads, frogs or snakes secreted about his anatomy. The only time he ever had a meal with us a small green snake slipped from the pocket of his ragged shirt and glided over the table.

"Do you think he is *human*, ma'am?" Salome asked, with bated breath, after he was gone.

"He is a born naturalist," said Dick. He is making a special study of ants this summer, it appears. Snakes are only a side issue at present. If he could be educated he would amount to something."

There did not seem to be much likelihood of this. T. B. himself had no illusions on the subject.

"There ain't any chance for me—never was and never will be," he once told me gloomily.

"Perhaps your grandmother would help you," I suggested.

T. B. grinned.

"Perhaps—when stones bleed," he said scornfully. "I don't s'pose the old beast has enough money. None of us knows how much she *has* got, she just doles it out. But she wouldn't give *me* any if she had pecks. She hates me. If there's any money left when she dies—s'posen she *ever* does die—Joe's to get it. He's her baby."

If Joseph—T. B. was the only one who ever called him Joe— was Granny's favourite he was not the favourite of anybody else. However we of the Tansy Patch might differ concerning the other members of the Conway family we all united in cordially detesting Joseph. He was such a sly, smug little wretch—"a born hypocrite, that child is, ma'am," declared Salome solemnly. We had no proof that it was really he who had cut off Doc's whiskers, but there was no doubt that it was Joseph who painted poor Una's legs with stripes of red and green paint one day. Una came home in tears, quickly followed by T. B. and Aunt Lily, the latter in tears also.

"I would rather have lost my right hand than have this happen, dear Mrs. Bruce," she wailed. "O, do not cherish it against us. Your friendship has been such a sweet boon to me. And turpentine will take it off—it can't be very dry yet."

"Jest wait till Granny goes to sleep and I'll lambaste Joe within an inch of his life," said T. B.

He did, too. When Granny wakened from her nap she heard the sobbing Joe's tale and shrieked objurgations at T. B. for an hour. T. B. sat on the fence and laughed at her; we could hear him and hear Granny also. Granny's vocal powers had not failed with advancing years, and every word came over distinctly to the Tansy Patch through the clear evening air.

"May you be eaten by pigs," vociferated Granny, and we knew she was brandishing her stick at the graceless T. B. "I'll bite your face off! I'll tear your eyes out! I'll rip your heart out! You blatant beast! You putrid pup!"

"O, listen to that awesome woman ma'am," said Salome, shuddering. "Ain't it a wonder she isn't struck dead?"

But Granny was every inch alive—except that she could not walk, having what Aunt Lily called "paralatics in the hips." She was confined to a chair, generally placed on the back verandah, whence she could command a view of the main road. From this point of vantage she could scream maledictions and shake her long, black stick at any person or objects which incurred her dislike or displeasure.

Granny was of striking appearance. She had snow-white hair and dead-white face, and flashing black eyes. She still possessed all her teeth, but they were discoloured and fang-like; and when she drew her lips back and snarled she was certainly a rather wolf-like old dame. She always wore a frilled widow's cap tied tightly under her chin, and was addicted to bare feet.

It was war to the hilt between Granny and Salome from the start. Granny attacked first, without the slightest provocation. Salome had gone through the spruce wood to call the children home to dinner. Perhaps Granny found Salome's expression rather trying. Salome always did look very well satisfied with herself. At least, something about her seemed to grate on Granny's nerves.

"Yah!" she shrieked vindictively, "your grandfather hanged himself in his horse stable. Go home, jail-bird, go home."

Outraged, Salome was too much overcome to attempt a reply. She came home almost in tears.

"Ma'am, my grandfathers both died most *respectable* deaths."

"You mustn't mind what Granny says, Salome," I said soothingly.

"Indeed, ma'am, nobody should mind what a lunatic says. But it is hard for a decent woman to have her grandfathers insulted. I do not mind the name she called me, ma'am, but she might respect the dead."

Granny respected nothing on earth. T. B., who, although he hated her, had a certain pride in her, told tales of her repartée. On one occasion a new minister had stopped on the road and accosted Granny over the fence. He was young and callow, and perhaps Granny's eyes disconcerted him, for he certainly worded his question rather inanely.

"Can you tell me, madam, where I am going?" he asked politely.

"How should I know where you are going, gosling?" retorted Granny. Then she had burst into a series of chuckles which had completed his discomfiture. The poor young man drove hastily away, crimson of face, "looking like thirty cents," declared T. B. with a relish.

On another occasion Granny routed an automobile. One, filled with gay hotel guests, had stopped at the gate. Its driver had intended to ask for some water, but Granny did not allow him to utter a word.

"Get out of this with your demon machine," she yelled. She caught up the nearest missile, which happened to be her dinner plate, and hurled it at him. It missed his face by a hair's breadth and landed squarely, grease and all, in a fashionable lady's silken lap. Granny followed this up by a series of fearsome yells and maledictions, of which the mildest were "May ye never have a night without a bad dream," and "May ye always be looking for something and never finding it," and—finally—"May ye all die tonight. I'll pray for it, that I will."

The dismayed driver got his car away as quickly as possible and Granny laughed loud and long.

"My old Granny's the limit," declared T. B.

If Joseph was Granny's favourite, poor Charity was her pet detestation. Charity was the oldest of the family; she was eighteen and a good-hearted, hard-working creature. Almost all the work that was done in that house was done by Charity. Consequently, she had little time for visiting, and her calls on us were few. She was a dark, rather stocky girl, but had her share of the family's good looks. She had dusky red cheeks and a very pretty red mouth. Granny vowed that Charity was "a born fool"; Charity was very far from being that, but she certainly did not possess very much "gumption," as Salome said. She had no taste in dress and went about one summer wearing an old rose gown with a bright scarlet hat.

"O, if only something would happen to one of them, ma'am, before they dislocate my eyes," groaned Salome.

One day, something did happen. A glad Salome told us of it.

"Charity Conway won't wear that dress again, ma'am. Yesterday when she was going to church she found a nest of five eggs in the field. So she put them in the pocket of her petticoat and when she got to church she forgot all about them and sat down on them and the dress is ruined, ma'am. It is a good thing, but I am sorry for poor Charity, too, for Granny is mad at her and says she won't buy her another dress this summer."

Part II

If Charity came to see us but seldom, Dorinda made up for it. Dorinda was a constant guest. Dorinda was sixteen and Dorinda wrote poetry—"bushels of it," so said T. B.

The first time Dorinda came she wanted to borrow some mutton tallow.

"I have chapped hands and I find it difficult to write poetry with chapped hands."

"I should think you would, Miss," said Salome; she got out the mutton tallow.

Dorinda bored us to death with her poetry. It really was the most awful trash. One line, however, in a poem which Dorinda addressed to the returned soldiers of the Boer War, always shone like a star in our family memory: "Canada, like a maiden, welcomes back her sons."

But Salome thought it wasn't quite decent!

"If there was only a wood-pool near here!" sighed Dorinda, "I can write my best only by a wood-pool."

"Why not try the pond?" suggested Salome.

"My Muse," said Dorinda with dignity, "only inspires me by a wood-pool."

I cannot remember the names of all Dorinda's poems. Some of them were "Lines on a Birch Tree," "Lines to My Northern Birds," "A Romantic Tail," and "Lines Written on a Friend's Tansy Patch."

Dorinda was stout but very good-looking. She had magnificent hair: great masses of silky brown curls. She always dressed it beautifully, too. But, like all mortals, Dorinda was not satisfied.

"I wish I was sylph-like, Mrs. Bruce," she sighed. "A poetess should be sylph-like."

The relations between Dorinda and Aunt Lily were not as cordial as their common addiction to literary pursuits might pre-suppose. There was some antagonism between them, the cause of which we never knew. But it resulted in T. B. hating Dorinda with an unbrotherly hatred and deriding her poems unmercifully.

One little white blossom of pure affection bloomed in the arid desert of T. B.'s emotional life. He loved his Aunt. She sympathized with his pursuits and, in spite of her lackadaisical ways, was not afraid of his snakes. T. B. would not allow Granny to abuse Aunt Lily.

"How did you stop it?" queried Salome anxiously.

"The first time she turned her tongue loose on Aunt Lily I went up to her and bit her," said T. B. coolly.

"You ought to bite her oftener," said Salome vindictively.

"There ain't none of the rest of us worth standing up for," said T. B. "Granny's tough biting."

T. B. figured conspicuously in Aunt Lily's diary. She seemed to centre her maternal affection in him.

"I wish I could educate T. B.," she wrote, "but alas, I am poor. How bitter a thing is grinding poverty! My poor brother is a genius, but he makes no money. And I fear he will never find the treasure he seeketh. Like myself, he is misunderstood and un-appreciated. My beloved T. B. lacks many things which should pertain to youth. I patched his best trousers to-day."

Many of T. B. speeches and exploits figured in the diary.

"For, perhaps, in spite of all, he may be famous some day," wrote Aunt Lily, "and then this neglected diary, written by a wom-an whose hopes in life have been blighted, will be of inestimable value to a biographer in search of material. I have noticed that the boyish pranks of great men are of surpassing interest. I could wish that T. B. used less slang. But English undefiled is seldom heard to-day. Alas, for it! I feel that T. B.'s association with the refined family who are now sojourning at the Tansy Patch may be of great help to him."

I don't know that we "helped" T. B. very much, but Salome tried to do him good in a spiritual way. She was much horrified to find that T. B. was a skeptic and prided himself on it. Accordingly, Salome took to lending him books and tracts and bribing him to read them, with doughnuts. One of them was the *Memoir of Susanna B. Morton*, an account of the life and early death of a child of extraordinary piety. Salome used to read it and weep over it Sunday afternoons. T. B. enjoyed the book, but scarcely, I fear, in the way Salome desired.

"Ain't Susanna a holy terror?" he would say to me with a grin. T. B. had a sense of humor and that book tickled it.

Una, too, told him sweetly that she meant to pray for him but this roused T. B.'s dander instantly.

"You ain't! Don't you dast! I won't be prayed for," he shouted.

"O, T. B., aren't you afraid of going to the bad place?" whispered poor Una, quite aghast.

"Nix on that" he said contemptuously. "I don't believe there's any hell or heaven either. When you die that's the end of you."

"Wouldn't you like to go on living?" asked Dick, who enjoyed drawing T. B. out.

"Nope. There's no fun in it," said the youthful misanthrope. "Heaven's a dull place from all the accounts I've heard of it. I'd like a heaven full of snakes and ants and things, though. There'd be some sense in that kind."

"How are your ants coming on?" I queried.

T. B. was transformed in a moment. He sat up, eager, alert, bright-eyed.

"They're durned int'resting," he exclaimed. "I sat all day yesterday and watched their doings in that nest below the garden. Say, but they're quarrelsome little cusses—some of 'em like to start a fight 'thout any reason, far's I can see. And some of 'em are cowards. They gits so scared they just double theirselves up into a ball and let the other fellow bang 'em round. They won't put up no fight. Some of 'em are lazy and won't work. I've watched 'em shirking. And there was one ant died o' grief 'cause another ant got killed—wouldn't eat, wouldn't work—just died. Tell *you*, I wish humans was as interesting as ants. Well, so long. I must be gitting home to dinner."

Always in the winter, which we spent in our town home, the children kept up a correspondence with T. B. He wrote very interesting letters, too, allowing for eccentricities of grammar and spelling. Aunt Lily wrote me wondrous underlined epistles, full of sentiment, and Dorinda sent us a poem every week—on "Memories of Other Days" or some kindred subject. We often wondered what life must be in the house beyond the spruces in winter, when Granny must perforce be cooped up indoors. Salome shuddered over the thought of it.

It was not until our fourth and last summer at the Tansy Patch that we were ever asked to partake of a meal in the Conway establishment. One day, not long before our final departure, T. B. came over and gravely handed us a formal invitation, in Aunt Lily's handwriting, on a soiled, gilt-edged correspondence card. We were asked to supper the next evening at seven o'clock. Salome got one, too.

"Surely, ma'am, you'll never try to eat a meal in that house!" she exclaimed. "Why, I *have* heard that they've been known to mix up cakes *in the wash-pan*, ma'am. And remember the dog and the soup, ma'am."

"But they threw the soup out," said Una.

"I think Mr. Bruce and I must go," I said. "I do not want to hurt Aunt Lily's feelings. But you can please yourself about going, Salome."

Salome drew a deep breath.

"I'd rather go to supper with the king of the Cannibal Islands, ma'am," she said. "But if you are determined to go, I'll go, too, and we'll all be poisoned together."

I really believe Salome was curious. She wanted to see what sort of meal "them lunatics" would put up.

We all got a surprise. The Conway supper table was as pretty a one as I have ever sat down to. The linen was spotless. The china and silver old and good—evidently relics of Granny's palmy days. The decorations of ferns and wildflowers were charming, and the awful lamp, with its hideous red globe, which stood on a corner table, cast a very becoming rose light over everything.

"You see, we can put on style when we want to," said T. B. slyly.

All the family were dressed up for the occasion. "Paw" in a dark suit and white shirt, was handsome and presentable. Aunt Lily for once had her hair done nicely and she and the girls, in their pretty muslins, looked quite charming. Even Granny had on a new black silk and a fresh cap; if she could only have held her tongue, she might have passed for a decidedly handsome and aristocratic old dame. But that Granny could not do.

"I hope you've got more in your head than you carry on your face," she said when Dick was introduced.

Having said that, however, she behaved herself quite well during supper.

The bill of fare presented to us was surprisingly good and—what was still more surprising—quite fashionable. Charity must have studied household magazines to some effect. Everything was so delicious that we could not help but enjoy it, despite sundry disconcerting recollections of gossip concerning snakes and wash-pans. We had angel cake that night and, whatever it was mixed up in, it was toothsome. Salome, in particular, was much impressed by the "style" and menu. She never spoke quite so scornfully of them afterwards.

"They may be lunatics, ma'am," she said, as we went home. "But that silver was solid, ma'am, and that cloth was double damask and there was initials on the spoons. And when all's said and done, ma'am, there's *family* behind them whatever they've come to."

"I hope you got your craws full," was Granny's parting salutation.

We all noticed how pretty and chipper Aunt Lily was that night. She was quite bright and animated. The reason therefore was disclosed soon after when Aunt Lily informed us that she was going to be married. She was very well satisfied about it, too, in spite of her tired heart and blighted life. We discovered that the bridegroom-elect was a common-place farmer living near the hotel.

"He's no beauty," T. B. informed us, "and Granny twits Aunt Lily with it. But Aunt Lily says she'd marry him if he was as ugly as a gorilla because it is his soul she loves. I dunno nawthing about his soul, but he's got the dough and he's going to educate me. Aunt Lily told him she wouldn't have him if he didn't. I'm going to live with 'em, too. Say, won't I be glad to get away from Granny's tongue and Dorinda's poetry? It makes me feel young again."

"How on earth will that woman ever keep a house, ma'am?" said Salome. "I pity that poor man."

"He is very well able to keep a servant," I said, "and I have always had a suspicion that Aunt Lily is not by any means as die-away as her looks, Salome. The woman who arranged that supper table must have something of what you call 'gumption.' Anyhow, everybody is so well satisfied that it seems a pity to carp."

"O, I like the creature and I wish her well, ma'am," Salome re-joined, with a toss of her head. "And I'm glad poor T. B is to have his chance. But say what you will, ma'am, George Black is marry-ing into a queer lot, and that is my final opinion, ma'am."

Aunt Lily meant to give up keeping a diary, so she informed me.

"I shall not need it," she said. "I can pour out my soul to my husband. I have put the past and all its sadness behind me. Will you help me select my bridal suit, Mrs. Bruce? I *did* want to be wedded in a sky-blue gown—the tint of God's own heaven, Mrs.

Bruce. But George says he would like a plain dark suit better and I believe that a wife should revere and obey her husband. I am no new woman, Mrs. Bruce, and I believe in the sacredness of the conjugal tie. The secret of life is devotion, Mrs. Bruce."

"I'm very glad you are taking T. B. with you," I said.

"I could not dream of leaving him behind, Mrs. Bruce. My heart is knit to his. I trust that in my home his surroundings will be more uplifting than they have hitherto been. In an atmosphere of calm and joy I feel sure that he will develop, Mrs. Bruce."

The next week Aunt Lily and T. B. went to the new atmosphere of calm and joy and we departed regretfully from the Tansy Patch. As we drove away in the still evening we heard "Paw" fiddling gloriously on his stoop. As we turned the corner of the road and passed the house Granny shook her stick at us with a parting malediction,

"May your potatoes always be rotten," she shrieked.

But "Paw's" fiddle followed us further than Granny's howls, and our memories of our Tansy Patch neighbours were not unpleasant ones.

"When all is said and done, ma'am," was Salome's summing up, "them lunatics were interesting."

√ ∛

Editors' note: This story, with an illustration by Canadian artist E. J. Dinsmore, was found in *Canadian Home Journal* (August 1918) by Carolyn Strom Collins. A note at the beginning of the story implies that another of Montgomery's stories, "The Cats of the Tansy Patch," had been published in an earlier issue of *Canadian Home Journal*, however, that issue has not yet been found. Both of these stories are listed in the "Unverified Ledger Titles" section of the 1986 bibliography.

Montgomery, with her two young sons—Chester, age six, and Stuart, age two and a half—had spent two months of the summer of 1918 in Prince Edward Island. Much to Montgomery's relief, the Great War was coming to an end after four arduous years. She would later recount much of the war's influence from the point of view of Canadians on the home front in *Rilla of Ingleside* (1920). Readers familiar with *Rilla of Ingleside* and other "Anne" books will notice a resemblance between "Salome Silversides" in this story and "Susan Baker," the housekeeper at "Ingleside."

Just after "Our Neighbours at the Tansy Patch" was published, Montgomery finished her work on *Rainbow Valley* which would be published in 1919. Another new story, "Garden of Spices," had been published earlier in 1918 and several of her stories and poems were republished that year.

THE MATCHMAKER
(1919)

"There is not a single baby in Lancaster," said Mrs. Churchill. "There is not *one* young married couple in Lancaster. And what's worse: nobody is getting married or has any notion of getting married. It's a disheartening state of affairs."

Mrs. Churchill was talking to her friend, Mrs. Mildred Burnham, as they sat on her verandah in the clear, spring twilight. They were both middle-aged widows and had been chums since they had shared the same desk at school. Mrs. Burnham was a tall, thin lady, who admitted that she had a sensitive disposition. Mrs. Churchill, who was a large, placid, slow-moving person, never jarred on this sensitiveness; so they were very fond of each other.

"Well," said Mrs. Burnham, "all the people who have been married in Lancaster for the last ten years have gone away. Just now there doesn't seem to be any candidates. What young folks there are hereabouts are *too* young—except Alden Churchill and this new niece of yours—what's her name?"

"Stella Chase."

"Now, if *they* would take a notion to each other?" suggested Mrs. Burnham.

Mrs. Churchill gazed earnestly at the rose in her filet crochet. She had already made up her mind that her nephew Alden should marry her niece Stella, but matchmaking is something requiring subtlety and discretion, and there are things you do not tell, even to your intimate friend.

"I don't suppose there's much chance of that," she said, "and if they did it wouldn't be any use. Mary will never let Alden marry as long a she can keep him from it; the property is hers until he marries and then it goes to him, you know. And as for Richard, he has never let poor Stella have a beau in her life. All the young men who ever tried to come to see her he simply terrified out of their senses with sarcasm. He is the most sarcastic creature you ever heard of. Stella can't manage him—her mother before her couldn't manage him. They didn't know how. He goes by contraries, but neither of them ever seemed to catch on to that."

"I thought Miss Chase seemed very devoted to her father."

"O, she is. She adores him. He is a most agreeable man when he gets his own way about everything. He and I get on beautifully. *I* know the secret of coming it over him. I'm real glad they've moved up here from Chancy. They're such company for me. Stella is a very sweet girl. I always loved her, and her mother was my favourite sister. Poor Loretta!"

"She died young?"

"Yes, when Stella was only eight. Richard brought Stella up himself I don't wonder they're everything to each other. But he should have more sense about Stella's marrying. He must know he can't live forever—though to hear him talk you'd think he meant to; he's an old man—he wasn't young when he married. And what is Stella to do after he's gone? Just shrivel up, I suppose."

"It's a shame," agreed Mrs. Burnham. "I don't hold with old folks spoiling young folks' lives like that."

"And Alden's another whose life is going to be spoiled. Mary is *determined* he shan't marry. Every time he's gone about with a girl she puts a stop to it somehow."

"Do you s'pose it's all her doings?" queried Mrs. Burnham, rather drily. "Some folks think Alden is very changeable. I've heard him called a flirt."

"Alden is handsome and the girls chase him," cried Mrs. Churchill, up in arms against any criticism of her favourite. "I don't blame him for stringing them along a bit and dropping them when he's taught them a lesson. But there's been one or two nice girls he really liked and Mary just blocked it every time. She told me so herself. Told me she went to the Bible—she's always 'going to the Bible,' you know—and turned up a verse, and every time it was a warning against Alden getting married. I've no patience with her and her odd ways. Why can't she go to church and be a decent creature like the rest of us in Lancaster? But no, she must set up a religion for herself, consisting of 'going to the Bible.' Last fall, when that valuable horse took sick—worth four hundred if he was a dollar—instead of sending for the Clancy vet as we all begged her to do, she 'went to the Bible' and turned up a verse: 'The Lord gave and the Lord taketh away. Blessed be the name of the Lord.' So send for the vet she would not, and the horse died. Fancy applying that verse in such a way! I call it irreverent."

Mrs. Churchill paused, being rather out of breath. Her sister-in-law's vagaries always made her impatient.

"Alden isn't much like his mother," said Mrs. Burnham.

"Alden's like his father—a finer man never stepped. Why he ever married Mary was something we could never fathom. Of course, she had lots of money but *that* wasn't the reason. George was really in love with her. I don't know how Alden stands his mother's whims. *He* rather plumes himself on his liberal views—believes in evolution and that sort of stuff. Going, are you? What's your hurry?"

"Well," sighed Mrs. Burnham, "I find that if I'm out in the dew much my neuralgia troubles me considerable. We're getting old, Ellen."

"To be sure we are," agreed Mrs. Churchill. "*My* rheumatism takes hold this spring, too, if I'm not mighty careful. Good-night. Mind the step."

Mrs. Churchill continued rocking on her verandah, crocheting and plotting. When her brother-in-law, Richard Chase, had moved from Clancy to Lancaster, Mrs. Churchill had been delighted. She was very fond of Stella and, as Clancy was ten miles away, she had never been able to see as much of her as she wished. And she had made up her mind that Stella and Alden Churchill must be married off to each other by hook or by crook. Stella was twenty-four and Alden was thirty and it was high time they were married, so Mrs. Churchill thought.

"I've no doubt I can bring it about," she said to herself. "But I'll have to be careful; it would never do to let one of them suspect a thing. It's going to mean a lot of trouble and bother, and some fibbing as well, I'm afraid. But it's all in a good cause. Neither Alden nor Stella will ever get married to anybody if I don't lend a hand, that's certain. And they won't take a fancy to each other without some help, that's equally certain. Stella isn't the kind of girl Alden *thinks* he fancies—he imagines he likes the high-coloured, laughing ones. But we'll see, Ellen, we'll see. *I* know how to deal with pig-headed people of all sorts."

Mrs. Churchill laughed comfortably. Then she decided she must get to work at once. Stella had been living in Lancaster for three weeks and the new minister was casting sheep's eyes at her. Mrs. Churchill had caught him at it. She did not like *him*—he was too anemic and short-sighted—she was not going to help *him* to Stella. Besides, Alden, who hadn't been dangling after any girls all winter, might begin at any moment. There was a new and handsome school-teacher down on the Base Line Road and spring was a dangerous time. If Alden began a new flirtation he would have no eyes for Stella.

As yet, they were not even acquainted. The first thing to do was to have them meet each other. How was this to be managed? It must be brought about in some way absolutely innocent in appearance. Mrs. Churchill racked her kindly brains but could think of only one way. She must give a party and invite them both. She did not like the way. She was intensely proud of her beautiful, beautifully kept house with its nice furnishings and the old heirlooms that had come down to her through three generations. She hated the thought of its being torn up by preparations for a party and desecrated by a horde of young romps. The Lancaster boys and girls were such romps. But a good cause demands sacrifices. Mrs. Churchill sent out her invitation, alleging that she was giving the party as a farewell send-off for her cousin Alice's daughter, Janet, who was going away to teach in the city. Janet, who hadn't expected Aunt Ellen to come out like this, was rather pleased. But Mrs. Churchill's other cousin, Elizabeth, two of whose daughters had gone away without any such farewell party, was bitterly jealous and offended, and never forgave Ellen.

Mrs. Churchill cleaned her house from attic to cellar for the event and did all the cooking for the supper herself, help being impossible to get in Lancaster. She was woefully tired the night before the party. Every bone in her body ached, her head ached, her eyes ached. But instead of going to bed she sat out on the verandah, in the chilly spring night, and talked to Alden, who had dropped in, but would not go into the house. Mrs. Churchill was very anxious to have a talk with him, so she braved the damp and the chill.

Alden sat on the verandah steps with his bare head thrown back against the post. He was, as his aunt had said, a very handsome fellow: tall, broad-shouldered, with a marble-white face that never tanned, and dead-black hair and eyes. He had a laughing, velvety voice which no girl could hear without a heart-beat, and a dangerous way of listening to a woman—*any* woman—as if she were saying something he had thirsted all his life to hear. He had gone to Midland Academy for three years and had thought of going to college. But his mother refused to let him go, alleging Biblical reasons, and Alden had settled down contentedly enough on the farm. He liked farming—it was free, out-of-doors, independent work—he had his mother's knack of making money and his father's attractive personality. It was no wonder he was considered a matrimonial prize.

"Alden, I want to ask a favour of you," said Mrs. Churchill. "Will you do it for me?"

"Sure, Aunt Ellen," he answered heartily. "Just name it. You know I'd do anything for you." Alden was very fond of his Aunt Ellen and would really have done a good deal for her.

"I'm afraid it will bore you," said Mrs. Churchill anxiously. "But it's just this: I want you to see that Stella Chase has a good time at the party to-morrow night. I'm so afraid she won't. She doesn't know the young people here, and they're all so much younger than she is...at least the boys are. Ask her to dance and see that she isn't left alone and out of things. She's so shy with strangers. I do want her to have a good time."

"O, I'll do my best," said Alden readily.

"But you mustn't fall in love with her, you know," said Mrs. Churchill, laughing carefully.

"Have a heart, Aunt Ellen. Why not?"

"I'm in earnest. It wouldn't do at all, Alden."

"Why not?" persisted Alden.

"Well—confidentially—I think the new minister has taken quite a shine to her."

"That conceited young ass!" exploded Alden, with unexpected warmth.

Mrs. Churchill looked mile rebuke.

"Why, Alden, he's a very nice young man—*so* clever and well-educated. It's only that kind of man who would have any chance at all with Stella's father, you know."

"That so?" asked Alden, relapsing into his indifference.

"Yes, and I don't even know if *he* would. Richard thinks there's nobody alive good enough for Stella. He simply wouldn't let her *look* at a farmer like you. So I don't want you to make trouble for yourself falling in love with a girl you could never get. I'm just giving you a friendly warning."

"O, thanks—thanks! What sort of a girl is she anyhow? Looks good?"

"If you'd gone to church as often as you should, Alden, you'd have seen her before now. She's not a beauty. Stella is my favorite niece but I can see what she lacks. She's pale and delicate; she'd never do for a farmer's wife. That's why I'd like to see her and the minister make a match of it. To be sure, she's too fond of dress—she's positively extravagant. But they say Mr. Paxton has money of his own. To my thinking, it would be an ideal match, and that's why I don't want you to spoil it."

"Why didn't you invite Paxton to your spree and tell him to give Stella a good time?" demanded Alden rather truculently.

"You know I couldn't ask the minster to a dance, Alden. Now, don't be cranky, and do see that Stella has a nice time."

"O, I'll see that she has a rip-roaring time. Good-night, Aunt Ellen."

Alden swung off abruptly. Left alone, Mrs. Churchill chuckled.

"Now, if *I* know anything of human nature, that boy will sail right in to show me and Richard that he can get Stella if he wants her, in spite of us. And he rose right to my bait about the minster. I declare, it's easy to manage men if you're half cute. Dear me, this shoulder of mine is starting up. I suppose I'll have a bad night."

She had a rather bad night, but the next evening she was a gallant and smiling hostess. Her party was a success. Everybody seemed to have a good time. Stella certainly had. Alden saw to that—almost too zealously for good form, his aunt thought. It was going a little too strong for a first meeting that after supper Alden should whisk Stella off to a dim corner of the verandah and keep her there for an hour. But on the whole, Mrs. Churchill was satisfied when she thought things over the next morning. To be sure, the parlor carpet had been practically ruined by two spilled saucerfuls of ice-cream, her grandmother's Bristol glass candlesticks had been broken to smithereens, and one of the girls had upset a pitcherful of rainwater in the spare room which had soaked downwards and discoloured the dining-room ceiling in a tragic fashion, but on the credit side of the ledger was the fact that, unless all signs failed, Alden had fallen in love with Stella. Mrs. Churchill thought the balance was in her favor.

Later on, she discovered another and more serious debit item. In a fortnight it transpired that Mrs. Burnham was deeply offended because she had not been asked to the party. That it was strictly a young people's party and that no elderly people were invited did not matter. Mrs. Burnham's sensitive nature was terribly hurt, and she told sundry neighbours that she would never feel the same to Ellen Churchill again. She came no more for friendly evening calls and was frostily polite when they met elsewhere. Mrs. Churchill was very blue about it. She missed Mildred terribly, though she thought she was absurdly unreasonable. But she was repaid on the evening she came upon Alden and Stella, loitering along arm in arm in the leafy by-road east of the village which Lancaster folks called Lover's Lane. Mrs. Churchill perked right up. She had not been able to find out if her party had produced any lasting results. Now it was evident things were going all right. Alden was caught, but what about Stella? Mrs. Churchill knew that her niece was not the sort of girl to fall ripely into any young man's outstretched hand. She had a spice of her father's contrariness, which in her worked out in a charming independence.

Stella came to see her aunt the next evening and they sat on the verandah steps. Beside Stella the big "bridal wreath" shrub banked up on its June-tide whiteness, making a beautiful background for the girl. Stella was a pale, slender thing, shy but intensely sweet. She had large, purplish-grey eyes, with very black lashes and brows, and when she was excited a wild-rose hue spread over her cheeks. She was not considered pretty but nobody ever forgot her face.

"I was very sorry to see you strolling in Lover's Lane with Alden Churchill yesterday evening, Stella," said Mrs. Churchill severely.

Stella turned a startled face towards her aunt.

"Why?"

"He isn't the right kind of beau for you at all, Stella."

"He is your nephew, Aunt Ellen, and I thought you were so fond of him."

"He's my nephew by marriage, and I like him well enough. But he's not good enough for you, Stella. He has no *family* behind him. Why, his mother's grandfather *hanged himself*; and her father made his money hawking a medicine he concocted himself around the country. The Churchills all felt dreadful bad when George Churchill married her—and the Churchills themselves weren't strong on family. I have to admit that, though I did marry one myself. But that's not the worst. Alden's awfully fickle, Stella. No girl can hold him long. Lots have tried and they all failed. I don't want to see you left like that the minute his fancy veers. Now, just take your aunty's advice, darling, and have nothing to do with him. You know how fond and proud of you I am."

"I know you've always been awfully good to me, Aunt Ellen," said Stella slowly, "but I think you're mistaken about Alden."

"No fear. I've known him for thirty years and you've known him for two weeks. Which of us is most likely to understand him?

THE MATCHMAKER   115

He'll act as if he was mad about you for a few months and then he'll drop you. You can't hold him—you're not his type. He likes the bouncing, jolly girls, like the Base Line teacher, for example."

"O, well, I must be going home," said Stella vaguely. "Father will be lonesome."

When she had gone, Mrs. Churchill chuckled again.

"Now, if *I* know anything of human nature, Miss Stella has gone off, vowing she'll show meddling old aunts that she *can* hold Alden, and that no Base Line schoolma'am shall ever get her claws on him. That little toss of her head and that flush on her cheeks told me that. *I* can read these young geese like a book."

When it became a matter of common gossip that Alden Churchill was "going with" Stella Chase, Mrs. Churchill looked out of her door one night with a sigh.

"The wind is east and I wish I could stay home to-night and nurse my rheumatism but I must go a-matchmaking. It's high time I tried my hand on Mary. She'll be the hardest nut to crack. But *I* know how to tackle her. Everyone has a weak point and I found Mary's out long ago."

The Churchill farm was a mile and a half from Lancaster, and Mrs. Churchill was very tired when she got there. Mrs. Mary Churchill did not welcome her too effusively either—she never did. The two sisters-in-law had never cared much for each other. But Aunt Ellen did not worry over Mary's coolness. She sat down in a rocker and took out her filet, while Mary sat opposite to her in a stiff-backed chair, folded her long thin hands, and gazed steadily at her. Mary Churchill was tall and thin and austere. She had a prominent chin and a long, compressed mouth. She never wasted words and she never gossiped. So Ellen found it somewhat difficult to work up to her subject naturally, but she managed it through the medium of the new minster, whom Mary did not like.

L. M. MONTGOMERY

"He is not a spiritual man," said Mary coldly. "He believes the kingdom of heaven can be taken by brains. It cannot."

"He's a very clever young fellow," said Ellen, rocking placidly. "His sermons are remarkable."

"I heard but one and do not wish to hear more. My soul sought food and was given a lecture."

"O, well, Mary, you know other people don't think and feel as you do. Mr. Paxton is a fine young man. He has quite a notion of my niece Stella Chase, too. I'm hoping it will be a match."

"Do you mean a marriage?" asked Mary.

Ellen shrugged her plump shoulders.

"Now, Mary, you understand what I mean well enough. And it would be just the thing. Stella is especially fitted to be a minister's wife. By the way, I hear that Alden is going with her a bit. You ought to put a stop to that, Mary."

"Why?" asked Mary, without the flicker of an eyelid.

"Because it isn't a bit of use," responded Ellen energetically. "He could never get her in this world. Her father doesn't think anyone is good enough for her—except a minster or doctor or something like that. He'd show a plain farmer to the door in a moment. You'd better tell Alden to give up all notion of Stella Chase, Mary. He'll find himself thrown over before long and made a laughing stock of, if he doesn't. Look at all the girls that have flirted with him and then dropped him. If that goes on much longer he'll never get a decent wife. No nice girl wants shop-worn goods."

"No girl ever dropped my son," said Mary, compressing her thin lips. "It was always the other way about. My son could marry any woman he chose. Any woman, Ellen Churchill."

"O?" said Ellen's tongue. Her tone said, "of course I am too polite to contradict you but you have not changed my opinion," Mary Churchill understood the tone and her white, shrivelled face warmed a little. Ellen went away soon after, very well satisfied with the interview.

"Of course, one can't count on Mary," she reflected, "but if *I* know anything of human nature I've worried her a little. She doesn't like the idea of folks thinking Alden is the jilted one. I s'pose she's busy turning up Bible verses now to solve the problem. Lord, how my shoulders ache! East winds were invented by the old Nick. But I feel I've done Alden and Stella a good turn to-night. There's only Richard to manipulate now. I wonder if he has the slightest idea that Stella and Alden are going together. Not likely. Stella would never dare take Alden to the house, of course. I'll tackle Richard next week."

Mrs. Churchill tackled him, according to programme. He was sitting in his little library reading, but he put his book aside when his sister-in-law came in. He was always courteous to her and they got on surprisingly well. He was a small, thin man, with an unkempt shock of grey hair and little twinkling, deep-set eyes.

Ellen sat down but said she could not stay long—she had just run up to borrow Stella's recipe for snow pudding.

"I'll sit a minute to cool off. It's dreadful hot to-night. Likely there'll be a thunderstorm. Mercy, that cat is bigger than ever!"

Richard Chase had a familiar in the shape of a huge black cat. It always sat on the arm of his chair while he read. When he put his book away it climbed over into his lap. He stroked it tenderly.

"Lucifer gives the world assurance of a cat," he said. "Don't you, Lucifer? Look at your Aunt Ellen, Lucifer. Observe the baleful glances she is casting upon you, from the orbs created to express only kindness and affection."

"Don't you call me that beast's Aunt Ellen," protested Mrs. Churchill sharply. "A joke's a joke, but that is carrying things too far."

"Wouldn't you rather be Lucifer's aunt than Neddy Churchill's aunt?" queried Richard Chase plaintively.

"Neddy Churchill is a glutton and a wine-bibber, isn't he? You've often given me a catalogue of his crimes. Wouldn't you rather be aunt to a fine, up-standing cat like Lucifer with a blameless record where whiskey and tabbies are concerned?"

"Poor Ned is a human being," retorted Mrs. Churchill. "I can't abide cats. It's the only fault I have to find with Alden Churchill. He's got the strangest liking for cats, too. Lord knows where he got it—his mother and father loathed them as I do."

"What a sensible young man he must be," said Richard Chase ironically.

"Sensible! Well, he's sensible enough—except in the matter of cats and evolution—another thing he didn't inherit from his mother!"

"Do you know, Ellen," said Richard Chase solemnly, "I have a secret leaning towards evolution myself."

"So you've told me for the last thirty years," retorted Mrs. Churchill. "Well, believe what you like, Richard. Thank God nobody could ever make *me* believe that I was descended from a monkey."

"You don't look it, I confess, you comely woman," said Richard Chase. "I see no simian resemblances in your rosy, comfortable, eminently respectable physiognomy. Still, your great-grandmother a million times removed swung herself from branch to branch by her tail. Science proves that, Ellen, like it or leave it."

"I'll leave it then. I'm not going to argue with you on that or any point. I've got my own religion and no ape ancestors figure in *it*. By the way, Richard, Stella doesn't look as well this summer as I'd like to see her."

"She always feels the hot weather a good deal. She'll pick up when it's cooler."

"I hope so. Loretta picked up every summer but the last, Richard, don't forget that. Stella has her mother's constitution. She's far from strong. It's just as well she isn't likely to marry."

"Why isn't she likely to marry? I asked from curiosity, Ellen, rank curiosity. The processes of feminine thought are intensely interesting to me. From what premises or data do you draw the conclusion, in your own delightful, off-hand way, that Stella is not likely to marry?"

"Well, Richard, to put it plainly, she isn't the kind of girl that is popular with the men. She's a dear, sweet, good girl but she doesn't take with them."

"She has had admirers. I have spent much of my substance in the purchase and maintenance of shotguns and bulldogs."

"They admired your money bags, I fancy. They were easily discouraged, too. Just one broadside of sarcasm from you and off they went. If they had really wanted Stella they wouldn't have wilted for that—any more than for your imaginary bulldogs. No, Richard, we might as well admit that Stella isn't the girl to win desirable beaus, especially when she's getting on in years. Loretta wasn't, you know. She never had a beau till you came along."

"But wasn't I worth waiting for? Surely Loretta was a wise young woman. You would not have me give my daughter to any Tom, Dick, or Harry, would you? My Star, who, despite your somewhat disparaging remarks, is fit to shine in the palaces of kings?"

"We have no kings in this country," said Mrs. Churchill, getting up. "I'm not saying Stella isn't a lovely girl. I'm only saying the men are not likely to see it, and considering her constitution, I think it is decidedly a good thing. A good thing for you, too. You could never get on without her; you'd be as helpless as a baby. Well, I'm off. I know you are dying to get back to that book of yours."

"Admirable, clear-sighted woman! What a treasure you are for a sister-in-law! I admit it: I am dying. But no other but yourself would have been perspicacious enough to see it or amiable enough to save my life by acting upon it. Good-evening, pearl-of-in-laws."

"Of course, there's never any knowing what effect anything you've said has had on him," mused Mrs. Churchill as she went down the street. "But if I know anything of human nature, he didn't like the idea of Stella not being popular with the men any too well, in spite of the fact that their grandfathers were monkeys. I think he'd like to show me! Well, I've done all I can—I've interested Alden and Stella in each other and I've made Mary and Richard rather anxious for the match than otherwise. And now I'll just sit tight and watch how things go."

Two evenings later Stella came up to see her Aunt Ellen. It was a hot, smoky evening, so they sat on the verandah steps again. Stella seemed absent-minded and quiet. Presently she said abruptly, looking the while at a crystal-white star hanging over the Lombardy at the gate.

"Aunt Ellen, I want to tell you something."

"Yes, dear?"

"I am engaged to Alden Churchill," said Stella desperately. "We've been engaged ever since last Christmas. We've kept it secret just because it was so sweet to have such a secret. But we are going to be married next month."

Mrs. Churchill dropped her crochet and looked at Stella, who still continued to stare at the star. So she did not see the expression on her aunt's face. She went on, a little more easily.

"Alden and I met at a party in Clancy last September. We—we loved each other from the very first moment. He said he had always dreamed of me – had always been looking for me. He said to himself, 'There is my wife,' when he saw me come in at the door.

And I felt just the same. O, we are so happy, Aunt Ellen. The only cloud on our happiness has been your attitude about the matter."

"Bless me!" said Mrs. Churchill feebly.

"Won't you try to approve, Aunt Ellen? You've been like a mother to me. I'll feel so badly if I have to marry against your wish."

There was a sound of tears in Stella's voice. Mrs. Churchill picked her filet up blindly.

"Why, I don't care, child. I like Alden—he's a splendid fellow— only he has had the reputation of being a flirt...."

"But he isn't! He was just looking for the right one. Don't you see, Aunty? And he couldn't find her."

"How will your father regard it?"

"O, father is greatly pleased. He has known it all along. He took to Alden from the start. They used to argue for hours about evolution. Father said he always meant to let me marry as soon as the right one came along. I feel dreadfully about leaving him, but Cousin Delia Chase is coming to keep house for him and father likes her very much."

"And Alden's mother?"

"She is quite willing, too. When Alden told her last Christmas that we were engaged, she went to the Bible and the first verse she turned up was, 'A man shall leave father and mother and cleave unto his wife.' She said it was perfectly clear to her then what she ought to do and she consented at once. So you see everyone is pleased; and won't you give us your good wishes, too, Aunty."

"O, of course," said Mrs. Churchill rather vaguely. There was not much heartiness in her voice and Stella went away a little disappointed. After she had gone Mrs. Churchill took stock of the preceding weeks.

She had burdened her conscience with innumerable fibs; she had confirmed her rheumatism; she had ruined her parlor carpet, destroyed two treasured heirlooms and spoiled her dining room ceiling; she had alienated the affections of her dearest friend, perhaps forever; she had given Richard Chase something to tease her about the rest of her life; she had put a weapon into Mary Churchill's merciless hand, which, if she, Mrs. Churchill, knew anything about human nature, Mary would not fail to use upon occasion; she had got in wrong with Alden and Stella and could only get out by a confession too humiliating to make. And all for what? To bring about a marriage between two people who were already engaged.

"I have had enough of matchmaking," said Mrs. Churchill firmly.

❧ ☙

Editors' note: "The Matchmaker," illustrated by O'Carter, was published in *Canadian Home Journal* in September 1919. It was listed in the "Unverified Ledger Titles" section of the 1986 bibliography and was found by Carolyn Strom Collins and Donna Campbell. It is available to view online in the Ryrie-Campbell Collection.

Montgomery reworked this story slightly for Chapters 15–17 of *Anne of Ingleside*, published in 1939. In those chapters, Anne herself is "the matchmaker" with identical results.

The "filet crochet" (or "filet") that Aunt Ellen had with her constantly is worked in a grid of small open squares resembling a net (or "filet" in French). A design is plotted on graph paper and worked by filling in the squares of the design with extra crochet stitches.

Aunt Ellen's prized antique "Bristol glass candlesticks" that were "broken to smithereens" at her party had come from Bristol,

England, where deep cobalt-blue glass items had been made for over one hundred years.

This story appeared about the same time that the first film version of *Anne of Green Gables* was released. It was a black-and-white silent film, starring Mary Miles Minter and directed by W. D. Taylor. The film has been lost but still photographs exist, some of which were published in an L. C. Page edition of *Anne of Green Gables*.

THE BLOOM OF MAY
The Story of an Old Apple Tree
and Those Who Loved It
(1921)

The apple tree grew in a big green meadow by a brook. It was an old tree—so old that hardly anybody remembered when it had begun to grow. Nobody had planted it; it had sprung from some chance-sown seed, and had grown so sturdily and valiantly that Miser Tom's father had let it live when he discovered it. Now Miser Tom's father had been dead for forty years, and the tree was living still—a great, wide-branching thing known to all the country round as "Miser Tom's apple tree." Miser Tom cared nothing for it—the sour green apples it bore were fit only for pigs to eat—but somehow the countryside had a sort of prescriptive right to it, as it had to the little cross-lots road that ran past it; and though there were few things Miser Tom dared not do for the sake of making and hoarding, he never dared to cut down the tree or shut up the road.

In Maytime "Miser Tom's tree" was a wonderful thing. The blossoms were snow white with no tint of rose, and they covered its boughs so thickly that hardly a leaf could be seen. It always bloomed; there were no "off" years for it. Old homesteads, sacred to the loves of the living and the memories of the dead, were all around it. Violets grew thickly in the grass at its roots, and the little cross-lots path ran by it and looped lightly up and over the hill—a little, lovable, red path over which the vagabond wandered and the lover went to his lady, and children to joy, and tired men home.

Years before one of Miser Tom's hired men had built a little wooden seat under the tree. Miser Tom did not keep him long—he was lazy, it seemed—but the seat remained, and almost every hour of the day some passer-by would step aside from the path to rest a while under the great tree, and look up into its fragrant arch of bloom with eyes that saw it or saw it not, according as they were or were not holden by human passions. The slim, pale girl, with the delicate air and the large wistful brown eyes, did not see it as she sat there with the young man who had overtaken her on the path. She had loved him always, it seemed to her; and there had been times when she thought he loved, or might love her. But now she knew he never would. He was joyously telling her of his coming marriage to another girl. She was so pale she could not turn any paler, and she kept her eyes down so that he might not see the anguish in them. She forced her lips to utter some words of good wishes, and he was so wrapped up in the egotism of his own happiness that he found nothing wanting; she had always been a quiet, dull little thing. When he was gone she sat there for a long time because she was too unhappy to move. "I shall hate this place forever" she said aloud, looking up at the beautiful tree. She walked away full of bitterness when she saw two men coming along the path.

They turned in and sat down under the tree. One was the minister of the community and the other a visiting friend, and they were deep in a profound discussion concerning the immortality of the soul. The friend was doubtful of it, and the minister desired greatly to convince him; but at the end his friend looked up with a smile and said: "After all, John, this tree is a better argument than any you've advanced. When I look at it I feel I'm immortal."

"That is better than believing," said the minister, with a little laugh. They felt suddenly very near to each other. "Our love—and our old friendship—of course it's immortal," he said. "It couldn't be anything else. One knows that.... Here, I have wasted my breath."

When they went away, two lovers came along the path through the blue of the afternoon. They held each other openly by the hand, as people dared to do on the by-path; and when he asked her, seriously, to sit for awhile on the bench under the old tree, she assented tremblingly, for she knew what he was going to say. She was very young and very pretty and very sweet—as sweet and virginal as the apple blossoms. When she said "yes" to his question, he kissed her and both sat silent for joy. They hated to go away and leave the darling spot.

"How I shall always love this dear old tree," she said. "This place will always be sacred to me."

The old tree suddenly waved its boughs over them as if in blessing. So many lovers had sat beneath it; it had screened so many kisses. Many of the lips that had kissed were ashes now, but the miracle of love renewed itself every springtime.

In the early evening came a little orphan boy on his way to bring home the cows from pasture. He was very tired, for he had been picking stones off a field all day, so he sat down for a few minutes to rest his weary little bones. He worked for Miser Tom, and no one who worked for Miser Tom ever ate the bread of idleness. He was a shy, delicate lad, and the other boys tormented him because of this. So he had no playmates and was often very lonely. Sometimes he wished wistfully that he had just one friend; there seemed to be so much love in the world and none of it for him. He liked the old apple tree; it seemed like a friend to him, a great, kindly, blooming, fragrant creature, reaching protecting arms over him. His heart grew warm with his love for it, and he began to whistle; he whistled beautifully, and the notes of his tune blew across the brook valley like drops of elfin sound. He was very happy while he whistled, and he had a right to be happy, for he had lived a good day, though he did not know that and was not thinking about it. He had done faithful work: he had saved a little bird from a cat; he had planted a tree—a little wild, white birch which he had brought home from the field and set out at the gate, Miser Tom giving a surly assent because it cost him nothing. So the lad whistled blithely. Life was all before him and it was May and the world was abloom. Long after he had gone up the path to the pasture the echoes of his music seemed to linger under the tree. Many children had sat under it and the old apple tree seemed to love them.

At sunset an old man came to the dim, spring valley and sat for a while, seeing visions and dreaming dreams. He was an ugly old man, but he had very clear, beautiful, blue eyes, which told you that he had kept the child heart. His neighbours thought that he was a failure; he had been tied down to farm drudgery all his life, he lived poorly, and was sometimes cold and sometimes hungry. But he dwelt in an ideal world of the imagination, of which none of his critics knew anything. He was a poet, and he had composed a great many pieces of poetry, but he had never written any of them down. They existed only in his mind and memory. He had recited them all a hundred times to the old tree. It was his only confidant. The ghosts of many springs haunted it for him; he always came there when it was in bloom. He was an odd, ridiculous figure enough, if anyone had seen him bent and warped and unkempt, gesticulating awkwardly as he recited his poems. But it was his hour, and he felt every inch a king in his own realm. For a little time he was strong and young and splendid and beautiful, an accredited master of song to a listening, enraptured world. None of his prosperous neighbours ever lived through such an hour; he would not have exchanged places with one of them.

The next visitor to the tree was a pale woman with a pain-lined face. She walked slowly and sat down with a sigh of relief. She had seen the old tree blossom white for many springs, and she knew she would never see it again. She had a deadly disease, and her doctor had told her that day that she had only a few more weeks to live. And she did not want to die; she was afraid of death.

A young moon set behind the dark hills, and the old tree was very wonderful in the starlight. It seemed to have a life and a speech of its own, and she felt as if it were talking to her, consoling her, encouraging her. The universe was full of love, it said, and spring came everywhere, and in death you opened and shut a door. There were beautiful things on the other side of the door— one need not be afraid. Then suddenly she was not afraid any longer. Love seemed all about her and around her, as if breathed out from some great, invisible, hovering Tenderness. One could not be afraid where love was—and love was everywhere. She laid her face against the trunk of the old tree and rested.

She had not been gone long when old Miser Tom came himself, walking home from market, and sat down with a grunt. He was tired and he did not like it because it meant that he was getting old. He had a thin, pinched, merciless mouth, and he looked around him with eyes that held nothing in reverence. All the land he could see around him belonged to him—or he thought it did. Really it did not belong to him at all, but to the old dumb poet and the little orphan who loved it. Miser Tom thought he was very rich, but he was horribly poor, for not one living creature loved him, not even a dog or a cat. His heart was poisoned and his thoughts were venomous because a neighbour had got higher prices at market that day than he had. He scowled up at the tree and wished he dared cut it down for firewood. It was no good and it spoiled several yards of the meadow. Yet, even as he scowled, a thought came to him. What if he hadn't made money his God, and scrimped and starved mind and soul and body for it? What if, long ago, he had married the girl with whom he had sat here one evening in his youth? What if he had had a home and children like other men? It was only for a moment he thought thus— the next minute he was Miser Tom again, sneering at such questions. A lavish wife and a spend-thrift brood—not for him. He had been too wise. That girl was no longer fair. She was a faded, drab, married woman, ground down with hard work, gnawing her heart out over the boy whose unknown grave was somewhere in France. Poor fool! O, yes, he had been wise. But he would not cut the old tree down—not just yet. It was a pretty thing, so white in the night's dim beauty. He would leave it be. After all, some shade enhanced the value of the pasture.

After Miser Tom had shuffled away, an old man and his wife came along the path and turned aside to rest. It was the anniversary of their wedding, and they had been spending it with their daughter in the village but now they were on their way home. They, too, loved the old apple tree.

"I sat here for a long time the night before our wedding day, Jean," the old husband said. "It was a small tree then, barely large enough to cast a shade, but it was as white as it is now. It was the first spring it had bloomed. There was no seat here then, so I sat on the grass under it and thought about you."

He began to dream of youth and his bridal day, murmuring bits of recollection aloud. But the old wife sat very silent, for it was not her wedding day she was thinking about, but her little first-born son, who had lived a year—just one year. She had brought him here once, when her tired old eyes had been young and eager and laughter-lighted, and had sat with him on the grass under the tree, and he had rolled over in it and laughed, and clutched at the violets with his little dimpled hands. He had been dead for forty years, but he was still unforgotten. She always felt that he was very near her here by the old tree—nearer than anywhere else, by reason of that one day they had played together under it. When she went away she had an odd idea which she would not have uttered for the world—of which she was even a little ashamed, thinking it foolish and perhaps wicked—that she left him there, playing with the gypsies of the night, the little wandering, whispering, tricksy winds, the moths, the beetles, the shadows, in his eternal youth under the white, enfolding arms of Miser Tom's old apple tree.

∽ ∾

Editors' note: "The Bloom of May" was published in the *Canadian Home Journal* (May 1921), illustrated by G. W. L. Bladen. It was listed in the "Unverified Ledger Titles" section of the 1986 bibliography and was found by Donna Campbell. It is available to view online in the Ryrie-Campbell Collection.

L. M. Montgomery was fascinated by her great-uncle, "Uncle Jimmy" Macneill (1822–1899), an eccentric individual who happened to be a wonderful poet and, like the old man in this story, he recited them frequently but never wrote any of them down. He was also the inspiration for "Cousin Jimmy" in the *Emily of New Moon* books.

The Macneills planted many apple trees on their farm in Cavendish, naming each one for a family member or a friend. Some of those trees are still living today.

On April 8, 1921, Montgomery wrote in her journal that they were enjoying an early spring in Leaskdale, but on April 17, she wrote that they had been "pitchforked" back into winter with bitter cold and an ice storm. It was a month of spring cleaning the Manse, an especially unpleasant task as her maid, Lily, was behaving in a sullen and insolent manner and was difficult to work with.

Montgomery published few stories in 1921: in addition to "The Bloom of May," her story "White Magic" appeared in *Women's Century*, a few poems were published, and three were included in a slim volume of poetry—*Verse and Reverse*—published by the Toronto Women's Press Club. However, she was discussing a new series of novels with her publisher and would begin the first one, *Emily of New Moon*, in August. Her novel *Rilla of Ingleside* was published in 1921.

HILL O' THE WÎNDS
(1923)

Chapter I

Mrs. Edward Wallace puffed up the Hill o' the Winds. Having called her Mrs. Edward Wallace once by way of conventional introduction, I shall hereafter call her Cousin Clorinda because everybody who knew her called her that, even those who were of no relation at all. And few ever left off the "cousin" in spite of the indefinable awkwardness of it. Nobody could call her Mrs. Wallace, and yet there was something about her that forbade plain Clorinda to all but her husband and a few old, intimate contemporaries. She was so sweet and lovable and dignified. You see, she had been born a Cooper.

She was a fat, sonsy lady who, at sixty, still retained the asking eyes of a girl and yet had something about her capacious maternal bosom that made you want to lay your head on it if you were tired or troubled. You could tell without half looking that she was a perfect cook, and that her children rose up and called her blessed.

She was addicted to wearing light-tinted dresses which she admitted calmly were far too young for her. She wore one now, a pink-flowered muslin, and a shade hat trimmed with clouds of pink tulle and daisies. She looked like a big, full-blown cabbage rose in it, and as she had all the outdoors of the sun-steeped summer afternoon around her for a background, she was not unpleasing to the aesthetic sense.

This is quite enough to say of a woman who is not the heroine of this story.

Cousin Clorinda did not come up to Hill o' the Winds very often. Elizabeth Cooper, who reigned there, was only a second cousin who kept up all the Cooper traditions and disapproved strongly of Cousin Clorinda's flower-hued dresses and daisied hats. Cousin Clorinda drove up on a duty visit once a year and was painfully polite to Elizabeth, who was painlessly polite to her.

But Cousin Clorinda, weighing one hundred and eighty, would not have walked up to Hill o' the Winds on a hot, dusty afternoon to see Cousin Elizabeth if she never saw her. She was going up now to see Romney Cooper, walking because she could not get a horse that day and to have waited another day without seeing Romney would have killed her. She had loved him as her own son in his boyhood days when he had spent his vacations nominally at Hill o' the Winds and actually down on her seashore farm. But she had not seen him for ten years and she was hungry for a sight of him. He *had* been such a darling.

He was, in the strict way in which the Coopers tabulated relationship, her "first cousin once removed." Elizabeth was his aunt. Elizabeth didn't deserve such luck, thought Clorinda. Romney had gone into journalism in a distant city when he was through college and had ceased to come to Hill o' the Winds for his vacations. But he had had pneumonia in the winter, followed by some complications, and had been ordered to rest wholly for the summer. So much Cousin Clorinda knew because Elizabeth had so told Doctor John Cooper, who told Clorinda. But there were a million other things she wanted to know if she had breath enough left to ask them after she had reached the top of that terrible hill.

She stopped at the gate when she did get up and leaned against it thankfully. Really Hill o' the Winds was a lovely spot. It was the old Cooper homestead so Clorinda had a prescriptive right to be proud of it, although she herself had never lived there. The old house was a fine, stately, white building hooded in trees that had taken three generations to come to that wide-spreading, leafy luxuriance. There was an old, formal garden with clipped cedars, thick, high hedges, and broad paths beautifully kept; the view of the big, green, sunshiny valley all around below, with gauzy hills on one side and the long, silvery sand shore of the hazy blue sea on the other, was something strangers always raved over. The Coopers themselves never said much about it; they were too proud of it to talk of it.

"It's an awful place to get to," sighed Clorinda, "but when you do get here you've something for your pains. I wonder who Elizabeth will leave all this to when she dies. I know it won't be me or any of mine, so I can wonder about it with a clear conscience. John Cooper is rich enough already and has no sons. But she hates almost everybody else. She ought to leave it to Romney, but she disapproves of him. She likes him well enough but she disapproves of him. So *he* has no chance. Now I must go in and talk to her a few minutes first, I suppose. Good Lord, send me something to say!"

Few of Cousin Clorinda's associates would have supposed she could ever be in want of something to say. But she always found it very hard to talk to Elizabeth, that high-bred, stately, old maiden Lady of the Hill, who could—so Doctor John was wont to aver—be silent in all the languages of the world. At least Cousin Elizabeth never talked the language of gossip, and gossip was Cousin Clorinda's mother tongue.

Perhaps the good Lord, whom Cousin Clorinda invoked, thought it would be easier to prevent an interview with Cousin Elizabeth at all than to furnish conversation for it. Elizabeth met Clorinda at the door of the dim, cool old hall and said distantly: "I suppose you have come to see Romney. Go right upstairs to the tower room. I've given him that for a sitting room for the summer."

Cousin Clorinda swam up the stairs. Cousin Elizabeth looked up at her from the hall.

"An old ewe dressed like a lamb," she thought contemptuously.

She herself wore dark purple velvet with a real lace collar. It was old fashioned but very handsome. She returned to her embroidery with the comfortable feeling born of a justified contempt for somebody we have never really liked.

But then Cousin Clorinda didn't care.

"What luck!" she thought as she made her way to the tower room.

"Cous-in-Clor-in-da!" said Romney between hugs.

"So you really know me?" said Cousin Clorinda complacently.

"Know you! You haven't changed a particle! Know you! Could I ever forget you?"

"I'm much fatter," said Cousin Clorinda with a sigh.

Then she held him off and looked at him. Yes, he was just as handsome as ever; his dark, reddish hair was just as thick and wavy, his gray eyes just as kind and luminous and twinkly, his figure just as fine and well bred. Cousin Clorinda was strong on breeding. But he was far, far too thin.

"Kiss me again," she said. "And then we'll sit down and talk. I've come up to pump you. I'm going to ask you about everything. You've got to tell me about everything."

"Of course," said Romney. He found her hatpins for her, pulled them out and took her hat off. He looked admiringly at her thick, brown-gold hair lying in sleek waves in which was not a thread of silver.

"You darling thing, you're as young as ever," he said. "I was a little afraid you might have grown old. I was coming down to see you to-night—did you know it?—you and your jam closet. *Have* you a jam closet still?"

"I couldn't wait for to-night; I want what I want when I want it. And of course I have a jam closet. While I live and move and have my being I'll have a jam closet."

"And a dairy full of cream? Do you remember how I used to steal cream out of your dairy?"

"The dairy is there all right. But we separate the cream now."

"Uh, cousin, I'm sorry! No more delightful big, brown panfuls to skim! But you'll give me plenty to drink, won't you. I *must* have plenty of cream, Cousin Clorinda; the doctors insist that I must have oceans of cream. And raspberry vinegar—they didn't tell me I must have raspberry vinegar because they didn't know anything about it. They would have, if they had known. Mind the time I stole a bottle of it to christen a boat? And you smacked my ear for it? I've been lopsided ever since."

"You haven't changed much," said Cousin Clorinda in a satisfied tone.

"Of course not. Sit here, dear thing, right by the window. I've been sitting here for an hour, musing on the Edgelow garden. When all's said and done it's finer than the Cooper garden."

Cousin Clorinda gave a scornful glance at the Edgelow garden as she filled the big chair with her pink billows, arranged them to her liking and leaned back as ineffably contented as a cat with its tail folded about its paws. She had not climbed Hill o' the Winds to discuss the comparative merits of Cooper and Edgelow gardens.

"How do you feel, Romney?" she asked anxiously.

"Lazy and contented. I've always been lazy but never before have I felt contented. As for the rest, I'm as poor and orphaned as I ever was. Lordy, but it's good to see you again! I'm going to stretch out on this sofa and feast my eyes on you. I love you in that pink. Why do ladies of sixty—excuse me, of course I'm not implying that *you* are sixty, ageless being!—generally go about so soberly and dourly clad? Sixty is the very time they should bloom out into gorgeousness like autumnal trees."

"I always liked bright colours," said Cousin Clorinda complacently. "I shall wear 'em till I die. They can bury me in black if they like, but as long as breath is in me, I'll have pink ribbons in my nightdress. Dear Elizabeth is likely throwing a fit down in the parlor now because of this pink dress. How have you been getting along in journalism, Romney?"

Cousin Clorinda spoke rather doubtfully. No other Cooper had ever "gone in" for journalism. It seemed a foolish, inconsequential occupation for a Cooper. The Coopers had been solid folk.

"I haven't made any money. I'm poor as a rat," admitted Romney. "But I've had a darned interesting time. Have *you* had *that*, Cousin Clorinda?"

"No," said Clorinda, one of whose charms was honesty.

"Nor any of the other Coopers hereabouts?"

"I suppose not," reflected Clorinda. "No, I think they've all been as dull as I. But if you can't make any money at your profession, Romney, how are you ever going to keep a wife and family?"

"But Cousin Clorinda, darling, I haven't a wife and family to keep."

"Don't you ever expect to have?" Cousin Clorinda was slightly severe. The Coopers had always thought it a highly respectable thing to be married. "You are thirty, Romney. It is time you were married."

"O, cousin, did you come all the way up here to lecture me on getting married? To twit me with my single cussedness?"

"No, I didn't—"

"And at sixty—you have annoyed *me*, cousin, by casting my years up to me, so I won't pretend you aren't sixty—you shouldn't be interested in marrying and giving in marriage!"

"I thank my stars that I didn't lose interest in youthful things when I lost my youth," retorted Clorinda. "I've lots of sentiment in me still and I'm not afraid to show it."

"That's what makes you so adorable." Romney stretched out his hand, possessed himself of hers and kissed it. "If there were a young Cousin Clorinda about I'd snap her up. But as there isn't, I'm afraid I'm doomed to die a bachelor. They tell me it's an easy death."

"Why won't you be serious?" reproached Clorinda. "When you were in your teens you used to tell me all about your love affairs. Do you remember your desperate flirtations with those Merrowby girls down harbour?"

"Of course I do. Say, those girls were delicious! What became of them? But I've no love affairs now, darling, or I'd certainly tell you all about them. I am not, never have been and never will be actually in love."

"Why?" said Cousin Clorinda.

"Because I have an ideal."

"Shucks, we all have. *I* had an ideal forty years ago. He was tall, like you; gray-eyed, like you; curly-haired; musical. And I married Ned Wallace, who was short and had hair so straight it wouldn't even brush and who couldn't tell 'God Save the King' from 'Money Musk.' As for his eyes, I've lived with him thirty-five years and I don't know even now what colour they are exactly. I *think* they're green. But I've been happy with him."

"I can't fall in love with anybody but my ideal," said Romney obstinately.

"What is she like?"

"Her name is Sylvia."

"Sylvia. You *have* met her then?"

"I have not. But her name is Sylvia. She is tall and has very black hair, which she always wears brushed straight back from her forehead as only a really pretty woman can dare to brush it. Of course she is fortunate enough to have a widow's peak. Then she wears it in a heavy, glossy braid around her head. She has intensely blue eyes, with very black lashes and straight black brows. She has a pale creamy face with a skin like a white narcissus petal, but a red, red mouth—and lovely hands, Cousin Clorinda. A beautiful hand is one of the chief charms of a beautiful woman. Sylvia's hands are—O, I wish you could see Sylvia's hands! I wish *I* could see them! But I never shall. It's a depressing thought, cousin. But haven't you a nice girl or two 'round to amuse me? You always used to have, shoals of them."

"That was when my girls were home. They don't come any more. Girls are scarce, it seems to me. Soon as they grow up now they're off and away. I've the school-teacher boarding with me. She might do—she's cute and pretty. And it would be quite safe for both of you," concluded Cousin Clorinda solemnly, "because you would never really fall in love with *her* and she has a young man of her own."

"Maybe the young man would object."

"O, he's away out west. She writes to him every day. You'll find her good company."

Romney hid a smile behind his hand. Cousin Clorinda was so deeply in earnest in regard to providing amusement for his summer, the darling, thoughtful old thing!

"I've been chumming with Samuel Rice since I came," he said. "Our acquaintance is only twenty-four hours old but we are sworn friends. Know him?"

"No. He's Elizabeth's man's son, isn't he?"

"Nephew—orphan nephew. Aged ten. The most amazing compound of mischief and precocity I've ever come across. Aunt Elizabeth detests him and frowns on our league of offense and defense. But you'd love him. He's taken on all our traditions because

his uncle works for us, even the old family feud. He ⸻
Whispering Lane, whistling impudently, and last nig⸻
him firing stones over the hedge into the Edgelow g⸻
quite indignant because I stopped him."

"Why did you stop him?"

"Why—did I—*why*? Cousin Clorinda, do you think I should
have let him go on firing stones over there?"

"Of course. It would serve old Jim Edgelow perfectly right, and
give him the exercise he needs throwing them back again, the lazy
old sinner!"

"You don't mean to say that *you* keep up the old feud still? Of
course Aunt Elizabeth does, but you—a moldy old scrap like that.
Do you even know who and what began it?"

"I do not, and it's no difference. A feud's a respectable thing
and should be kept up like all the other family customs."

Romney examined Cousin Clorinda's face and eyes to see if
she was being sarcastic or facetious. He concluded that she was
neither, but wholly in earnest, and the wonder of the thing almost
staggered him.

"It's the only honest-to-goodness passion in our existence,"
continued Clorinda. "It lends spice to everything. I'd get tired
to death of going to church if it wasn't for the fun of sweeping
past Mary Edgelow from Clifton, and staring her brazenly in the
face without a hint of recognition every Sunday. But I admit that
the feud isn't what it was once. There are fewer Coopers, and no
Edgelows at all except Mary and old Jim. When they die the feud
will die with them. But he's only sixty and most of the Edgelow
men lived well into the eighties."

"The men, but not the women."

"Well, the men killed them, of course, in different ways. All
quite legal. I never knew a happy Edgelow woman. Look at that
old cream-brick house there—nice, chubby old place all grown

er with vines. Yet it's been full of tragedies. Old Jim tortured his wife to death for thirty years, by denying her everything she wanted and showering on her everything she didn't want. She was smothered and starved. Of course in the first place he really courted her to cut out Ronald Cooper. Then, when he got her, he lost his enthusiasm. Now they say he's lonely. I'm glad of it, though I'm afraid it's too good to be true."

"He doesn't look any more amiable than of yore," said Romney. "I saw him glowering at me from his front doorway last night precisely as he glowered at me twenty years ago. Wouldn't you think anybody'd get tired of glowering in twenty years? I smiled at him at shouted 'Good evening.' He went in and banged the door."

"You shouldn't have demeaned yourself." Cousin Clorinda was as severe as she could be with Romney.

"Cousin Clorinda, where is the sense of keeping it up?" he pleaded.

"There isn't any. But hate's a good lasting passion. You get over love but never over hate. And as for the sense of it, there's no sense in heaps of things we do. There's no sense in your forswearing marriage and the comforts of home because you've got an impossible ideal. Still—you do it."

"Still—I do it," echoed Romney in a melancholy tone. "You're right, perfectly right, divine one. Man cannot live by bread alone; he must have either feuds or ideals. My ideal means everything to me, everything, even though I shall never find her."

"O, maybe you will yet," said Cousin Clorinda with cheerful optimism. Cousin Clorinda couldn't believe that tall, wax-skinned girls with black hair and blue eyes were as scarce as Romney seemed to think.

"Never," said Romney in a tone of profound conviction. "She is chatelaine only of my castle in Spain. I shall never find her in the flesh."

He sighed and went to the window, looking down into the Edgelow garden. He stood there for a few seconds. Then he said calmly: "There she is now, down in the Edgelow garden."

Cousin Clorinda gasped, got up, and went over to the window. There was a girl in the Edgelow garden, walking about bareheaded, pulling a flower here and there. She was a slender thing with heavy, glossy black hair. She was too far away for her eyes to be read, but her skin was as creamy as a lily and her mouth was crimson. She wore a dress of pale green and one great pink rose was stuck in the braid of her hair over her ear.

"You've been making fun of me," said Clorinda severely. "You knew all about that girl. You've been describing her to me. You—"

"Cousin Clorinda," interrupted Romney solemnly, never taking his eyes from the girl, "your suspicion is natural but unjust. I give you my word of honour that I never saw her before, save in my dreams. I didn't even know there was a girl over there. Who is she?"

"It must be Dorcas Edgelow," said Clorinda, compelled to believe him.

"Dorcas. Nonsense! Her name is Sylvia, *must* be Sylvia."

"I never heard of a Sylvia Edgelow. But I did hear last spring that old Jim was expecting his niece Dorcas for a visit this summer. She's Martin Edgelow's daughter from Montreal, you know."

"Well, whoever she is, she's mine. It's a staggering thing, Cousin Clorinda, to look out of a casual window thus, and see the very girl you've been dreaming about all your life."

"But Romney, you can't marry *her*! She's an Edgelow!"

"I don't care. I told you I had cast off the Edgelow feud with the shackles of the past. That girl there is mine—"

"She's old Jim Edgelow's heiress, too. He's worth nobody knows how much. She'll be very rich; she won't—won't—"

"She will. I don't care whose heiress she is nor how rich… at least I don't *now*. At three o'clock to-night I'll probably care horribly. But now I'm drunk, Cousin Clorinda, I'm drunk just with looking at her! I've seen all my fancies, ideals, hopes, dreams in a human shape. She looks like love incarnate. I *know* her eyes are blue and her name is Sylvia."

"Dorcas—Dorcas."

"Sylvia! Look at her hands. Did you ever see anything so perfect?"

"The Edgelow hands," admitted Cousin Clorinda. "They were always noted for fine hands. O, she's a lovely thing, Romney, and it's not likely you're the first man that's noticed it. She's likely engaged already."

"Not a bit of it. She was predestined for me. Look, she's smiling to herself, cousin! I do like to see a woman smiling to herself. Her thoughts must be so pleasant and innocent. I wish she'd look up. Can't I rap on the glass?"

"She'd think you were crazy, Romney. This was just how you carried on over the second Merrowby girl when you were eighteen."

"Slanderer! I did not, nor with the first nor third Merrowby girl—rollicking, soulless young nonentities! Of course I'm crazy. She's driven me crazy, so she might as well know it."

Before Cousin Clorinda could prevent him Romney had thrown up the window and leaned out. He put his hands to his mouth and sent a long, tender, persuasive "Co-oo-e-e" down into the Edgelow garden.

The girl looked up, startled. Romney waved his hand at her and smiled. For a moment both he and Cousin Clorinda thought she was going to smile back. Then she coolly turned her back on them and walked into the big cream-brick house and shut the door.

Romney pulled his head in and sat down.

"Have I made an awful ass of myself?" he said doubtfully.

"You have," said Cousin Clorinda comfortingly. "But," she added as an afterthought, "either she liked it, or she is a born flirt."

"Her rose fell out of her hair as she went in," said Romney. "It's lying there on the porch. I wonder if old Jim Edgelow would shoot me if I went over and got it. I think I'll risk it."

"Romney!" gasped Cousin Clorinda. But Romney had gone. She looked out of the window in helpless fascination, saw him appear below, saw him cross the Cooper garden, open the gate, go along the road to the Edgelow gate, disappear, reappear again round the corner of the house, and pick up the rose in triumph.

The door opened and old Jim Edgelow came out.

"What are you doing here, you impertinent pup?" he growled.

"Why be so unoriginal?" asked Romney cheerfully. "Anybody could call me a pup. Why not think of something worthy of the Edgelows? Besides, I'm not a pup really. I'm quite a middle-aged dog. I just came after your niece's rose. I'm going to marry her, you know."

"Will you get out of this before I kick you out?" asked old Jim with dangerous calmness.

"O, I didn't mean to stay. I'd have been gone before this if you hadn't detained me, uncle-that-is-to-be."

Romney took out his pocketbook, carefully placed his rose therein, shut it, restored it to its place, bowed low to his ancient enemy, and returned to the tower room with the air of a conqueror.

From a vine-hid upstairs window of the cream-brick house Miss Edgelow watched him as long as he was in sight.

Chapter II

It was morning and Romney was on his way to the sand shore for a swim with his bathing suit rolled up under his arm, a gayly striped bath towel hung over his shoulder, and his coppery head bared to the sun. He was in excellent spirits, although his three o'clock musings had been of an unsatisfactory character.

At three o'clock it had seemed preposterous to dream of marrying an Edgelow heiress and senile to fall in love with her. He had laughed at himself and now he felt very wise and prudent. She was his ideal, but between them her wealth and his poverty stood like grim, unconquerable ogres. The feud counted for nothing in his eyes, but one couldn't marry on an income that served only, in its most flexible moments, to keep life in one. There was nothing like looking facts squarely in the face and accepting their logic. He couldn't afford to fall in love with Dorcas Edgelow—but her name *must* be Sylvia!—and therefore he would not do it. She must remain for him only an exquisite might-have-been.

She could be only his dream girl.

Meanwhile life was good. It was worth while having been ill to realize the tang and savor of returning health again on a morning like this when a sea wind was blowing up over the long green fields.

"There's nothing on earth like a sea wind," said Romney, filling his lungs with it, snuffing rapturously at it. "What a tang, what a zip, what a message from vast, interminable spaces of freedom! What a magic of adventure! I feel as if I'd exchanged my shopworn soul for a fresh one, fire-new from the workshop of the gods. 'Who is Sylvia—what is she,' compared to this incomparable morning, wind and sea? 'I am the master of my fate, I am the captain of my soul!' Sylvia shan't rock my canoe!"

He whistled gayly and strode on. Everything was good. He felt like a boy again. The rice lilies were as thick as ever in the shore fields and the margin of the pond as pink with water witches. Beyond, in the dunes, was a wild, sweet loveliness of salt-withered grasses and piping breezes. Far out, the sea was dotted with sails that were silver in the magic of morning sunlight.

L. M. MONTGOMERY

He would have a glorious dip, a glorious wallow on sun-warm golden sands, then, after a glamorous walk home, one of Aunt Elizabeth's delightful dinners, then an afternoon of hammock dreams in the garden. He would not even look across the hedge. For him Edgelow estates and heiresses had ceased to exist. He would not look at, speak to, nor think of Sylvia again.

With this, he looked at her. He had reached the brink of the deep little "run" by which the pond waters ran out through a gap in the dunes to the sea. On the other side of it, barely five yards away, Sylvia was standing, her arms full of water witches, looking in dire perplexity at the water. Then she looked at him.

For a moment or two—or an aeon or two, according to whatever measurement of time you prefer—they stood so and looked at each other. Romney, who had just sworn never to look at Sylvia again, fairly devoured her with his eyes. She wore green again and she looked like a long, slender, green flag lily with the exquisite blossom of her face a-top of it. Had there ever been such a pretty woman in the world before? Had any woman ever had such an exquisite line of neck and chin? What were all the renowned, unhappy Edgelow beauties compared to her? They were dead and gone, broken-hearted, but she was here in her exquisite flesh and blood, looking as if no sorrow ever had, or ever could have, touched her.

"Good morning," said Romney, who wanted to say, "Hail, goddess!"

Miss Edgelow looked at him and smiled. Her smile was very faint and mysterious, like a half-opened rosebud. You felt that the full flower could not be quite so wonderful.

"The plank is gone," she said plaintively. "It was here when I crossed an hour ago."

Romney pointed to some men who were making marsh hay up along the pond.

"Likely they have taken it."

"And how am I to get across?" she asked. "It's so deep—and cold. I can't wade it."

"No reason why you should," said Romney. "I was sent here by the Powers That Govern for this moment. It was predestinated in the councils of eternity that I should be here at this precise moment to carry you across."

"Then I hope it is likewise predestinated that you won't drop me! The water looks fearfully cold and black, and I'm sure there are horrible slimy things at the bottom."

Romney coolly stepped into the run, though he felt slightly dubious as to what bottom he might find. Sand and mud are a treacherous combination, and to wade in icy-cold water to your knees is an experiment for a man not too long over pneumonia. But what cared Romney? Luckily the bottom of the run, though oozy and squdgy, was no worse, and he got across without trouble. He was very near to her now. Seen close, she was not quite so beautiful but infinitely more charming. Her creamy skin was powdered with delicious little golden freckles. They made her less a goddess and more a woman.

"You must let me carry you over," said Romney. "I won't drop you, and I won't wet you…but," he added internally, "I won't swear that I shan't kiss you before I set you down."

"I'm afraid it will be too much for you," she said. "You've been ill, haven't you? And you're dripping wet with that cold water."

She must have been asking about him to know that he had been ill. James Edgelow would never have volunteered the information. Romney glowed from head to foot.

"I'm all right. As for being wet, I came down to get wet."

"But not in your clothes. That," she said practically, "is what makes it dangerous. Why didn't you take off your shoes and socks and roll up your trousers?"

"That would have kept you waiting."

"You are a very imprudent young man," she said; then added, as if by way of afterthought, "I wouldn't have minded being kept waiting."

What did she mean? Romney imagined several things she might mean. He stood, staring at her. What a delicious mouth she had! Her hair was like midnight under her wide green hat. But her nose *was* slightly irregular—well, let us say crooked. How nice! And her voice was a sweet, throaty, summery drawl. What a voice for love making! Romney stood there and imagined her making love in it.

"Did I frighten you last night by my crazy hoot?" he asked.

"O, no. I have been told that the Coopers are eccentric."

"You've been brought up on the feud, I suppose," said Romney sulkily. "Well—are you going to let a vile, contemptible Cooper carry you over the run?"

"Yes, but I won't speak to him while he's doing it," said Miss Edgelow. She smiled again; it made Romney want to seize her in his arms and press kisses on the smile until he had found the heart of its mystery. This Edgelow girl had the smile of Mona Lisa, the everlasting lure and provocation that drives men mad and writes scarlet pages in dim historical records.

He picked her up and waded through the run with her. He did not hurry. Every time he took a step he felt carefully about to make sure of his foot-hold. He did not go straight across, but anglewise, with no explanation offered. Finally, however, he had to make land. Then he set her down—reluctantly—without kissing her.

"Thank you," she said. "I hope you won't take cold for this."

"There are no such things as colds in the seventh heaven," said Romney. He felt that it was an incredibly stupid thing to say. Why couldn't he think of something clever? He could think of clever things easily when there was nobody to say them to. His magazine stories were noted for their sparkling dialogue. Yet now he could only be clumsy. His fiction heroes talked superbly to heroines of all sorts. They never made asses of themselves.

Miss Edgelow ignored his feeble attempt properly.

"You must go and take your saltwater dip directly," she commanded. "And dry your clothes in the sun before you put them on. Be *very* particular about that."

"I am going to stand here," said Romney, folding his arms, "and watch you out of sight. And to-night—what about to-night? Can I come over into the Edgelow garden and talk to you?"

Miss Edgelow smiled.

"The dead Edgelows would turn over in their graves."

"Excellent exercise for 'em," commented Romney. "Be honest. I don't believe you care a hoot for the dead Edgelows and their feuds any more than I do."

"No, I don't," she said candidly. "But one living Edgelow is worse than all the dead ones. Last night my uncle commanded me never to speak to you, look at you, nor in any way become cognizant of your existence. He was…emphatic."

"Which means that he didn't scruple to enforce his decree with some fine old Edgelow oaths. Do you intend to obey him?"

"A man," said Miss Edgelow reflectively, "is master in his own demesne. At least I cannot invite you into his garden. Neither, of course, can I go to yours."

"The Whispering Lane is debatable ground," said Romney.

"So I have heard," said Miss Edgelow. Before she turned away she looked at him once from under her broad hat. Something in the look made Romney suddenly recall Cousin Clorinda's pronouncement: "Either she liked it, or she is a born flirt."

Was she a flirt? That look—was it invitation, lure, provocation? It held more than mere friendliness, Romney knew. There was even a hint of defiance in it, though more, it seemed, of feuds and prohibitions than of him. He had a feeling that Sylvia—hang it, her name *couldn't* be Dorcas—might come to walk in the Whispering Lane as much to "show old James Edgelow" as for any other reason.

"I will be prudent," said Romney to himself as she went away. "I shall remember the fatal hour of three o'clock. I shall not make myself miserable howling for the moon nor humiliate myself to furnish a summer holiday for a bored beauty. Only prudence is such a shoddy sort of virtue by times. One always feels ashamed of it. If I had been prudent I would not have waded through this icy run water and so would never have held that delicious armful for thirty seconds I would never have had that exquisite white hand resting on, clinging to, my shoulder. There was no engagement ring on it, by the way. Nevertheless, there are certain things I must remember henceforth."

Romney held up his left hand and checked them off on his fingers: "First, she is an Edgelow, therefore born to hate me; second, she is an heiress, therefore taboo; third, I am poor as a rat and likely to remain so, therefore out of the running; fourth, I think she *is* a bit of a coquette, therefore to be shunned; and fifth—" Romney paused for a moment. "And fifth, she is the sweetest, most adorable, most desirable thing that ever looked allurement at a man out of a pair of—of—of—heavens, I've forgotten after all to find out what colour her eyes were. Therefore, I am a besotted fool!"

He caught up his impedimenta and hurried over the dunes to the beach. He would certainly be prudent henceforth. He would devote himself to Cousin Clorinda's school-teacher by way of double prudence. He plunged into the surf thinking: "Her lashes are so long it's no wonder I couldn't rightly see her eyes. And her eyebrows are straight and dark. I'm sure of *that*, anyhow."

The lady referred to was not the school-teacher.

At dinner that day, sitting in the cool, dim dining room of the Hill, looking out on the golden valley, Romney was not above trying to pump Aunt Elizabeth about her new neighbour, but he got nothing for his pains. Aunt Elizabeth knew nothing about her, and plainly did not want to know.

She contrived to give Romney the impression that Edgelows did not really exist. They might imagine they did, but they were mere emanations of the Evil One, to be resolutely disbelieved in by any one of good principles and proper breeding. You did not speak of the devil in good society; neither did you speak of the Edgelows. This imagined girl might be an imagined Dorcas Edgelow or she might not. Aunt Elizabeth relegated the whole Edgelow clan, connection, and cash to limbo with one wave of her thin, unbeautiful Cooperian hand. Edgelows, indeed!

Thus checkmated, Romney swore inwardly that he would never ask anyone about Miss Edgelow again—and a quarter of an hour later was asking Samuel about her. He simply couldn't keep from talking to somebody about her.

Samuel lived in a little house in a hollow on the side of Hill o' the Winds. He was never called Sam. It simply could not be done. He was a handsome urchin of ten with an elfin beauty of face which Aunt Elizabeth considered clearly diabolic. Jet-black eyes, limpid with mischief, laughter, lawless roguery; brown curls, bare to the sunlight; cheeks rose-red beneath golden tan; a shirt, half a pair of suspenders, what was left of a pair of pants originally fashioned for a much older boy—that was Samuel. He generally had a snake, dead or living, concealed about him, and he had never heard of the Ten Commandments. By nature he was honest, but he never spoiled a good story by sticking too closely to the truth, and he was as thorough a young pagan as ever ran wild on the heath.

Romney loved him.

"Do you," said Romney shamelessly, "happen to know who the enchanted princess is who walks occasionally in yonder fair pleasance beyond the cedar hedge?"

"Meaning old Jim's garden?" asked Samuel, transferring a vicious-looking little brown snake from his pants pocket to his shirt pocket. "'Zat what you mean?"

"Yes."

"Don't know nothin' of her. Watched her through the hedge last night. She'd be good looking if 'tweren't for her freckles. Gee, but they're thick!"

Romney glared. Samuel winked at him impudently and, on second thought, restored the snake to the pants pocket.

"How can you touch those horrible things?" said Romney, shuddering. He hated snakes.

"This snake's dead," said Samuel contemptuously.

"Then you have no information to give me concerning our mysterious stranger?"

"Nope. I kin find out all about her though if you're so set on it. What," asked Samuel seriously, "what makes you like her so well?"

Romney was flabbergasted. He thought he had been very cool and impersonal and detached in his questions, and here was this imp.

"Samuel, my boy, you have a very vile habit of jumping at conclusions. Simply because I betray an entirely natural curiosity regarding a lady who is my next-door neighbour, why do you absurdly suppose that I have a deep personal interest in her?"

"'Cause you don't talk English when you ask questions about her," rejoined Samuel, fishing up another snake, a very live one this time. "All them big words mean you're bashful talking about her."

"Has she been here long?" asked Romney, reverting to English.

"Never saw her 'round 'fore yesterday." Samuel explored a third pocket with a disappointed expression. "There, he must 'a' slipped through that hole! Just my durned luck! He was the finest snake of the bunch. Say, don't worry. I'll know all there's to be known about her 'fore to-morrow night. But you oughtn't to be hankering after her—one of that gang over there."

The Cooperest of all Coopers could not have expressed more contempt for "that gang" than Samuel, who had never heard of them a month previously. Samuel had an instinctive recognition of a foe to all boys in old Jim, and had adopted the feud as a convenient excuse for hostility.

As for Romney, he was by now far from the three o'clock mood and he wanted so badly to talk of his dream lady that he must needs talk of her to Samuel, no fitter confidant offering.

"I want you to find out that her name *isn't* Dorcas."

"But it *is*," said Samuel. "I heard old Jim shouting after her this morning, when she went to the shore: 'Dorcas, you remember my dinner hour is twelve.'"

"Well," thought Romney, turning away in disgust, "I can think of her as Sylvia anyhow. And that is all that matters, since she is an Edgelow and an heiress and a coquette. Dorcas is not for me, but Sylvia has always been mine. Samuel," he added aloud, "do you wish you were rich?"

"Yep."

"What is the first thing you would do if you were rich?"

"Buy Joe Perkins' trotter," said Samuel unhesitatingly.

"And *I*, Samuel, if I were rich, would marry the young lady we've been speaking of."

"Would she hev you?" asked Samuel.

Chapter III

Miss Edgelow was walking at sunset in the Whispering Lane. This land ran through the beech wood at the back of the Cooper and Edgelow estates. It had been a bone of contention for generations. Both families claimed it and both used it determinedly to prove their claim. For the past twenty years no particular fuss had been made over it. Miss Elizabeth walked through it on principle twice a year when she knew James Edgelow would see her; and James Edgelow always went to church that way, when he did go, though it was the longest way around.

Samuel joined Miss Edgelow as she loitered along under the great, gray-boughed beeches. Perhaps Miss Edgelow had been expecting someone else; perhaps not. She did not betray any disappointment and she smiled at Samuel in a chummy fashion and proceeded to get acquainted with him.

Miss Edgelow had, so it seemed, a "way" with boys. Samuel liked her but kept his head. After all, he was the retainer of a clan that was at feud with hers. When he found out that she was not afraid of snakes he respected her also, but for all that he had made up his mind that he was not going to have any "courting" between her and Romney.

Samuel wanted Romney wholly for himself; he loved him and he wanted him for chum and playfellow. This would, Samuel knew with a deadly, instinctive certainty, be all spoiled if he began running after a "skirt." Men were no good when they began running after skirts. Besides, this particular skirt was an Edgelow, and you couldn't trust an Edgelow. She would likely as not make a fool of Romney. Sarah Dean, down at Clifton, had made a fool of Homer Gibson and Homer had hanged himself. Samuel was not going to have any hangings at Hill o' the Winds. This Edgelow girl must have her claws clipped in time.

Samuel had been thinking over the matter all day and knew just what he was going to do. Meanwhile he sat on the log and appeared so simple and charming and naïve that Miss Edgelow thought him a delightful child.

"What is your name?" asked Samuel.

"Dorcas Edgelow."

"I told him that. He wouldn't hardly believe it."

"Told who?"

"O, Romney. He was quizzing me about you."

"O, indeed! And why wouldn't he believe my name was Dorcas?"

"Dunno. He's full of queer notions. He says," went on Samuel shamelessly, "that if he was rich he'd marry you."

Miss Edgelow crimsoned. She looked very angry for a moment, but Samuel, intent on shifting a snake to more comfortable quarters, did not notice this.

"But he's poor—always was and always will be, so he says. He's a writer man, you know. He likes to spoon about with girls and then put them in his stories."

"O, so that is what he does," said Miss Edgelow, still looking a little dangerous. "Did he tell you so?"

"Yep. He wants to get acquainted with *you* so that he can put you in a book. Honest. That's his idea. Would you like to be put in a book?"

Miss Edgelow bit her lip.

"Did he tell you this, too?"

"Yes," assented Samuel unblushingly. "Thought I ought to warn you. And he told me he always tells a girl just what he thinks she'd like to hear. Don't let him fool you."

"O, I won't." Miss Edgelow looked as if there was not the slightest danger of it.

"He thinks you ain't bad looking o' course," supplemented

Samuel, "only he doesn't like your freckles. Say, do you know what will cure mange in a bulldog—a *half* bulldog?"

Just at this moment Romney came along the lane on his way to have supper with Cousin Clorinda. He was dressed in white flannels and was bareheaded. His eyes were luminous and his thin, delicately cut face was dreamy and remote. He did not see Miss Edgelow until he was quite opposite to her, did not see her because he was thinking of her. Then he halted in confusion and bowed rather stiffly.

Miss Edgelow stood up. He saw at once that she wore a dark red hat, very wonderful and droopy and becoming, and the palest of pale pink dresses. She turned away, but as she turned she flung him a brief, mysterious smile, a surprisingly nice smile considering the expression that it had replaced. Romney wanted to follow her but dared not. He went on feeling exceedingly and foolishly happy. He was quite as well aware of the foolishness of it as of the exceedingness.

Miss Edgelow walked away also, forgetting Samuel, who, however, was satisfied, feeling that he had done a good bit of work. Miss Edgelow communed with herself as she went back home.

"So that is what he does—studies girls for 'types' and puts them in his stories! Mr. Cooper, you need a lesson. I believe Uncle Jim was right when he said all Cooper men believed that every girl who looked at them fell in love with them. So you would marry me if you were rich. Condescending, insufferable young man! Wait till I'm through with you! And you don't like my freckles." Suddenly Miss Edgelow stopped and laughed. "Why should I blame you for that? I don't like them myself."

"What do you find in this forsaken hole that is so amusing?" asked old Jim Edgelow, coming around a corner of the cedar walk.

"Uncle Jim," said Miss Edgelow, "if you were a young man trying to make love to a charming young woman—I *am* charming, am I not?—would you object to her freckles?"

"Who's been making love to you?" demanded old Jim fiercely.

"Nobody. That's the trouble. Nobody has made any love to me. I flung myself quite boldly in Romney Cooper's way to-night and he passed me by. He objects, so I understand, to my freckles. Uncle, do you suppose I could make him fall madly in love with me in spite of my freckles, and then spurn him in true, dramatic Edgelow fashion? Do you suppose it would make any difference if he knew I don't have freckles in winter?"

"I think you're quite mad," said old Jim. "No, don't smile at me like that. Let me tell you, Miss, that you trade too much on that smile. It may work with silly young asses but it won't work with *me*. I won't have you associating with this Cooper imbecile, do you hear me? Am I to be defied at my age by a chit of a girl?"

"He says he won't marry me," said Miss Edgelow plaintively.

"Good Lord, girl, have you asked him to marry you?"

"Not yet," said Miss Edgelow. "I'm afraid it wouldn't be any use. He doesn't like my freckles, as I've said."

Old Jim snorted and stamped off, too angry to speak. Besides, he suspected that this girl was making fun of him.

"If there's one thing that I like more than another," Miss Edgelow remarked to the weeping beech, "it is tormenting the men."

Romney went down the lane and across the windy fields and along the shore. The sea was ruffled into a living crimson under the sunset. The fishing boats were coming in. One incredibly white little star was just visible where the pale pink of the upper sky shaded off into a paler green. Down low in the southwest there was a new moon. He saw it over his right shoulder, and wondered if Sylvia saw it too. She was not out of his thoughts for a minute during his whole walk, but he thought this was because he allowed it—never that it was because he could not help it.

Cousin Clorinda's house was so near the sea that the sound of waves always filled its rooms—a gray old house fronting the sunset, with leagues of satiny-rippled sea before it, purple headlands, and distant, fairylike, misty coasts.

"What a view old Mark Wallace picked out when he built his homestead!" said Romney admiringly. "What a thing to have the sea at your very doorstep like this! How delightful it would be to live in this old remote place with Sylvia and walk along that shore with her in the moonlight. Heigh-ho, if it were only possible!"

"If what were only possible?" queried Cousin Clorinda, billowing down the walk in blue muslin and a cherry-hued scarf.

Romney told her.

"And why isn't it possible?"

He stared at her. This incredible woman scarcely twenty-four hours ago had warned him against having anything to do with Miss Edgelow, and had quoted feuds to him. And now she didn't seem able to believe that the idea was absurd.

"Adorable and adored cousin, why this right-about-face? You amaze me."

"Haven't you faced about yourself?" retorted Clorinda. "Yesterday afternoon you were going to marry her out-of-hand. Now you are groaning that it isn't possible!"

"I told you three o'clock would bring wisdom. Three o'clock in the morning is the wisest and most accursed hour of the clock. At three o'clock I saw clearly how impossible it all was."

"At three o'clock *I* saw that is was quite possible," averred Clorinda. "Why not?"

"She is, or will be, disgustingly rich."

"All the better. You can't live on love."

"Nor on my wife's money, either."

"Can't you make enough to live on?"

"I've always made enough to live on myself. But I couldn't ask Sylvia to live in a garret with me."

"Any other reasons?"

"She is a flirt, I think. No, I'll say a coquette. That sounds better, infinitely more alluring and gracious."

"A girl like her always flirts till the right man comes."

"I don't suppose she'd look at me."

"She's half in love with you already."

"And finally, her name isn't Sylvia."

"I won't discuss the matter if you're not going to be serious," said Cousin Clorinda, really annoyed. She had lain awake most of the night constructing a gorgeous castle in air for Romney, and it was aggravating to find that he refused to inhabit it, and refused so frivolously.

"Dear young thing, I *am* serious. Isn't it serious that that exquisite dream maiden should be named Dorcas? Serious! Why, it's a tragedy!"

"I have known several excellent women," said Cousin Clorinda severely, "who were named Dorcas."

"I grant it. Excellent women, beyond a doubt! But had those excellent women beauty, charm, distinction? Did they walk and speak like queens? Could they afford to comb their hair straight back from their faces?"

"No," admitted Cousin Clorinda after a few moments of honest reflection, "no, I don't suppose they were—did—could."

"You see," said Romney triumphantly, "of course she shouldn't be named Dorcas! But don't let's talk of her, cousin. I had an attack of temporary insanity at four by the clock yesterday. I am sane now. I am not in love with Miss Edgelow. I am not *going* to be in love with her. I think I will put her into my next magazine serial as a heroine. That is her proper environment. She is not meant for human nature's daily food. I couldn't ask her to darn my socks or fry my bacon. Lead me to your jam closet, lady fair! Comfort me with raspberry vinegar, for I am sick of Aunt Elizabeth's sweetish ginger cordial. And stay me with an armchair. Your armchairs always fitted my kinks."

"I've got supper ready for you in the dining room. I want you to eat it and tell me I'm a good cook. I'm dying for a compliment. I never get any now that I'm old."

"Where is your school-teacher?"

"In her room, correcting exercises. No, I am not going to call her down. If Dorcas Edgelow doesn't interest you then—"

"But she *does*. Haven't I told you that I'm going to write a story about her? Interest me! Why, I held her in my arms to-day for thirty blissful seconds! I won't say but what I held her a shade more tightly than was absolutely necessary. But then I had to be careful not to drop her, hadn't I? Fancy if I had dropped her in the run!"

"Rom-ney Coop-er!"

"They didn't put the hyphens in when they christened me. Strawberry shortcake! Cousin of my heart, you're—"

"You shan't have one crumb of my strawberry shortcake until you've told me what you've been doing. Romney, you're overacting. You are dying to talk to me of Dorcas Edgelow, and yet you pretend you aren't."

"I came down here to talk about Samuel Rice," protested Romney with warmth. "I'm really interested in Samuel. He is a gifted, engaging orphan. I want to do something for him, uplift him. For instance, couldn't we persuade him to go to Sunday school? *You* can help me, Cousin Clorinda. A good woman's influence—"

"I don't care a hoot about gifted orphans, just now, anyhow. I'm dying to hear all about Dorcas Edgelow and you. I've never known a romantic love affair, not even my own."

"Would you sacrifice my happiness, ruin my life, break my heart, to gratify your lust for romance?" demanded Romney. "Cousin Clorinda, I *won't* talk of her. She is charming; you've no idea how charming she is! Her freckles are enchanting; an atmosphere of perfume seems to surround her and yet I swear she doesn't use perfume. She has a nice little way of cuddling in your arms when you are carrying her about. And her smile, Cousin Clorinda—"

"I am a patient woman, Romney, but if you don't tell me without any further preamble what you mean by carrying her about I'll smack your ears."

Romney told her. Also he told her of the meeting in the Whispering Lane.

"She was in the Whispering Lane?"

"Yes, by chance or God's grace and she wore—"

"She went to the Whispering Lane after you had suggested it as a sort of neutral ground? And you didn't stop and talk to her? You didn't—"

"I had an engagement with you, divinity."

"You are a hopeless goose! You have thrown away a golden opportunity. *And* you have insulted her."

"Cousin Clorinda, you don't really mean that you think she went there to meet me?"

"Of course she did," said Cousin Clorinda. "When she smiled at you as you say she did you should have followed her, even if you broke forty engagements with me; followed her to the very den of old Jim himself, if necessary."

"What about the feud?"

"A feud," said Cousin Clorinda solemnly, "is an unchristian thing. Besides, it would be a treat to see Mary Edgelow's face if Dorcas married you."

"I give up trying to understand you," said Romney. "Anyhow, I've told you all there is to tell, so now may I have my shortcake?"

It was starlight when Romney went home. A white filmy mist was hanging over the river valley. He crossed the sea fields and climbed Hill o' the Winds. The dew was cold and the night was full of mystery and wonder and sheer magic. The two houses on the hill and their old gardens were veiled in it. It was an expectant night, a night when things intended to happen.

Romney halted on the porch for a moment. There was a blot of white in the Edgelow garden, just across the hedge. As he looked at it something was thrown over the hedge and struck him in the face, a soft, odorous something. He stopped and picked it up. It was a wide-blown rose, damp and exquisite with dew, a rose white enough to lie in her bosom or to star the soft, dark cloud of her hair.

When Romney straightened up and looked across to the Edgelow garden the blot of white was gone.

He kissed the rose.

"It's too dear a night to go to sleep," he said. "I will lay me down in the hammock and dream sweet, wonderful, foolish dreams that will be all the more wonderful and foolish and sweet because they can never be anything but dreams. I will dream of a world where there is no three o'clock in the morning."

In her room Miss Edgelow was looking scrutinizingly in the glass.

"They really don't show so much by lamplight," she said.

Chapter IV

There is, unfortunately, a three o'clock every night, and the fire of Romney's enthusiasm was in white ashes again by morning. He got up and repeated several times aloud to himself: "She is an Edgelow. Her father is rich. Her uncle will make her richer. Her name is Dorcas," by way of fortifying his determination to think no more of her and see no more of her.

He was full of prudent resolution. He would not so much as look toward the Edgelow garden; he would never go near the Whispering Lane; if he ever met Dorcas Edgelow by accident he would bow with easy courtesy and pass on. It did not matter a particle whether her eyes were gray or blue.

Then it occurred to him that it was odd that it should require such a tremendous amount of resolution to avoid a girl whom he had not even seen forty-eight hours ago. It would not be forty-eight hours until four o'clock that afternoon.

Romney whistled uproariously all the time he was dressing. One window of his room looked out on the Edgelow garden, but he never glanced that way. He talked to Aunt Elizabeth all through breakfast of his work and his ambitions and his idea for his new serial, but he did not tell her he meant to use Dorcas Edgelow for a heroine. He did not mention Edgelows at all. The curious thing is that he thought himself quite heroic because he did not.

After breakfast he rushed off to the shore for a surf dip, never glancing at the Edgelow garden at all. Not that he would have seen anything if he did look. Dorcas Edgelow, being no doubt a lazy, luxurious, pampered little thing, was still asleep in bed.

Halfway to the shore Romney suddenly remembered that he had left the rose she had tossed him in a glass of water in his room. What if Aunt Elizabeth flung it out! She would be sure to, never dreaming that a faded flower was of any value. He turned and rushed madly home again, getting there just in the nick of time. He met Aunt Elizabeth carrying the rose downstairs.

"O, aunty, give me that. It's very much mine."

"It's faded," said Aunt Elizabeth in astonishment.

"I kissed it to death," said Romney.

"It is not," said Aunt Elizabeth coldly, "the sort of flower you should have in your possession at all."

So she knew it for one of the Edgelow roses.

"It's a rose of Eden," said Romney. "Do you know the legend of the Rose of Eden, Aunt Elizabeth?"

No, Aunt Elizabeth did not know it. She knew only that she wanted to get downstairs and that Romney was blocking up the way.

"Don't you know your Kipling, Aunt Elizabeth?"

"What is a Kipling?" asked Aunt Elizabeth patiently.

"Why—er—ah—Kipling is a poet." Romney was very flat.

"Was he any relation to Longfellow?"

"No, I think I may safely say they were not connected. But he wrote a poem about the Rose of Eden. When Eve left Eden she contrived to carry off with her one of its roses, and wherever one of its blood-red petals fell sprang up a Rose-of-Eden tree. You find 'em here and there all over the world. And every daughter of Eve—and every son of Adam, though Kipling doesn't mention that—shall once at least 'ere the tale of his years be done' smell the scent of an Eden rose, have his one glorious moment when he sees his dream, even though he may never grasp it. And that one moment, Aunt Elizabeth, makes life worthwhile, even though all the rest of it be roseless."

Aunt Elizabeth looked down at him. She was not a stupid woman even if she did not know her Kipling, and she understood his meaning. An old, old memory stirred in her heart; a whiff of ghostly fragrance, painfully sweet, blew through the deserted chambers of her soul. Without a word she handed Romney his rose and went on down the stairs. But at the foot she turned and looked up, already repenting her weakness.

"She is of the race of our enemies," she said warningly and disapprovingly.

It was too late now to go to the shore. The sun would be too hot for the return walk. Romney went down to the hollow and hunted up Samuel. Again he never looked at the Edgelow garden. Yet although he did not look, he saw her there quite plainly, strolling up and down the acacia walk bareheaded. When he had disappeared without looking, Dorcas Edgelow went back to the house and remarked to her uncle, who was reading in his library.

"I hate that young man next door."

"It would please me much better, Miss, if you thought nothing at all about him," said her uncle.

"And therefore," continued Miss Edgelow, "I am going to break his heart; or if that is impossible by reason of his having none to break, I shall hurt his pride so dreadfully that he will suffer still more. I should like, Uncle, to humiliate that young man to the very dust."

"So he has snubbed you, has he? Serves you right for throwing yourself at his head."

"I only threw a rose," said Miss Edgelow plaintively.

"Don't make a fool of yourself," said her uncle comfortingly. "I haven't any authority over you, of course. I invited you here for the summer because your father told me plainly that he wanted to feel you were in some safe place while he had to be in Mexico. I did not know then that Elizabeth Cooper was going to have a young jackanapes next door. Likely she brought him there on purpose. I don't believe a word of his being ill. He looks fit as a fiddle. But remember this, Miss. If you throw yourself away on that penniless fortune hunter not a cent of my money will you ever see."

"Throw myself away on him! Uncle, do you realize that I've just told you I hate the creature?"

"See that you keep on hating him then, miss. There's a proverb, if I remember aright, to the effect that hate is only love that has missed its way."

Old James looked very fierce and relentless. Miss Edgelow sighed and went away. It was frightfully dull at Hill o' the Winds. It was a detestable old place. It was out of the world. No decent people abode there. She would rather be in Mexico.

O, why had she been so silly as to throw him that rose? Why did night and faint starlight and scented winds make people do such absurd tings? She had been warned, hadn't she? Samuel had warned her. Well, then, why had she done it?

"I suppose," she thought resentfully, "that he doesn't even find me interesting enough to study for material. Detestable creature! I am not going to think about him again."

Romney, meanwhile, was talking to Samuel. He was resolved that he would not mention Miss Edgelow to Samuel. It will never be known whether he would have kept this resolution or not, because Samuel mentioned her at once.

"Her name *is* Dorcas," he announced triumphantly. "She told me herself."

"Dorcas it is," said Romney airily. "Not that it matters. Dorcas or Titania or Melisande—all is one. Her last name is Edgelow."

"Her father had to go to Mexico for the summer—he's a civil engineer—so she came to stay with her uncle, and she's twenty-three years old," said Samuel.

"Did she tell you her age, too?"

"Nope. I found that out down at Clifton last night. 'Pink' Raymer told me. Pink is old Mary Edgelow's chore boy. He heard her telling old Mrs. Franklin all about her. She's an awful flirt, old Mary says, and her father sent her to Hill o' the Winds 'cause he had to go to Mexico and dasn't trust her home alone. She can't help making eyes at any man who happens to be 'round, old Mary says. She's even been engaged a lot o' times, old Mary says, but always broke it off. She means to marry rich when she does marry, old Mary says. She's so extravagant, nobody but a rich man could keep her, old Mary says. Her dress bill every year is awful!"

"Samuel, do you realize what an abominable thing gossip is?" demanded Romney sternly. "I'm sorry to find you so addicted to it."

"You told me to find out all I could about her," protested the aggrieved Samuel.

"Did you then find out whether her eyes are blue or gray?"

Samuel stared a second.

"No," scornfully.

"You see the only important thing, the only thing I really wanted to know about her, you have failed to find out. And yet you were sitting beside her on a log in the Whispering Lane for some time last night. Unobservant Samuel! But never mind. Her name is Dorcas and there is no reasonable doubt in my mind that her eyes are fishy blue. Let's go a-fishing."

"Let's," said Samuel, brightening up. "Say, I've called my pig after old Jim Edgelow."

So Dorcas Edgelow was a heartless coquette who broke hearts and ruined lives for her amusement, a cold-blooded schemer who meant to ensnare a rich husband! Romney did not know that Samuel had made up all these accusations out of whole cloth, that he had never been at or near Clifton the preceding evening, that Pink Raymer was only the name of the hero in a lurid dime novel Samuel was secretly devouring. Nobody could have suspected such a thing of Samuel, the frank-eyed, open-faced, red-lipped child.

He seemed too frank and honest.

Doubtless old Miss Mary Edgelow exaggerated somewhat, thought Romney; ancient maiden ladies of seventy-odd seldom erred on the side of charity in their judgment of their young relatives. But the fact remained. Dorcas Edgelow was a calculating coquette. Dorcas Edgelow was mercenary. Dorcas Edgelow must be avoided.

Therefore Romney went fishing.

Chapter V

He fished all day and wrote in the tower room all the evening. He would not let himself look down into the Edgelow garden. Dorcas Edgelow was sitting there reading a book; at least she had a book on her lap. At intervals she religiously turned a page. She sat facing the tower room and the hedge, but she never looked at them—noticeably.

She was bareheaded and she had thought a great deal about her dress before she put on her primrose silk. She wore a starlike cluster of pink and white daisies in her hair. She knew she looked very well. But what difference did that make when there was nobody to look at her?

She read until eight o'clock and then got up and went indoors in a huff. I am afraid she banged the door. She would die in this stupid place—yes, die! Then perhaps people might be sorry for their behavior. Her cruel father, for instance, who had doomed her to this solitude and exposed her to unparalleled impudence from the cub editors that infested it. There was no doubt that Miss Edgelow was very much annoyed.

Five minutes after she had gone in Romney went to the window and looked down into the Edgelow garden. Nobody was there. What an intolerable, prim, antiquated, formal, unattractive place it was! How could anybody endure year after year those endless stiff walks and clipped hedges and old-fashioned roses. How could anybody live at Hill o' the Winds anyhow? How thankful he would be when his doctor would let him get away from it!

Romney stared at the Edgelow garden for ten minutes longer; then he tried to write again, failed, threw down his pen, looked at the Edgelow garden, still deserted, and betook himself to the hollow to seek Samuel.

Samuel he could not find. Samuel was at that moment talking to Miss Edgelow in the Whispering Lane, imparting to her a few facts and considerable fiction. So he went for a walk to the shore instead. It was dark when he got back and there was still no one in the Edgelow garden. Romney was sure of that because he went to the hedge and looked it over thoroughly.

He did not sleep a great deal that night. Neither did Miss Edgelow. It was a warm night and the mosquitoes were troublesome. Samuel slept dreamlessly. He had told Miss Edgelow that Romney thought she was quite stuck on him, and he had told Romney that Pink Raymer had heard old Mary say that there was a certain millionaire in Montreal to whom Miss Edgelow would be engaged in the fall. It was an understood thing, according to the mythical Pink.

Therefore for two days Romney wished and wrote and ignored Miss Edgelow and thought continually about her. And for two days Miss Edgelow read novels and avoided the garden and sang so loudly and cheerfully that old Jim told her to shut up. He had no particular ear for music. So Miss Edgelow went to the Whispering Lane. She knew there was no danger of meeting that detestable young man there because she had seen him striding down the hill half an hour before.

Of course Romney was there; he had only been down as far as the hollow and when he came back he saw a white figure, which was really that of old Jim's housekeeper, disappearing in the distance along the valley road to the shore. He was sure it was Sylvia—*pshaw*, Dorcas!—so the lane would be safe.

They met face to face. They smiled at each other as if they had expected to meet. Romney said it was a lovely evening and Miss Edgelow said it looked like rain—it didn't—and then they walked on together because there was nothing else to do.

Each of them thoroughly distrusted the other but neither wanted to be anywhere else. Miss Edgelow told herself again that it would be a pleasant and righteous thing to teach this young man a lesson. Romney told himself that if Miss Edgelow wanted to flirt, well and good; he would play the game with zest and get as much amusement out of it as she did. So they were both ready to be surprisingly agreeable to each other and both of them felt suddenly that Hill o' the Winds was a dear, old, quaint, romantic spot, full of poetry and steeped in romance. Romney as he walked beside her felt perfectly happy and satisfied.

"Now why?" one part of him asked the other. "I've often walked in lanes before. It can't be the lane. Dorcas Edgelow is a beauty, but I've walked with women just as beautiful. Why?"

There was no answer so he gave up asking the question and enjoyed his satisfaction. The Whispering Lane was a delightful spot. The warm air was full of elusive wood fragrances that mingled distractingly with the faint perfume that exhaled from Sylvia's—no, confound it, Dorcas'—dress. Shafts of sunlight fell through it; now and then one struck athwart Sylvia's hair and intensified its blue-black sheen.

Robins whistled here and there. Little ferns brushed Sylvia's silken ankles. There were openings in the trees like green, arched windows, and one saw enchanting little landscapes through them.

There was a gate at the end of the lane and when they came to it they leaned against it and looked down into the valley. The gate was narrow and crowded with dogwood bushes, so that they had to stand close together. Occasionally Romney's shoulder touched Sylvia's or a frill of her lacy sleeve brushed his hand.

They watched the valley in a long, delicious silence. It was luminous in hazes of purple and pearl. Great clouds piled themselves up in dazzling masses over the iridescent sea, thunderclouds with white crests and gorges of purple shadow.

Miss Edgelow did not try to talk much. She knew exactly the value of significant silences when you were teaching a certain kind of lesson. She knew that foolish women chattered too much, that wise ones let nature talk for them.

When she did talk she talked of Samuel, his engaging deviltry, his amusing precocity. She said she was very fond of Samuel; Romney said he was, too, and felt that it was a link between them. He told her how he had loved Hill o' the Winds in childhood and how glad he was to find it unchanged, a place unspoiled by the haste and rush of modernity, a place where one might dream dreams and cherish feuds and other impossible things.

Then they were silent again in as many languages as Aunt Elizabeth herself could have been. In fact, when Romney lay awake half the night to think over that half hour in the Whispering Lane he was surprised to find how little they had talked and yet how much more he seemed to know of her. At first he struggled against thinking of her; then philosophically decided that the more he struggled the more fictitious importance the thought of her would assume. Better think her out and have done with it.

So he gave himself over to his memories of her and gloated over them, the delicate, half-mocking, half-alluring undertones in her voice, the delicious golden spots on her face, the charming gestures of her wonderful hands. O, she was quite perfect, just as he had always known she would be.

There was no danger of his falling in love with her. There were a score of indisputable reasons for safeguard. So there was no danger in dwelling on her perfection, no danger in recalling her ways and words and glances—but he had forgotten after all to find out the real colour of her eyes!—no danger in dreaming of what might have been when one knew it couldn't possibly be. In short, there was no danger in a skillful flirtation when both parties knew exactly what they were about.

"I have been walking in the Whispering Lane with Romney Cooper," said Miss Edgelow to her uncle.

"Humph!"

"He is a very nice young man."

"Humph!"

"He is, I think, the nicest young man I ever met."

"Humph! I thought you said you hated him."

"So I did. So I do. I hate him all the more for being so nice. What business has he to be so nice when he is poor and designing and a Cooper and utterly out of the question?"

"Out of the question for what?" grunted old Jim.

"I'm glad you didn't say 'humph' that time," said Dorcas reflectively. "It was getting monotonous."

It was a week later that Romney went to see Cousin Clorinda again, through a weird, uncanny twilight following a rainy day. The sea was like gray satin before Cousin Clorinda's old house. The sky was curdled all over with pale gray clouds. Cousin Clorinda wore flowered organdie and kissed him.

"Cousin Clorinda, she is divine."

"Who?" said Cousin Clorinda indifferently.

"Why, Sylvia—Dorcas—if you must have it."

"O, yes, the niece of old Jim's," said Cousin Clorinda as if she just now heard of her for the first time. "Try some of my shortcake, Romney. You used to be very fond of it."

"She's the most charming thing in the world, Cousin Clorinda. I am not in love with her. Please don't imagine I'm in love with her."

"O, I wouldn't imagine it," Cousin Clorinda seemed a trifle absent.

"But I could be in love with her overwhelmingly if she weren't as rich as wedding cake, and a man-eater. I could adore her. She is adorable. The only thing I'm really sorry for is that I didn't kiss her that day I carried her over the run. The gods will never send me such a chance again."

"My white hen stole her nest and brought out ten of the dearest yellow chicks to-day."

"Chickens! Cousin Clorinda, I'm talking of Sylvia—Sylvia! It's such a luxury to call her Sylvia when I speak to you instead of Miss Edgelow or that abominable Dorcas! This morning when I woke up she was helping Mrs. Gould weed the kitchen garden and singing like a seraph. I love to hear a woman singing at her work. Everybody should sing at his work."

"Nonsense," said Cousin Clorinda. "Fancy a butcher singing at his work! Or an undertaker!"

Romney ignored the interruption.

"You can't believe how deliciously her hair kinks at the nape of her neck on a rainy day. You can't believe how golden her freckles are on her creamy skin. She isn't like any other woman in the world."

"Nobody is," said Cousin Clorinda. "Is Elizabeth troubled with rheumatism this wet day?"

"Cousin Clorinda, I didn't expect to find you so unsympathetic," reproached Romney.

"Is it unsympathetic to ask about Elizabeth's rheumatism? I would have thought it quite the reverse."

"Darling, I came over here to-night to talk about Sylvia to you. I wanted to tell you that, lovely as she looks in flower-hued robes, she is still lovelier in a gray Mackintosh and a rubber cap; that, exquisite as she is when she's talking, she's ten times more exquisite when she's silent; that I'll go mad if I can't solve the mystery of her smile—and you're not a bit interested!"

"No, I don't think I am. In fact, you bore me when you rave about Dorcas Edgelow. Don't be so emotional."

Romney stared incredulously, reproachfully.

"And the last time I was down here you were urging me to marry her!"

"I was not," said Cousin Clorinda brazenly. "I was only teasing you. I regarded the whole matter as a joke. The idea of your marrying Dorcas Edgelow is quite absurd. She wouldn't look at you."

"Why wouldn't she? I am kind and amiable when I feel like it. I never lose my temper, though I may mislay it occasionally. I go to bed early at least once a week. I bear other people's misfortunes with equanimity. And I *never* tell anyone that he has a cold. I'd really make an admirable husband."

"And your salary wouldn't keep her in boots for a month."

"Cousin Clorinda, you've been lying awake at three o'clock too often and too long. That is what is the matter with you."

"Anyhow, I'm not going to talk or be talked to about that Edgelow puss," said Cousin Clorinda decidedly. "The world is full of other subjects."

"Don't you believe it," said Romney.

But Cousin Clorinda was pink and white and blue-draped adamant. She fed him royally, but not a word would she hear of or say of Sylvia. He went away disgruntled.

"You'll be sorry when I'm dead," he warned her.

But Cousin Clorinda sat back in her rocking-chair and laughed.

"The less we talk of her the more he'll think of her," she reflected. "If I had let him pour out all he wanted to tell me he'd have gone home empty, resolving to be sensible and eschew her and all her beguilements. Now he's gone home determined to show me he can't be shooed away. Besides," added Cousin Clorinda, "he took a whole week before he came down to tell me about her. I am not going to put up with being ignored in that fashion by a young snip I pampered with cream while he was a baby!"

Chapter VI

There were some transactions between Miss Edgelow and Samuel whereby the former became possessed of two adored orange-hued kittens, fluffy morsels of fur and mischief that gambolled about her feet as she walked in the Edgelow garden and frisked after her in the Whispering Lane.

She did distracting things with them—at least Romney found them distracting. She cuddled them under her lovely chin and kissed the sun-warm tops of their round, velvety heads. Romney knew she was doing it deliberately, on purpose, out of malice aforethought to drive him crazy, and she very nearly succeeded in spite of his knowledge of her arts. Sometimes he gloomily wished he could wring the necks of those little beasts. Only a conviction that Samuel would get her more prevented him from putting them out of the way in some underhanded fashion.

Yet often the pretty picture Sylvia and her little cats made in the prim, stately, haunted old garden charmed him. He wished that he were an artist and could paint her. Failing that, he wrote her into his new serial so vividly that she took possession of it and played hob with his plot. It would never do for the magazine he meant it for, or any other, and his summer's work would go for nothing and he would be minus several hundred dollars and be on short commons for the winter. But still he wrote on at it, and would have nothing to do with any other tale.

Occasionally he talked to Samuel about it and Samuel told of it, what seemed good unto him, to Miss Edgelow. Samuel was not satisfied with what he had done. He had meant to keep those two apart and had not succeeded. He had meant to keep Romney to himself, and Romney spent all the time he was not in the tower room at work, mooning about in the Whispering Lane with Miss Edgelow. Samuel was disgruntled, and took his revenge as he might.

Both Romney and Miss Edgelow made a great pet of him, but that did not worry the vacuum where his conscience wasn't in the least. He was an artistic liar and never told either of them anything that sounded out of keeping. So they kept on believing him and mistrusting each other and hankering for each other and meeting each other. Aunt Elizabeth and old Jim were not supposed to know anything about it and perhaps they didn't.

Miss Edgelow was very curious about the story Romney was writing of which she was the heroine. But he never mentioned it to her and she would not betray Samuel by mentioning it to him. She vowed, though, that he should have a final scene for it which he would never forget, and, with this in view, she was as sweet to him as if she had really been the coquette he believed her—and perhaps she was.

At least, she was secretly much dissatisfied with her progress. Romney said delicious things to her and looked things still more delicious and played the part of devoted admirer to perfection. But Miss Edgelow wanted more than admiration. To spurn admiration would inflict no real wound, teach no lasting lesson. She wanted him to love her, so that he might feel it to the core of his soul when she finally laughed at him and dismissed him.

And so far, in spite of three weeks' delectable companionship and pretty speeches and prettier silences and moons and stars and kittens, she could give herself no assurance that he really cared a penny's worth for her. Her failure annoyed her and caused her to say sarcastic things to old Jim.

Romney considered that he was still a wise and prudent young man. He congratulated himself on his ability to refrain from loving not wisely but too well when there was such temptation to it. Not many men, he reflected, would have kept their heads in the face of such provocation, even though they knew her for a professed flirt and themselves for paupers. They would have been fools and fallen fathoms deep in love without being able to help themselves. Now he, Romney, was not a fool.

True, sometimes at three o'clock at night wisdom and prudence seemed rather ugly and sordid virtues, and Romney thought it might have been just as well to let himself go, to put his neck under her scornful little foot and let her play with his heart and throw it away, and spend all his wealth and power of loving in one splendid, unreasonable, unreasoning burst of folly. But around the rest of the clock he was complacent and kept telling himself he had done well to keep fast hold of his heart.

This was his state of mind when Clifford Hughes came to see him. Hughes was the owner of the string of magazines for one of which Romney had once intended his serial. Hughes wanted to know about the serial and was disgruntled because Romney told him it would never do.

But that was not really what Hughes had come to talk about. He had fallen hopelessly in love and got himself engaged and he was so blindly, besottedly happy that he had to tell somebody all about the affair, and Romney was the only fellow he could tell about it. Romney had always been a dreamy, romantic chap. Romney would sympathize with him. So he sat in the tower room and raved for hours.

Romney listened and sympathized, and grew more dismayed every minute. This fellow Hughes was saying about his lady just what he, Romney, wanted to say about Sylvia. This fellow Hughes was disgustingly happy in the very way he, Romney, wanted to be happy—in the very way he *could* be happy if Sylvia loved him as Hughes' lady loved him. Romney was shocked and alarmed and upset, and didn't know what he was saying to Hughes half the time. He only realized that a truly dreadful state of affairs had come about all at once.

He loved Sylvia, loved her just as wholly and madly as ever a man loved a woman. How could he have been so blind and besotted as not to have known it before? Why, he had loved her from the moment he had first seen her in the Edgelow garden! And she didn't care a snap for him, and he couldn't ask her to marry him if she did, and how was he ever to get himself past three o'clock *that* night? *Then* he would realize his position to the full. And even now it was quite unbearable.

"Hello," said Hughes, looking out of the window. "Who's the pretty girl over there, Cooper?"

"Pretty girl!" Hopeless idiot! Blind bat! Couldn't he see that Sylvia was the most beautiful woman in the world?

"Syl—Dorcas Edgelow," said Romney indifferently.

"Know her?"

"I've a nodding acquaintance with her," said Romney indifferently. "You know there's an old feud between the families. It has petered out pretty well in our generation, but it doesn't make for cordiality."

"I see. Pity. She's really quite nice looking." Then Hughes dropped the subject. To prevent any possible return to it Romney took him fishing. He forgot to ask Samuel and Samuel was so furious that he went straight to Miss Edgelow and told her that he *had* been fishing with them and heard them talking about her, and Romney had told the city man that she was a nice small thing and that he could have her for the asking, but didn't mean to ask because he was too poor and a wife was a nuisance anyway.

Samuel, being angry, was less artistic than usual and for the first time Miss Edgelow wondered if he was not painting the lily. He looked so guileless and cherubic that it was hard to believe it of him; but really Romney Cooper didn't seem like a man who would say such things to a friend about any girl. Nevertheless, Samuel couldn't be making it *all* up out of whole cloth; *something* must have been said.

She was very disdainful and saucy when Romney came that night to the Whispering Lane. But all her disdain and sauciness didn't keep her away from the lane nor from making a very careful toilet before she went there nor from looking radiantly entrancing when she got there.

"So your friend has gone?" she said.

"Yes, thank Heaven," said Romney. "If he had stayed any longer I should have gone crazy."

"Do your friends always have that effect on you?

"No, not always. But he is engaged to be married. He was so insultingly happy that I couldn't tolerate him. And he kept talking about *his* lady fair when I wanted to be talking about mine."

"O, so you have one?" Miss Edgelow tucked a kitten under her chin and spoke only with languid interest.

"Yes. I've never told you about her, have I?"

"Not that I remember."

"May I? I suppose I've caught the infection from Hughes. I want to talk about her to-night. You don't mind?"

"O, no," quite graciously.

"Her name," began Romney gravely, "is Sylvia. It couldn't be anything else. Sylvia is the only name in any language that absolutely suits and expresses her."

"We had an old black cook once named Sylvia," murmured Miss Edgelow reminiscently. "Go on."

"Her name is Sylvia. She is about five feet six. She has

jet-black hair that grows off her face in a widow's peak. She has a creamy skin and lips as red as the rose of love. She has wonderful hands. She has straight black brows. She has eyes that are—why, I swear they are dark, dark blue! It has only come home to me this minute what colour they really are. She has such a trick of veiling them with her lashes, you know."

"She has no imperfections, of course," said Miss Edgelow, a trifle contemptuously.

"O, yes. She isn't Tennyson's *Maud* at all; not 'faultily faultless,' not she. She has a number of little golden freckles and her nose is—is—"

"Crooked?" suggested Miss Edgelow.

She smiled a bit.

"No, no—not crooked. I swear it's not crooked. Just a trifle more than aquiline."

Miss Edgelow was quite angry. She knew—let it be accounted unto her for vanity or not—that Romney was describing her to her face. He was trying out a scene for his story in all probability.

"It will be very witchlike when she grows old, no doubt."

"Sylvia will never grow old," said Romney. "She is the incarnation of eternal youth."

"Does this paragon return your affection?" dared Miss Edgelow.

"Alas, no. She laughs at me. She mocks me. She doesn't care for me at all. It's just as well, of course. I can't marry her, you see."

"Why not?" Miss Edgelow's lashes hid her eyes very securely.

"She is rich and going to be richer. I am poor and will probably be poorer. Besides, as aforesaid, she doesn't and couldn't care for me."

"This," thought Miss Edgelow, "is the point in the story where I should say, 'Have you asked her?' with the soft pedal on. I shall not say anything of the sort. Instead I shall say:

"You are very likely correct in your opinion."

"I know I am," said Romney, folding his arms and scowling ferociously at space. "I know I am. But O, you have no idea how madly I love her! How madly I shall always love her!"

"How many girls have you loved—always—before her?" asked Miss Edgelow impertinently.

"Not one. I never even fancied I loved before."

"How interesting. Now I—" Miss Edgelow paused, and went through the motions of a blush. "I have been in love, or imagined myself in love, several times. Three, to be exact. Yet I am soundly heart-whole at the present moment. So you see there is hope of your ultimate recovery."

"I shall never recover. I don't want to recover. Why didn't you marry those men?"

"It is not permitted to marry three men," said Miss Edgelow plaintively. "And there were other reasons. One of them was a young lawyer. He was the handsomest man I have ever known."

"He had piggy eyes. I swear he had piggy eyes," said Romney viciously.

"He had *not*. And he made love *so* artistically. It was quite a pleasure to listen to him."

"He must have had heaps of practice"—still more viciously.

"The same idea occurred to me," said Miss Edgelow composedly. "I think that was why I didn't marry him. A man with a talent like that *couldn't* bury it in a napkin. He'd have to keep on using it. The second object of my affections was a professor of McGill. He was the cleverest man I ever met."

"Moon-face, pursy-mouth, tortoise-shell glasses! I can see him," said Romney.

"He was very intellectual looking," murmured Miss Edgelow. "And yet he asked my opinion about things. That was his way of making love. It was agreeable. But I had a presentiment that after we were married he would stop asking my opinions. That would *not* be agreeable."

"There was a third, I think," said Romney, seeing that Miss Edgelow had lapsed into apparent reverie.

"O, yes, there *was* a third. Note the tense. He is—was—moderately good looking and moderately clever. I think I liked him better than any of the others."

"Why didn't you marry him?"

"He didn't ask me to. He…he told me he loved another lady. He even described her to me, talked to me about her. I couldn't with any self-respect care for him one moment after that, could I?"

Miss Edgelow shot an upward glance at Romney before her concluding words. Romney remembered what Samuel had said old Mary Edgelow had said, "She can't help making eyes at any man who happens to be around."

"She is luring me on," he thought miserably. "I won't *be* lured. She can laugh at me in her sleeve but she shall not have the satisfaction of laughing at me openly!"

He strode on in silence. They turned at the gate and walked back. At the entrance to the lane they paused. The old Edgelow house and garden, drowned in lilac sunset light, incredibly delicate and elusive, lay below them in a dip at the long Hill. They stood and looked down on it.

After a long silence Miss Edgelow said dreamily: "It is a house of memories. I am haunted by them. So many Edgelow women, and all unhappy! There has never been a happy Edgelow woman; or if they were happy they were never happy long. Some of them deserved their unhappiness; some of them didn't. I wonder—" Miss Edgelow looked reflective "—in which class I shall belong."

"She has taken a new tack. She is trying to play on my sympathy now," thought Romney. "She is not content with my veiled avowal. She must have my scalp to dangle openly at her belt. She can't claim it yet because her name is not Sylvia."

"Some of the Edgelow men were to blame for their women's unhappiness, weren't they?" he said.

"Yes, some. I think Uncle Jim must have been a horrid sort of husband. I was here one summer when I was a little girl. I have never forgotten Aunt Fanny's eyes. She died by inches through the years. Most of the other tragedies were sudden and speedy."

"Tell me about them—if you don't mind talking about them."

"O, I don't. I'm rather proud of my family ghosts and demons. I shall be one of them some day, and I shall come and haunt this old place. Our house in Montreal isn't really ghostable. I shall wander about this old garden and my ghost chum will be Thyra Edgelow, Great-uncle Fairfax's bride. Just a few weeks after her marriage she went gayly out to those woods away over there to gather nuts and never returned."

"What happened to her?"

"That question has been asked a thousand times and never answered. She simply vanished from among the living that autumn afternoon. No trace of her was ever discovered. Some thought she must have been drowned in the river and her body swept out to sea. Some thought—but there were all sorts of surmises. She hadn't wanted to marry Fairfax Edgelow, it seems. She was a gay, merry creature.

"Then there were Tom and Dorothy Edgelow. They were married children; he was nineteen and she was seventeen. They had one glorious summer in that old house at least. He was Grandfather Edgelow's brother. They both died in the same week of typhoid. Great-aunt Edith was a wonderful musician and very ambitious. One of her hands was so mangled by a door slamming on it that she could never play again. She went insane brooding over it. Uncle Jim's sister, Aunt Lilian, was killed by lightning in the room I sleep in, struck while trying on her wedding dress. The Edgelow fate seems to have a special hatred of our brides. None of us have been happy in our love affairs. It's the old Edgelow curse, you know. We have a family curse as well as a family feud, you see."

"I never heard of the curse. What of it?"

"My great-great-great-grandfather, Thomas Edgelow, was a harsh creditor. He sold out at a chattel mortgage sale the household possessions of a poor old woman. She cursed him and his descendants. 'Your women shall never be happy,' she said. 'One and all they shall die in sorrow, as I die.' She hanged herself that night. Do you believe in curses? I don't. But it is the truth that there has never since that day been a happy Edgelow woman, whether she was Edgelow by birth or Edgelow by marriage.

"Uncle Jim's father was blinded by an explosion of his gun three months after he was married to Cora Graham, the great beauty. And after that he made her life wretched through his jealousy for fifty years. For they lived together that long and he never seemed to realize that she had grown old. He was as madly jealous of her when she was seventy as when she was twenty.

"Katherine Edgelow was jilted by her lover. She never went out of that house afterward except once. When her false lover was married in Clifton Church she dressed herself in widow's weeds and went to the wedding. She stood a little behind the bridal party during the ceremony; nobody dared interfere with her. The bride fainted when she turned and saw her. Katherine was living when I was here that summer long ago. She was incredibly old and I was terribly frightened.

"But the bitterest of our ghosts must be my great-great-grandmother Edgelow. She was jealous. She thought her husband loved Adella Cooper. That was the beginning of the Edgelow-Cooper feud, you know."

"No, I didn't know. I never knew what began it; I thought it was something trivial. What did your great-great-grandmother do?"

"She met her husband one night when he was returning, so she thought, from Adella, and threw vitriol in his face. He was blinded for life."

Romney shuddered. The sun had dropped into a bank of western cloud and a chill and a shadow swept over Hill o' the Winds and rolled down its sides to the valley.

"At least she was in earnest. She didn't play at loving," he said, as they turned away.

"No; but wouldn't it have been better if she had?" retorted Miss Edgelow.

"Undoubtedly. Yet I think I rather like ladies who love in earnest."

"Would your Sylvia love in earnest?"

"If she loved me at all. But you see, she doesn't."

"Are you quite sure she doesn't?"

"Quite."

"And you are quite sure you couldn't marry her if she did?"

"Quite."

"So it is a blessing she doesn't?"

"Exactly."

Miss Edgelow turned to the gate that opened from the Whispering Lane into the Edgelow garden.

"I think," she said, "that I am going to be very busy for the rest of my stay here."

"I shall be—busy—too," said Romney gloomily.

"O, yes, you have your serial to finish."

Romney wondered how she knew he was writing a serial. He had never said anything to her about it.

"Yes," he said very briskly. "I must really hurry up with it. My time is nearly up: only three weeks more."

"And since we are both going to be so—busy—we may as well say a polite good-bye now," said Miss Edgelow. She held out her hand. Romney took it, gave it the requisite friendly pressure, dropped it.

"Good-bye, Miss Edgelow," he said. He lifted his hat and went away whistling. Miss Edgelow, holding her head very high, went back to the Edgelow house.

Old Jim was, as usual, reading in his library.

"Romney Cooper has just told me that he can't marry me."

"Did you ask him to, pray?"

"I think I did."

"And he refused you."

"Practically."

"Then he has more sense than any Cooper ever had before," said old Jim, returning to his book.

"Nobody takes me seriously," mourned Miss Edgelow. "I suppose I must be fundamentally light. Well, isn't that better than destroying my husband's sight with vitriol, Uncle Jim? Wouldn't *you* rather have a wife who laughed at you than one who threw vitriol at you?"

"*My* wife did neither," said old Jim significantly.

"But she died young," thought Miss Edgelow. She did not say it aloud; there were some things it would not do to say to old Jim. She went up to her room and peeped out. There was a light in the tower room.

"He is busy at his story," said Miss Edgelow. "I don't think he got much material for it from me this evening—of the kind he wanted, anyhow. I wonder what a subeditor's salary is."

Then, oddly enough, Miss Edgelow lay down on her bed, buried her face in a pillow and cried.

Romney was not writing. He was bunched moodily up in a chair. Aunt Elizabeth was knitting lace. Samuel was building a pen in the back yard for a couple of pet snakes. Samuel was very happy.

Chapter VII

Samuel was happier still for the next two weeks. Romney was his own again. He kept no more trysts in the Whispering Lane, but devoted himself to Samuel. They fished and swam and lounged together. The tower room was forsaken and Romney's pen rusted on his inkstand.

Sometimes he saw Miss Edgelow and her golden balls of fluff in the Edgelow garden, but she never looked his way. Quite often he heard her singing gayly. Soon after that he always whistled gayly. Peace and contentment apparently brooded over Hill o' the Winds.

Only Aunt Elizabeth was slightly worried. Romney's appetite was poor. Her choicest delicacies did not tempt him; neither did Cousin Clorinda's. Romney had been down to see Cousin Clorinda quite often through the summer, but he had never talked to her of Sylvia, and Cousin Clorinda could not ask him to. Now he went down on another cool, rainy evening when the fogs were coming in on the east wind and the valley was gray and hidden.

"Beloved, how long can two weeks be?" he asked her.

"That depends," she said.

"On what?"

"In your case I think it would depend on Sylvia," said Cousin Clorinda boldly and anxiously. She did not like Romney's lack of appetite and hollowness of eye any better than Aunt Elizabeth.

"There is no such lady as Sylvia," said Romney. "She is such stuff as dreams are made of."

"What about Miss Edgelow then?"

"An amusing young person. I haven't been talking to her lately."

"For two weeks, to be exact," said Cousin Clorinda. She rocked slowly in her chair and looked at him very maternally. Romney had a queer fleeting feeling that he would like to lay his head on her breast and cry as he used to do long ago when he got hurt, and have her stroke his head and say, "Never mind, be brave; you'll soon feel better."

"Make a clean breast of it to me," said Cousin Clorinda.

"You weren't very sympathetic the last time I tried to talk to you about her."

"I don't suppose I'll be sympathetic now either. But it'll do you good to talk it out. What did you quarrel over?"

"We didn't quarrel. She just dismissed me. I suppose she had got all the amusement out of me that she expected—or wanted."

"Tell me every word both of you said," ordered Cousin Clorinda. Romney did. He had no difficulty in remembering them; they were all too deeply impressed. Cousin Clorinda listened and rocked gently. After he had finished she continued to rock so long that Romney wondered if she meant to say anything at all. Finally she said: "Poor girl!"

"Poor—*what?*"

"Poor girl," repeated Cousin Clorinda.

"Why do you pity *her?*" cried Romney, aggrieved.

"Because it must be very hard to be as deeply in love as she is with a young man so utterly insensate and blind and pig-headed as you," said Cousin Clorinda calmly.

"Why, thank you." Romney was very sarcastic. "Thank you. I haven't received so many compliments for a long time. Insensate?"

"Yes, insensate. A girl like Dorcas Edgelow practically offers herself to you and you practically flout her."

"Cousin Clorinda!"

"Blind because you can't see that she's dying for you. Pig-headed because you would rather destroy her happiness and your own than ask Jim Edgelow's heiress to marry you."

"Dearest, you are simply darkening counsel by words without knowledge. Miss Edgelow doesn't care a snap of her lovely, slender fingers for me. I came to you for the bread of comfort, Cousin Clorinda, and you give me the stone of ridicule."

"Go back to Hill o' the Winds; go to Dorcas Edgelow; say to her: 'I love you. Will you marry me?' Then if she says 'no' come back to me and I'll give you all the comfort and sympathy you can desire."

"I can't do that," said Romney stubbornly. "Besides, I have done it—practically, as you say. I've told her I loved Sylvia. She knows well enough who Sylvia is."

"Yes, and immediately after telling her you informed her that you were too poor to marry her. Romney, are you really so very poor?"

"I am. Worse, I'm in debt to my doctor. I've been depending on paying him off with the cash I'd get for my serial this fall. And now I can't get it written, not in a salable way anyhow. Job's turkey was a capitalist compared to me."

"And have you no chance of promotion?"

"Not at present. Not for years, if ever. I suppose the truth is I'm lacking in enterprise, Cousin Clorinda. I'm not a pusher. And I've dilly-dallied a bit, I know—drifted. You see, it didn't seem to matter. As long as I could pay my own way and enjoy life after my own fashion I was contented. I didn't believe I'd ever really meet Sylvia. So I've rather been sidetracked."

"Get back to the main line and hustle," said Cousin Clorinda.

"Too late. I can't ask her to wait for years for me. Besides, she wouldn't."

"Then forget her."

L. M. MONTGOMERY

"I can't."

"Then for goodness' sake," said Cousin Clorinda in exasperation, "try some of my ginger snaps."

So, after all, Romney didn't get much sympathy from Cousin Clorinda. He went back to Hill o' the Winds feeling that she thought him a rather poor sort of critter. Well, so he was. He was a failure, an utter, arrant failure. He had failed in everything in which a man ought to succeed. No wonder Sylvia laughed at him! No wonder Sylvia mocked him! He even wondered that she thought him worthwhile flirting with. How deep her eyes were, how perfect the curve of her throat, how kissable the sweet red curve of her mouth! Romney groaned.

"Matter?" queried Samuel, appearing suddenly halfway up the Hill, his wet, laughing face dimly visible in the rainy twilight. "Sick?"

"No. But you will be here in this cold east rain with nothing on your back but a torn shirt. Hustle home and dry yourself! You have a cold now."

"O, I'm a fish," said Samuel. "Rain never hurts me, no more'n a frog. But *you* had new ammonia. You gotter be careful."

"I'm not going to be careful," said Romney recklessly. "It would have been better for me if the pneumonia had made an end of me. Samuel, were you ever so unhappy that every beat of your heart hurt you?"

"Nope," said Samuel laconically. "You feeling that way?" he added uneasily.

"Samuel," said Romney, "if I could just be snuffed out to-night—like a candle—I'd like it."

"All on account o' that Edgelow skirt, I s'pose," said Samuel, less disdainfully than usual, however. A close observer might have thought that he felt a trifle less satisfied with himself than before.

"Samuel," said Romney, "never fall in love."

Samuel thought this warning totally unnecessary. But he was worried. He knew Romney well enough by this time to know that the more airily he talked of anything the more deeply he felt. When Romney was indifferent he talked quite earnestly. Samuel, when he went to bed that night, wished that after all he had not told Miss Edgelow certain things. He wished it hard for quite a while and then he gave up wishing anything except that he might get warm and stop shivering. Next day his uncle sent for the doctor.

Samuel was sick for a week before Miss Edgelow heard of his illness through her uncle's housekeeper. She went right down to the hollow. Romney was there, waiting on him. Samuel would have no one else, though they had brought a nurse up from Clifton. He was delirious but he always knew Romney.

"Pneumonia?" asked Miss Edgelow.

Romney nodded. He looked worn and ill himself, for he had not slept much during the week and he was worried over Samuel. He didn't know how fond of Samuel he was until the doctor looked grave over the child.

"Yes, double pneumonia. We're doing all we can for him. But he's worried over something. It's against him."

"What is it?"

"We don't know. He keeps saying, 'I wish I hadn't told her,' and begging me to put things straight. I promise to do so, but I haven't an idea what he means and I don't think he has any confidence that I'm doing what I promise."

"Can I see him?"

"O, yes. But it isn't likely he'll recognize you."

Samuel was lying on his bed, staring at the ceiling with dull, fevered eyes. It was not clear whether he recognized Miss Edgelow or not. But he appealed to her.

"They was all lies, you know. You'll tell her, won't you?"

"Yes, yes, dear."

She was very gentle and motherly as she took Samuel's thin, strangely white and clean little paw. Romney saw a look on her face, an expression of her spirit that he had never seen before.

"He never said one of those things. I made 'em up. Tell her that. *You'll* get it straighter than *he* would. *He'd* mix it all up. *He* talks all round things. *He* never goes to the point. *You* tell her."

"I'll tell her. I'll make her understand," promised Miss Edgelow.

"What'll they do to me for telling lies?" queried Samuel.

"Who, dear?"

"The fellers up there," Samuel pointed to the ceiling. "God and the rest."

"O! O, they'll forgive you, dear, if you're sorry."

"I am sorry. I wisht I hadn't. It's made him want to be snuffed out. I don't want him to be snuffed out. *You* won't—" Samuel gripped her hand "—*you* won't let her snuff him out, will you?"

"She shall not snuff him out," promised Miss Edgelow solemnly.

"I made Pink Raymer up, too," said Samuel. "There ain't no Pink Raymer, only in a book. I took him out of the book. You'll put him back in the book, won't you?"

"Yes, dear."

"And shut the cover tight?"

"Yes."

"Now, mind, you mustn't let her snuff him out," said Samuel.

The nurse came in then and Miss Edgelow went out. She did not look at Romney. She paid very little attention to Romney for the next week, though she saw him every day when she came to see Samuel. Samuel was delirious at times yet, but he had evidently given up worrying. Only when he saw Miss Edgelow he always said, "You won't let her snuff him out, will you?" and Miss Edgelow always replied, "No, I won't let her snuff him out."

But she never looked at Romney.

On the evening of the day when Samuel "took the turn" for the better, Romney went to the Whispering Lane. It was three weeks since he had walked there. Miss Edgelow was standing in the shadow of the beeches. Their gloom threw still darker shadows on her glossy hair and deepened the luster of her long blue eyes. She had a kitten on her shoulder and her dress was a young-leaf green with a scarlet girdle. Beyond her were tossing young maples whitening in the wind, with glimpses of the purple valley beyond them.

Romney came up close to her and looked down at her. He was tired and pale but there was an air of triumph about him.

"Your name isn't Sylvia—" he began.

"But it is," said Miss Edgelow. "Sylvia Dorcas Edgelow. I am always called Sylvia at home. Uncle Jim hates the name. He has always called me Dorcas."

Romney tried again.

"You are your uncle's heiress, and I—"

"I am not. Uncle Jim hasn't ever had any intention of leaving me a cent. His will was made years ago; he has left everything to found a library in Clifton. He thinks I don't know that but I do. Old Cousin Mary told me."

"You have been brought up in luxury and—"

"I was brought up in comfort and father gave me a year at school in Paris. After I came back I graduated in domestic science at Macdonald. I can make bread, I can make my own clothes… the number of useful things I can do is quite appalling."

"I am poor but—"

"Honest."

"Sylvia, you *must* stop interrupting me! I cannot allow my wife to interrupt me."

"You are too poor to keep a wife."

"I'm *not*. I have a letter here in my pocket—hear it crackling?—from Clifford Hughes, offering me the head-editorship of the four magazines he owns. The salary will keep us very comfortably. Besides, 'to him that hath shall be given.' Aunt Elizabeth told me this morning that she had made her will when she took that trip down to Clifton last week and had left everything she owned to me, except the Chippendale sideboard, which is to go to Doctor John, and the coloured egg dish, which is to go to Cousin Clorinda. As it happens, the sideboard and the coloured egg dish are the only things of Aunt Elizabeth's I've ever coveted. But it means something to me to know that some day my—my—let us say my grandchildren will inherit this old place. So now will you be good?"

"Have you finished your serial?" asked Miss Edgelow inconsequently.

"No. I'm working it up to the grand climax now, though. It's coming out better than I expected. How did you know about it?"

"Samuel told me. He also told me you experimented with girls and put their reactions into your stories. At least, he did not use those words, but that is what he implied."

"Little beast! But I *did* put you in that serial, Sylvia. Only you were so unmanageable after I had got you in, you persisted in snuffing the hero out."

"Well, you know—" Sylvia looked straight into his eyes "—I promised Samuel I wouldn't do that anymore."

It might have been an hour or a hundred years afterward that Romney said: "I want to kiss each of your freckles one by one. It will take some time."

"Aren't you afraid to marry me?" asked Sylvia. "There is the curse, you know."

"*You* will be a happy woman. A curse is worked out in four generations. You are the fifth. It has spent its force, as all evil things must do. The Edgelow tradition of unhappiness will vanish with the old feud. *You* will not disappear nor go insane nor throw vitriol at your husband."

"And you," said Sylvia, "will not open my letters, nor give me a silk dress I don't want and refuse me a new hat I do, nor jilt me?"

"It's a bargain," said Romney.

Old Jim Edgelow was reading in his library.

"Uncle Jim," said Sylvia, "I am going to marry Romney Cooper in six weeks' time."

She was really afraid. Nobody ever knew just how old Jim would react to anything. But old Jim Edgelow had been governed by contraries all his life. He loved to disappoint people. He would rather disappoint them agreeably than not at all. He shut his book, took off his glasses, and said: "Marry him then and be hanged to you! It will infuriate old Elizabeth Cooper, anyhow."

"She didn't seem very angry," said Sylvia.

"What! Does she know of it already?"

"O, yes. We went right to her as soon as we became engaged. She said, 'God bless you.' It was old-fashioned, of course," said Sylvia meditatively, "but I think I liked it."

Uncle Jim replaced his glasses and opened his book.

"Those whom Elizabeth Cooper has joined together let not James Edgelow put asunder," he said.

❧ ❧

Editors' note: This story, really more of a "novelette," was published in the March 17, 1923, issue of *Love Story* magazine and was illustrated by P. J. Monahan. It is listed in the "Unverified Ledger Titles" in the 1986 bibliography. It was found by Donna Campbell and is

L. M. MONTGOMERY

available to view in the Ryrie-Campbell Collection.

The character of "Cousin Clorinda" in "Hill o' the Winds" may remind some readers of other characters in Montgomery's fiction, such as "Miss Cornelia Bryant" in *Anne's House of Dreams* and "Mrs. Ellen Churchill" in her story "The Matchmaker" in this volume. As for Cousin Clorinda's style of dress, Montgomery was pondering the changes in fashion at that time and remarked in her journal on February 6, 1923, that "My day for the frilly gowns of organdy and lace is over—henceforth I must wear the richer hues and materials of the matron." She was forty-nine years of age at the time.

Montgomery's reference in Chapter II to "Who is Sylvia?" is from Shakespeare's poem of that title from his play *The Two Gentlemen of Verona.* She also quotes the famous line in William Ernest Henley's poem "Invictus" in that same passage: "I am the master of my fate, I am the captain of my soul."

Dorcas' remark that she had studied domestic science at Macdonald College was a reference to Montgomery's dearest friend, Fredericka Campbell Macfarlane, who had followed that same path. "Frede," as she was called, died of pneumonia in 1919.

In 1923, L. M. Montgomery was involved in lawsuits with her first publisher, L. C. Page and Co., one of which was eventually tried before the US Supreme Court. Montgomery finally won both lawsuits.

In January 1923, Montgomery had received a letter from the Secretary of the Royal Society of Arts in Great Britain, inviting her to become a Fellow, the first Canadian woman to be so honoured. (In 1935, Montgomery would be made an Officer in the Order of the British Empire.)

JIM'S HOUSE
(1926)

"Friend Cat," said Jim Kennedy, "I am going house-hunting to-day."

Friend Cat, sitting on a stool beside Jim, blinked his topaz eyes a trifle insolently and then looked bored. He never condescended to get excited. But Jim was evidently very much excited about something, and Margaret Irwin gazed at him across the breakfast table with shy, friendly interest.

She had not seen Jim Kennedy excited about anything in the week she had been boarding with his sister-in-law. Excitement became him, she thought. It thrilled his lazy, musical voice with delightful cadences, and lighted illuminating fires in the depths of his golden-brown eyes.

Margaret Irwin had known Jim only a week, but she felt better acquainted with him than with any man she had ever met—which is not saying a great deal, since she seldom met men, and never got really acquainted with them when she did. It was very pleasant to sit across from Jim at meal times, listening to his gentle, whimsical talk, and watching him smuggle tidbits to Friend Cat when Mrs. Kennedy was not looking.

"You'll have an awful job to find a house," said Mrs. Kennedy placidly. "I don't know of one in the village either for rent or for sale, except the big Ormsby house. And you don't seem to care for that."

"It is an impossible house," said Jim solemnly. "Not because of its size, but just because of its impossibility. Miss Irwin, you saw it yesterday. What was your first impression, if you don't mind telling me?"

"I felt," Margaret said, responding to the challenge in Jim's eyes, "as if I wanted to get a broom and sweep off all the gingerbread and frippery and wooden lace."

"Exactly! *Any* sensible woman would feel the same."

"It's an elegant house," said Mrs. Kennedy, a trifle warmly. Her brother had built it; the matter was slightly personal.

"It *is* elegant, with all the term implies," agreed Jim gravely. "Far too elegant for a humble schoolmaster like me. It would own me, body and soul. I'd have to carry it with me wherever I went—on my back, like a snail. I want a house I can love, and that Friend Cat can boss. O, I'll find one! I don't know where, but I feel it in my bones: luck's just waiting round the corner for me. My house is somewhere, wanting me as badly as I want it. Come, Friend Cat. We'll walk up the spruce road and talk it over."

Jim went out, flinging a smile back from the door. Friend Cat ambled after him. Mrs. Kennedy smiled indulgently.

"Jim's in great spirits this morning. I don't wonder. He had a letter from Isabel Bartlett last night. And at last she's coming home to marry him. They've been engaged five years. *That's* why he's going house-hunting. I must say I'm glad. Jim has been very patient, but the long wait has been hard on him. He's always been crazy about Isabel. And he's thirty—it's time he settled down and had a home of his own. Though I'll be sorry enough to lose him. He's boarded with me ever since I came here, and a nicer man never lived, odd as he is.

"For he *is* odd, nobody can deny it. You may have noticed the queer things he's always saying. My husband wasn't a bit like him. You'd never have thought they were brothers. Still, I'm fond of him, and I'm glad he's going to be happy. I've been worried for fear Isabel would take up with someone else and throw him over—and that would break his heart. I always wondered at her liking him. She's so pretty and attractive she could marry most anybody. But Jim was her choice, it seems, and she hasn't changed, and I'm thankful for his sake. She'll make him a wonderful wife, just the kind he needs."

Mrs. Kennedy paused for lack of breath, to Margaret's regret. Jim's affairs interested her. She had known he was engaged—Mrs. Kennedy had told her, and intimated that there was a romance linked up with it. Margaret loved romance. It had never touched her own life—never would touch it. She wanted quite greedily to hear all about Jim's.

"It's no secret," Mrs. Kennedy assured her. "Everybody in Glenby knows about Jim and Isabel. It's a wonder Jim hasn't told you—he loves to talk about her. I never heard of a man so wrapped up in a girl. That's why I've been worried for fear she wouldn't come back to him. It began six years ago. Jim was just through college and had been taken on as principal in the High School. Isabel had come to live in Glenby then, with the aunt who brought her up. It was love at first sight with Jim, and no wonder, for she was the prettiest thing: just seventeen and slight as a reed, with the loveliest golden hair—*yards* of it—and big blue eyes.

"And such a happy little thing! Her laugh was *catching*, as Jim said. Everybody liked Isabel and she had dozens of beaux, but from the first it was Jim and nobody else. People wondered—Jim was eight years older and always had been an odd stick. He's not as handsome as some, but he has a taking way with him, as you may have noticed."

Yes, Margaret had noticed it.

"They were engaged, and meant to be married right off. And then the aunt, Miss Bartlett, got sick and the doctors told her her lungs were affected and she must go to Colorado. And she didn't know what to do. She couldn't go alone, and there wasn't a soul to go with her except Isabel. Isabel and she were alone in the world, and she was one of the clinging, dependent sort of women.

"But Isabel said right out she'd go with her, and Jim agreed that it was her duty, though it was mighty hard on him. When they went away they didn't think she'd be away more'n a year; but here it's been five years. This spring Miss Bartlett up and married an old widower she'd met out there—no waiting for *her* once he came to time—and poor Isabel was free at last. That was the news Jim got last night—that, and the fact that she was coming home to him. She's to be here in September and I s'pose Jim'll spend the summer hunting up a house for her and talking the ears off his cat. He's *got* to talk to someone about her, and the cat's the only creature that's willing to listen for hours on end."

"I hope he'll find his house," said Margaret dreamily.

"I don't know why on earth Jim has such a spite against the Ormsby house. He seems to hate it as if was a prison. And it's such a nice house. Perhaps it's a little fussy on the outside; I think myself a bay window or two could be spared. But it's so convenient! Hot and cold water, electric light, hardwood floors, two bathrooms—why, it's equal to a city apartment. And so near everything: shops and churches and the park. Cassell Street's the liveliest in Glenby—there's a string of motors passing all the time on the way to the lake. Perhaps the price staggers Jim, but he has money saved up, and Ormsby would sell it for half its value to settle up the estate."

"I don't think the Ormsby house belongs to Jim," said Margaret.

Mrs. Kennedy stared.

"No, of course it don't belong to him. It is part of the old Ormsby estate."

"It might belong to him for all that," said Margaret. "Have you never seen houses that you felt belonged to you—no matter who owned them?"

No, Mrs. Kennedy had not, nor had she a glimmer of a notion what Miss Irwin meant. So she got up and began to clear away the dishes and Margaret went out to the garden and lay in a hammock under the trees, doing nothing.

O, how sweet it was to do nothing in the beautiful silence! Margaret had been working in a department store for twelve years, and she hated it. She always felt that she was in the grip of an octopus that was slowly devouring her, and would never let he go as long as there was a bone left to crack. She had two weeks' vacation once a year, and had to spend it on a lonely farm with the grouchy old uncle and aunt who had brought her up and who expected her to work hard at weeding and milking and pie-baking, all her little two weeks.

She always felt more tired when she went back to work than when she had left it. But she had never rebelled. There was nothing of the revolutionary in her. She was a little brown thing; her dark brown eyes were too soft and shadowy to be black, and apart from her eyes she was neither pretty nor ugly, just insignificant. She had had two chances of marriage; but though in the abstract she had thought she would marry *anybody* who would take her out of that horrible transfer and change department, when it came to the concrete she found she couldn't do it. Nobody would ever marry her now. She must go on at her counter and her little wicket forever and ever and ever, until she got too old to work.

Her uncle and aunt had died in the winter. Margaret was not very sorry and did not blame herself because she wasn't. They had always been tyrants—cruel, selfish tyrants. She was too gentle and sweet to hate anyone, or she would have hated them. They did not leave her anything—everything went to their own daughter. But Margaret had an odd, stifled feeling of freedom. She would have a *real* vacation—the first she had ever had.

It was to be a longer vacation than she had counted on, for she felt so miserable in the spring she was obliged to go to a doctor. He told her that she must take three months off or a worse thing would befall her. Margaret didn't see how she could. Then she suddenly made up her mind to do it, even if she lost her place. But the manager of the transfer department became human for five minutes, and told her he would keep her place for her, so she decided to make one wild, reckless plunge. She would take enough of her small savings and find a nice boarding house in some quiet place where there was no *noise,* and no abominable cabbage-y smells. O, to be where there was no noise!

For the transfer and change department, in the middle of the big hardware basement, was the noisiest place in the great hive. There were all kinds of noises—ceaseless, meaningless noises that hammered on her tired brain and numbed her soul. The other girls in the transfer got used to the noises—never noticed them, so they said. Margaret didn't believe them—it seemed so impossible to her. But now, for the whole golden, blissful summer she was going to forget them.

Jim did not come home to dinner. Somehow it seemed a rather flat meal. But he was there at supper time, radiating triumph.

"I told you it was my lucky day," he said. "I've found my house and bought it; paid cash down for it before Jack Petersen could change his mind. I wouldn't take any risks on that house. It's mine—mine this blessed minute. Why, it's such good luck as to be almost uncanny."

"Jack Peterson?" said Mrs. Kennedy. "You don't mean to say—"

"I do. I mean to say it all. I've bought Jack's house—or rather the house he owned by a legal quibble. It's always been really *my* house, you know: built for me, predestined for me. But I had no hope of ever getting my own. I thought he wanted it for himself and *his* bride. I couldn't believe any man who owned that house could dream of selling it. And to-day has literally flung it into my hands."

"That little Petersen house!" said Mrs. Kennedy, aghast. "Why it's old and shabby and so small, and out of the world!"

"You've said it! It's most gloriously out of the world. That's one reason I love it. And it is old and shabby; that's why I can afford it. I'm going to fix it up. I've got two months to work at it. I mean to do everything with my own hands."

"Do you think Isabel will like to live away up in that lonely place?" demanded Mrs. Kennedy.

Jim looked at Margaret and smiled. "Do *you* think she will?" he asked.

"She can't help it," said Margaret.

Mrs. Kennedy snorted.

"Well, I suppose it's no use saying anything—"

"Not a bit. The fatal deed is done. I, Jim Kennedy, am a landed proprietor, owning a house, a garden, and a spruce wood an acre in extent. I, who this morning hadn't a square inch of this big earth to call my own. Friend Cat, be excited for once, I implore you—that's a duck of a cat."

Friend Cat still refused to be excited. He purred placidly and winked one eye at Margaret.

"I want you to do me a favor, Miss Irwin," Jim went on, when Mrs. Kennedy had gone out. "I want you to come up to my house—*my* house, my *house*!—excuse me, I have to say it—I *have* to try how it sounds every way—and look it over; tell me what you think of it. I want to make it convenient for Isabel, for I'm not such a fool as to imagine that a woman can keep on loving a man who doesn't provide her with proper cupboards."

"I'll be delighted!" said Margaret sincerely. Jim looked grateful.

"You're too good to be true—almost," he said. "What nice things women are! Women and dear little houses with kind, quiet trees about them! Hurry up and finish eating. I want to take you right up to mine. There's a short cut to it up the hill. Never mind a hat—you don't want a hat on an evening like this. I like the thought of that smooth brown head of yours slipping through the gray-green trunks and the long green boughs. Your hair is just the brown that belongs to the woods."

As they went out, Margaret remembered that this was the first compliment she had ever received—if it were a compliment. Yes it was—Jim's eyes told her that. She tasted it all the way up the long hill. The little, winding path was so narrow they had to walk in single file. Margaret went first and Friend Cat followed, waving his tail, and Jim brought up the rear. It was a lovely path; ferns grew all along it and the dew-moist air was pungent with the aroma of young, sun-steeped firs. Before the last turn Jim overtook her with one long stride and put his hands over her eyes.

"Go on like this" he commanded, "and don't open your eyes till I say you can."

Margaret obeyed delightedly. A few more steps and Jim took his hands away.

"O!" gasped Margaret. "O!" Something seemed to sweep over her soul. Her eyes suddenly filled with tears. It *hurt* her to look at Jim's house, yet she liked the hurt.

It was a little gray house that looked as if it had never been built, but had just grown up in that wild, ferny, woodsy corner like a toadstool. It was low-eaved, with odd, little diamond-paned windows. Its gray roof was mottled with fat cushions of moss like green velvet mice. Two big pine trees joined their branches right over it. There was a porch over the front door, covered with honeysuckle. Behind it tall spires of fir stood out against gray-pink shades of evening. Robins were whistling wildly in the firs. The woods were all around the house except on the south sides, where the land fell away in a long hill, looking down on Glenby. Between the house and the view, but not hiding it, was a row of wonderful Lombardy poplars. And between their trunks, far away through the crystal-clear evening air, rose a great, round, full moon.

"Girl, you're crying!" said Jim.

"It's all so lovely—it hurts," said Margaret.

"I knew you'd like it, but I didn't expect you'd like it as much as that," said Jim. "You don't know half its charms yet, either. Wait until it gets dark and you see the lights of Glenby twinkling out down there and all over that hill. And this hill is full of squirrels—I love squirrels, don't you? Friend Cat likes them, too. He catches them—I've got to break him of it. There are any number of shy rabbits, too. And bats! It's a great place for bats. I like 'em—nice, queer, creepy, mysterious creatures, coming out of nowhere. There's one now—s-s-woop! And there's a little mossy hollow behind those young firs that's full of violets in spring—violets! 'Sweeter than the lids of Isabel's eyes, or Isabel's breath.'

"Isabel's a nicer name than Cytherea or Juno, isn't it? And I want you to notice especially that little gate over yonder. It isn't really needed; it opens only into the woods. But *isn't* it a gate? I love a gate like that; it's full of promise. There *may* be something wonderful beyond. A gate is always a mystery anyhow: it lures, it is a symbol. That's a nice bit of garden, too, don't you think? Of course I haven't much land, but the sky is all mine."

Margaret thought she could have stood there forever listening to Jim's lazy, laughing voice at her shoulder. But Friend Cat flew through the garden after a bat and Jim led her into the house. It was as dear and lovable inside as out. It was a house where there had been brides and mothers, and their happiness seemed to linger in it like a perfume. Margaret fancied she saw Isabel there—lovely, golden-haired Isabel—flitting through the little rooms, laughing under the firs, sitting hand in hand with Jim before the fireplace.

"Will you let me help you fix this house up for you, for Isabel?" she said softly.

"O, will you?" he cried. "How I wanted to ask you, and I was afraid you'd hate to be bothered. I need a woman's help in heaps of ways. My brother's wife is a jewel, but certain things are holden from her eyes. *You'll* know just what Isabel would like—I was sure of that the moment I saw you. And you'll help me! O, you nice little thing! You *nice* little thing!"

He was squeezing her hands so hard that he hurt her, but she did not flinch. She had never been so happy in her life. What a joy it would be to help fix up this darling place for beautiful Isabel. Margaret felt she loved Isabel herself, for her beauty, her charm, her loyalty, her laughter. She would do her very best to make this house, where Isabel would be queen, perfect in its way.

"I won't paint it," said Jim. "I want it left its own woodsy gray. But inside it must be painted and things bought to put in it. That's where I need your help. I don't know a darn thing about furnishing a house and I've precious little money left. I wasn't going to have a cent of debt on this place. But I must get things for her somehow."

"We'll get them," said Margaret. "I'll help you paint. I can paint beautifully."

"And you're *sure* it won't be a nuisance?" said Jim anxiously. "You ought to be resting, I suppose—you're not strong."

"It will be the greatest treat of my life," cried Margaret. "And it will be the right kind of a rest. O, we've been here half an hour and I feel as if I'd known this house all my life. When you and Isabel are living here I'm coming to visit you whether you ask me or not—but I won't stay long. I'll just come and look at the house—and see if you're using it right and if you *deserve* it—and then go away again."

"I know you're too nice to be real," said Jim. "I'm sure I've dreamed you. But I hope you'll get my house furnished before I wake up. And when Isabel comes you'll love her, too.

She's—she's—she's *Isabel. Do* let me talk about her to you. You needn't answer, you needn't even let on you hear me, just let me talk."

"Talk, dear lover," laughed Margaret. She wondered a little at herself. It seemed so easy to chatter with Jim, somehow—as easy as talking to herself.

She lay awake quite late that night planning for Jim's house. As long as she could remember, life had been dull and colourless. Now she had come to a little patch of violets, purple and fragrant, hers for the plucking. She would advise Jim to paint the living-room in tones of deep cream and brown; she would see that he picked the right kind of paper. She would get him to put up shelves in the chimney recess, and a rose trellis over the wildwood gate, and replace the worn-out wooden steps of the porch with red sandstone. And make a new button for the pantry door…and she was asleep, the first sound sleep she had had for weeks.

The next two months seemed like one dream of rapture to Margaret. She was so absorbed and happy that she never thought about herself, and she worked so hard in the daytime that she slept like a log at night.

They painted and papered the house, and Margaret got her own way in everything. Then they borrowed Mrs. Kennedy's fat old brown mare and jogged far and wide looking for furniture—quaint, old-fashioned bits that belonged in the little house. Margaret knew one whenever she saw it, and she was such a good bargainer that she always got it for a song.

When they got it up to Jim's house they tried it in a dozen different places and were not satisfied until they found the right one; and sometimes they could not agree about it, and then they would sit on the floor and argue it out. And if they couldn't settle it, they got Friend Cat to pull a straw with his teeth and decide it that way.

Margaret found a delightful old dinner set of real willowware at a farm auction, and snapped it up in a frenzy. Not a piece was missing and it had shallow thin cups and deep saucers, and scalloped plates and fat, knobby tureens. She knew Isabel would be crazy over it—Jim had told her Isabel loved pretty dishes. She regarded that set as her greatest treasure, though the old chest of drawers with the white china knobs was a close second. She polished the chest until her elbows ached.

Not all the things that went into the little house were bought. Jim had several bits that had belonged to his mother: an old rosewood piano; two tall, lovely brass candlesticks; lots of round, braided rugs; a grandfather clock; a big, brass coal scuttle; a gilt-framed mirror with fat cupids gambolling in a panel over the glass; a battered little silver teapot of incredible age; and a quaint Japanese rose-bowl.

Margaret made potpourri for the bride in this, from the roses that grew in the garden, and she was quite reckless with her scents and spices. She paid for them herself, not telling Jim, for she wanted to give the house something of her own. Finally she made jam—heaps of it: raspberry and cherry and blueberry and plum (the strawberries were over before she thought of it)—and sealed it up in lovely little blue-and-white jars, dozens of them, which Mrs. Kennedy had stored away in her attic, relics of a departed brother's drugstore.

They had queer names printed them, over which Margaret and Jim had lots of fun. But Margaret made dainty little labels, carefully written and ornamented with curlicues, and pasted them on. She filled the pantry shelves and the swinging shelf in the cellar with them, and she loved them best of all the things in the house.

They had glorious minutes of fun whenever they stopped to rest. There was a little bluebird's nest in the rosebush under the living-room window, which they watched and protected from

Friend Cat. They made friends with an old rabbit that often came hopping out of the woods into the garden. They had a game as to who could count the most rabbits and squirrels in the daytime and the most bats in the evening.

For they did not always go home as soon as it got too dark to work. Sometimes they sat out on the porch steps and watched the twilight creep up from the valley, and the lights twinkle out on the opposite hill, and the shadows waver and advance under the fir trees, and the white, early stars shine over the big guardian pines. Friend Cat sat and purred beside them, or swooped madly about in pursuit of bats. Jim recited some of his poetry to Margaret in these hours. She thought it wonderful—perhaps she was not very critical. But Jim's voice and the charm of the half-light would have made a masterpiece of anything.

And then, at last, everything was done. They looked at each other one September evening and realized that Jim's house was ready for Jim's bride.

"There's absolutely nothing more we can do," said Margaret. "We can't even *pretend* there's anything more."

"I suppose not," agreed Jim. His voice sounded a little flat. He looked about the living-room wistful, he looked at Margaret, sitting like a little brown elf on the oak settle in the chimney corner; he looked at the fireplace where kindling and pine wood were laid ready for a fire. His eyes lighted again.

"Yes, there is," he cried. "How could we have forgotten it? We've got to see if the chimney will draw properly. I'm going to light that fire."

Margaret had laid the fire, meaning that Isabel should light it with her own hand the first evening she came as Jim's wife to Jim's house. But she made no effort to dissuade Jim. She only nestled down a little closer in her corner. She had come suddenly to the end of everything. *Everything.* Life seemed simply *cut off.* It sickened her to think of the transfer department. She would not think of it. For a little while she would just think of her home—yes, *her* house—and of Jim. Not even of Isabel.

When the fire blazed up, Jim came over and sat down on the settle beside her. Friend Cat hopped up and sat between them. Up blazed the merry flames; they shimmered over the old piano, they glistened on the brass candlesticks, they danced over the glass doors of the cupboard where the willowware dishes were, they darted through the kitchen door, and the row of brown and blue bowls Margaret had arranged on the dresser winked back at them. The room was full of the scent of the rose-jar on the sideboard—a haunting scent like all the lost perfumes of old, unutterably sweet years.

"This is home," said Jim softly. "It's lovelier than I ever dreamed it being. And it's your creation, Margaret."

Margaret did not answer. She was looking at Jim, as he gazed into the fire—his black hair, his smiling eyes, his whimsical face. She was recalling all his friendly looks and jests and quips and subtle compliments. It was all she could ever have of him. For just this half hour she would give herself up to enchantment. The future was Isabel's, but this half hour was *hers*. She shut her eyes and prayed: "Help me to remember *every moment* of this—never to forget one single breath of it."

When she opened her eyes Jim was looking at her.

"We've been good friends," he said.

Margaret nodded.

"We'll just sit here and think about it all," he said. "We won't talk. But we'll think it all over—everything—until the fire burns out."

The fire crackled and snapped; the great clock ticked; Friend Cat purred; a little slender young moon shone down through the pine boughs straight on them through the window. It was worthwhile to have lived long dreary years for this and to live them again looking back on it, thought Margaret.

When the fire died down into white ashes, Jim got up.

"Let's go," he said. "Little friend and chum and comrade, there's nothing to do but go."

Margaret wondered if he guessed—if he was sorry for her. She did not care. She didn't mind his knowing, somehow. He would never laugh at her. He belonged to Isabel. Isabel would have the little house and the jam-pots, and the rabbits and the blue dishes. But Isabel could never have this perfect, enchanted half hour.

She was in her room at sunset, crumpled up in a chair, listening. Jim had gone to bring Isabel over. Isabel had arrived in Glenby the night before and was with her cousin, Mrs. Alden, up the road. Jim had met her at the station and spent the evening with her. At breakfast that morning he had been even more whimsical than usual and Mrs. Kennedy had thought him in remarkably good spirits. Then he had gone to school—it opened that day—promising to bring Isabel over that night.

And now they were coming. Margaret, peeping from the window, saw them in the distance and shrank back in her chair. A few minutes later a peal of laughter floated up to her from the front porch—a frank, hearty, generous peal of laughter, evidently welling up from a friendly, uncritical heart. Margaret stared straight before her. That could not be Isabel's laughter! Impossible! Isabel's laughter was like—what had Jim said it was like? O, yes, the tinkle of a woodland brook. This sounded more like rich cream gurgling out of a big jug. Margaret gave a queer, choked, half-hysterical little giggle.

Mrs. Kennedy called her. She went down slowly, wishing herself anywhere else in the world—even in the transfer department, or in her cheap boarding house with its stale cooking smells. She paused for a moment in the doorway of the sitting room. She saw

Jim back in the twilight corner, smiling his twisted, enigmatical smile. Then—

A billowy whirl of white and blue surged across the room to her, a pair of plump white arms were around her, a gay voice was exclaiming: "This is Marg'ret—I know this is Marg'ret!"

And she was heartily kissed—no, *smacked*!

Margaret was ashamed all the rest of her life of what she did then. She said stiffly,

"My name is Margaret."

She gasped with repentance the next moment. How insufferably rude and silly she was! But Isabel only threw back her big golden head and laughed again – that great, full, jolly laugh of hers. Then she seized Margaret once more and gave her a hearty hug.

"So it is! Do forgive me," she said frankly. "*I* know how horrid it is to have your name mangled. I could murder and devour without sauce any boob who calls me 'Is'bel.' I guess it *was* cheeky of me to call you by your name like that, but I just couldn't help it. I seem to know you by heart; Jim's written so much of you and how good you've been helping him fix up our house and all. I don't know how we're ever going to thank you, you darling thing. But I do know I'm just going to love you forever and ever, amen. I'm like that. I just fancy a person at first sight or I never do. And I—love—you."

Isabel emphasized each word of her last sentence with a squeeze that nearly expelled every particle of breath from Margaret's slender body. Then she went back and sat down on the settee by Jim, sending Friend Cat spinning to the floor with a cheerful slap and a "here now, puss, this is *my* place." Margaret dropped into a chair and stared like one fascinated at Isabel who began talking gaily to Mrs. Kennedy. Outraged, Friend Cat got up on Jim's knee and Jim stroked him absently.

And this was Isabel! What had Mrs. Kennedy said of her? "A slight reed of a thing?" Isabel was a big, buxom, deep-bosomed creature, altogether splendid in her way. Naturally, one would expect some difference between a girl of seventeen and a woman of twenty-two. And Mrs. Kennedy had been right—perfectly right—in calling her beautiful. She was so beautiful that her beauty struck you in the face. Margaret had heard of "stunning" girls. Well, Isabel was stunning.

Her head was crowned with masses of wavy golden hair held in place by many jeweled pins. Her cheeks were pink, her eyes big and brilliantly blue; she had a crimson mouth, through which bursts of laughter came at the end of every sentence; and superb white teeth, most of which she showed when she laughed.

She had a marble-white neck, a splendid figure, large, capable, dimpled hands, well-ringed, and a very high instep, silken-sheathed. She radiated health and good humour. Never had Margaret felt so brown and skinny and insignificant. And never—never!—had she been so helplessly furious over anything as over the idea of this magnificent girl queening it in Jim's little gray house. It was outrageous—her house had been furnished for the Isabel of her dreams. And *that* Isabel had no existence.

"O, yes, I had a perfectly delightful trip home," Isabel was telling Mrs. Kennedy. "Everybody was so kind. I made friends all along the way. And when I got to Redway—you know how horrid and confusing it is there with that big station and those new lines built since I went away—I *was* all muddled up and I met the nicest young fellow. He looked after everything for me—said his name was Ned Rogers and he lived in Glenby."

"O, he's our new veterinary surgeon," said Mrs. Kennedy. "Yes, he *is* a nice young fellow. Everybody likes him—except Jim here."

"O, *Jim!*" Isabel turned and chucked him under the chin. "Now, what fault have *you* to find with him, Jim?"

"None—none whatever," said Jim solemnly. "It can't be his fault exactly that he's a horse doctor; these things are predestined. He's good-looking, well-off, a church member, and has—they tell me—a great knack with colic."

Isabel threw back her head and let out a laugh that flooded the sitting-room, large as it was.

"Isn't that like him?" she appealed to Margaret. "He's jealous, that's it. You needn't be, honey." She chucked Jim under the chin again. Margaret quivered. It was sacrilege. Jim should be kissed, should have his cheek patted, and his thick black hair stroked softly. He should never, never be chucked under the chin! Then Margaret wanted to laugh hysterically. She had to clutch hold of her chair.

"I s'pose Jim's told you of the house he's got for you? " Mrs. Kennedy said, smiling.

Isabel laughed as if it were a huge joke.

"Yes, I thought he was hoaxing me at first. Then when I found he wasn't, I said he must be dippy—didn't I, honey?"

"I *told* him you wouldn't like it," said Mrs. Kennedy.

"Like it? Me? Buried alive up there in the woods! Not for mine! But we'll have to put up with it for a while, I guess, till we can find a better place. I wondered why he was so mysterious in his letters about the house—never *would* tell me where or what it was—just kept saying he had a surprise for me. Well, it was a surprise all right."

Isabel's laugh made the pendants on the hanging lamp tingle. Jim did not laugh. He continued to stroke Friend Cat slowly and rhythmically.

"Well, I'll make the best of it till we can mend it," said Isabel. "I haven't been up to see it yet—I want to put off the evil day as long as possible. I know I'll have a conniption when I do see it. Let's talk of something cheerful."

They talked—at least Isabel and Mrs. Kennedy did—of births and deaths and marriages and engagements, and motor cars and movies. And when Isabel went away she put on her big hat and came across to Margaret again.

"You sweet little thing. I want another kiss. I don't know when I've seen anybody I liked so much. And you're going to love me, too, honey, aren't you? We're going to be special friends, aren't we!"

"I—I hope so," stammered Margaret. Behind Isabel she saw Jim smiling in a curious way, and Friend Cat winking impudently at her.

"Of course we are," Isabel kissed her again, waved her hand to Mrs. Kennedy, linked her arm in Jim's and swept out, goddess-like in her liveliness.

"Isabel hasn't changed a mite," said Mrs. Kennedy complacently. "Except to fill out. She's going to be big like her mother, I guess. Mrs. Bartlett weighed two hundred and fifty. But she's just the same dear, bright, friendly girl. Isn't she breezy? And hiding her disappointment over the house so well—that's Isabel, always making the best of things—never a word of reproach to Jim for doing such a fool thing."

Margaret fled to her room. "Breezy? Why—why," gasped Margaret, "she's a *tornado*!"

Margaret held onto herself—she would not let herself go—she would relapse into helpless, hysterical laughter if she did.

"I hate her, I hate her," she gasped. "And I *could* like her awfully—yes, the creature's abominably likable—if only she weren't going to live in *my* house! That's desecration. O, *what* does Jim think of her? I suppose he's perfectly satisfied—she's so beautiful—she's as she always was, Mrs. Kennedy says. It's just that I've been a fool with my imagination of something entirely different. O, to think of her washing my lovely dishes with those horrible fat, pudgy hands of hers."

Margaret looked at her own thin, brown hands. Was she jealous of Isabel's smooth, dimpled fingers! No, she was not. She had expected to be jealous of Isabel and she was not—not the tiniest bit. She only hated to think of her in Jim's house, laughing at it. She could wring Isabel's satin neck for laughing at it.

"Anyhow, Friend Cat doesn't like her. He knows—and I know—that she is the kind of woman who likes cats 'in their place,'" said Margaret vindictively, and took immense satisfaction out of knowing it.

The wedding was fixed for October. Isabel was busy getting her trousseau. She pleaded with Margaret to stay and be her bridesmaid, but Margaret said her leave would be up the week before and she must go. Jim came and went and smiled and quipped, and took very little notice of Margaret. Margaret told herself this was only what was to be expected and it really did not worry her much.

The only thing that worried her was her dear, unappreciated house. She never went near it—she couldn't bear to. Isabel went to see it and came down and said it was quite sweet and quaint and would do nicely until they could get something better.

"I don't mind the furniture being so old-fashioned; I know Jim hasn't much money. But that queer old piano! I'm going to have a Victrola—I'll have enough money for that after I get my things, and I must have *something* to cheer me up in that little hole, 'steen miles from anywhere. I *could* stand the furniture, but I can't stand the location. Jim is peeved that I don't like it, so I don't say much to him. And he could have had that lovely Ormsby house and wouldn't take it! Can you beat it, honey!"

"I think Jim's house is lovely," said Margaret.

Isabel patted her hand.

"*You* did your best, anyhow, pet. Don't think I'm not grateful. Men don't understand things, do they? We've got to humor them sometimes."

For a wonder she did not laugh after she had said this. She looked thoughtfully across the autumn fields.

"You know, honey," she said slowly, "there are times when I think—"

But just then, Jim came up the porch steps and Margaret never knew what Isabel thought.

Margaret was packing her trunk. She was going away the next day. She went slowly down the stairs. The front door was open and the sunset came flooding in. Isabel was standing in the hall, superbly beautiful in a warm, golden-brown suit. It was her going-away suit, and Margaret wondered what on earth she had put it on to-day for. She ought not to wear it until her wedding day.

Isabel put her arms around Margaret, drew her into the parlor and shut the door.

Evidently she was very much excited and—if such a thing could be imagined of Isabel—a little nervous.

"Marg'ret, honey, I want you to do something for me."

"What is it?"

"Will you—will you go and tell Jim something?"

"Tell him what?" cried Margaret.

"Tell him—that I—was married to Ned Rogers in Redway— this afternoon."

Margaret stared at Isabel without saying anything. Isabel, the confession over, was herself again. She laughed and caught Margaret's hand.

"You *do* look flabbergasted, honey! Now, don't scold. It isn't a bit of use. Just sit down by me on the sofa and let me explain. I haven't much time. Ned's waiting for me down the road in his lovely new car—we're going to take the Montreal train to-night. O, I know you're shocked to death, honey. But it had to be. Ned and I fell in love with each other the day I came home. But I'd promised Jim, and I meant to be true to him. You know, I was just wild about Jim five years ago. Even yet I like him—better than Ned in some ways—and if it wasn't for that crazy house of his… but I *couldn't* swallow *it*. And Jim's so stubborn he was *bound* to live there.

"Ned's bought the Ormsby house and is going to furnish it handsomely. Really, honey, everything's better as it is. Ned and I are much better suited to each other than Jim and I."

"Yes, I think you are," said Margaret coolly. She was one whom great shocks render cool.

"But why didn't you tell Jim *before* you did this?"

"O, honey, I know I *should* have. But I was afraid, honestly. Jim has such a wheedling tongue. If I wasn't really married to Ned he'd talk me out of it. I had to do it this way. Now you just go and tell him, angel, and break it to him gently. He'll take it better from you than from any one else—he thinks so much of you—and so do I. You *mustn't* blame me for this. I know you won't. You're such a sweet little thing. And I know Jim will feel awful. But he'll get over it—they always do. There was a fellow in Colorado—gracious, I *must* go—we haven't too much time. *Goodest*-bye, honey, and tell him I'm awfully sorry, but that house got on my nerves."

She was gone. Margaret went at once to Mrs. Kennedy. The hideous thing she had to do must be done while her curious numbness of thought and feeling lasted. When sensibility returned she could never do it. She had to break Jim's heart, and it must be broken quickly.

"Where's Jim?" she asked.

"O, up in that blessed house of his, I reckon," replied Mrs. Kennedy. "Anyhow, I saw him and Friend Cat going up the path not long ago."

Margaret stepped out of the back door and went up the path— that little, sequestered path up the hill—where Jim and she had always to walk in single file. It was a perfect evening, full of nice whispery sounds. Summer had stolen back for one more day of dream and glamour. When she reached the little house the Lombardy poplars were in dark purple silhouette against a crocus sky, and there was one milk-white star over the big pines, like a pearl on a silver-green lake.

The robins were whistling sleepily in the firs and the moist air was fragrant with the tang of balsam. O, how lovely and dear it all was. But the little house looked very pathetic to her: a casket rifled of its jewels, a lamp with the flame gone out.

"Anyhow, she won't eat my jam," she whispered suddenly, and then hated herself heartily for the contemptible thought.

She had never been up to the house since the evening Jim and she had sat together by the fire. She found Jim there now—only there was no fire—nothing but the ashes of the one they had left. It seemed that another one had never been laid.

Margaret stood before him, straight and tense and white-lipped. It was horrible to think that Jim would always connect her with this dreadful news.

"Jim, I have something to tell you."

"Yes?" Jim went on stroking Friend Cat.

"She said to break it gently but I can't—I don't know how. You've *got* to know it: Isabel married Ned Rogers in Redway to-day. They've gone on the Montreal train. That's all."

Margaret turned to go and tripped over Friend Cat, who had suddenly bounded—or been tumbled—to the floor. Jim caught her just in time.

"You'd have given yourself a nice bump if you'd struck that fender! Why don't you look where you're going, elf?"

"I'm sorry," said Margaret dazedly, trying to wriggle herself out of Jim's arms, and not succeeding.

"*I'm* not. It gave me an excuse for grabbing you just this much sooner. Don't squirm like that—you're worse than Friend Cat when he wants to break loose. So Isabel and Ned have eloped. God bless them! Now you and I can get married right off."

"Married!"

Margaret stopped squirming and stood quite still.

"Of course. You can't live here in this house with me unless we do. There'd be talk. And you've *got* to live here; it's *your* house! It's *always* been your house!"

"But—don't you care—Isabel—"

"Isabel's a darling," said Jim. "She's saved everybody heaps of trouble. I love her bushels. But you…you're *mine*! I knew that, way back in summer. That's why I lit that fire here that night. I didn't care a hoot whether the chimney drew or not. I just wanted to sit here with you and pretend we were a honeymoon couple.

"I thought it would be all I ever could have. I meant to do my duty and marry Isabel, of course. I was such a vain, besotted fool I really believed she wanted me. Point of honour, and all that. That angel of a girl has solved everybody's problems. I'm going to give her a corking kiss for it when she comes back. And so will you— *won't* you now, Mrs. Jim Kennedy?"

"O, I will—I will," said Margaret, not knowing in the least what it was Jim had asked her to do.

"But give *me* one first—now," said Jim.

◈   ◈

Editors' note: "Jim's House" was published by *People's Home Journal* in July 1926 with illustrations by Charles Andrew Bryson. It was listed in the "Unverified Ledger Titles" section of the 1986 bibliography and was found by Sarah Riedel and Donna Campbell. This story is available to view online in the Ryrie-Campbell Collection.

In February 1926, L. M. Montgomery and her family moved from Leaskdale, Ontario, to Norval where her husband, Ewan Macdonald, became minister in the Presbyterian churches at Norval and nearby Union. Her novel, *The Blue Castle*, was published in 1926, and she continued working on the third volume of her "Emily" trilogy, *Emily's Quest*, which would be published in 1927. Four stories that were the beginning of her work on *Magic for Marigold* (1929) were published in the May, June, July, and August 1926 issues of *The Delineator*.

THE MIRROR
(1931)

S he was alone at last. She had asked them all to go out and leave her alone for the last hour before the ceremony that was to make her the happy bride of Lester Barr. They went out with jest and smiles—all but Old Ellen. If Old Ellen had ever smiled or jested it had been so long ago that nobody remembered it. Old Ellen went out bent and smileless. But before she went out she did something quickly and furtively, in a dark, shadowy corner of the room. She turned at the door and looked for a long moment at Hilary standing wraith-like in her shimmer of satin and tulle. It was no look to fall on a bride. Hilary shivered slightly amid all her glow. But then, Old Ellen had really never liked her. Hilary had always known that, but she forgave Old Ellen for it because she had loved Star so much.

"Ellen, Mr. Barr will be here in half an hour. Let me know when he comes."

"Ay," said Old Ellen ungraciously. As she closed the door she muttered contemptuously: "Him and his carneying voice! Ay, he'll soon be here for his bonny bride. But will she look in it first – will she look in it?"

Hilary heard the mutter, though not the words. She smiled again. Old Ellen hated Lester, of course, because she liked Alec Stanley. Hilary knew Old Ellen would not have been so dour and grim on this bridal day if Alec were the bridegroom.

She was glad Old Ellen had gone out—glad they had all gone out—though they were all dear girls. She wanted to be alone with her wonderful happiness for an hour before she gave herself to him forever.

She looked at her reflection in the mirror. She was too pale for a bride and she had never been beautiful. She had a sweet, dark face, with eyes that no one ever quite knew for blue or gray or green, richly quilled about with black lashes. Her eyebrows might have been drawn in soot, so finely dark they were against her white face. But apart from her eyes she was insignificant, which made all the more marvelous the miracle of Lester Barr's love. Out of a whole world of beautiful women, his for the asking, he had chosen *her*.

"This mirror always makes me look a wee bit green," she thought with girlish petulance.

There was another mirror in the room—a mirror that would not have turned her green—but Hilary had no intention of looking into it. It hung on the wall in the corner by the window. A long oval mirror with a beautiful back of beaten copper. Hilary had turned its face to the wall when she had come to be mistress of Glenwood. She liked the beautiful mellow copper oval, which Old Ellen kept meticulously polished; but there was another reason for her action.

She did not think the mirror was her friend.

She went over to the high, arched, Georgian window looking out on the lawn. What a wretched day it was for a wedding. The sky at sunrise had been blood red, which soon darkened into sullen gray. The waves were moaning drearily on the sandshore. A snarling, quarrelsome wind, which blew an occasional bitter splash of rain against the window, was tormenting the boughs of the big aspen poplar Star had loved. Why could she not help thinking about Star—Star who should have been here to drape her veil and arrange her roses; Star, who had died, nobody knew why, one dark, haunted November afternoon just like this three years ago. She wanted to think of Lester and their exquisite love and the wonderful life before them—and she could think of nothing but Star. She had thought of Star when she wakened that morning to see that wild red sunrise through the trees; she had thought of her all the forenoon of hurry and preparation; and now it almost seemed that Star was with her in the room.

Star, who kept everyone laughing; Star, with her body like a young sapling not to be broken, however it might bend; Star, with her eyes like brown marigolds flecked with glints of gold; Star, with her soul of fire and snow. Glenwood was full of Star; everything about it held some memory of her. Star, running out at bedtime to kiss the flowers good-night; Star, chasing the reflection of the moon along the wet sandshore; Star holding buttercups under her saucy chin; Star with the new red boots she hated, deliberately putting her feet in a pail of buttermilk to ruin them; Star, with a wreath of ox-eye daisies on her bronze hair; Star, singing in the old Glenwood garden lying fragrant and velvety under the enchantment of a waning moon; Star, dancing—why, her very slippers would have danced by themselves the whole night through; lovely Star who loved everything beautiful; and now she was lying in the cold, damp grave in the churchyard and the long grasses and withered leaves must be blowing drearily around it.

Hilary shivered again. What thoughts for a wedding day! But when Lester came he would banish them.

Glenwood, with its colourful, pine-scented garden, full of wind-music and bee-song, that dropped in terraces to the harbour shore where there was always the luring sound of "perilous seas forlorn," had always been a vital part of her life. She and Star, orphans who lived for the most part with Uncle Paul and Aunt Emily Tempest, spent every summer of their childhood there. Cousins came from everywhere to that old house—cousins who all worshipped Star and thought little about shy, plain Hilary. All but Alec Stanley who lived next door. He had never been fascinated by Star. There had never been anyone but Hilary for him, from the day when he had rescued her from Old Ellen's ferocious gander. With what a lordly air he had caught the furious hissing creature by its snaky neck and hurled it over the fence. With what boyish tenderness he had turned to poor little seven-year-old Hilary, standing tranced in her childish terror. She had always felt so *safe* with Alec after that—dear Alec, whom she still liked so much—still loved, if only he were content with that kind of love. But Alec had known, too, from the day of the gander that Hilary had something in her hand for him if he could ever prevail on her to open her hand and give it. And nothing else would do him.

How furious Alec had been with old Great-Uncle Neil who, when he saw Hilary for the first time, had shaken her earnestly by the hand and said,

"Eh, nae beauty—nae beauty." Alec never forgave people who preferred Star to Hilary. But Hilary found it easy to forgive them. She loved Star so much herself. Who could help loving Star? Her very look said "Come and love me." Whenever she came into a room everyone in it felt happier. Aunt Mildred loved her and it was common surmise in the clan that she meant to leave Star her money and Glenwood. It was a proof of how greatly Star was loved that no one was jealous because of this.

Even Old Ellen loved Star. Old Ellen had always lived at Glenwood; she was some kind of a cousin of Aunt Mildred's long-dead husband. Even then she seemed to the children incredibly old. Both Star and Hilary were terribly frightened of her. She always sat in a corner knitting and watching. They thought she must have sat there knitting for a hundred years. She never smiled but sometimes she looked at certain people and laughed maliciously and slyly. Her face was all dead except her eyes which were most horribly alive under the white frost of her hair. Star began by calling her Ancient of Days but soon dropped it. Even Star could not make a joke of Old Ellen.

"She's a witch," she told Hilary, "and rides on a broomstick over the harbour at nights."

"Do you really think so?" whispered Hilary.

"Of course. She always knows what we're thinking of. That shows she is a witch."

The mirror hung on the wall of Aunt Mildred's bedroom— a great long, softly gleaming thing in its ruddy frame. Aunt Mildred's great-grandfather had brought it home from some- where abroad and all the children who came to Glenwood were always eager to get into Aunt Mildred's room and have a peep into the mirror. All but Hilary. Hilary was afraid of the mirror. Sometimes it seemed to her like a friend, sometimes an enemy. She never could decide which. Yet her very fear attracted her to it—she wanted to see if there were really anything to be afraid of. Who knew what face might look out of it—all the shadowy ladies who had once looked into it? Once, when Aunt Mildred had shut her in the room alone for some childish peccadillo, she had fan- cied for a moment she *had* seen a face looking at her out of it – a malicious, sneering face. She rather liked to talk to herself in it, but Old Ellen caught her at it once and frightened her from ever doing it again.

"Why mayn't I talk to it," she had asked rebelliously.

"Because that looking-glass isn't like other looking-glasses," said Old Ellen mysteriously. "There's a curse on it. Your great- great-grandfather was a bad man. And a woman he scarred with a blow looked in the glass and when she saw her face she cursed it. Ay, her curse is on it. And there's stories told of it."

Hilary knew that. She had heard most of the stories at differ- ent times, though never in any detail. There was Aunt Mildred's little sister, Claudia, who had seen—something—in the mirror and had never been "quite right" again. And there was Great-Aunt Kathleen who had gone to meet her lover and go away with him. The lover, coming to her, had been killed in a train wreck and beautiful, selfish Kathleen had hurried back home, thinking no one would know. But the doors were closed against her; her husband had looked in the mirror.

Margaret Tempest had seen her husband dying on a South African veldt in the Boer War on the night he died. And nobody ever knew what Lucia Tempest had seen for Lucia Tempest had dropped the lamp she was holding and her dress caught fire and she was dead in two hours.

Yet the mirror was not always malevolent. Rachel Tempest had known her lover was alive, shipwrecked on the Magdalens, when everyone else was sure for a whole winter that he was drowned. And Jennie Tempest had seen a ghostly minuet danced in it once, and had been none the worse of seeing it.

Not everyone could see things in it. Aunt Mildred had never seen anything, though it had hung in her room for forty years. She laughed at the silly stories that were told of it, and warned the children to put no faith in them. Star did not worry her sunny head about the mirror and its spooks. But Hilary continued to be afraid of it. When she let herself feel it, she always felt that the mirror was going to hurt her dreadfully some day.

So they had grown up. Everybody in the clan took it for granted Alec and Hilary would be married, though no actual engagement existed between them. Star had no acknowledged lover, though she had more beaus than would have been good for the average girl. It did not spoil Star. She was as dear and charming and lovable a girl as she had been a child. There was not a grain of bitterness or envy in her nature.

When Aunt Mildred died suddenly and an amazed clan found that she had left everything to Hilary instead of Star, it had been

L. M. MONTGOMERY

Star who was the first to fling her arms about Hilary and congratulate her whole-heartedly.

"It should have been you, Star, darling, it should have been you," protested Hilary, furious with Aunt Mildred.

Star stopped the protesting lips with a kiss.

"I shouldn't. You are the right one for Glenwood. Besides—" Star was roguish "—it joins the Stanley estate. And again besides—" Star was flushed and dreamy "—*I* couldn't live there anyhow for long. I've been wanting to tell you, Hilary: up at Aunt Jean's this summer, I met—"

Hilary never knew who Star had met, never knew who had called that dream into her eyes and that flush into her face. There was an interruption, Star went home in Aunt Jean's car, and when Hilary got home herself, she found Aunt Jean had carried Star off for another visit.

Hilary wondered who Star's lover was. It must be a lover—that look, that blush. Well, she would know when Star came back.

But Star never came back. Two days later she had gone out from Aunt Jean's house—gay, laughing, happy—and next day they had found her dear, drenched little body in the pond below the rock garden.

After a while Hilary came to Glenwood to live. She had never thought she could bear it. But Aunt Emily had died and Uncle Paul wanted to go to live with his daughter. So there was nothing for her but Glenwood—Glenwood without Star, who was in her grave, with a white marble shaft above her.

Stella Tempest. Died November 10th 1925, aged eighteen.

Died, yes. But why? Hilary never ceased to ask that question. Why had Star, who had so much to live for, drowned herself?

At first she could not bear Glenwood. She felt that it was a terrible house full of old tragedies. And it was so strangely empty since Star's laughter had gone out of it—that sweet laughter that had echoed so often through the twilights of the old place. O, surely Star could not be dead. Not Star. Would she not come stealing up by the birches or along the silvery solitude of the sandshore, wearing her youth like a golden rose? She could not have borne it had it not been for Alec. And after a while the pain grew a little less terrible and she loved Glenwood again with its mad galloping March winds, its winter birches with stars in their hair, its snow of cherry petals in spring and the low continuous thunder of the sea on the harbour bar. Life began to beckon once more; and there was always Alec.

Old Ellen was still at Glenwood. She looked no older—perhaps because it would have been impossible—and she still sat and knitted. When Hilary came she looked at her and said: "It should ha' been Star."

"Yes," said Hilary gently, "but it's not my fault that it isn't, Ellen."

"I'm not saying it is," muttered Ellen. "But ain't ye goin' to find out who sent her to her death, Hilary Tempest, afore ye settle down to your own ease and happiness?"

"How could I find that out? I've tried, I've tried," said Hilary wildly. "Nobody knows anything—not even who it was she went to meet. There's no way of find out."

"Eh, but there *is* a way," said Old Ellen, and would say no more.

Hilary chose Aunt Mildred's room for her own. It was the nicest room in Glenwood with the finest view. She had it redecorated and refurnished; yet still there seemed something strange and alien in the room, something a little hostile. But is there not something strange about any room that has been long occupied? Death had lurked in it. Love had been rose-red in it. Births had been there—all the passions, all the hopes. It was full of wraiths. No wonder people saw things in the mirror.

The mirror still hung in its old place. She had given up believing those funny old stories about it, but she was still afraid of it.

She would have taken it down if Old Ellen had not held up her aged darkened hands in horror over the idea. To pacify Ellen, Hilary left it there, but she turned its face to the wall. Ellen muttered a good deal even over that.

Then she had met Lester Barr. He had kissed her at their second meeting—carelessly, on her cheek. Hilary had never been kissed before. Alec had never dared, and no other man had wanted to. The world still thought Hilary a cold shy girl, but that night she lay in her bed with thoughts that made her cheeks burn hotly in the darkness. The glow at her heart was with her when she woke, and went with her through the day.

He came again to her that evening. His beguiling eyes looked deep into hers, with a look that was a kiss. It sent a strange shiver of delight and terror all over her. She thought of Alec. She tried to be faithful to him and to their implied understanding. But she knew she was fighting a losing battle. Sooner or later Lester would win, if he seriously wished to win. And he left her in no doubt that he did wish to win. There came a night when she sat in the moonlight and looked at the two roads she might walk on through life. One with Lester, one with Alec. She thought of Alec curiously and pityingly—and a little disdainfully. He had given her up very easily; he had not put up any fight to keep her. Well, she knew Alec was like that. He would not want her if she did not want him. She was sorry for him, for somehow she knew, in spite of his passivity, that he was suffering. But he would get over it. She dismissed him very lightly from her thoughts and knew the path she had chosen. Her engagement to Lester Barr was announced. They were to be married in November and spend their honeymoon in Bermuda.

Hilary seemed to move and breathe in a trance of happiness. She could not get used to the miracle of finding herself engaged to Lester Barr. She could not get used to the wonder of her own passionate love for him. And once she had imagined she had loved Alec. Hilary smiled. She knew the difference now. There was only one drop of bitterness in her intoxicating cup: if only Star were here to share and understand and sympathize! She knew her clan rather disapproved this over-speedy wooing. After all, nobody knew much about Lester Barr. He was handsome and well-educated and nobody could deny that he was the newspaper correspondent he called himself. He was one of the Montreal Barrs—a good family, no doubt. After all, Hilary was old enough to please herself. It was a pity about Alec Stanley, but really he was a little slow. He shouldn't have let Hilary keep him dangling so long. Everybody admitted Lester was charming. Everybody except Old Ellen, who hated him. But then Old Ellen would have hated anyone who was not Alec Stanley.

"But I love Lester and I don't love Alec, Ellen," Hilary protested, wondering why she did protest. Why care what Old Ellen thought?

"Ay, I've heard infatuation called love afore now," said Old Ellen dourly.

A car was coming through the gate. It was Lester's car, and Hilary turned away from the window with a sudden crimson flush. Then she paused. A strange little icy ripple ran over her. The wind for a moment was still and the ensuing silence seemed to hold some profound and terrible meaning. What was the matter with the room? It seemed more hostile and furtive than ever. There was a change in it. Its very shadows were heavy with doom. But in the dim corner where the mirror hung, there was light.

The face of the mirror was turned outward.

Hilary took a step forward. She did not mean to look in it; she meant to turn it back again. This was Old Ellen's work. Andy why? Hilary seemed to feel a bodiless emotion in the room. She knew she was waiting for something evil and terrible.

Then, before she could help herself, she looked in the mirror.

Hilary never knew how long nor how short a time she stood there. What she saw was not her room, nor her own bridal form. It was as if she looked through a window, not a mirror, at a scene she knew well.

There was a pond under dun, branching, leafless trees and a path heaped with sodden, fallen leaves. And coming along the path to the man who waited for her—Star! Star, an exquisite, shimmering young thing, with face and eyes that were love and rapture incarnate. What was said to her that wiped all that exultant emotion out of her face in a few terrible moments? She held out her hands—Star had had such lovely hands—and said something. The man turned—Hilary saw his face, his handsome, arrogant, beloved face—and laughed. Laughed, and went swiftly away along the dim path. Star watched him go, then she looked straight at Hilary with her terrible tortured young eyes. The next moment, the dull shadowed waters of the pond closed over her.

Hilary sprang forward with a shriek and half fell, half hurled herself against the mirror in a mad effort to get through it to reach Star. But there was nothing there—nothing but a silvery-gleaming glass in a copper frame, reflecting her ghostly face and dark, cloud-like hair.

Hilary stared helplessly about her, sick and cold with agony to the depth of her being. The room was just the same. It seemed indecent that it should be so. The wind at the window seemed living—a bitter malignant thing. Old Ellen hobbled in without a pretense of knocking.

"He's below," she said contemptuously. "In the library. What's your will?"

Hilary did not answer. She went slowly out, past Old Ellen and down the hall, down the stairs, to the room where Lester Barr waited.

He came to meet her, with his eager eyes and seeking lips, but Hilary raised her hand.

"Stop," she said. "don't touch me. You—*you* were Star's lover. She killed herself because of you."

"Who told you?" he cried, and betrayed himself. "Hilary, what foolishness is this—"

She silenced him with a look. Now her eyes were neither blue nor green not gray but a flame.

"No one told me. I *know*. Merciful heavens, that men like you should live!"

For a moment his handsome eyes looked like a snake's.

"O, well—if you are going off the deep end! There was no need for that little fool of a sister of yours to drown herself. She should have known I couldn't marry a girl with nothing. Come, Hilary, don't you be a fool, too. You can't draw back now; think how you'd be laughed at."

"As if that matters. I will never look on your face again. You made love to Star because you thought she was Aunt Mildred's heir—and you pretended to love me for the same reason. You *dared*!"

Then he laughed. She had known that sooner or later he *would* laugh, as he had laughed Star to her death.

"What man would marry you for anything but your money? You and your superior airs."

She was glad he had said that. It set her free. She could despise him now. He went out laughing. Old Ellen was in the hall and Old Ellen was laughing, too—noiselessly. She laughed as she shut the door behind him; but the laughter went out of her dreadful old eyes as she faced Hilary.

"Ellen, send them all away. Tell them there will be no wedding."

In her own room Hilary tore off her bridal finery. The mirror gleamed tranquilly. She did not turn it to the wall. She was not afraid of it any more.

But she felt desolate and cold and helpless as she looked from her window into the fog that was creeping up around Glenwood.

"What is there in life for me now," she thought drearily.

Through the dreamlike landscape of the fog went Alec Stanley, crossing his lawn with his old dog slouching at his heels. What mad unreality, what unbelievable nightmare had come between them?

Hilary knew at last that the mirror was her friend.

❧ ❧

Editors' note: "The Mirror" was published in *Canadian Home Journal* (February 1931), illustrated by Roy Fisher. It is listed in the "Unverified Ledger Titles" section of the 1986 bibliography and was found by Carolyn Strom Collins.

The "Magdalens" referred to early in this story are the Magdalen Islands, located in the Gulf of St. Lawrence, between Prince Edward Island and Newfoundland. L. M. Montgomery's father, Hugh John Montgomery, was shipwrecked there before his marriage to Clara Woolner Macneill early in 1874.

Another Montgomery story, "Some Fools and a Saint," was published in *Family Herald* in May and June of 1931. Her novel, *A Tangled Web*, was also published that year.

TOMORROW COMES
(1934)

Judith Grayson—whose mother called her Judy and whose grandmother called her Hester—was born expecting things to happen. That they seldom did happen, even at Bartibog, under the watchful eyes of Grandmother and The Woman, never blighted her expectations in the least, especially at Bartibog. Things were just bound to happen at Bartibog. If not today then tomorrow. Of course The Woman had once said dourly, when Judy had promised to do something tomorrow: "Tomorrow never comes, Hester." But Judy knew better. Tomorrow *would* come sometime. Some beautiful morning at Bartibog you would wake up and find it was Tomorrow. Not Today but Tomorrow. And then things would happen—wonderful things. You might even have a day when you would be free to do as you liked, unwatched by Grandmother and The Woman, though that seemed almost too good ever to happen, even in Tomorrow. Or you might find out what was along that road—that wandering, twisted road, like a nice red snake—which led to the End of the World. You might even discover that the Island of Happiness was at the End of the World. Judy had always, all through her seven years of life, felt sure the Island of Happiness was somewhere if one could but find it.

But how could you explore for it, or for anything else, when Grandmother and The Woman bossed you all the time and wouldn't let you out of their sight? Bossing was not Judy's word. She had taken it over from Timothy Salt and thought it very expressive. Judy especially resented being bossed by The Woman.

She did not like it in Grandmother, of course, but you felt reluctantly that perhaps a grandmother had a right to boss you. What right had The Woman?

The Woman's name was really Martha Monkman, as Judy knew perfectly well, but once, long ago, she had heard someone say that Martha Monkman was old Mrs. Sinclair's "woman" and Judy never thought of her as anything else after that. It suited her so well, especially when spelled, as Judy always saw it, with a capital—a great big, forbidding W, as full of angles and corners as Martha Monkman herself.

"I hate her," Judy had once said passionately to Mother.

"Hush, hush." Mother was always hush-hushing. Both Grandmother and The Woman would not have any noise about the house. Everybody had to move softly, speak softly, even, so Judy felt, think softly. Judy often felt perversely that she wanted to yell loud and long. She *would* do it sometime—when Tomorrow came—and O, how she would enjoy the look on The Woman's face!

"Do *you* like her, Mother?" demanded Judy.

"Martha is very honest and faithful," said Mother wearily. "She has been your grandmother's companion for forty years."

Judy did not think this was an answer at all.

"She hates *me*," said Judy.

"Judith Grayson! Martha doesn't—"

"She does…and Grandmother, too. They both do. You know they do, Mother."

Mother looked aghast. She tried feebly to change Judy's mind but she did not seem to be able to think of any good arguments. Judy brushed them all aside.

"Why do they hate me, Mother?"

"You are an absurd child. Grandmother and Martha are both old people and old people are easily disturbed and worried. Of course you annoy them sometimes. And…and…when *they* were young, children were brought up much more strictly than they are now. They cling to the old way." There was no use in trying to extract anything from Mother. Judy knew this and gave it up. But she permitted herself one satisfaction…although she looked carefully around first to make sure the door was shut.

"Grandmother and The Woman are two tyrants," she said deliberately, "and when Tomorrow comes I'm going to escape from them forever."

She had expected Mother would nearly die of horror—I am afraid Judy really said that hoping to make a sensation—but Mother only looked at her strangely. And said a strange thing: "There is no escape for either of us now. Tomorrow will never come. As for you…they need not be so afraid to let you out of their sight. There is no fear of anyone kidnapping you."

Mother laughed bitterly. It was unthinkable but Judy almost thought Mother was really sorry that there was no danger of her being kidnapped. And yet Judy knew that her mother loved her fiercely and tenderly and wholly…knew it just as indisputably as she knew that Grandmother and The Woman didn't love her at all. Why, they never spoke of her by her name, even her middle name, if they could help it. It was always "the child." How Judy hated to be called "the child," just as they might have spoken of "the dog" or "the cat." Only there was no dog or cat in Grandmother's house.

"When Tomorrow comes," Judy told Grandmother once, "I will have a million dogs and forty-five cats."

Grandmother's face had grown dark and angry. Judy had been punished for impertinence.

But at least she was at Bartibog. They always came to Bartibog in the summer. Judy loved it. She hated Grandmother's gloomy, splendid town house in which everything seemed unacquainted with her, although she had lived there as far back as she could remember. But when they came down to Bartibog everything changed magically. She couldn't step outside the door there without stepping into something romantic. She lived in a world of romance once she came to Bartibog. Instead of a long, grim, stately street there was beauty wherever you looked. Luckily Grandmother and The Woman couldn't prevent you from look- ing, though Judy had no doubt they would if they could. The lighthouse down on the green point, painted in odd red-and- white rings; the dim blue shore where there were happy golden hollows among the dunes and the bones of old vessels; the little silvery curving waves; the range-lights that gleamed through the violet dusks…all gave her so much delight that it hurt. And the sea sunsets! Judy always went up to the north dormer to watch them and the ships that sailed out of the harbour at the rising of the moon. Ships that came back, ships that never came back. Judy longed to go in one of them on a voyage to the Island of Happiness. The ships that never came back stayed there…where it was always Tomorrow.

She could see the harbour from the north dormer with its smoky islands and its misty bays. She had never seen it any closer but she knew the mysterious road ran in that direction and her feet itched to follow it. When Tomorrow really came she would fare forth on it and perhaps find an island all her own, where she and Mother could live alone and Grandmother and The Woman could never come. They both hated water and would not put foot on a boat for anything. Judy liked to picture herself, standing on her island and mocking them, as they stood vainly glowering on the mainland shore.

"This is Tomorrow," she would taunt them. "You can't catch me anymore. You are only in Today."

What fun it would be!

And there was Timothy Salt. At least, there had been Timothy Salt last summer and Judy fervently hoped he would be this summer, too. Of course Grandmother and The Woman would disapprove of him as they had done last summer; but they could not do away with him altogether because he was the nephew of Tillytuck Salt—which was a name out of Tomorrow if ever there was one—the man who took care of Grandmother's house at Bartibog and was so useful in various ways that they dare not offend him. Tillytuck stood on his dignity and let it be known that his nephew was good enough for anybody to play with, take it or leave it. Grandmother took it and, under many restrictions, Judy had been allowed to play with Timothy. The most galling restriction, of course, was that they were never to go out of sight of the house. What wonders of adventure and romance might they not have discovered had it not been for that! At least they would have explored the Road to the End of the World. *Where* did that bewitching road lead? Sometimes Judy thought she would burst if she didn't find out.

In spite of all restrictions she and Timothy had a good deal of fun together. They made sand pies and swung on the side gate and talked. Judy liked to hear Timothy talk. He always said such nice slangy things. He was always very polite, too—Tillytuck had told him he would lick the stuffing out of him if he wasn't polite—and had a nice lean, brown face with round blue eyes and a delightful grin. He was about a head taller than Judy, which made her wonder what on earth The Woman meant by saying he was beneath her. Judy went to bed that night rather sadly because she had as yet seen nothing of Timothy. Perhaps he had gone away. It was a lonesome night, too. The first few nights at Bartibog were always like that till you got used to the moan of the sea and the sigh of the wind. Judy wished she could sleep with Mother. But Grandmother wouldn't allow that. Mother couldn't even put her to bed. Judy couldn't understand why but she knew she was never left alone with Mother any oftener than Grandmother could help.

"I'm always so afraid of things in the night," she had told Grandmother piteously. And Grandmother had said there must be no cowards in her house.

Alone and lonesome though she was, Judy went conscientiously through her little ritual of retiring. She folded her clothes and cleaned her teeth and brushed her long straight brown hair with the glints of red in it that always angered Grandmother... Judy couldn't imagine why. Of course it wasn't like Mother's lovely golden hair with the ripples in it and the little love-locks that curled about her ears. She didn't look a bit like Mother anyhow. Her skin was creamy and colourless where Mother's was pink and white, her eyes were as russet as her hair where Mother's were the most heavenly blue, and her chin was square and cleft where Mother's was pointed and little. Of all the things about her Judy knew it was her chin Grandmother hated most.

"It gets more like His every day," Judy had once heard Grandmother say to The Woman.

Whose?

Before Judy got into bed she opened one of the drawers in the high, black, polished old bureau and took a carefully-hidden picture from under a pile of handkerchiefs. She had cut it out of a piece of newspaper that had come wrapped around a parcel. A man's picture...she didn't know whose because the name had been torn away. But she liked the face tremendously. The chin was like her own. She thought if she had had a father she would have liked him to look like that. Her father was dead, so Grandmother told her, looking at her so vindictively that Judy knew her father had been hated by this grim, bitter old woman. Mother never would say anything about him. She had forbidden Judy to mention him.

"Your father did not love you," she said, her eyes dark with some kind of feeling and her little red mouth trembling. "He… hated you."

Judy wondered why. She had, so they said, been only three when her father died. Why should anyone hate you when you were so small? Could you be worth hating? But Judy never mentioned her father to anybody again.

"Good-night, dear Man." She kissed the picture and returned it to its hiding place. Then she climbed into bed and cuddled down under the blankets, for the June nights were cool enough at Bartibog and the sea breeze searching. There was more than a breeze tonight. It whistled and banged and shook and thumped and raged, and she knew the waves were dashing wildly down on the shore. What fun it would be to steal down close to them under the moon! But it was only in Tomorrow one could do that.

Judy lay awake a great deal at nights when the grown-ups were asleep, thinking out things and asking herself questions that were never answered. Why was Mother always so sad? And why was Grandmother angry with her because she was sad? And tonight she had a new mystery to ponder over. She had overheard Grandmother say to Mother: "*He* is here."

"How—how do you know?" Mother had asked in a queer, choked voice.

"Tillytuck told Martha. He is visiting his uncle down at Flying Cloud. James Markham is very ill…he is not expected to recover. And *he* will probably stay there until the end."

"It—it doesn't matter to me." Mother had spoken breathlessly and defiantly. It was almost like a cry.

"It shouldn't. But you are always so terribly weak, Elaine."

"Why have you told me he was here at all?" cried Mother.

"To prepare you. You might meet him somewhere unexpectedly. And the child must be kept under strict watch and ward. If he thought he could get a hold on you by kidnapping her he would do it in a minute, hate her as much as he may"

"Why should he kidnap her? The law would give her to him if he cared to invoke it."

"He will not go to law. That clan hates publicity. That is why he has never attempted to get a divorce."

"He won't bother his head about Judy. He cares nothing for her...or me. You have told me that often enough, Mother."

Mother was crying now. Judy clenched her fists. How dare Grandmother make Mother cry? But Grandmother often did that with some queer little speech Judy couldn't understand. Only she always felt that there was far more in what Grandmother said than her words themselves said.

"Is Grace with him?" asked Mother.

"Probably. She wouldn't trust him near Bartibog alone."

"Then," said Mother bitterly, with a little laugh so sad it nearly broke Judy's heart, "you need not be afraid of my meeting him."

Grandmother had come out into the hall and her face darkened when she saw Judy.

"Eavesdropping!" It was only one but what venom Grandmother could put into a word.

Judy thought it over until her head whirled. Who was "he?" Where was Flying Cloud? What a name! Out of Tomorrow again. It was maddening to be so near Tomorrow and not be able to get into it. What had "he" to do with Mother or herself? Kidnapping! Judy quivered, hardly knowing whether she were frightened or thrilled. But it was all nonsense. People weren't kidnapped in Bartibog. That only happened in the papers. But she would ask Timothy Salt about it tomorrow. How the wind blew! The waves sounded nearer, nearer...one of them was a great dark wave of sleep that rolled right over her...and Judy drowned in it with a delicious sigh of surrender.

She could not ask Timothy about it next day for there was no Timothy. For three days there was no Timothy. Judy simply couldn't stand it any longer so she waylaid Tillytuck and asked him where Timothy was. It was a tremendous relief to learn that Timothy was only visiting another uncle and would be home by the end of the week.

"I was afraid he might have got into Tomorrow ahead of me," Judy confided to Tillytuck.

"Ye're an odd little skeesicks," said Tillytuck. Then added, as if speaking to himself, "And it's my opinion them two old dames are a sight too hard on you."

Timothy was there the next Monday morning, as brown and polite as ever, and at least an inch taller. It was good to see him. Judy smiled to him over the gate with her shy sweetness and said, "What's the news in your neck of the woods?"

Being safely out of Grandmother's and The Woman's hearing she could indulge in a bit of slang. It sounded daring and adventurous. She felt as if she has slipped from some invisible shackle when she said it. Timothy and she swung on the gate the whole forenoon while he told her the news in his neck of the woods. Occasionally The Woman came to a window and scowled at them. But not as often as usual because Grandmother was in bed and The Woman was waiting on her. It was such an unheard-of thing for Grandmother to be in bed in the daytime. Judy couldn't recall such a state of affairs before. Of course, Grandmother wasn't really ill. She just had a pain, The Woman said. So Judy felt that it was not altogether too awful of her to be glad that Grandmother had to stay in bed.

"Let's hope," said Timothy cheerfully and unashamedly, "that she will have a pain for a week."

Judy felt a bit guilty because she couldn't help thinking it *would* be rather nice. And she felt guiltier still when the doctor had to be sent for after dinner.

From then on she didn't feel anything but amazement and bewilderment over the rush of events. Everything was in a whirl of excitement. Grandmother had appendicitis and must be taken to the hospital at once. The Woman went with her. She would not let Mother go; Mother must stay and look after the child. There was nobody left in the house except Judy and Mother and the cook. But Tillytuck promised Grandmother he would sleep in the garage loft at night.

That night Judy slept with Mother. It was almost as if Tomorrow had really arrived. And how heavenly to wake in the morning and see Mother's face on the pillow next to her, all flushed and sweet like a rose, and the little gold knob at the nape of her white neck. Mother was always so beautiful in the morning. Only Mother's eyes looked sad and restless as if she had not slept a great deal. When Judy laughed in her face Mother shuddered.

"Do *his* eyes still laugh?" she whispered to herself. Judy's quick ears caught it.

"Whose eyes?"

"Never mind. Somebody I used to know."

"Somebody you liked an awful lot," said Judy shrewdly. But she was more taken up with her own hopes than with anything else just then. It was so wonderful that Grandmother and The Woman were gone and she was alone with Mother. The cook and Tillytuck didn't count. But Timothy did. And Timothy made a proposition when he came that fairly took Judy's breath away.

"Say, I've got to go down the harbour way on an errand for Uncle Tillytuck. You come with me."

"O, I couldn't," gasped Judy.

"Why not? The old ladies are away."

Why not, indeed! Judy took a huge gulp of freedom.

"How long will it take?"

"Not more'n two hours. You'll be back in time for dinner. We'll see where that road goes to."

That settled it. This must certainly be Tomorrow. Judy decided then and there to take a chance on it. Mother had gone to lie down with a headache and Judy wasn't going to disturb her, especially as it was quite possible Mother would forbid such an expedition—"put the kibosh on it," as Timothy said. It was probably wicked to go without asking permission but things were all upset anyway and old standards had gone by the board…and she couldn't resist the lure of that road which had called her so long.

"Now you can yell," Timothy told her as soon as they were out of sight around the first S bend.

Strange! She no longer wanted to yell, now that there was nothing to prevent her doing so. She just wanted to walk quietly on…on…on, towards that blueness at the end of the world, drinking in the loveliness all around her. Every turn and kink of the road revealed new beauties, and it turned and kinked interminably, following the twists of a tiny river that seemed to have appeared from nowhere.

On every side were fields of buttercups and clover where bees buzzed. Now and then they walked through a milky way of daisies. Away to the right the sea laughed at them in silver-tipped waves. On the left, the harbour, ever drawing nearer, was like watered silk. Judy liked it better that way than it was pale-blue satin. They drank the wind in. The very sky was glad. A sailor with gold rings in his ears—the kind of a person one would meet in Tomorrow—smiled as he passed them. Far out on the bar was a splendid low thunder. Judy thought of a verse she had learned in Sunday School: "The little hills rejoice on every side." Did the man who wrote that mean the golden dunes at Bartibog?

"I think this road leads right to God," she said dreamily.

"No, it just goes down to the back shore," said Timothy matter-of-factly. "Look, you can see the end from here. Soon as I've done my errand we'll go on down to the end. Here—we turn off here. We've got to go over to that island."

"That island" was a long slender one, lying out in the harbour about a quarter of a mile from the shore. There were trees on it and a house. Judy had always wished she could have an island of her own with a little bay of silver sand in it just like this. But how to get to it?

"We'll row out in this flat," said Timothy, picking up the oars in a small boat tied to a leaning tree.

Judy shrank back for a moment. Even in Tomorrow....

"You're afraid," taunted Timothy.

"I'm not." Judy stepped into the boat. She *was* a little, but she was not going to let Timothy see it.

"Good stuff," said Timothy approvingly.

He could row. Was there anything Timothy couldn't do? By the time they reached the island Judy had got over her fright and wished the distance were twice as long. But this island was a fascinating place where anything might happen. Of course it was in Tomorrow. Islands like this didn't happen except in Tomorrow. They had no part or lot in unadventurous, hum-drum Today.

Timothy's errand was to a certain Mrs. Thompson who appeared to be the housekeeper. A nurse who met them at the door told Timothy he would find her on the far end of the island picking wild strawberries. Fancy! An island where wild straw-berries grew! Timothy went to hunt her up and Judy was asked to wait in the living room.

It was a beautiful room, with flowers everywhere and wild sea breezes blowing in. There was something about the room Judy

loved. Especially she loved the mirror over the mantel which reflected the room so beautifully and, through the open window, a
glimpse of lowland and dune and sea.

And then Judy got the shock of her life. Propped up against the
mirror was a large envelope with a typewritten address:

James Markham,
Flying Cloud,
Bartibog.

This island was Flying Cloud! Here was the mysterious "he" who
might kidnap her! And there he was, coming through the door.

Judy stood frozen in her tracks, all dismay and terror and
something that was neither. For this was the man whose picture
lay in her bureau drawer! And he looked even nicer than in his
picture, with his crinkly russet eyes and his sleek, red-brown hair.
Judy decided, in one swift flash of intuition, that she didn't care an
awful lot if he did kidnap her.

"Who are you?" asked the man, smiling.

"I'm…I'm me," faltered Judy, still in a swither of various
emotions.

"O, to be sure…you. Popped out of the sea, I suppose…come
up from the dunes…no name known among mortals."

Judy felt she was being made fun of a little. And she liked it.
But she answered a bit primly.

"My name is Judith Hester Grayson."

There was a silence—a very queer silence. The man looked
at her for quite a time without saying anything. Then he merely
asked her politely to sit down.

"I'm waiting for Timothy," she explained. "He's gone to tell
Mrs. Thompson something. When he has told it we are going
back to Bartibog"

Now, if you have any notion of kidnapping me, Mr. Man!

"Of course. But meanwhile you might as well be comfortable. And a spot of light refreshment perhaps? What would you like?"

Judy sat down. She felt oddly happy and at home.

"Can I have just what I like?"

"Yes."

"Then," said Judy triumphantly, "I'd like some ice-cream with strawberry jam on it."

The man rang a bell and gave an order. The ice-cream and jam came. Yes, this must be Tomorrow. No doubt about it. Ice-cream and strawberry jam didn't appear in this magical manner in Today.

"We'll set a share aside for Timothy," said the man.

They were good friends right away. The man didn't talk a great deal but he looked at Judy very often. There was a tenderness in his face…a tenderness she had never seen before in anybody's face, not even in Mother's. She felt that he liked her very much.

"I have your picture in my bureau drawer," she told him.

He looked startled.

"My picture! Who gave it to you?"

"Nobody. I cut it out of a paper. It hadn't any name but I liked it. Do you notice—" Judy was very grave "—that our chins are something alike?"

"Something," agreed the man. Then he laughed bitterly. Did all grown-up people laugh like that? No, Tillytuck didn't. But this man was looking as bitter as his laugh now. He wasn't happy. Judy wished she could make him happy. People who lived in Tomorrow shouldn't be unhappy.

Timothy came in and ate his share of the treat. Then there was nothing to do but go. Judy knew the man hadn't the slightest notion of kidnapping her and she felt the strangest, most unaccountable sensation of disappointment.

"Good-bye and thank you," she said politely. "It is very nice here in Tomorrow."

"Tomorrow?"

"This is Tomorrow," explained Judy. "I've always wanted to get into Tomorrow and now I have."

"O, I see. Well, I'm sorry to say it isn't Tomorrow for me. And *I* wouldn't want to get into Tomorrow. *I* would like to get back into Yesterday."

Judy was very sorry for him. She looked longingly back to Flying Cloud as Timothy rowed away. Why did Grandmother hate this man? There was nothing hateful about him. Her heart yearned back to Flying Cloud. Even on the road she turned again for a last, longing look at it.

"Look out!" screamed Timothy.

The room went around oddly. The furniture nodded and jigged. The bed...how came she to be in bed? She couldn't remember going to bed. Somebody with a white cap on was just going out of the door. What door? How funny one's head felt! There were voices somewhere—low voices. She could not see who was talking but somehow she knew. Mother and the man. What were they saying? Judy heard stray sentences here and there, bobbing out of a confusion of murmuring.

"I—I thought you always hated her," said Mother. There was a sound of tears in Mother's voice, and a sound of laughter, too. Laughter with no bitterness in it.

"My own baby! I loved her," said the man. "Always. But I never knew how much till Timothy Salt came rowing over to tell me she had been struck ... and killed by a car."

"I knew you loved her as soon as I got here and saw your face bending over her," said Mother.

More murmurs. The room went around again, jigged up and down, then steadied itself.

"I admit I was jealous of her. I thought you cared nothing for me any more…you seemed so wrapped up in her."

If that room would only stay put! Really, things behaved very queerly in Tomorrow. Judy hadn't heard what Mother said. The man was speaking again.

"It was your mother told you that. She never liked me or anything about me. You remember she would never call Judy anything but Hester because Judith was *my* choice of a name— my mother's. Elaine, you know it was your mother and Martha Monkman who made all the trouble between us."

"Not all." Mother seemed to be spunking up in a rather half-hearted defence of her family. "Not *all*. You know your sister hated me…*she* made half the trouble."

"Grace was always a mischief-maker I admit. But I wouldn't have believed her if I thought you still cared. And Judy seemed afraid of me. I thought you were bringing her up to hate me."

"O, no, no, Stephen! She *was* frightened of you, I didn't know why. I think—now—Mother and Martha told her things. And I thought you couldn't forgive her for not being a boy."

"Woman!"

What a delightful way he said "woman." Judy could fancy his smile. She wished she could see him but when she tried to turn her head round went that room again.

"We were both young fools," Mother was saying when it stead-ied once more.

"Is it too late to be wise, Elaine?" said the man.

Judy strained her ears for Mother's answer. Somehow, she felt it would be of tremendous significance to everybody in the world. But she could hear nothing, only sobs. Judy gave a long sigh of despairing resignation.

There was a brief silence. Then they came over to her bed, Mother and the man. She could see them now. Mother, all pale and tearful, looking as if she had been through some terrible experience, but with some strange inner radiance shining behind it all—a radiance that seemed part of the golden sunset light which suddenly flooded the room. The man was smiling triumphantly. Judy felt they both loved her very much.

"Are you feeling better, darling?" said Mother.

"Have I been sick?"

"You were knocked down by a car over on the mainland road," said the man. "Timothy came for help. To use his own expressive language, the liver was scared out of him. We brought you over here to Flying Cloud and sent for the doctor—"

"And for me," said Mother happily.

"The doctor said you had a very slight concussion—nothing serious. You'll be all right soon. Only you must keep very quiet for a few days."

He had such a delightful voice…you loved him for his voice. And he had his arm around Mother.

"This is your father," said Mother, "and—and—we are not going to be separated anymore."

"Father is dead," said Judy. "So I suppose I am dead too."

"Father and you are both very much alive, sweet." Father bent down and kissed her. "When you feel quite up to listening you shall hear the whole story of two very proud, very silly, very unreasonable young people who were not all to blame for what happened and who have learned wisdom through suffering."

The woman with the white cap was coming in again. Somehow Judy knew that whatever she had to say must be said before she quite got in.

"Will we live here?"

"Always…when we're not living somewhere else," said Father gaily.

"And will Grandmother and The Woman live with us?"

Father seemed as bad as Timothy for slang.

"Not by a jugful," said Father.

The sunset gold was fading and the nurse was looking her disapproval. But Judy didn't care.

"I've found Tomorrow," she said, as Father and Mother went out.

"*I* have found something I thought I had lost forever," said Father as the nurse shut the door on him.

৬১   ৫৯

Editors' note: This story was published in *Canadian Home Journal* (July 1934) with illustrations by Seymour Ball. It was listed in the "Unverified Ledger Titles" in the 1986 bibliography and was found by Carolyn Strom Collins and Donna Campbell. This story is available to view online in the Ryrie-Campbell Collection.

In 1934, Montgomery was living in Norval and working on *Mistress Pat*, the sequel to *Pat of Silver Bush*. Her first grandchild, Luella, had been born in May. Later that year, the "talking" movie version of *Anne of Green Gables* premiered.

Readers of L. M. Montgomery's novels will recognize many similarities between this story and *Jane of Lantern Hill*, published in 1937.

In addition to "Tomorrow Comes," two more Montgomery stories were published in 1934: "From Out the Silence" and "The Closed Door."

THE USE OF HER LEGS
(1936)

Tillie John—known to the postmaster of Upper Bartibog but to nobody else as Mrs. John Page—set a freshly baked batch of pies on her shelf, looked at her work, and saw that it was good. There was no one in Upper Bartibog who could match her for pies, she complacently reflected. Other things contributed to her complacency. It was a lovely day after the April rainstorm the day before—a bit cool but clear and sunny. She was going to town to spend the day with her sister Annie and help her plan her daughter's wedding. The only thing that marred her enjoyment was leaving Amanda alone. They seldom left her alone but it couldn't be helped to-day, for John had to go to town on business that couldn't be postponed, and Mrs. Harrow, the only near neighbour who could be asked to come and stay with her, was also away. Really, there was no danger. Tramps never came to Bartibog—it was too much out of the world—and Amanda was perfectly healthy, except that she hadn't the use of her legs, poor thing. Tillie John sighed again. She was glad that so far John had resisted all the solicitations of persistent agents to sell him a car. She had never felt safe in one since Amanda's accident ten years before. Amanda had gone out in a friend's car, there had been a collision, and Amanda had never walked again.

Amanda Page was sitting in her wheelchair by the kitchen window, looking like a mediaeval saint and probably quite aware of the fact, at least if you left the mediaeval out. Mediaeval saints may never have worn dresses of blue print with an elaborate Irish crochet collar around the neck, but they sometimes had smooth braids of rippling auburn hair wound around their heads, placid creamy faces, and large, brilliant, gray-blue eyes set at a slant, calculated to give the face a peculiarly appealing sadness. At any rate, Amanda Page had them and the lashes of a Hollywood star into the bargain. She was thirty-five but you would never have guessed it to look at her. Tillie John sometimes scowled at her own wrinkles and warped hands and resented Amanda's timeless beauty a little. No wonder Amanda looked pretty and young! She spent her time between her bed and her wheelchair and was waited on hand and foot. Then Tillie John would reproach herself. After all, when you hadn't the use of your legs....

"That north blind is an inch lower than the other. Would you mind making them even?" said Amanda in the soft pathetic voice she had always affected since her accident.

Tillie John gave the north blind a jerk that sent it whizzing to the top. Then repented her impatience and adjusted it carefully. After all, the Pages were like that. John himself was as fussy as an old maid about trifles.

Amanda surveyed the blind with an air of plaintive triumph. Then she looked at the lunch Tillie John had set out for her on one end of the long kitchen table, on a trim little red-and-white checked cloth.

"Is there anything else you'd like, dear?" Tillie John asked solicitously, to atone for her momentary petulance about the blind.

"You could set that chocolate peppermint cake out," said Amanda gently. "I might fancy a crust of it, though I haven't any appetite. But then you know I never have. I wonder what it would be like to feel hungry again. Ah, you people who can take exercise—do you ever stop to think how fortunate you are? Thank you, dear. I'm sure I'll get on very nicely. Have a good time at Annie's and don't worry about me."

"I will worry, though," said Tillie John. "It doesn't seem right to leave you alone. Dear knows what might happen."

"What could happen? No tramps ever come here—"

"Suppose the house took fire."

"I could get out in my wheelchair somehow if it did. Besides, it won't. You've always worried too much, Tillie. You're as bad as old Daniel Random, you really are."

"Speaking of old Daniel, he's gone off again," said Tillie.

"Has he ever been on?" inquired Amanda. "As long as I can remember Daniel Random has had rats in his garret, especially when it came to religion."

"Well, you know he's worse at some times than others. And they've been holding revival meetings up at Prospect Head, with them go-preachers, and Daniel never missed one."

"No doubt he's had a glorious time, too."

"Well, his wife hasn't. She's worried to death about him. He thinks the end of the world is coming. And I hear he got up in Prospect church last Sunday and asked the minister questions."

"He'd get a real kick out of that," said Amanda, "and so would everybody else who was there. Daniel has always been very peculiar. If I could have laughed over anything I'd have laughed at the look on his face that Sunday last fall when him and Captain Jonas were here and Daniel was shooting off some of his fine talk. 'All humanity are my brothers,' he boomed, big-like. And Jonas said, winking at me, 'That's too much of a family for the average man to carry, Daniel.' Daniel went off mad and has never been back since."

"Which is a mercy," said Tillie John devoutly. "I never did feel easy when he was about. He gives me the creeps. One of his crotchets just now, they tell me, is that it isn't right to cut your hair or beard. He's letting his grow. They're both to his waist already. Won't he be a sight? He's been seeing a great army in the sky and painting texts everywhere about his place. Mrs. Peter Cary told me it got on her nerves just to walk through his yard with all the awful warnings staring her in the face from the barn walls. His wife says he's used up five dollars' worth of paint already and them mortgaged to the ears. And he kneels down and prays whenever the notion takes him—when he's ploughing or watering the horses or feeding the pigs. He prayed for half an hour in Henry Beckett's store at Prospect Centre last Tuesday and got fearful mad when the boys laughed at him. Of course they shouldn't of laughed at an afflicted man, but you can imagine. He ought to be shut up till the spell passes. Well, I think I've arranged everything for you as well as I can. I hope you won't be lonesome. Likely—" she said slyly "—Captain Jonas will be up sometime through the day."

Amanda smiled mysteriously. "O, no, he won't, Tillie. Jonas won't be coming back any more—except to my funeral. He said so yesterday."

Tillie John knew something had happened the previous afternoon. She had meet Captain Jonas starting out, when she came up from her trip to the harbour for fresh fish, looking as indignant as a cat you had just put off your knee. She supposed he had lost patience with Amanda at last. Well, it wasn't any wonder. Any man got tired of being a doormat in time. She could never understand his infatuation for Amanda, when he could have got plenty of reasonable women—with full use of their legs—for the asking. However, since nobody but Amanda would suit him, it was a pity Amanda was so stubborn.

"I can't see why you won't marry Captain Jonas, Amanda," she said a bit crossly.

"And me with no use of my legs!" Amanda eyed her reproachfully. "I may be selfish, Tillie—no doubt I am—but I'm not so selfish as that."

L. M. MONTGOMERY

"If he doesn't mind your legs I don't see why that should hinder you. He can afford to hire Matilda Wiggins to do the work and wait on you. He never goes on long voyages now and that new house of his at Lower Bartibog is fitted up with everything. You could do all the sewing and nothing else to do but just look pretty. And he's real good-looking with such a nice flat stomach."

Tillie John, recalling John's paunch, sighed.

"I know I'm a terrible burden to you." Amanda looked like a wounded gazelle—at least like the picture of a wounded gazelle in the African explorer's book on the clock-shelf, which John read on rainy Sundays. "I know—I feel—you'd like to be rid of me and I don't blame you, Tillie, not a speck do I blame you. I often wish I could die and be no more trouble to you."

"I *don't* want to get rid of you," protested Tillie in exasperation. "It's just that I think you'd be happier if you married Jonas, that's all."

"I'd marry him if I had the use of my legs," said Amanda, "but since I haven't I'll never, never burden him with my affliction. I made him understand that finally yesterday, Tillie. That was when he got mad and said he wouldn't come here again 'til he came to my funeral. It may not be so long as that."

"Captain Jonas will die before you do," snapped Tillie. Tillie was always snapping and then instantly repenting. "Everybody says he's fretting himself to death because he can't get you."

"No one in the Haye family has ever died of love," smiled Amanda. "Of course I'll miss him coming here—I've always enjoyed his company—but you know it keeps people gossiping and wondering, so it's better as it is. Now, Tillie dear, don't worry about Jonas and me any longer. Just go off and enjoy yourself. You might bring me my red bedroom slippers with the fur 'round the tops. My shoes are hurting my feet a bit. And you might hand me my pale blue chiffon scarf, in case anyone should come in. It's in the third box from the top in my middle bureau drawer. I'll finish embroidering that gingham cushion to-day. Thank goodness I have the use of my hands at least. I'm not absolutely good for nothing."

"You're the most wonderful sewer I ever saw," said Tillie John. "I don't know what we'd do without you if it comes to that." She knew it was of no use whatever to plead the cause of the faithful Captain Jonas any further. Amanda was inflexible. She had always been like that, Tillie John reflected; always sweet but always going her own way.

"It's little enough for all your kindness and care," said Amanda, with a break in her voice. "Sometimes—Tillie, I've never spoken of this but O, I've thought of it—sometimes I wonder if you believe what that English doctor from the convention said when he was at the Bartibog Hotel. You remember? He said there was nothing to prevent me walking now if I wanted to—*wanted to*. As if there is anything on earth I want more! You don't believe him, do you, Tillie?"

"Of course I don't. Amanda, you haven't been brooding over that?"

"Sometimes in the night when I can't sleep. I wonder if you and John think I'm a fraud."

"Amanda Page, stop talking like that! As for that doctor, he didn't know what he was talking about. Anyhow, we never heard the rights of what he did say. Something about the trouble being in your sub—sub-something mind."

"I've only got one mind! I wish *he* had to sit here year in and year out, a helpless burden on his friends. He'd know then whether I wanted to walk or not. Perhaps Jonas thinks it, too, since he's always worrying me to marry him. Well I'll try not to think of it. There's John with the buggy. You might sprinkle a whiff of violet on me before you go. There's a little left in the atomizer. I'm fond of violet perfume. It reminds me of happier days."

"I'll bring you home a new bottle," promised Tillie. The violet perfume cost a dollar, and dollars were hard to come by. But she could take one of the three she had saved for a new hat. The hat could wait.

Amanda heard the buggy drive away down the lane with a secret smile of satisfaction. It was really nice to be alone once in a while. Tillie was a dear but there were times when she got on your nerves. She really was rather stupid. And she was always trying to cheer you up and entertain you and amuse you when you didn't want to be cheered up or entertained or amused. Amanda generally found quite a bit of entertainment and amusement in her day-dreams. Gorgeous fantasies of luring princes and ruling empires—she, Amanda Page, of Upper Bartibog. If she had the use of her legs she would have been quite content to lure and rule Captain Jonas, but since she hadn't it was fun to fly a bit higher in imagination.

She gazed complacently in the mirror on the wall opposite her chair. She really looked quite nice. Her hair gleamed like polished mahogany in the sunlight. Amanda had always been very proud of her beautiful hair, and her complexion was above the average. The Pages had all been born with good skin. There were not many women in Bartibog with as few wrinkles. That scarf around her full white throat was certainly becoming. It was rather a pity there was no likelihood of anyone—well, of Jonas—seeing it. Jonas noticed things like that, more than most men. She would certainly miss Jonas' visits, and his lean, lined, kindly face smiling at her. Jonas *had* a nice smile. But it wasn't fair to keep him dangling around when she could never marry him. She had made that very clear to him yesterday. It had all been rather dramatic and exciting. Amanda laid down her gingham cushion, leaned back in her chair, and savored her recollection of it. Captain Jonas had come in with an armful of pussywillows for her and had arranged

them in her favorite vase. He was given to delicate little atten-
tions like that. They had had their usual pleasant chat but at the
end Captain Jonas had spoiled it all by again pleading with her to
marry him.

"You know I can't marry you—or anyone—when I haven't the
use of my legs," Amanda had told him sadly for the umpteenth
time. Her eyes had filled with tears. She could cry whenever she
wanted to, which was a great asset because she could cry and
be beautiful. She never made noises or grimaces. The tears just
brimmed over and got tangled in her long fringing black lashes. It
was them eyelashes did the trick, Captain Jonas told himself. No
man could resist them.

"I don't care a hoot whether you've got the use of your legs
or not," said Captain Jonas bitterly. She ought to know that by
this time. It wasn't her legs he wanted her for…though they were
shapely enough, at least, what he could see of them below the blue
dress. Amanda did not hold with too brief dresses. At any rate he
had a fine view of her ankles and he reflected that he had never
seen finer ankles in his life, and he had been around a bit in his
time.

But the ankles were only incidental. He wanted Amanda to be
waiting for him when he came home from a voyage. He wanted
to sit beside her when rain drifted over the gray sea beyond the
bar, when fogs crept up the harbour and made everything—even
the ugly old houses at the fishing village—lovely and mysterious. He wanted to watch the evening star with her and the silvery
moonlight paths over the water, the far dim shores jeweled with
home lights. He wanted her to admire his delphiniums and his
gorgeous splashes of nasturtiums than which there was nothing
finer in either of the Bartibogs. It would be wonderful just to have
her living in his house—his fine new white house with its red
roof and its dormers at Lower Bartibog. He liked to think of her

sitting there at his fireside, warm and cosy, while the winter winds ravened outside and the shadows of wild black cloud tore over the sands. He could never get things like this to her. Every word he uttered sounded clumsy when he talked to her. But he had made it clear to her for many years that he wanted her and only her for a wife, and never could want any other woman. And to have her turn around and say coolly that if he hunted about a bit he could find himself another girl was really too much to endure. For the first time in his life Captain Jonas felt that he was mad at Amanda.

"I never argue with a lady," he said, "and I'm not looking for another girl. But I'm through with coming here and being advised to marry someone else. I'll not come back again unless it's to your funeral, since you seem to think you've got one foot in the grave the way you talk. So put that in pickle."

"Dear me, I hope you'll be in a better humor when you come back," sighed Amanda. One tear succeeded in making its escape from her lashes and rolled down the round enticing cheek, which Captain Jonas in wild moods pictured himself kissing. But, possessed by all the anger of a patient man, tears, even Amanda's tears, had no influence on him now.

"I'm not coming back. When you want me you can come to me. You know where I live: Journey's End, Lower Bartibog, at your service. And so good-day to you, Miss Amanda Page."

Captain Jonas had marched off and Amanda permitted herself the luxury of a few more tears while Tillie John was walking up the lane. What hurt her was Captain Jonas' speech about going to him if she wanted him. When he knew she hadn't the use of her legs! Or did he believe what the English doctor had said? Well, he was gone and for good. He would probably be sorry for what he had said when he cooled off, but the Hayes, like the Pages, never broke their word when it was once passed. And it was better so—far, far better so. Amanda was Tranquil and composed by the time Tillie John reached the house and had assumed her Madonna look.

The day passed quite agreeably to Amanda: she embroidered her cushion diligently; she ate her dinner, contriving to dispose of a fair amount of food despite her lack of appetite; she wistfully decided that a third slice of peppermint chocolate cake might be better left uneaten; and she was quietly arranging herself for a nap in her chair when Daniel Random opened the door and stood for an impressive moment on the threshold, his flaming red beard sweeping across his breast. His grizzled hair reached to his shoulders and he was hatless. His six feet of bone and sinew was clothed in a faded red sweater and ragged, faded blue overalls. Altogether, he was a rather extraordinary-looking creature with his red-hot brown eyes blazing in his very long, very narrow, deeply wrinkled face. There was undoubtedly something sinister about him but Amanda was not in the least alarmed. She had known old Daniel Random all her life and, years before, had laughed with the rest of the young fry over his religious spasms of prophetical fervor and strange frenzy. She had not seen him in any of them of late years and had heard they were growing worse but it would never have occurred to her to be afraid of poor crazy old Daniel Random. On the contrary she thought it would be rather amusing to hear what he had to say…a welcome break in the monotony of the day.

"Well, Daniel, and how are you?" she said cordially.

"I am *seeking*," he said mysteriously. "Seeking for my soul."

"Dear me, have you mislaid it?" queried Amanda with mild sarcasm. "You Randoms were always terrible careless creatures."

Daniel advanced a few steps into the room.

"I have been told by the Heavenly God what I must do if I am to find my soul," he said.

"And what is it? But won't you have a chair?"

Daniel ignored her invitation. His eyes blazed. Really, thought Amanda, the poor man was terribly strung up.

"Sacrifice," he said hollowly. "Sacrifice! I have been told to offer a sacrifice and I dare not disobey the Voice. Then I shall not only find my soul but the people of this community will be compelled to realize the danger of delaying any longer their acceptance of the truth that the end is near at hand. O, how lofty are their eyes! And their eyelids are lifted up. But they shall be brought low, those children of wrath, those sons of Beelzebub. They have trusted in the blood of bulls and of goats but a nobler sacrifice is demanded. And I—I, Daniel Random—have been chosen by the Heavenly God for this high office."

"And what are you going to sacrifice, Daniel?" inquired Amanda, still easily, as she threaded her needle. You had to humor such people, she reflected. But he really ought to be shut up when these spells came on. There was no knowing what he might do. Kill somebody's cow, as like as not.

"You—you, Amanda Page, are the appointed sacrifice," said Daniel solemnly, taking a few steps nearer.

"O, me?" said Amanda, aroused. "I wouldn't do at all, Daniel. I haven't the use of my legs. You mustn't offer up an imperfect thing to the Heavenly God, you know. That's in the Bible, isn't it?"

"You are not deformed and you are very beautiful, Amanda Page. The Heavenly God took the use of your legs away from you because you danced. That was an offence to the Heavenly God."

"You used to dance yourself, Daniel, if I remember aright," retorted Amanda. His burning eyes were beginning to make her a little uncomfortable but she smiled over the recollection of Daniel Random leaping and shouting furiously as he danced an eight-hand reel at a party in Lower Bartibog years ago.

"I did, I did," said Daniel wildly. "That was how I lost my soul: I danced it away. Danced it to damnation. But it is not yet too late. I have got a word from the Heavenly God. To-day he spoke to me and I have seen the light. I have been waiting for a sign and lo, it is here."

He was quite close to her by this time and Amanda felt a sudden stab of fear. She had never heard of him being so bad as this.

"Don't you touch me. Don't you dare touch me, Daniel Random," she said sharply, trying to keep her voice steady. It did not do to let lunatics see that you were afraid of them. And this man was clearly mad! Not "off" or "cracked" or "goofy," but simply mad.

Daniel laid a bony hand, with long and very dirty nails, on her smooth, plump arm. There was a certain horrible gloating in his touch.

"I shall not speak smooth things to you, Amanda Page," he said sternly. "High and lifted up you have always been, proud of your long hair and your eyes that bewitch the hearts of men. But your hour is come. Prepare to meet the Heavenly God. I will wash my hands in your blood…it will be a glorious experience, O, my sister. The parched ground shall become a pool and Daniel Random, priest of the Heavenly God, shall find his soul."

"You'd better run away home, Daniel," said Amanda faintly, when his ridiculous farrago of phrases and tags had eased temporarily for want of breath. "I'm very tired…and I always take a nap in the afternoon."

For all answer Daniel picked her up as if she were a child. Amanda tried desperately to free herself but he had her arms imprisoned between their bodies and she could not get them loose. O, if she could only kick him! Faugh, what a terrible breath he had! Was this a nightmare?

"Blue and purple and scarlet and fine-twined linen!" shouted Daniel, suddenly exultant, as her chiffon scarf blew across her face in a sudden gust of wind from the open door. "He that sitteth in the heavens shall laugh…ay. He shall laugh!"

Daniel laughed himself, horribly. He lifted Amanda high in the air for a moment, then laid her on the kitchen table, holding her down with one hand while he reached across the table with the other.

Amanda was momentarily paralyzed with horror. Her hands went clammy. This—this was one of the things you read about in books and newspapers but which could never happen in real life.

Daniel had got what he reached for: Tillie John's old, long, wickedly thin and sharp carving knife. His burning eyes gazed into Amanda's terrified orbs with all the irresponsible light of insanity as he raised the carving knife with both his hands gripping the handle.

Amanda knew all at once and indisputably that this madman meant to kill her. Something in her screamed although no sound passed her lips. She made one wild, convulsive spring from the table. She went out of the door and down the steps and down the lane, running as she had never run in all her life before. The use of her legs had returned with a vengeance.

Daniel was close behind her, still clutching the carving knife. In his momentary stupefaction at her unlooked-for escape he had allowed her to get the lead but he was rapidly overtaking her. Not a living soul was in sight. Amanda flew across the road, her chiffon scarf, held by the pin of her collar, streaming behind her, and down the old, disused wharf below the Page place. Eliza, escaping from pursuers and bloodhounds, had nothing on Amanda as she leaped over the gaping holes in the ragged structure to the very end where two rowboats were tied. With one final, frenzied jump Amanda landed in John's boat. But the rope was tied in a firm knot and Daniel was already in sight. Amanda snatched up a hatchet which John had providentially left there and severed it at a blow she caught at the oars and pulled wildly. She had been a good rower ten years before and under the stress of terror and stark necessity all her old skill came back combined with the strength of desperation. For Daniel had climbed into the Harrow boat and was coming after her. It was not so very far to Lower Bartibog where the little river debouched into the harbour. And once around the point Captain Jonas' house was near. Could she hold out? She would…she must.

Captain Jonas, standing where his lane ran out from his garden, smoking a pipe and scowling viciously at things in general, saw something. He had been all over the world and had seen all kinds of incredible things but never anything quite so incredible as this. In fact, he didn't believe he saw it. It couldn't be…it simply wasn't happening. He was dreaming or drunk or crazy. Ay, that was it: crazy, as a man might well be after such a night as he had spent. Hadn't there been a yarn that his father's cousin's great-aunt had been in the asylum? Those things run in families, you couldn't deny it.

Captain Jonas saw, or thought he saw, Amanda Page—who hadn't put a foot under her for ten years—running madly up his lane with Daniel Random one jump behind her, flourishing an implement which everybody in both the Bartibogs would have recognized as Tillie John's favourite carving knife. Amanda was almost staggering and was uttering the most piteous little cries. Her hair had come loose and streamed madly in the wind, her cheeks were whipped to a brilliant scarlet, her blue dress was spattered from head to foot with mud and her red bedroom slippers would never be the same again.

"Jonas…save me…save me…" she gasped, as he ran to catch her.

Captain Jonas had already decided that he was not crazy—after all, that great-aunt had been on the cousin's mother's side—but only dreaming. Still, you had to do something even in a dream. Captain Jonas dreamed that he put the shaking Amanda carefully down on a stone bench and packed Daniel Random a wicked wallop on the jaw. There was something so solid and satisfying in the impact that Captain Jonas felt a conviction that the scene was real.

Daniel sat down abruptly in the muddy lane and put a hand to his face. The carving knife had flown from his grasp over the hedge into the garden, where Captain Jonas found it next day and restored it to Tillie John who could never have cut another slice of bread in her life if she hadn't regained it.

"What does this mean, Daniel Random?" demanded Captain Jonas.

Daniel looked about him vacantly.

"The Heavenly God—" he began.

"We'll leave God out of this," said Captain Jonas. "There's evidently been a miracle and it's probably His doing but you're not going to take His name in vain in your condition. I'm asking you what has happened."

Daniel tried again.

"The Heavenly God—"

Captain Jonas lost all patience.

"Git up and git."

Daniel Random got up and got. He was crying bitterly as he stumbled down the lane but his frenzy was over for the time being at least, as his harrowed wife thankfully realized when he arrived home in tears.

Captain Jonas turned to the disheveled, mud-splashed Amanda and gathered her up in his arms. She sobbed out a disconnected account of what had happened.

"O, Jonas, it's been like a terrible nightmare…but it's over…and I can walk again. O, Jonas…that English doctor must have been right…but you don't think I was deceiving you all these years, do you? Maybe I *have* got a sub—sub-whatever-it-was mind."

"My loveliest girl!" Captain Jonas tightened his grip. "You ought to know me better than that. Now, now, darling, don't be hot and bothered any longer. He's gone and you are safe. You'll just come in and have a bit of supper first, before we do any more talking. Mrs. Wiggins is getting it ready…it'll set you up."

Amanda lifted her head from his shoulder and sniffed. A heavenly smell of fried codfish cakes and salt pork floated out on the crisp April air.

"I could do with a cup of tea," she said. "O, Jonas…you said I'd have to come to you…and I came. It—it's an act of God, Jonas."

"Act of God—or act of Daniel Random—you're going to marry me right straight off, Amanda Page."

"Well," sighed Amanda happily, "since I've got the use of my legs…."

❧   ❧

Editors' note: "The Use of Her Legs," illustrated by James and Charlotte Billmyer, was published in the September 1936 issue of *Canadian Home Journal*. It is not listed in the 1986 bibliography but was found by Benjamin Lefebve and Donna Campbell. Lefebvre discovered that Montgomery wrote the story on the backs of the pages of her original manuscript for *Jane of Lantern Hill* (1937), which is kept in the Confederation Centre Archives in Charlottetown, PEI. The published story is available to view online in the Ryrie-Campbell Collection.

Readers of *Kilmeny of the Orchard* (1910), Montgomery's third novel, will notice similarities in the two plots: a young girl is paralyzed (in *Kilmeny's* case, she is unable to speak) but a terrorizing situation frees her from her "subconscious" (the word "Tillie John" and "Amanda Page" tried to remember) paralysis. The character "Daniel Random" might remind some readers of "Marshall Elliot" in *Anne's House of Dreams*. Elliot had refused to cut his long hair and beard until the "Grits" were voted back into office: a fifteen-year-long commitment.

The comparison of Amanda to "Eliza, escaping from pursuers and bloodhounds" refers to the enslaved Eliza Harris in *Uncle Tom's Cabin* (1852) who was running for her life and that of her baby, trying to reach the Underground Railroad and freedom.

The fictional town of "Bartibog" was also used in Montgomery's story "Tomorrow Comes," published in *Canadian Home Journal* two years earlier (July 1934), and also found in this collection.

Montgomery used the word "crotchets" early in the story to mean "a perverse or unfounded belief or notion," not to be confused with "crochet" as in the use of a special hook to make handmade lace.

Captain Jonas' home, "Journey's End," bore the same name Montgomery had given to her own home in a suburb of Toronto on Riverside Drive. She and her husband had bought this home on his retirement from the ministry in the spring of 1935 after living in Presbyterian manses in Leaskdale and Norval, Ontario, for about twenty-five years. She died in this home in April 1942.

Montgomery's *Anne of Windy Poplars* was published in 1936. Eight of the stories (adapted) from *Anne of Windy Poplars* were published in *Family Herald and Weekly Star* (May 6–July 1); some of these are available to view online in the Ryrie-Campbell Collection along with another story, "Brother Beware," published in *Country Home* in June 1936.

JANET'S REBELLION
(1938)

"I wonder, Jink," said Janet, "whose dress it will be this time. I almost wish I were like you and had just the one neat, furry, grey coat to wear all the time. You have the comfort of feeling that it is your own, Jink, haven't you? You don't have to wear other kitties' skins and know that all the other cats know it. I don't exactly wish I were a cat, Jink: it's a pretty nice thing to be a girl. I like being a girl .But O, dear me, Jink, I *don't* like wearing other peoples' cast-off finery, even if it is pretty and becoming.

"Jink, listen sympathetically to my tale of woe: I went to Nora Marr's party in April and I wore Cousin Alice's last year's blue voile. It was pretty and almost as good as new, but everybody knew it was Alice's. I felt like a rag-picker. Then in May came the Veterans' concert and I had to sing. And I wore Cousin Theodora's last summer's yellow organdie that she left for me when she went away. And everybody knew it was Cousin Theodora's. I didn't feel like Janet Stannard at all—I felt as if I were in the wrong body, Jink. I didn't sing half as well as I should have, and nobody knew why.

"And, Jink, it's always been the same. I've always had to wear my city cousins' dresses after they got through with them. They mean to be kind, Jink; I appreciate their good intentions and I love them dearly. But O, I'd so much rather have just one plain, cheap new dress of my very own than a dozen lovely second-hands. How would you feel, Jink, if you were a girl sixteen years old and had never had a dress of your very own in your life?

That is: a nice dress, not counting a gingham or flannel once in a while for school wear? Fancy what it's like, every time you go anywhere, to know that people are scanning you to see whose dress you've got on now? And I can't say a word of protest, Jink. They would all think me so ungrateful and I wouldn't have them think that for the world. They've all been so good to me and I *am* grateful, but I can't help my poor little feelings.

"I've got rather used to wearing other girls' dresses to church and other places, where you're only one of a crowd, after all. But these special occasions will be the death of me, Jink. And there's another of them looming up now: Jennie Reever's wedding. The invitations came to-day. I'm invited, too, Jink, and I don't know yet what I'm to wear. Alice's voile got stained at the party all across the front breadth. No, Jink, I did *not* do it accidentally on purpose. Polly Marsden ran into me with a cup of coffee, so that's out of the question. I've grown out of Theodora's organdy since May. It's too tight everywhere. Jink, it's my one beautiful hope— I'm growing so fast that some day I'll be bigger than anybody in the connection and then I can't wear their dresses. As for Jennie's wedding, Aunt Lena and Helen and Louise are holding solemn conclave in the breakfast room this very minute and my fate will soon be settled. It has done me good to have this little growl to you, Jink. I feel ever so much better."

Janet laughed, patted Jink's sleek grey head, and ran down-stairs. She was a tall girl with curly, reddish-brown hair and hazel eyes. All her life she had lived with her Uncle Charles and Aunt Lena Stannard and she had a very happy home. But money was sometimes scarce and her cousins, older than herself and out in society, needed so many things. And so the family habit, begun when Janet was a baby, was to fit her out with made-overs and cast-offs. They never thought Janet minded it. Her clothes were always pretty and much more costly and dainty than most of her girl friends wore. They would have been amazed and grieved had they known how Janet really felt about it.

Aunt Lena and Louise were, as Janet said, planning out their costumes for the wedding and Helen came in presently and joined in the discussion.

"What is Janet to wear?" asked Helen just as Janet came in.

Louise always settled such questions, so she looked at Janet critically.

"She has grown so tall I really think that lovely white muslin dress that Cousin Amy sent out in the box will be the very thing. It's beautiful and I can easily fix the sleeves over with puffs. Janet has such pretty arms and elbows. She can wear your pale blue sash, Helen."

Janet, making no sound outwardly, groaned in spirit. She had been afraid of this. That dress of Amy's! Amy had worn it the preceding summer during her visit in Pinewood: everybody would recognize it, for it had attracted notice wherever it had been seen. It was a lovely dress, but Janet had hated it from the start, for she knew it would probably be left to her or sent to her when Amy had grown tired of it. Janet felt a sudden new, hot rebellion sweep over her, but she said nothing. In the days following Louise got out the white muslin dress and pressed and puffed and altered the skirt; it was a dream of a thing and suited Janet to perfection. But Janet could not bear the sight of it.

Just as the Stannards were going upstairs to dress on the day of Jennie Reever's wedding, all Uncle James's folks arrived, having driven over from Milledge. Somebody must get them their meal and that somebody was Janet.

When the meal was over all the rest went to the Reevers', leaving Janet to dress alone.

"You'll have plenty of time," said Aunt Lena kindly. "There is an hour yet. We'll go right over, for Mrs. Reever wants Helen to help her, and Louise promised to arrange Jennie's veil. Never mind the dishes, just leave them in the pantry."

Lingeringly, Janet climbed the stairs to her room, Jink springing up before her with his striped tail erect. Rebellion was still smouldering in Janet's heart. It burst into fierce and sudden flame at sight of Amy's muslin dress spread out on her bed, with Helen's blue sash and Cousin Margaret's kid slippers. They were all so kind, the darlings, yet she couldn't wear it, no, she couldn't and she wouldn't! The recollection of how Cissy Carel and Marjorie Street had laughed behind her back at Nora's party about her "second-handedness" swept over her with a flush of shame.

"I'd rather wear my gingham," she said bitterly; and then stopped short and glared so fixedly at Jink that Jink looked scared and shrank away.

Why not? Why not wear her gingham? It was new. It was neat. It was her very own. She would!

Without another second of hesitation Janet flew to her closet. Out came the Alice-blue gingham made for school wear. On it went. Janet looked at herself in the glass with satisfaction. Her cheeks were crimson with excitement, her eyes starry and bright. She had never looked better in her life; and O, how self-respecting she felt! Aunt Lena and the girls might be angry, but Janet was past caring for that. She couldn't, no, she *couldn't* wear Amy's dress. Sixteen years of patient second-handedness came to an end in that wild revolt of the blue gingham dress.

Janet was very nearly late. The bridal party were descending the Reever staircase just as she turned into the dressing-room. She flung off her hat and coat and slipped down, taking a seat near the door of the big living-room. Aunt Lena and Louise were opposite her, across the room. The ceremony was over before Louise's eyes fell on Janet. Louise stared as if she couldn't believe her senses.

"Mother," she gasped in a low tone, "is that really Janet over there? Janet!"

Mrs. Stannard looked. "Yes, it is, Louise. In that blue gingham! What has happened? What can have possessed her?"

"She must have torn the muslin or something," groaned Louise. "But to come in that gingham! O, this is terrible. What will people think? What will they say? *What* shall we do? Janet must go home at once."

"*We* can't do anything now," said Mrs. Stannard. "She is here and everybody has seen her. They only thing to do is to ignore the matter until we go home. Dear me, what possessed the child? I feel so mortified."

Meanwhile, Janet was beginning to enjoy herself. It was delightful to be able to go about with a single mind, with no dread of hearing somebody whisper behind her, "Amy Ladelle's last summer's muslin." She had never enjoyed a social function so before. Ted Reever took her into supper and didn't seem to mind the fact of her gingham frock at all. And afterwards Mrs. Reever came up and asked her to sing.

Aunt Lena and Louise across the room knew what Mrs. Reever was saying and fervently hoped Janet would have the sense to refuse. But Janet had forgotten all about her dress and consented at once. She stood up beside the piano, a tall, girlish figure: her eyes were shining and her cheeks were like roses; there was not a girl present—in muslin or silk or lace—as pretty as Janet Stannard in her plain blue dress.

She sang beautifully and was encored twice, the guests crowded around her to congratulate her; Mrs. Mayfair, the wealthy aunt of the Reevers who lived in Toronto, asked to be introduced. Aunt Lena and Louise groaned in spirit. That child in her gingham dress! What would Mrs. Mayfair think?

The evening was a triumph for Janet. When it ended she

slipped off home with a party of girl friends, and when Aunt Lena and her cousins came they found her sitting bolt upright on a living-room chair, waiting for the vials of family indignation to be poured out on her head. She didn't care; she had had a splendid time, and she would do the same thing over again!

"O, Janet, how could you?" exclaimed Aunt Lena with a catch in her voice.

Janet's defiance crumpled up with a suddenness that left her limp. She had been prepared for anger, but this mild reproach was much worse. For the first time she looked at the matter through Aunt Lena's eyes. It had not occurred to her that people might make her gingham dress a hissing and a reproach to Aunt Lena— Aunt Lena, who had been so good to her!

"O, Auntie," she cried, with tears springing to her eyes, "O, I'm sorry—I really am. I didn't think that it would make you feel badly. I forgot that it would reflect on you or I would never have done it."

"But why *did* you do it?" said Aunt Lena. "What happened to Amy's dress?"

"Nothing happened to it, only just that it *was* Amy's dress" answered Janet. "O, Aunt Lena, I was so tired of wearing other people's dresses, even if they were nice. And some of the girls make such fun of my 'second-handedness,' as they call it. I just felt that I couldn't wear Amy's dress to the wedding. So I put on my gingham because it was new and my own. But I'm sorry."

Aunt Lena said nothing for a few seconds. Then she said, very gently: "You should have told me how you felt about it, Janet."

"I—I couldn't," faltered Janet. "I was afraid you would think me ungrateful. O, please forgive me, Aunt Lena."

"Yes, yes, dear. Perhaps there is a little need for forgiveness on both sides. We didn't think, that was all. Don't cry any more, my dear. Run away to bed, you're very tired."

When Janet had gone Aunt Lena and Helen and Louise looked seriously at each other.

"The poor child," said Louise. "I had no idea she felt so."

"When you come to think of it," said Helen, "we wouldn't like it either if we were in her place. It was well enough when she was a child. But we have all forgotten, I think, that Janet is really growing up."

"I've made a mistake," said Aunt Lena, "and I'm glad my eyes are opened to it, even if it took a little mortification to open them. I'll have a good talk with Janet in the morning and set myself straight with the child."

"O, Jink," said Janet to her kitty next day, "I'm so happy. Aunt Lena is going to get me a party dress of my very own and a new tweed suit. And she says I'll never have to wear second-hands any more. O, Jink, I pity you because it isn't possible for a cat to have an aunt like Aunt Lena."

⤳ ⤶

Editors' note: "Janet's Rebellion" was published in *Girl's Own Paper*, an English magazine, in December 1938, with illustrations by Muriel Harris. It was listed in the "Unverified Ledger Stories" section of the 1986 bibliography and was found by Christy Woster and Donna Campbell. This story is available to view in the Ryrie-Campbell Collection.

Girl's Own Paper had republished Montgomery's 1913 story "How We Went to the Wedding" in October, and her 1904 story "Elizabeth's Child" in 1937.

Montgomery finished her twenty-first book, *Anne of Ingleside*, on December 8, 1938.

MORE BLESSED TO GIVE
(1939)

The fresh spring sunshine was coming through the tall, narrow windows of the college library, casting banners of light on the floor and tables, and lighting up the somber nook between the wall and the historical bookcase that was known as the "English corner."

There were but few students in the library, and those few seemed bent on amusing themselves rather than on studying seriously. Lectures were over and exams nearly so; there was nothing more to come except the announcement of the results.

Eleanor Dennis and Irene Cameron were together at the magazine table, talking in the low tones required in the library—not so low, however, that the girl curled up in a chair in the English corner could hear all that was said. She had been dreamily turning over a volume of essays and listening to the rollicking chorus of a class song sung by some irrepressible girls in the grounds outside; but at the sound of a name on the other side of the historical bookcase the listless expression left her face and was replaced by one of keen interest.

"It is such a pity that Helen Lewis can't come back to college next year," Irene Cameron was saying. "She is certainly the cleverest girl in the junior class."

"She is the cleverest girl in the college," said Eleanor Dennis decidedly. "She has carried all before her this year and no doubt would do the same next year. In fact, I believe she would stand an excellent chance of graduating with 'great distinction,' and you know that no co-ed has ever done that here yet. For the honour of the co-eds as well as for her own sake I wish she could complete her course."

"There is no chance of her coming back after all, I suppose?" said Irene.

"None at all, I fear. I suggested something of the sort to her, but she answered quietly that it would be impossible. She said frankly that she could not afford to come, owing to business losses which her father had suffered."

"She must feel terribly disappointed."

"Yes, I am sure she does. But you would not have supposed so from her manner or from anything she said. You know she has always been a very reserved, independent girl. So I merely said that we would be very sorry if she could not come back."

"The class will be lost without her next year," said Irene. "She has always been the leader in everything. It is such a loss when a brilliant girl like that has to drop out of the ranks. Everyone was proud of her talents in an impersonal sort of way. They reflected honour on the class. That is really the only reason why I am inclined to envy those clever girls—they mean so much to their class. There are dozens of fairly bright girls, like most of us, to one girl like Helen Lewis, and so it seems a double pity that she should be the very one who is not able to go on. Do you know what she intends to do?"

"From a remark she made I imagine she will have to go to work at once, at whatever she can get to do, I suppose. It will be hard for her, with all her ambition, but she is plucky and self-reliant. I suppose she hopes to earn enough to come back some time and complete her course; but that will be a very different thing from going straight to the end with all her class-mates."

"If it were a girl like Winifred Fair, now," said Irene rather scornfully, "it wouldn't matter. She is hopelessly dull, but she has any amount of money and so she can stay here when a girl like Helen Lewis has to go. It is horribly unfair."

"Hush," said Eleanor softly, with a little motion of her hand towards the gold-tinted bob plainly visible above the somber volumes of Motley's *Dutch Republic*. Irene recognized it and coloured. She had forgotten that Winifred Fair was reading in the English corner, and wished she had not spoken so loudly. Winifred was certainly not clever, but she was a girl whom everybody liked. Irene was sorry for her careless words.

Winifred, however, had possibly not heard and certainly had not heeded them. Nobody knew better than herself that she was dull. For that very reason she admired the talented girls all the more earnestly, and she had a girlish admiration for Helen Lewis. It was a little sentimental, perhaps, for Winifred Fair, in spite of her three years at college, was as much a schoolgirl at heart as she had ever been. All the same, it was very warm and real, and the news that Helen could not come back to college to take her degree with honours and cast still more lustre over the class was to Winifred nothing short of a calamity.

She sat in the English corner a long time after Eleanor and Irene had gone, with her chin propped on her hand and her blue eyes filled with perplexity. Finally she, too, rose, replaced her book, and went out. In the hall she met a tall, dark-eyed girl with thoughtful brown eyes and a plain yet striking face. She smiled brightly at Winifred and the two walked together down the entrance steps and across the grounds, where the musically minded were still celebrating. It was not until they had left the grounds and turned down a quiet elm-shaded street that Winifred ventured to speak of the subject uppermost in her mind.

"Is it really true, Helen, that you are not coming back to Lakeside next year?"

"Quite true," answered Helen calmly.

"O, I'm so sorry!" cried Winifred impulsively. "We can never get along without you, Helen. Are you sure there is no chance?"

"Not the foggiest, darling. You know my family isn't rich. It has always involved a good deal of self-sacrifice on their part to send me here, but I expected to be able to make it up to them some day. I had a letter from mother a few days ago. Father has met with business losses and it will be quite impossible for me to come back next year. It will be necessary for me to find something to do at once. I may be able to come back some time, but that is uncertain. Just now the only thing for me to do is to make it all as easy for mother as I can. Of course, I can't deny that it is a great disappointment, but I mean to think as little about it as possible."

"O, Helen, if it's only a question of money, you needn't be disappointed," cried Winifred eagerly. "You know I have plenty of my own—ten times as much as I need. I'm really disgustingly rich. Let me help you, Helen. Do! I'd be so glad!"

Helen had turned crimson and then pale, but she answered very steadily: "Thank you so much, Winnie, but, of course, that's impossible. I could not borrow money not knowing when I could pay it back."

"I don't want it repaid," protested Winifred. "O, Helen, can't you take a gift from me after we've been such friends?"

"That would be still further out of the question," said Helen rather coldly. "I know you mean it in all kindness, dear," she added hastily, seeing the crestfallen look on Winifred's face, "and I thank you with all my heart for your offer. I simply couldn't accept such a favour from anyone."

"I wish you would let me help you, Helen," said Winifred sadly, as she turned up the street that led to her beautiful home.

Helen walked rapidly down the street to her boarding-house. Alone in her own room, the pride and courage that had sustained her before her friends almost failed, and she sat down in a chair by the window with tears in her eyes. She had been eager, so ambitious! Her three years at Lakeside had been filled with triumphs and she had looked forward so radiantly to next year, when she had hoped to graduate with honours. Then would come the proud and happy home-going and after that the finding of a worthwhile place among the world's busy workers.

"Well, this is the end of my dreams," said Helen bitterly. "But at least Mother shan't suspect how bad I feel. She is worrying so about my having to give up college. I mustn't make her more miserable."

From somewhere through the open window the sound of voices drifted up to her. At the window of the room below her own two other girls were talking. Margaret Mitchell, a senior girl, was saying in her high, clear voice: "To accept a favour gracefully is one of the hardest things to learn. Anyone can refuse. Independent people make a merit of refusing. It's only ungracious pride not to grant a friend the privilege of helping us."

Helen smiled involuntarily. Margaret was rather noted for laying down the law about everything. Then she winced a little. She wondered if her refusal of Winifred's impulsive offer could be classed under the head of "ungracious pride." Upon reflection she decided it could not. Certainly she couldn't possibly take money from Winifred Fair. No one could blame her for that. Not wishing to hear more, she shut her window and began to study half-heartedly for the last examination of the term.

The afternoon waned slowly, and at last a creamy-golden sunset began to reveal itself above the housetops. Helen did not go down to tea. Her head ached and she felt that she could not bear the gay talk and laughter of the other girls that evening. They would be talking of their plans for next year and the fun they expected to have as seniors. She would only sit among them silent and unhappy.

When it grew too dark to study she went to the window and watched the glow of sunset along the hills over the lake and the crystal glimmer of a star above the woods that crested them. She was still sitting there when somebody tapped softly at her door and Winifred Fair came in.

She came over to Helen and sat down on the low stool at her feet. Winifred's pretty face was flushed and her eyes sparkled in the dusk.

"Helen," she said, speaking more rapidly than usual, "I've come down to tell you something and ask you something. I couldn't keep from thinking about you after I left you to-day. No, don't say anything until I finish, please. I want to explain it all to you if I can, but it is so hard for me to put into words just what I feel. You are clever and perhaps you will understand. You see, dear, it's this way. I'm stupid, awfully stupid. I know I am. I know I can never do anything to make my class or my college proud of me. I'll be lucky if I just manage to scrape through; but I love Lakeside so much and I do so want to do something for it. You are brilliant, and we are all so proud of you, and it's a great thing for our class to have you in it. Don't you understand, Helen? If you would let me help you to come back next year it would seem somehow as if I, poor stupid I, were doing something for my class. It wouldn't be I who was conferring the favour at all. It would be you, and I should be so grateful and so proud.

"I felt all this to-day, but I couldn't express it then. I had to go home and think it out. O, don't refuse, my dear. You don't know how much it means to me. I wouldn't feel so useless, so super-fluous. Nobody need ever know but you and me. My money is my own—Aunt Grace left it to me—and it seems to me that I never had any chance before to do any good with it. It is your pride that makes you refuse, Helen, and it is a selfish pride, for it takes away from me the chance of doing something for my dear old class, and I never can do anything for it in any other way. Let me help you, Helen. Do try to understand what it means to me. You can look upon it as a loan if you will. That isn't what I care about."

Winifred leaned forward and touched Helen while she looked pleadingly up into her face. Helen did not answer at once. She was thinking earnestly. For perhaps the first time in her life she tried to put herself fairly in another girls' place and look at the matter through Winifred's eyes. She understood her friend better than the latter had dared to hope. Her own love of class and college helped her to understand. Margaret Mitchell's words came back, too. "Ungracious pride." Yes, perhaps it was. To refuse Winifred would be to wound her deeply.

"You will, won't you?" whispered Winifred.

"Well, my dear—" Helen stopped suddenly, too overcome for words. Then quickly: "O, thank you, thank you," she said with a little break in her voice. "It means so much to me."

"Not half as much as it means to me," said Winifred gravely. She reached over and kissed Helen's cheek. The action was spontaneous. The girls were great friends and understood each other perfectly.

When Winifred had gone Helen opened her window again. Three jolly students passed along the street below, shouting out a class ditty with all the fervor of youthful lungs. Far out over the maze of roofs the lights gleamed from the cottage at Lakeside where the senior class were holding a reception. At the window next to her own two girls were chatting gaily about the class work for next year. Helen's heart thrilled happily. She would be back again to share in it all. Her place next year would not be vacant.

"It is hard for some of us to learn to accept favours, but the lesson is worth learning," she said softly.

Editors' note: This story was published in *Girl's Own Paper* (December 1939), illustrated by George Clark. It was not listed in the 1986 Bibliography but was found by Christy Woster and Carolyn Strom Collins, while they were both in the process of updating references for Montgomery's stories and poems, and Donna Campbell. This story is available to view online in the Ryrie-Campbell Collection.

Montgomery must have reflected on her own college experience to some extent when writing this story—she had attended Prince of Wales College in Charlottetown in 1893–94. In 1895–96, she managed one year at Dalhousie College but could not afford to stay any longer. How she might have wished for a friend such as "Winifred Fair" to offer to help her!

Other stories published in 1939 were "The Little Black Doll" and "An Afternoon with Mr. Jenkins" (both also published in *Girl's Own Paper* and both available to view online in the Ryrie-Campbell Collection) and a series of eight "Ingleside" stories in September and October issues of *Onward*, selected from *Anne of Ingleside* which had been published earlier that year.

Also in 1939, Montgomery began writing a sequel to *Jane of Lantern Hill* (1937). Due to the ill health of her husband and her own health problems, that book was never completed. For the first half of 1939, Montgomery was negotiating with RKO Pictures to make films of *Anne of Windy Poplars* and perhaps *Anne's House of Dreams*. *Anne of Windy Poplars* was debuted in 1940 and starred "Anne Shirley" (formerly "Dawn O'Day"), the actress who had played "Anne" in the 1934 version of *Anne of Green Gables*. *Anne's House of Dreams* was never made into a film.

L. M. MONTGOMERY

RESOURCES

Canadian Home Journal. Toronto: Consolidated Press Ltd., August 1918; September 1919; February 1931; July 1934; and September 1936.

Children's Companion Annual. London, England: The Children's Companion, 1924.

Collins, Carolyn Strom, ed. *An Annotated Bibliography of the Stories and Poems of L. M. Montgomery.* Charlottetown: The L. M. Montgomery Institute, 2016.

Girl's Own Paper. London: Lutterworth Press, December 1938 and December 1939.

Kentuckian, The. Hopkinsville, Kentucky, November 14, 1907.

Montgomery, L. M. *Anne of Green Gables.* Boston, Massachusetts: L. C. Page Co., 1908.

———. *Jane of Lantern Hill.* Toronto: McClelland and Stewart, 1934.

———. *Anne of Ingleside.* Toronto: McClelland and Stewart, 1939.

New York Tribune. New York, October 23, 1910, Sunday Edition.

People's Home Journal. New York: F. M. Lupton, July 1926.

Pictorial Review. New York: American Fashion Company, August 1909.

Rubio, Mary and Elizabeth Waterston, eds. *The Selected Journals of .L. M. Montgomery (Volumes I–V).* Toronto: Oxford University Press, 1985–2004.

Russell, Ruth Weber, D. W. Russell, and Rea Wilmshurst. *Lucy Maud Montgomery: A Preliminary Bibliography.* Waterloo: University of Waterloo Library, 1986.

True Story. New York: Street & Smith Corporation, March 17, 1923.

Western Christian Advocate. Cincinnati, Ohio: Methodist Episcopal Church, May 9, 1906; May 16, 1906; June 5, 1907; June 12, 1907; November 13, 1907; August 26, 1908; and September 29, 1909.

৶ ৶

For more information on L. M. Montgomery's stories and poems, consult *An Annotated Bibliography of the Stories and Poems of L. M. Montgomery,* published by the L. M. Montgomery Institute at the University of Prince Edward Island in 2016.

EDITOR BIOGRAPHIES

Carolyn Strom Collins is the author of *The Anne of Green Gables Treasury* and other "Anne" companion books (published by Penguin Canada); she has also published companion books on *Little Women* (Viking Penguin), *The Secret Garden* (HarperCollins), and Laura Ingalls Wilder's "Little House" books (HarperCollins). Carolyn wrote two chapters for *The Lucy Maud Montgomery Album*—"Green Gables" and "The Scrapbooks"—published by Fitzhenry and Whiteside (1999), and has presented papers at many L. M. Montgomery Symposia at the University of Prince Edward Island, including pieces on the arrival of the Montgomery family in PEI (published in *Storm and Dissonance: L. M. Montgomery and Conflict*, Cambridge Scholars Publishing [2008]), the 1919 black-and-white silent movie *Anne of Green Gables*, Montgomery's stories that were based on actual events, Montgomery's publications during the Great War, Montgomery's Island scrapbooks of memorabilia, and Montgomery's poems about women.

In 2010, Carolyn helped found The Friends of the L. M. Montgomery Institute at UPEI in order to raise funds for enlarging and maintaining their Montgomery collection of publications and other materials. She also founded the L. M. Montgomery Literary Society, based in Minnesota, in 1992 with co-author Christina Wyss Eriksson. She has written many articles for the LMMLS annual newsletter, *The Shining Scroll*.

In addition to this volume of newly discovered Montgomery stories, Carolyn compiled *A Guide to L. M. Montgomery's Story and Poem Scrapbooks (1890–1940)* and edited *An Annotated Bibliography of L. M. Montgomery's Stories and Poems* (updating

Lucy Maud Montgomery: A Preliminary Bibliography, published in 1986 by the University of Waterloo); both the *Guide* and the *Annotated Bibliography* are published by the L. M. Montgomery Institute of the University of Prince Edward Island.

Christy Woster collected L. M. Montgomery materials for fifty years, beginning when she was just ten years old. Her goal was to have an original copy of everything Montgomery published, including over five hundred stories and five hundred poems, as well as first-edition books and related materials. She was nearly to that goal when she died unexpectedly in late April 2016, just a few weeks before this volume originally went to press.

In addition to co-editing this volume of stories, many of which she discovered, Christy also provided hundreds of new citations to the updated *Annotated Bibliography of L. M. Montgomery's Stories and Poems*. Her sleuthing skills were impressive—virtually unparalleled—and she was very generous to share her "finds" with the Montgomery community.

Christy attended most of the L. M. Montgomery International Symposia at the University of Prince Edward Island and presented papers at several of them, highlighting some of the many items in her Montgomery collection. She was a charter board member of The Friends of the L. M. Montgomery Institute and volunteered to chair the Silent Auction Committee for the last several years, helping to raise thousands of dollars for the Friends. She was also a charter member of the L. M. Montgomery Literary Society, contributing much of her time, talent, energy, and research to that group. Many of her articles were published in the LMMLS newsletter, *The Shining Scroll*.

ACKNOWLEDGEMENTS

Researchers in this project used a variety of resources to discover new citations and new stories: many public and university libraries in Canada, the United States, and Great Britain; websites devoted to digitizing magazines and newspapers from years past; online auction sites; and personal collections.

We would like to thank the independent researchers whose work has contributed to the current collection of stories as well as to hundreds of new references for an updating of Rea Wilmshurst's chronological listing of stories and poems in *Lucy Maud Montgomery: A Preliminary Bibliography* (Ruth Weber Russell, D. W Russell, and Rea Wilmshurst, University of Waterloo: 1986). The updated version of this bibliography, *An Annotated Bibliography of L. M. Montgomery's Stories and Poems,* also published by the L. M. Montgomery Institute of the University of Prince Edward Island, will identify some of the independent scholars, including Alan John Radmore, Benjamin Lefebvre, Donna Campbell, James Keeline, Joanne Lebold, Sarah Riedel, Mary Beth Cavert, and Janice Trowsdale and ourselves. Names of the researchers who found the stories included in this volume (and shared their discoveries with us) are listed with each story.

Some of the stories herein are included in the Ryrie-Campbell collection of Montgomery materials at UPEI and can be seen as they originally appeared in periodicals. Readers are encouraged to consult the L. M. Montgomery Institute website (lmmontgomery.ca) for more information about the *KindredSpaces* project launched at the 2016 L. M. Montgomery Institute conference.

At the University of Prince Edward Island Donald Moses, Mark Leggott, Simon Lloyd, Lindsey MacCallum, Dr. Philip Smith, and the L. M. Montgomery Institute management committee have provided encouragement and technical support in helping to produce this collection. Copies of L. M. Montgomery's story and poem scrapbooks are available in UPEI's Special Collections in Robertson Library (the original scrapbooks are kept in the Confederation Centre Archives in Charlottetown); Rea Wilmshurst's files on the Montgomery stories were donated to the L. M. Montgomery Institute at UPEI by her partner, the late Dr. Andrew Silber.

We are enormously grateful to Elizabeth Epperly for her careful reading of the stories during the final weeks of readying the stories for publication.

Proceeds from the sale of this collection go directly to the L. M. Montgomery Institute at the University of Prince Edward Island for the purpose of adding to and maintaining its collection of Montgomery artifacts, which are made available for study by Montgomery scholars and researchers all over the world.

—Carolyn Strom Collins and Christy Woster, March 2016